TREE
OF
ASH

Praise for Tree of Ash

"A riveting sequel full of twists and turns, Tree of Ash brings us deeper into the world of Evrópa and leaves you wanting more."

"For those who enjoy Norse mythology, the unbreakable bonds of friendship, magic, war, and learning to love and lose."

"Tree of Ash kept me on the edge of my seat the whole time! Get ready for a wild ride filled with plot twists, fierce best friends, sweet love-interests, dark villains, and wholesome humor."

"Stakes are raised, and the Fates are at work in this captivating sequel by Kayla Ann. Get comfy when you start this one because you won't be able to put it down!"

THE RUNIC SAGA
BOOK TWO

TREE OF ASH

KAYLA ANN

Kayla Ann Books

979-8-9884385-5-7 (ebook)

979-8-9884385-4-0 (paperback)

979-8-9884385-6-4 (hardback)

Library of Congress Control Number: 2024926640

Ebook, Paperback & Dust Jacket Cover Art by Etheric Tales

Hard Case Laminate Cover Art by Nemaiza Rhayne

Illustrations & Endpapers by Efa-finearts

Mapwork by Aaguirreart

Edited by Addison Horner

First Edition 2025

10 9 8 7 6 5 4 3 2

For my readers, who, like Halla, always wanted to fall into your
favorite book.
Your faith in my stories made this possible.

IYSTHEIM
1. The Wall
2. Intake Yard
3. Marketplace
4. Court of Aristocracy
5. The Palace

1
3

Tavsiden

1. The Outer Wall
2. Intake Yard
3. The Second Wall
4. Court of Aristocracy
5. The Palace
6. The Royal Garden

N
RANN'S SEAS
RANN'S SEAS
RANN'S SEAS
RANN'S SEAS
DIAMANT
Gjoll River
ISHJEM
TREHEIM
Undarbrunnk Lake
Nordryggen Mountains
RUBIN
SMARAGD
BRANNSIDEN
VIDNÁM
PERLE
Kvalven River
LYSTHEIM
SAFIR
HAVSIDEN
EVROPA
N

Part One

Heim

Power is a tremulous being
It shapes, destroys, and rebuilds
Until those who use it
Are but shadows of themselves.

-Urðr, *Book of the Past*

Prologue
Verðandi

Verðandi hummed as her fingers danced across the surface of the well. With each touch, the water rippled and golden light swirled up from its depths. Rays of illumination flashed across the leafy canopy that covered the expansive meadow. The thick roots of *Yggdrasil* snaked around the well and into the ground. Though Verðandi's tiny body lay at rest across the stones, her stomach clenched with anticipation and delight.

She'd planned for years. Now that her moment had come, Verðandi would not allow anyone to spoil it. Not even her sisters.

Perhaps Skuld, with her ability to see so far into the future, already knew what Verðandi was planning. Urðr would learn of it soon enough as she recorded the past. But *Ragnarok*—the war of the gods—had diminished her sisters, diminished them all. Without the mortals to worship the Norn, goddesses of fate, their own power would fade away until there was nothing left. They would become like the other surviving gods and giants: pathetic and weak leftovers of a broken world.

Verðandi shoved the thought aside, replacing it with the image she'd clung to during the darkness after *Ragnarok*. She imagined the mortals crying her name in adoration: Verðandi, their savior. The sounds of the imagined crowd died abruptly as *Yggdrasil*'s mighty branches rustled, alerting Verðandi to the presence of her long-awaited guest.

A woman's slim figure broke through the tree line, her feet crossing into the tall grass that brushed her waist. The mortal stiffened, her eyes roving up *Yggdrasil*'s giant trunk, tilting her head back as she attempted to make out the top of the great tree. Verðandi giggled, knowing the woman never could.

It was the giggle that brought the mortal's attention snapping down to the base of the tree. She narrowed her eyes in Verðandi's presence but lowered her head in a display of submission. Her vibrant white hair fell like a curtain around her face.

Verðandi clapped her hands in delight. She'd walked in this woman's dreams enough to know that the mortal distrusted the gods, blamed them for *Ragnarok*, but unlike so many of the others, this woman knew how to play the game.

"Welcome, Lif," Verðandi's soprano voice rang out. She leapt to a nearby root and opened her arms as though in a wide embrace. "You've made it; I knew you would!"

Lif raised her head and approached, her pace steady as though stalking prey. Her clothes were ragged and torn, even bloody in some places, and a large knife was strapped to her thigh. Mankind had been reduced to such primitive ways after *Ragnarok*, but that was all about to change. Lif stopped short of the well. "You called for me, Great Seer."

"I did," Verðandi's high voice trilled. "As I saved you from desperation once, I will save you again."

Lif's golden eyes clouded in apprehension. "I don't know what you mean."

Verðandi waved away the woman's words with a small hand. "Of course you do, or you wouldn't have come. It was my sisters and I that hid you mortals within the roots of *Yggdrasil* while the fires of *Ragnarok* ravaged this world. It was we who gifted mankind with innovation, arts, and endurance to ensure your survival. But like sheep walking toward cliffs of extinction, you've already fallen into desperation, killing one another without restraint. You lack leadership." Verðandi offered a girlish grin. "I can help."

"We've tried," Lif protested. "We're not lacking in leaders; we're lacking in those who can command authority. We're fractured into too many groups. If we keep fighting at this pace, you might as well have let us perish in *Ragnarok*."

Verðandi's bottom lip jutted out, irritated at Lif's ungratefulness. "What you *lack* is the direction of the gods. In your anger over *Ragnarok*, you've ignored us." She brushed back fiery strands of hair along with her irritation, replacing her pout with a smile. "What if I told you that I knew which leaders would be best suited for each people, and not only that, but I would give these leaders the power they need for everyone else to obey their authority?"

She scoffed. "I'd say that's impossible."

Verðandi's frown returned. "Not for a goddess."

Unfiltered power, animalistic in its raw state, pulsed from within Verðandi's small body, reminding the mortal woman who she was. Lif flinched as Verðandi's *galdr* washed over her like a storm cloud, showering her in a torrential downpour of power. She fell to her knees, cowering in the tall grasses, shaking even as the sun filtered in through the mighty branches. A perpetual child or not, Verðandi was a goddess, and her power was limitless; or at least, it would be again.

"Do you believe me now?" Verðandi's sweet voice echoed across the clearing while the might of the gods shook the ground.

"Yes," Lif gasped, not daring to lift her head. "But there's nothing I can do. I have no power, no authority."

Verðandi softened her voice. "Not yet, but you will. There is a test you must pass to gain the power you need."

"What test?"

Verðandi leapt from the root, placing a small hand under the woman's chin and lifting her face so that Lif's blazing golden eyes were unable to look away. Verðandi tilted her head like a bird. "Do you know how Óðinn discovered the language of the runes?"

Lif swallowed. "He impaled himself with his own spear, hung himself for nine days and nights on the tree of ash, and was granted the power of the runes."

"Not only the power of the runes, but power itself. *Galdr* is the magic of the gods, and with my connection to *Yggdrasil*, I can channel it into whomever I deem worthy." Verðandi tightened her grip on Lif's chin until the mortal winced. "You're worthy because I have made it so." She paused and giggled, releasing the mortal woman with a twirl. "That is, if you pass my test."

"And if I can't?" Lif asked, though fierce curiosity peeked through her apprehension.

Verðandi shrugged. "Then your soul will be sent as a gift to Hel." The goddess laughed at the horror on Lif's face. "I'm only playing! You mortals, always so serious. Your fate has already been set. You'll pass the test, and once you're done, you will no longer be called Lif, but rather Rúna, Queen of Perle, the first kingdom of Evrópa."

1

Initiation Day

Halla

HALLA FOCUSED ON THE dark curl plastered against Darien's forehead.

She'd woken from the fog jostled about in Darien's arms. The memory of the pale-eyed man and the *draugr* from the warehouse quickened her heartbeat as she stared at the sweat beading on Darien's hairline. They wove through the streets of Lystheim—the city of Perle—as cables swayed in the darkening sky above them. Darien's breaths came in short gasps, and blood dripped from a nick in his neck.

"Darien," she said, testing her voice.

"Halla!" Widening eyes glanced at her, relief evident on Darien's face.

Halla struggled to piece together what was happening. "Is someone following us?"

"Yes," he huffed.

She remembered the warehouse that stank of exhaust and fear, the blond man—*Kafteinn* Calder—who'd mimicked Darien's voice, Larissa's empty gaze, and the *draugr*. There was a vague recollection of the warehouse's ceiling opening up as it crashed down all around them, but Halla wasn't sure if that had only been a hallucination caused by the lump on her throbbing head.

"Where's Lara? And Anara?"

"Split up."

Her chin bumped into his chest as they barreled around the corner. Darien's body heaved for air, but he pushed forward, adjusting Halla in his arms.

"Darien, put me down," she insisted. "I can run."

He frowned, his feet never slowing. The muscles in his arms trembled.

"I can run!" she protested again.

The battle in Darien's face was brief. His arms shuddered as he lowered Halla to the ground. She had no chance to regain her footing herself before Darien's hand grasped hers, pulling her into a run. Her side cramped up, but Halla ignored it. She would not complain. She would be strong like Larissa.

They'd gone to Lystheim so Anara could find a contact to lead them to the Viðnám—the rebellion forming against the Empress. The Viðnám was supposed to keep them safe, but the sound of footsteps pursuing them only reminded Halla of the surrounding danger. On the next street, a group of sentries waited.

"There they are! In the name of the Empress, stop!"

Darien pushed Halla behind him. "Run, Halla!"

His sword clanged as he blocked a sentry's knife. Halla didn't know when he'd drawn it. She desperately wanted to stay, to help, but she'd promised Lara that if it all went wrong, she would run. Halla cursed her size, knowing she was too weak to be of any help. Tears gathered in her eyes as she fled.

The sound of the commotion behind her grew louder, loud enough that she had to look back. There were more sentries now, but these new sentries seemed to be fighting *with* Darien, not against him. She couldn't tell who was on whose side until one of the sentries drew his gun and pointed it at Darien who, engaged with another man, didn't see it. Just as the sentry pulled the trigger, a giant of a man tackled him to the ground. The bullet intended for Darien whizzed so close to Halla's face, it left a trail of heat against her cheek.

Halla turned, her small feet pounding hard down the alley. The corner was in sight, but before she could turn it, she found herself tangled in someone's arms instead. On his upper bicep, Halla saw the flash of a black-and-white armband belonging to the *thræll*—the Empress' slavers.

A strong hand wrapped around her long braids, yanking her head back and forcing her green eyes to meet unyielding gray ones. "Why're you running, girl?"

Halla froze in fear. She knew his voice. She'd heard it the night before, when the slavers had nearly caught them all hiding in the forest.

"Halla!" Darien cried out, his voice muffled by the distance.

She struggled against the *thræll*'s grip, her nails scratching at the hands that held her hair. "Let me go!"

"Fenris," said another voice from behind Halla's captor. "Those aren't all sentries fighting out there."

Halla's heart lifted. Could it be the rebellion they'd been searching for had actually shown up? But Halla's quick flame of hope was smothered by another yank on her hair.

Half a dozen men surrounded her, all sporting the black-and-white armbands of the *thræll*. They grouped behind the leader and shifted on their feet, watching the fight at the other end of the street with their hands on their weapons.

Fenris's eyes never left Halla; he seemed unfazed by her feeble attempts at freedom. With his other hand, he grasped Halla's face, pinching her chin between his fingers.

"Let the sentries figure it out. We've got our prize."

Halla's teeth found their mark with a swift snap. Immediately, Fenris howled, curses streaming from his mouth as he drew back his bloodied finger. His other hand clutched Halla's hair more tightly, winding his fingers in the mess of her braids, refusing to let go no matter how she struggled to turn back to Darien.

She never saw the fist that hit her.

ᚾᛁᛉᚱᛋᚾᛁᛉᚱᛋᚾᛁᛉᚱᛋᚾᛁᛉᚱᛋᚾᛁᛉᚱᛋ

Time passed without Halla's approval or awareness. When she awoke, cold seeped into her skin from the cement floor. The painful pulsing behind her left eye confirmed none of it had been a dream. She'd been taken by the *thræll*.

How long had she been unconscious? What would the *thræll* do once they realized she was awake? Halla squeezed her eyes, willing herself to fall back into unconsciousness, if only to prolong the moment before accepting reality.

She bit her lip, struggling against her desire to curl up and cry. Every part of her ached. She had to be brave like Larissa, like Anara, like Darien. In the darkness, an idea blossomed like a ray of light. If she could not be brave as herself, she would be brave like the goddesses from Pappa's stories. She would pretend that she was not Halla, but rather the goddess that Loki had once captured.

I am Iðunn, goddess of spring and keeper of immortality. I will survive this. What would Iðunn do? Get information. With her new persona in place, Halla dared to open her eyes.

There was little information to be found. Her cell had three walls made of stone and one of iron bars. Apart from the bucket in the corner of the cell that she refused to acknowledge, she was alone. Even the cells across the hall were empty. She was relieved not to see the familiar faces of her sister, Darien, and Anara. At least they had not been captured. But loneliness threatened to consume her. If Lara hadn't been captured, why hadn't she come for Halla?

At the sound of metal clanking and slamming, Halla flinched and scooted away from the door. Her hair, having fallen free from her braids, hung in waves around her face. Heavy footfalls echoed down the stone hallway. With every step, the light in the cell increased until the whole space was illuminated by an electric lantern.

Halla squinted against the light at the hand that held it. One of the fingers was bandaged. Her eyes traveled farther up, passing the slaver's armband, until she met the bleak gray eyes that mocked her very existence. Halla resisted the urge to look away.

She was Iðunn, goddess of life itself, and she would not be afraid.

The man called Fenris smiled, and Halla half-expected to see the fangs of a wolf snarling at his prey. "Look who's finally awake."

Halla rose to her feet. *I am Iðunn; I will be brave.* "Where am I? You can't keep me here!"

"Feisty thing, aren't you? Some bidders like that, I suppose." Fenris let his bandaged hand hang against the thick cell bars, hanging the lantern on a nearby hook. The hair on Halla's arms stood at the growl in his voice. "I don't. Submit, or you will receive worse than a black eye."

Halla swallowed. She was Iðunn, she reminded herself, but her bravery shriveled up inside and left her hollow with fear. Only one ray of hope remained: Larissa would come for her. Darien and Anara too. Maybe they'd found a way to the Viðnám after all, or even if they hadn't, they would come back for Halla. Halla just had to hold on until then.

Fenris chuckled at her silence. "You're learning already."

He slammed the key into the lock, opened the barred door, and advanced toward Halla, snatching her hands from her sides. Her chin jutted forward, though she clenched her teeth to keep it from trembling. Fenris strangled her wrists with the cold metal that cut into her skin, and Halla imagined him as the wolf from Pappa's stories, wishing that the god Tyre would bind him like the animal he resembled. As if sensing her thoughts, Fenris grinned—snarled, really—before pushing Halla in front of him toward the open hallway.

"Move."

Her bare feet protested against the cold ground. Fenris stalked behind, carrying their only source of light in the windowless prison.

To stop her fear from growing, Halla imagined that they were not in Perle at all, but rather the giant Thjazi's home where the Trickster Loki had abandoned Iðunn to her fate. She would bide her time until the giant was asleep, then make her escape. She would be braver than even the original Iðunn, who had needed rescuing.

At the end of the hall, Fenris opened the door and pushed Halla through it. Hot light blinded her, and she squeezed her eyes shut, but Fenris' impatient hands shoved her forward.

Bowing her head against the sun, she walked across a large, open compound. Several buildings no bigger than her farmhouse back home sat evenly spaced across the hard, compact dirt. There was no vegetation or life as far as she could see. Beyond the small structures were longer and narrower buildings. A tall, thick wall encircled the area—a miniscule mimicry of the Outer Wall that surrounded Perle—topped with coiled barbed wire. A *thrœll* patrolled the length of it.

The pressure on Halla's back increased, and though Halla knew there was no point in struggling, she couldn't help the instinct that made her thrash against her restraints. Ignoring her, Fenris dragged Halla along by her arm, kicking open the door of the nearest small building and flinging Halla inside.

Gray walls matched gray floors. A wash basin sat in the back corner, cupboards lined the walls, and an old woman bent over a small desk with a bright light in the center. Though there were several other desks around her, she toiled alone, her back a misaligned hump as she labored over her work. The woman's gnarled fingers layered strands of hair over the mannequin head that sat on her table. She briefly looked up at Halla's arrival before turning her attention back to the wig.

"Hair and clothes, then escort her to Barrack Four." Fenris ordered before turning toward the door. With one foot across the threshold, he turned to bare his teeth at Halla. "Behave, little girl, or I'll be back."

Halla flinched as the door slammed shut.

The old woman sighed, rising to her feet. "Come here."

Halla jolted at the gravelly sound. Lined with wrinkles particularly around the eyes and mouth, the woman's face was as foreboding as her tone. Halla followed her toward the large bin on the far wall, the handcuffs digging into her wrists. Yanking open a cabinet, the woman shoved clothes into Halla's arms.

"Put that on and clean the blood off your face."

Halla huffed, raising her arms and clinking the handcuffs together.

The older woman glared, as if the restraints were Halla's fault, and fished in the great wide pockets of her apron until she produced a key. Her eyes speared Halla with unflinching steel. "Don't even think about trying anything."

As the cuffs fell away, blood rushed back into Halla's fingers. She cried out in relief and pain at the abrupt sensation. The woman thrust the clothing at her again. Halla accepted the thick gray shirt and sweats, then looked for somewhere to change in private.

The woman's eyes narrowed with impatience. "I don't have all day."

Cheeks flaming, Halla stripped, swapping out her filthy clothes for the scratchy garments before turning to the basin. Letting the freezing water rush over her fingers, she wished there was a mirror, anything to look at herself in, but the metal walls were non-reflective. She dipped her face down and ran her fingers over her eyes, gentle with the left one that still throbbed from Fenris' assault.

A sudden tug at her scalp was followed by a loud snip. Twirling toward the woman, Halla flung her hand to the back of her head. Hanging from the woman's right hand was a pair of scissors; her left held a long lock of Halla's hair.

Halla grasped the ends of her cut hair, her eyes wide with horror. "Why would you do that?"

"Turn around." The woman reached for another handful of hair, her scissors flashing before Halla could protest.

She couldn't stop the tremble in her whisper. "Why are you doing this to me?"

Snip.

"Be grateful it's me and not Fenris. He doesn't care what the scissors cut."

Snip. Snip.

Halla's eyes smarted as the tears welled up within them. She stared into the water basin. She would not cry. Not as she felt every snip, or as she watched the stray blonde strands fall in the water. Her fingers clutched the basin's metal edge as she swallowed the whimper in her throat.

Done, the woman released her. Halla's fingers frantically searched the newly exposed scalp. Even the stale air raised goose-bumps across the back of her neck. She refused to acknowledge the woman beside her until she saw the clear bag in the woman's hand stuffed with Halla's blonde hair. Halla's eyes drifted to the woman's work table, where the black wig lay unfinished. She shivered.

The old woman led Halla out of the room and across the yard to the long buildings Halla had seen earlier. Painted on the side of each was a number. As they passed by, Halla's hands returned to her neck again and again, brushing the edges of her shorn hair. It hung just at her ears, and although it spiked out in all directions, Halla was grateful the woman had at least made it even all around.

They stopped before a building marked with the number four. Without a word, the woman opened the door and shoved Halla within, the door slamming behind her with the thunk of the lock.

Halla froze. Dozens of eyes landed on her face and all noise within the building ceased. Bunks lined each side of the long room, reaching all the way to the back of the building. On almost every bunk, a child sat, staring at Halla. Though some looked to be around her age, others seemed older, maybe fourteen or even fifteen.

Halla's lips went dry, matching the parchedness of her throat as the children continued to stare. Only one boy toward the back ignored her presence, nibbling at an apple in his palm. When a girl rose from her bunk, moving toward Halla, the other children looked away, returning to their food and hushed conversations.

The thin girl stopped in front of Halla, letting Halla examine her as openly as she did in return. She was close enough that Halla could see the bruises decorating her bare skin, particularly around her wrists. A thick bandage wrapped around her neck.

"I'm Juni," she said.

It took only a moment for Halla to match the voice to the face. She'd seen this girl before on the slave auction in Perle. Worse, Halla had heard her cries in the forest, begging for someone to save her as the *thræll* dragged her away. Halla gulped, wondering if the guilt in her heart was written in her eyes, but the other girl only looked at her curiously. Her black hair was like Anara's, but it had been cut short and ragged around her ears. Dark circles clung to her honey-colored eyes.

Seeming undaunted by Halla's lack of a response, Juni pointed to Halla's throbbing eye. "How'd you get that?"

Halla lifted her hand to touch her tender, swollen eyebrow. "The *thræll* hit me."

"You must have put up a fight." There was an odd note of praise in Juni's voice. "That's good. Only fighters survive here."

Halla looked away, unable to accept Juni's praise when she could still hear the girl's screams from the forest. She lifted a hand to tug at her braid only to find empty air. A sob crawled up her throat.

Stop it, Halla, she thought to herself. *You are Iðunn, and you will not cry. You are beautiful and strong no matter how long your hair is.*

"What's your name?" Juni prompted.

"Halla," she whispered.

"Come on, Halla," Juni said. "Let's find you a bunk. You hungry?"

Halla shook her head; she couldn't eat if she wanted to. They passed the rows of bunks filled with children who hunched over miniscule portions of food. Some jerky here. A piece of bread there. A can of green beans. There were just as many boys as there were girls. Some stared at Halla as she passed, their faces openly curious. Others ignored her. And some, Halla could hear, were crying into their mats.

Juni led her down the aisle, farther into the back where a handful of beds lay empty.

Halla stared at the bunk before her, unable to move. "Where am I?"

"These are the barracks," Juni said. "We're in the *thrœll*'s main compound in the city."

Halla looked around, noting the dark-haired boy who'd ignored her earlier seated on a bunk nearby. He picked at the apple in his hand but seemed to be listening to their conversation. Or perhaps Halla was just being paranoid.

"Are you all second-borns?" Halla asked.

"A few." Juni sat on the bunk—Halla's bunk. "Some of us are here to pay off our parents' debts; others were orphaned with nowhere to go, so the *thrœll* found a use for them."

"How long are we here?"

"Some are here for a week or two, depending on when the next auction is. They don't have them regularly, just depends on their stock." Juni's words were bitter. "Some are here longer, doing work to line the *thrœll*'s pockets."

The dark-haired boy turned his head in their direction. "Better to be here than the third option."

Halla's stomach clenched. So he *had* been listening. She faced him fully. "What's the third option?"

His onyx eyes met Halla's, and her stomach flipped. His dark hair matched his eyes. He was beautiful.

"The Empress pays well for new slaves," the boy said. "The *thrœll* consider it an honor when she makes a purchase from them."

"We could be sent to the Empress?" Halla squeaked.

"Stop scaring her, Kai." Juni's voice shook, with anger or fear, Halla didn't know.

The boy—Kai—leaned his head against the barrack wall, looking straight ahead. "I've been here for a year. I've seen it." He peeked at Halla from the corner of his eyes. "Just keep your head down and don't attract attention. If you're lucky, you'll be sold at the next auction."

Halla's knees shook. She'd hardly turned back to her bunk before collapsing upon it, not comprehending whatever Juni said next. Halla pulled her knees into her chest and stared at the metal wall. As the pressure behind her eyes mounted, Halla reassured herself that even Iðunn must have cried at least once during her imprisonment.

Yet, even after granting herself permission, Halla's tears would not come. There was an emptiness inside that allowed her thoughts to wander until they condensed on her only hope.

Lara, where are you?

2

The Spare

Darien

Darien pulled at the collar that constricted his throat. He started to scratch at the stubble covering his cheeks, but his fingers faltered at his father's stern glance. With controlled effort, Darien lowered his hands, doing his best to appear attentive yet relaxed. His older brother Aeron had mastered the balance with ease, but Aeron wasn't there, and Darien didn't want to remember why.

Darien, along with Anara, Torsten, and six additional council members, sat around the rim of the long oval table. The council members watched him from the corners of their eyes, measuring him against Torsten, king of Safír and Darien's father. Some of them were no doubt measuring him against Aeron as well. But no one knew that Aeron, the perfect Crown Prince, had become the Empress' War Dog who hunted them even now. Only Darien, Larissa, and Anara knew the truth.

One week had passed since their ill-fated trip into Lystheim, the city of Perle, with Larissa, Anara, and Halla. They'd found Halvor, a supposed shopkeeper who'd given them a rendezvous point to meet with Viðnám rebels, but they hadn't realized how closely they had been hunted. Before the rebels arrived, a *draugr* attacked Darien and Anara as *Kafteinn* Calder confronted Larissa and Halla. Their escape had come at a cost.

Halla.

Darien clenched his fists under the table. *He'd* lost Halla. Though Viðnám spies had successfully smuggled them out, Halla had been left to the mercy of slavers. Darien's guilt over Halla's capture soured his joy of seeing his father alive.

In the last week, Darien's time with his father had been short; he'd spent most of his days in *galdr*-induced exhaustion. Even with the rest, Darien struggled to focus. As King Torsten informed the council of Larissa's return, though he referred to her as *Lovisa*, the room faded away. In its place, the gnarled and runed roots of an enormous tree snaked across the room, beckoning Darien back into dreams he'd fought so hard to escape.

A sharp pinch in his side cleared the roots from his vision, bringing the council room back into focus. Anara side-eyed him, drawing Darien back into the discussion.

" . . . invite one representative from each family to attend, though we will still run out of room," Torsten instructed.

The dark-skinned man on Darien's left leaned forward, his elbows thudding against the table. "What of the Perle Princess?"

Darien stiffened at the impatience in the man's tone, glancing at Anara. Her shrewd eyes narrowed at the council member. He'd introduced himself as General Sture of the Smaragdian commonwealth. The electric lights drilled into the stone walls of the mountain glared against his dark, bald head. Emerald vines embroidered in the collar of General Sture's suit seemed to swirl against the cloth.

Torsten raised an eyebrow, his piercing blue eyes unblinking. "What of her?"

General Sture gestured to the empty chair among them, an emerald ring glinting on his fingers as he waved them about. "You tell us this Princess of Perle has returned to fulfill the prophecy of the False Empress' downfall. You expect us to rally our people for war. Yet we've not yet been given the opportunity to meet with her or hear the details of this prophecy for ourselves."

"Your people?" Torsten asked, a foundation of steel underlying his light tone. "All people within the Viðnám are under my command, General."

"Of course, your Majesty," the man to Sture's left agreed. He held his posture with rigid perfection, but his gray eyes shifted as he smoothed back his oiled black hair. "Though General Sture's question stands. Why is she not here? As the council of kingdoms, shouldn't we be the first to assess this princess before the rest of the people?"

"Do you doubt King Torsten's assessment, General Aiko?" Anara asked, her voice full of innocence.

The man's mouth tightened as he flicked a glance in Anara's direction. He shifted ever so slightly away from her. "Of course not."

"Our princess returned," muttered another general. He was older than the rest and seemed to be holding back tears. "Our people have waited for so long."

Darien remembered his name. Soren, the general of Perle.

"We could not risk this information spreading," King Torsten continued, addressing the previous general's concerns. "Not until we were ready for the entire Viðnám to know, General Aiko. It was only this morning that Princess Lovisa woke, which is why I called this council to order."

"A banquet has been arranged for you all to speak with the Princess tonight," Halvor added, pushing up his half-moon spectacles. Of all the council members, Halvor was the only one that Darien trusted. He'd encouraged Torsten to march on Perle and rescue Halla at Larissa's request. "The Jötnar have agreed to host us."

All turned to Speaker Skaði. The giantess leader of the Jötnar met their gazes with a serenity that undercut the tension in the room. Her skin, dark as the mountains, glowed with an unearthly sheen. Power seemed to sleep beneath her skin. Though Halvor had warned Darien to not use the term "giant," there seemed no other way to describe the Jötnar who lived in the Nordryggen mountains. Even the smallest Jötnar towered a foot over most men. Though they varied in appearance, all Jötnar had the same amber eyes that glowed even in the darkness of the mountain—a reminder they were not entirely human.

Torsten rose to his feet, signaling the end of their meeting. "You have my instructions. Gather the representatives of your people. Tonight, everything changes."

General Soren harrumphed at Torsten's understatement. Though Sture and Aiko opened their mouths as though to protest, neither spoke at the sight of Skaði rising from her chair. Her presence demanded obedience. She held her hand toward the door. "If you will, generals."

Darien glanced at the exit, his heart pulling him down the twisting tunnel halls to where he knew he could find Larissa still recovering from the return of her *galdr*. Though he longed to follow the council members out, his head reminded him of his duties. His father had to know about Aeron.

"I'm sure she's fine," Anara murmured.

Darien sighed in defeat. "You always know what I'm thinking, don't you?"

"Only when it's about *Larissa*." She grinned. "Which is most of the time."

Darien lowered his voice further. "The council doesn't seem too certain about Larissa."

"Politicians," Anara scoffed. "They just want to be reassured of their own importance. Halvor's banquet is sure to settle any rustled feathers."

"So." Torsten's booming voice cut off Darien's response. His vivid blue eyes locked onto Darien under bushy black brows. "What did you think of your first council meeting?"

"I—" Darien paused, sitting straighter in his chair. The words *didn't care for it* came to mind, but he was certain that wasn't the right answer. "I'm not sure why I was here. There wasn't anything I could add apart from retelling them our story."

"Your presence alone was everything," Torsten said. "For decades, I have guided the Viðnám, and though it is composed of people from every commonwealth, I have not forgotten the priority of my people. The Safírians rely on me to restore us to our home one day. But how can a people trust a king with no heir? Our blood is blessed with the power of the gods, and with your return, there is hope in the continuation of our strength."

Torsten smiled, but Darien's mouth went dry, his tongue sticking to the back of his teeth as the meaning behind his father's words washed over him. The power of a kingdom was dependent on its monarchs' Ancestral Blood. Tradition taught the stronger their *galdr*, the stronger the people. It was one of the reasons why many monarchs hadn't married beyond their borders for risk of diluting the power of the gods.

A sharp jab from Anara's finger in Darien's back prodded him to speak. "So you were putting me on display for the council?"

"In a manner of speaking, but it's so much more than that." Torsten glanced at Speaker Skaði who, to be honest, despite her enormous size, Darien had not seen return. It was eerie how one so large could make herself appear nearly invisible. Perhaps it was her *galdr*. Darien still wasn't sure exactly what the Jötnar could or couldn't do.

"If that's the case, why wasn't Larissa here?" he asked. "She's the hope of Perle, isn't she?"

From the corner of his eye, Darien caught Anara's smirk. Halvor looked down at the table.

The firm pressure of Torsten's lips revealed his distaste. "You mean *Lovisa*. I don't care what she calls herself in private, but to the world, she can only be known as Lovisa."

Skaði leaned forward, her dark hands spreading over the glossy surface of the table. "Lovisa is still recovering from recent events. She needed rest and to prepare for this evening."

"Precisely," Torsten agreed, his voice clearly signaling the end of the discussion. "Tonight we will announce Princess Lovisa's return and our plan to reclaim Perle, but there is more. Tonight, I will name you as the new Crown Prince of Safír."

It was the obvious decision, and yet Torsten's words landed like a gut punch. Darien hadn't been raised to be the Crown Prince; that had always been Aeron's role. "Faðir, there's something you need to know. Aeron, he isn't—" He struggled for words.

Anara cleared her throat. "He's alive."

Darien winced as her bluntness echoed in the following silence. Speaker Skaði's eyes widened, sending her thin black eyebrows up to her hairline. The grin on Torsten's face melted into a confused grimace.

"That's impossible," he said. "Aeron is dead. All the reports said so."

"The reports were wrong." The greatest courtesy Darien could offer his father was the truth. "The man we told you about, *Kafteinn* Calder, the War Dog that hunted us, he's Aeron. Anara and Larissa will tell you the same thing."

Not even Darien's use of *Larissa* had broken through the King's disbelieving stare. Anara shifted in her seat noticing how Darien watched his father in concern. Despite the fact that his *galdr* slowed his body's aging, at that moment, Torsten looked over a hundred years old. Gaunt and hollow.

"When I learned the gods had returned my second son," Torsten muttered, covering his eyes, "I wondered what it would cost. The Norn have set their faces against me. How many know the truth?"

"Anara, Larissa, Halla, myself," Darien answered quickly. "Now you, Halvor, and Speaker Skaði."

"No one else can find out." Torsten held each of their gazes for a moment. "The people would lose hope if they learned that their beloved Safír Prince was the one hunting them." His sigh was heavy and bitter. "It would have been better if he had truly died."

Darien froze in shock. It had been one thing for him to think such thoughts, but for his father to actually say them aloud seemed callous. As much as he hated Calder, Darien couldn't simply shove aside the obvious. "Should we consider rescuing him?"

"From what?" Torsten asked, dropping his hand from his face. "If everything you tell me is true, my son is long dead, and the sooner this man Calder follows, the better. It all falls to you now."

"What falls to me?"

"If the gods favor us, one day you will lead our people. Despite my best efforts, you are the last of our blood."

Best efforts? The question formed on Darien's tongue, but his mind refused to entertain the idea of his father taking another wife.

Besides, Torsten was still talking. "We must start your training immediately."

Knowing how his next words would be received didn't stop them from coming. "Faðir, I still have to help Larissa."

Torsten's eyes refocused on his son, hard and cold. "I need to speak privately with my son."

Halvor and Skaði rose without hesitance. Anara offered the briefest touch on Darien's shoulder before she too was gone.

Torsten held his gaze all the while. "I let you entertain your infatuation with *Lovisa* when you were a boy and when Aeron was to be king, but now, it is time for you to put aside childish habits. We have to keep our *galdr* strong. The Norn have returned you to me for a reason. You must be there to carry on our fight if anything was to happen to me. The Viðnám will need a leader. They will not trust Anara, not with her tainted blood. As for Lovisa, Larissa, whoever she is, she will be a good figurehead, but we both know that you were the one born to lead."

Except that wasn't true, was it? All of Darien's life, the pressure of the crown had fallen squarely on Aeron's shoulders. As Aeron had met with their father's counselors, Darien had walked along the sandy shore at Lovisa's side. As Aeron had undergone political training, Darien had professed his love to the Perle Princess. There had never been a time in his life when he had desired to change positions with his brother; Aeron had been the perfect successor, and Darien had been content to support him as he led their kingdom to prosperity.

Until now.

The thought of the responsibility and expectations that would be placed on him became overwhelming. The room seemed too small, the air too thick.

Torsten rose from the chair, taking his son's silence for acceptance. "Go and prepare for this evening. I will collect you. This is the will of the gods."

The dismissal in his tone was clear. Darien's feet carried him across the floor before his tongue could catch up with his mind.

Anara waited for him in the hall, leaning nonchalantly against the wall. Her dark hair rippled as she straightened, raising an eyebrow. "Hel looks better than you, and she's half corpse."

"He's naming me Crown Prince after Larissa's announcement tonight." Darien's voice sounded dazed, even to his own ears.

"So I heard."

"He wants to start training me to take his place."

"You didn't see that coming?"

Darien rubbed his face, his fingers scratching against the stubble that had only recently spread across his jawline. "Anara, you know me. I never wanted to be king. That was always Aeron's dream." He shook his head. "It should be Aeron."

"It can't be Aeron." Her voice was firm. Anara's hands moved to cover the injury that stretched across her abdomen where the *draugr* had gutted her on Aeron's orders, nearly killing her.

No, not Aeron, Calder, Darien reminded himself. *It was Calder who did those things, not Aeron.*

As though aware of what she was doing, Anara forced her hands back to her sides.

"Did you know? About Aeron surviving?" he asked.

To Anara's credit, she didn't hesitate. "I wondered. When Aeron's body was never recovered, it didn't seem right. After Shiko had total control, when Torsten and I founded the Viðnám, there were rumors of the Empress' *Kafteinn*. Very few saw him and lived. Of those, fewer made it to the Viðnám. Their descriptions made me think of Aeron, but Torsten was never open to the idea, and I had no proof, so I stopped pursuing it."

"That doesn't sound like you to just let something that important go."

"I didn't want it to be true."

Darien knew that feeling all too well. "You were right about my father. He's not the man I remember. He was strict, absent sometimes, but never so cold."

"To be fair, you're probably not the son he remembers either."

"He still thinks I care too much for Larissa and not enough about the crown."

She smiled. "Some things never change."

But Darien's thoughts were elsewhere, drifting into dangerous territory. Though his mind begged him not to ask the question, his mouth did not listen. "Anara, do you think Halla is alright?"

Her face hardened. "I think you shouldn't ask questions you don't really want the answers to. Let's focus on getting her back and getting out of here."

Darien caught the bitterness in her voice. "Are you alright, Anara? Being back here?"

She scoffed. "You noticed it too, huh?"

Throughout the meeting, he'd watched as the Generals had given Anara a wide berth, often glancing at her in trepidation. He nodded, waiting for her explanation.

"Let's just say that my *galdr* makes me a strong asset to the rebellion, but it also means they will never accept me. They see a shifter, but they wait for the day I'll change into a *draugr* with their hands already on their weapons."

"That's ridiculous—"

"The fears of lesser men are not my problem." Anara pushed herself off of the wall and walked away without checking to see if Darien would follow. She tossed her words over her shoulder. "We should get ready. Larissa will need us by her side tonight."

3

Seven

Halla

HALLA HATED THE SMALL brown-and-black beans that stuck to her sweaty fingers. In the past week, she'd been assigned to several rotations within the compound—knotting rugs, shelling the coffee beans, cleaning the barracks—but nothing frustrated her as much as weighing and packaging beans. After several hours, her fingers cramped and her hands spasmed.

Juni had been right. While Halla waited in dread of the next auction day, the *thræll* would work her for every ounce they could earn.

At least Juni shared Halla's rotation that day. The dark-haired girl kept Halla's sanity intact, whispering to her stories of her life living on the streets of Lystheim whenever the *thræll* walked out of earshot. They'd been kept in the barracks to sort the beans under the supervision of the *thræll*, who snapped his whip when they moved too slowly. At the end of the shift, he'd count and weigh each bag to record their production, but Halla suspected it was more about making sure the children did not eat the beans out of desperation.

Though Halla's eyes blurred from the beans and her knees ached from where she knelt, she did not complain, unwilling to bring any unwanted attention from the *thræll* upon her. Not that she was scared, she reminded herself; she was Iðunn. No, it would simply be easier for her to plan her escape if no one was watching.

And she was planning her escape.

She just didn't have a plan quite yet.

To distract herself, she would recite Pappa's stories in her mind, sifting through them as she tried to decide which story she would share with her bunkmates each night. At first, she couldn't think of Pappa's stories without crying, but on Halla's third night within the compound, a new child had been brought to their barrack—sold to pay off his family's debt. When the boy cried, Halla sat beside him and told one of Pappa's favorite stories. It wasn't until she was done that she'd realized the entire barrack had been listening to her tale of Thor's missing hammer and the mockery of a wedding that ensued afterward.

Her stories made her instant friends and brought back the warmth of Pappa's voice—if only in her mind. The following days, the other children would share a quick smile or just a short nod in Halla's direction. It was ironic that her enslavement had given Halla the opportunities for friendship she had always longed for.

She could only thank the Norn for this strange twist of fate.

"That's the last one." Juni threw the bag into the pile in the middle of the floor, then scratched absentmindedly at the bandage around her neck.

Halla had asked Juni about it, but the girl's face had darkened, and when she hadn't responded, Halla knew not to ask about it again. But she still wondered every time she saw Juni's hands touch the worn fabric.

"You, you, and you," the *thræll* barked, pointing at several of the children, "take these to the south tower and report back. The rest of you to your bunks."

Halla sighed in relief to not be one of the three unlucky souls chosen. Those hefted their loads over their shoulders, following the *thræll* out of the barrack. The sacks were heavy, and the southern tower was the farthest in the compound. As they left, children from other rotations were ushered back inside the barrack from their outdoor duties.

Released from her position on the ground, Halla limped on numb feet back to her bunk and collapsed from exhaustion, covering her eyes with her hands. Even with her eyes closed, the outlines of the beans were etched onto eyelids. She wondered if she would forever be counting beans before sleep even if Larissa were to find her.

When, she reminded herself in an unyielding mental tone, *not if*.

"Must be nice to sit inside and count beans all day." Kai's words hit Halla's ears just as she felt his body settle at the bottom of her bunk.

Halla groaned but didn't bother to open her eyes at the now-familiar voice. "My hands are wrecked."

"I had sewer duty."

Halla peeked at him through slitted lids. "You win."

Kai smiled in self-satisfaction, but the smile dropped quickly. Halla loved those brief glimpses; his smile softened his face and chased away whatever haunted him. When he smiled, he was even more beautiful than Darien—though Halla would never admit it.

"Come on, get up." He tugged at her elbow. "If you stay here, we'll only get crumbs for dinner."

Halla lowered her arms and sat up with a loud sigh. She leaned over to where Juni had collapsed on her own bunk. "Juni, food."

Juni grunted but pushed herself up from the bunk and made her way toward where the other children waited near the door. There were around twenty of them, though the number shifted regularly as more children were brought in and some were sent out into the city as laborers. Among them, Halla was the youngest. She'd turned thirteen two days ago. What would've been a momentous occasion at home had passed in the shelling of coffee beans with the threat of the *thræll*'s whip looming overhead. She hadn't spoken to anyone that day, not even Juni or Kai, preferring to escape into daydreams in which her parents still lived.

Kai rose from Halla's bunk, leaving her to stare as he walked away. He looked different from anyone she'd ever seen before in Perle or Safír. His skin was fair, but with warm undertones that came out in the sun. It contrasted against his jet-black hair that stuck up around his ears. His eyes always seemed to be laughing at her, yet Halla had never heard Kai laugh. The other children gave him space when he approached the door, as they typically did.

Halla's back nearly buckled as her feet hit the ground. She forced one foot in front of the other. Even on berry picking days, Halla had never felt this stiff. She remembered the way that Pappa would crack every joint in his hands at night only for Tucker to try and outdo him by cracking his knuckles in his toes. Halla's smile at the memory swiftly slipped from her face, and she closed her mind against the image, but the damage was done as other memories seeped into her thoughts.

"You okay?" Juni nudged her shoulder into Halla, but her words were faint compared to the sound of roaring fire in her ears.

In her mind, Halla was back in the barn, hiding under the trapdoor as smoke filled her lungs. She could hear her parents' screams as the *draugr* killed them. At least they'd been able to bury her parents, but Tucker's body had been left in the fields to rot. Saliva gathered in Halla's mouth as nausea threatened to empty her stomach.

"Halla. Halla!" Juni shook her shoulder.

Halla breathed in deep through her nose, doing her best to dispel the images that plagued her dreams. "Sorry. What?"

Juni's quizzical gaze was laced with sorrow.

The door to the barrack opened as a *thrall* threw in the bag of rations for dinner—the one meal they got per day. Madness reigned as the children scrambled to be the first to open it. Any fondness the others had for Halla's stories faded at the sight of the bag as Halla earned more than a couple elbows jabbed into her sides, fighting to get her hands on something edible. She'd learned early on that if she waited, there would be nothing left. Having secured herself a bottle of water and some type of bread, Halla escaped the melee and fled back to her bunk.

Not long after, Kai and Juni joined her. They were always better at scoring food. Kai had even captured an apple at some point, bruised on one side, but still.

Halla munched on her bread, grateful for the raisins baked into the dough. But the memory of Mamma's hands on her own in the kitchen came back with such ferocity that Halla gagged on the bread in her throat. Tears sprung to her eyes as she forced herself to swallow. Juni's pounding on her back, though ineffective, was appreciated.

When Halla's coughing had stopped, Kai leaned forward, his back turned toward the other children in the barrack who had retreated to their bunks to eat and rest. "I overheard something interesting from the *thræll*."

Juni threw up her hands in exasperation. "How is it that you always get to hear the interesting things?"

"I'm a better listener and have more patience than you," he shot back.

Juni wrinkled her nose, leaning away from him. "You also smell worse than me."

Halla ripped a bite from her bread. "Be nice, Juni. He had sewer duty."

"Sewer duty," she repeated, looking toward the back corner of the barrack.

Halla and Kai exchanged a glance including raised eyebrows and shrugs.

"Something you want to tell us?" Kai asked.

"Not yet." Juni's gaze sharpened. "So what did you hear?"

"Apparently there was some big commotion in the city last week," he whispered, looking over his shoulder before continuing. "The *thræll* aren't supposed to talk about it, but a whole warehouse was destroyed, and whoever destroyed it got away."

Halla paused with her bread hanging in the air. Her sister's shouts, the clang of Darien's sword, the screams of the *draugr* as Larissa brought the ceiling down on it all echoed in her mind. Halla dreamt of them almost every night. Twice, Juni had woken Halla to stop her screams before the *thræll* would hear. The previous night, it had been Kai who had wrapped Halla in her blanket after waking her and sat beside her in silence as her tremors passed.

Only last night's dream hadn't been her recurring nightmare. Halla had walked around the massive trunk of a tree while a girl giggled beside her. It hadn't been a frightening dream, yet neither had it been pleasant. She wouldn't have woken at all if not for Kai, who claimed she'd been tossing in her sleep.

His voice brought Halla back to the present. "Weren't you two captured around then? Did either of you see anything?"

"No, but I was probably already caught by that point." Juni touched the bandage, but Halla knew it was involuntary. "What about you, Halla?"

She shook her head, not trusting herself to speak.

Kai leaned in, his voice only a murmur. "There's more. Rumors are floating around about the Perle Princess. Some say that the Viðnám is going to make a move against the Empress, that they already did in the city."

Halla gasped, but Juni's bitter laughter drowned out the small sound. "The Perle Princess? Now, I know you're messing with us."

But Kai was watching Halla. "What do you think?"

She did her best to look away, certain that the truth about Lara would be plainly written on her face. His eyes caught hers. Halla didn't mind getting lost in those bottomless pools of ink and would have held his gaze, if she hadn't been worried about what secrets he might uncover. Blushing, she looked down. Two years older than Halla, Kai surely didn't see her as anything more than a child. Her size didn't help. Halla frowned at the thought.

The barrack door slammed open, cracking against the wall. Fenris' massive body silhouetted the doorframe, and the children rose from their bunks, standing at the edges of their beds. Though Juni and Kai had only moved far enough to stand in front of their own bunks, they might as well have been miles away with how alone

Halla felt in Fenris' presence. The last time Fenris had shown up in the barracks, he'd taken three of Halla's bunkmates to be sold to work in the loading bays. Now he prowled down their lines as another sentry walked beside him with a clipboard in his hand.

From several bunks away, Fenris' eyes passed over Halla, and a grin stretched his lips into an unnatural smile. Halla clasped her shaking hands, willing them to stop.

"Breathe, storyteller," Kai hissed under his breath, still looking straight ahead. "Don't let him see your fear."

Halla's jaw clenched, but she nodded. She was Iðunn; she was brave. She would be like Lara and Anara. Fenris stopped two bunks down and said, "Six."

The *thræll* behind him scribbled on the clipboard.

Fenris skipped Juni, then paused at Halla. "Seven."

Seven what? Halla wanted to ask, but she bit her cheek, having seen what consequences came from asking questions.

Looking almost disappointed at Halla's lack of a response, Fenris moved on, not bothering to spare Kai a glance. Most people treated him that way, as though he did not exist. Fenris moved back toward the front of the barrack, occasionally numbering a child on the opposing row of bunks.

On Halla's right, Juni looked at Kai, and mouthed, "What does it mean?"

Horror leaked through his guarded expression, and Halla knew Kai had seen something like the numbering before.

Juni leaned toward him, annoyance raising in the flush on her cheeks, "Kai, what does it mean—"

Her whisper transformed to a yelp of pain accompanied by the crack of the *thræll*'s whip against her body. Juni fell to the ground, wrapping her arms around her chest in preparation for the next hit.

Fenris approached from behind the sentry. "Haven't learned your lesson yet, slave?" Snatching Juni's wrist, he yanked her into the air until Juni whimpered from the pain. Fenris glared around the room, confirming that every child was watching. "Slaves are to be seen, not heard. A disobedient slave is a disposable slave."

Juni fell to the ground with a thud. Though Halla yearned to comfort Juni, her limbs were petrified stone that refused to move. There was nothing she could do, not while Fenris stood there, looking at Halla, daring her to intervene. In Juni's small cries, Halla heard the echoes of her screams in the forest.

Fenris' gray eyes pierced into Halla, reveling in the sorrow he caused. "Got something to say, little girl?"

Halla bit her tongue, thinking of all the things Anara would say. Gods, Anara would just rip out his tongue. Darien would persuade him to pull out his own tongue. Lara would shoot it off, but Halla was just Halla. She didn't have *galdr*; there was nothing she could do.

He chuckled, a low and unpleasant sound in the back of his throat. "You're learning your place." He nodded at the sentry behind him. "We're finished here."

The thuds of his footfalls echoed against the metallic walls in the silent barrack, followed by the slam of the door and the click of the lock. The children fell to their bunks, averting their eyes as Halla and Kai moved to Juni's side. Halla offered her hand. "Are you okay?"

Juni stood on trembling legs, fiddling with the bandage around her neck. She averted her eyes, as though ashamed of her own weakness. "Tell us a story, Halla."

The other children nearest turned toward Halla at Juni's request. Halla usually waited until after dark when the *thrall* were less likely to visit, but Juni had asked, and there was so much Halla wished she'd done for Juni. This she could do.

"Sure." Halla sat next to Juni on her bunk as the other children moved to sit on the cement floor in front of them. Kai sat on his own bunk. Half the time Halla was certain he wasn't even listening to her stories, but there were times when she'd catch his eyes on her. Halla racked her brain until she decided on the perfect story.

She remembered when Pappa had chased the wolf from their farm, and later that night, he'd told her the story of Fenrir.

"When the mighty god Loki fathered a giant wolf pup, he named the monster Fenrir . . ."

Like the children, Halla lost herself in the story. The pup was gifted to the gods, but due to his unusual strength, he'd been enslaved all of his life. Only during *Ragnarok* was he freed to wreak havoc on a dying world. As her story closed, Halla emerged as if from a trance. "And so Víðarr, son of Óðinn, ripped open the mouth of Fenrir, avenging his father and killing the wolf who had swallowed the moon and the sun."

The light had faded during Halla's story, leaving only the soft moonlight streaming in through the skylights to illuminate the wonder on the faces of the children around her. One by one they rose in silence to retreat to their bunks. It wouldn't be worth it to be caught out of their bunks after darkness, but as they walked away, Halla heard their whispers.

". . . if only the gods would kill Fenris like they did Fenrir."

"Shh, don't let anyone hear you say that . . ."

"Nice story," Kai commented. "Next thing you know, you'll be starting your own rebellion. Who needs a Perle Princess when we've got a storyteller?"

"Don't tease," Juni snapped in low whispers from her place sitting beside Halla.

Kai lifted his hands in a show of surrender. "Wouldn't dream of it. Who taught you these stories, Halla?"

She froze, the triumph of another story chased by her grief. "My Pappa."

Perhaps it was the sound of her voice that stopped Kai from pursuing that line of questioning. Now that her story was over, Halla remembered the reason for Fenris' visit, and her apprehension returned. "Kai, why was Fenris counting us?"

His thumb rubbed the inside of his other palm. "You don't want to know."

"But he counted me," Halla protested. "I need to know."

He sighed. "Every month, Fenris will do a count of the light-haired girls."

"And?" Juni demanded when Kai paused.

"They don't go to the auction block; he sells them directly."

Sweat coated Halla's palms. "To who?"

He wouldn't meet her anxious stare. "Word has it the Empress will pay anything for young, light-haired girls."

The bunk under Halla rocked as the sweat on the back of Halla's neck turned cold. She wished she still had hair to cover it. "What do you mean? Why does she want them?"

"Who knows?" He lifted his eyes, his mouth turning up in mockery. "Maybe to bathe in their blood to stay young and beautiful forever. She is a monster, after all."

Halla shrank away from him until her back slammed against the wall, and her heart thudded painfully in her chest. *The Empress?*

She was going to be sent to the Empress.

Juni's arm wrapped around Halla's trembling shoulders. She sent a glare in Kai's direction, but the boy lay back, staring unconcernedly at the ceiling. Halla's breath came in short bursts that did nothing to fill her lungs.

"What is wrong with you?" Juni hissed. "Why would you say that?"

"I was trying to lighten the mood. No one actually thinks the Empress is bathing in blood; it would ruin her complexion." He shrugged. "She's been rounding up as many light-haired girls as possible for as long as I've been here. I've heard she's looking for someone."

Halla froze, her breath hanging in that space between inhale and exhale, and a single thought consumed her. The Empress was looking for light-haired girls. Larissa's white hair blurred in Halla's mind. Had the Empress' one-child mandate all been a method of searching for Lovisa?

"Halla? Halla. Breathe!"

Juni's fingers snapped in front of her eyes. Halla's vision refocused around the black dots, blinking them away.

"Halla, there's no proof that life is any worse in Diamant than it would be here. I highly doubt the Empress bathes in anyone's blood." Juni's voice was less confident than Halla would have preferred. She rushed on, "Kai's just being Kai. He's bitter because no one wants him, and he's forced to live here for the rest of his days on sewer duty."

"I heard that," Kai muttered.

"You were meant to," Juni snapped.

"I can't go to the Empress," Halla whispered, her fingers digging into Juni's shoulders tight enough to bruise. "Please, Juni, you have to help me. There has to be a way out."

Juni was quiet for some time, stroking Halla's short hair. It wasn't fair for Halla to ask Juni for help. Not after Halla had abandoned Juni to her fate in the forest, not after Halla had left Juni to stand on that auction block, but still. Halla couldn't go to the Empress.

Finally, Juni whispered, "There might be a way."

4

Fulfillment of Fate

Larissa

Lost.

Larissa was lost, consumed by past and memory. Unblocking her mind had let forth an uncontrollable torrent of information that could not be organized or contained. Guilt and shame rose up to accompany the memories of that night. She remembered it all, her weakness as she did nothing but watch her father's brutal murder and her mother's bloody sacrifice. Her people halved by Shiko's anger at Lovisa's disappearance. No wonder she'd resisted remembering the trauma of that time.

Time passed in remembered dreams, and yet, time never moved. Larissa couldn't guess how long she'd been stuck in the storm of what her life had been, or how much longer she'd have to tread the murky waters of who she had become.

Somewhere in that place between reality and dreams, Halla's screams rent the air. A dirt path formed under her feet, and Larissa ran toward the sound, pressing through the all-too-familiar fog around her. Copper and burnt metal scents lingered in the air. Larissa's panting breaths were harsh in the vast emptiness of her mind. Even knowing this was only another dream did nothing to deter Larissa's adrenaline from rising. The fog solidified into tall grass that tickled her sides as she ran toward the tree, whose size claimed the entire horizon.

Ignoring the roots and the branches, Larissa frantically scanned for the source of her sister's screams. On one of the lower branches, a deer stared in mild disinterest before it bounded away. On the same *branch, a squirrel sat with its mouth open wide; only at Larissa's approach did it shut its mouth, cutting off Halla's screams.*

Larissa's feet stuttered beneath her.

Red, so brilliant that it looked like a living flame, caught her attention. Verðandi's feet dangled off the branch upon which she sat. "Halla is waiting for you, Larissa, and so am I."

The strange galdr of the child-goddess was alluring and repellent all at once. Already the scene was slipping through Larissa's grasp as her mind shied away from the raw power. Scenes from a previous life poured through the fog, and Larissa was lost again.

ᚾᛁᛗᛕᚿᚾᛁᛗᛕᚿᚾᛁᛗᛕᚿᚾᛁᛗᛕᚿᚾᛁᛗᛕᚿ

LARISSA CRUMPLED THE PAPER in her hand. The ink had long ago dried, and small rips around the note creeped farther into the page every time Larissa twisted the paper in her hands. The writing was nearly illegible at this point, but that didn't matter. Larissa had memorized the short message.

Bathe, eat, drink, and get dressed. Do not leave your room; you will get lost in the tunnels. I will come for you soon. - Halvor

The note, a tray of food, and a beautiful floor-length gown awaited Larissa upon her waking. She'd ignored the hot bath waiting for her, trying to make sense of the dreams that still danced across her vision. A clearing with grass as tall as her knees, a tree with branches that blotted out the sky, and a small red-headed girl who beckoned and said, *Come to me.*

Verðandi.

Though Larissa had only seen the child-goddess once before, she would recognize her anywhere. With the return of her memories, it was clear how Verðandi had intervened ever since her mother's death: by hiding Larissa within time itself, placing her on Dal and Vern's berry farm, sending her dreams that would remind her of her past, and finally empowering Larissa so she could to collapse the warehouse on Calder and his *draugr*. For better or worse, the goddess of fate had taken an interest in Larissa's life, and by the continued presence of the dreams, it seemed Verðandi was not done with her yet. But even a goddess could not hold Larissa's attention, not when she looked at the empty half of her bed where Halla should have slept.

Halla, whom Larissa had left in the hands of the *thræll*.

The thought, combined with her empty stomach, was enough to send the walls spinning. Larissa pushed her head between her knees, determined to hold it together. She had to. She had a plan. She had agreed to Torsten's terms. She would be Princess Lovisa, and in return, they would mount an attack on Perle to reclaim the commonwealth and rescue Halla.

With her plan in mind, Larissa forced herself to stand on wobbling legs, to bathe, to eat, to drink, and to dress, but she had not anticipated being thwarted so easily in her endeavors. Half-dressed before the mirror, she strained against the frustrating metal clasp that kept slipping from her fingers.

No matter how she bent or contorted her body, the zipper was stuck.

The material of the dress was as gentle as moonbeans and as smooth as a frozen lake. The hem of the pale-pink fabric was lined with hundreds of tiny runed stitches that seemed to burn with every movement. Though obviously meant to represent her royal lineage, the gown's off-the-shoulder, slitted sleeves were a nod to modern influences. The dress was a marvel, but Larissa seriously considered ripping the thing to shreds. She had faced *draugrs*, for Odinn's sake. Yet here she was, brought down by a zipper and satin.

Releasing her arms, Larissa winced as blood rushed back down to her fingers. But the tingle in her hands sparked an idea. She hadn't tried manipulating her *galdr* since she'd awoken, although the power gnawed inside her. Turning so that her back faced the mirror, Larissa glared over her shoulder at the troublesome piece of metal and focused her energy onto it. The ring on her hand grew warm, and her gut constricted as she pulled from the *galdr* that had sat dormant within her for so long. Reflected in the mirror, the zipper wiggled as though pulled by some invisible force.

Then it stilled, stuck in the fabric.

"Kings and Queens!" Larissa ground her teeth; her hands reached to tear the gown from her body. The slight creak of her door sent Larissa spinning, holding the loose dress against her shoulders.

"Relax, it's me." Anara slid into the room with the grace of a cat, closing the door silently behind her. A long red garment wrapped around her body, embedded with enough jewels that it moved and shimmered like an open flame. It paled in comparison to the pendant throbbing against Anara's tan chest like a second heart. Etched into the stone was Hagalaz, the rune of Rubin symbolizing chaos and change. Her hair had been gathered in three sections, lined with golden ribbons that matched the hoops hanging from her ears and the hoop in her nose. Tiny diamonds ran along her hair line and dipped down her back. For someone who had nearly died, she looked surprisingly well.

"Anara," Larissa breathed out, releasing her tensed shoulders. "You look amazing."

She flashed a grin, revealing the sharp points of her teeth. "I'm aware."

"No, I mean, you *are* stunning—but your wound, is it healed?"

"Turns out Torsten found a way to replenish his supply of nectar." A small jade vial flashed in Larissa's mind. The nectar within was made from blossoms of the Smaragdian commonwealth and could advance healing and restoration. Larissa had experienced its effects firsthand.

"And it worked?" Larissa pushed.

"Clean bill of health." Anara tilted her head, appraising Larissa's predicament. "Turn around."

Anara yanked the zipper and finished its journey to rest right beneath Larissa's shoulder blades. The gown clung to her waist, then flared out around her legs, the runes shimmering all the while as a show of royalty, heritage, and prestige.

There was just one problem.

"Your hair," Anara clicked her tongue.

Larissa ran her hand down the shimmering fabric. "I was thinking more about the fact that there's nowhere to hide my gun."

"Are you anticipating being shot?"

"Given what's happened lately, I wouldn't be surprised."

Anara rolled her eyes. "I'll find you something tomorrow. For now, you can't wear your hair in a braid when you greet your people. You're a princess again, not a farm girl. Sit."

It was impossible to resist the pressure of Anara's hands on her shoulders. Before Larissa had settled herself on the stool, Anara's hands were already in her hair, unwinding the braid she'd put in earlier. Her touch struck a memory of two young girls preparing for the Jóltide Festival. Even then, Anara would usually dismiss their attendants so they could prepare themselves together. As Anara's fingers molded her hair, Larissa swore she smelled the jasmine she always associated with the Rubinian.

Larissa caught her gaze in the mirror. "I missed you."

Anara's face softened. "I missed you too. I started to wonder if Lovisa would ever return."

Larissa dropped her eyes. "I still prefer Larissa."

"I figured as much." Anara pulled the brush through her hair. "It's clear you remember your past; *finally*, might I add. Do you want to explain why you insist on being called Larissa?"

"I don't know if you would understand."

"Try me," she muttered around the pins she held between her teeth.

"When I was Lovisa, I was never allowed to be Lovisa, not really. No one could know that I was Princess of Perle." Larissa's words faded.

Anara squeezed her shoulder. "They were just trying to protect you."

"I know." And she did know; her parents had said it often enough. The Norn had come to Queen Stjarna, warning that her child would be responsible for righting the chaos and bringing back peace, but death would follow. Believing this death to be Lovisa's, Stjarna had pretended to lose her child in birth, sending Lovisa from the palace as an infant. Only later was Lovisa brought back to the castle as a ward of the royalty. In private, she'd been embraced by her parents; in public, there was a necessary distance. The threat of the prophecy forever shadowed Lovisa's steps.

"I had Faðir and Móðir," Larissa continued, "but even then, our relationships could only exist behind closed doors. You, Darien, Aeron, you all *lived*. Your people knew you. The times we spent together were just moments of your life, but for me, those moments *were* my life. Larissa might have been built on a lie, but I was more honest as Larissa than I ever was as Lovisa. Even Torsten said he could never imagine Lovisa fighting a *draugr*, and he wasn't wrong. I did that because of who Larissa made me."

Anara pulled a pin from her mouth. "Maybe that's why you connected with Halla so immediately. You understood what it was like to live your life in the shadows."

Larissa shook her head. "I connected with her because she's my sister, and I love her. Call it insanity or the will of the Norn, but I believe she was always meant to be my sister."

"My Amma used to say the strings of the Norn connect us long before we're born, and we feel the pull of those strings in life."

All Larissa felt was the pit of despair gnawing away at her intestines, as it had ever since she'd woken up. "We have to get Halla back. How long was I asleep?"

Anara's movements paused. "Nearly a week."

Larissa's hands tingled, *galdr* crackling across her fingertips. The energy in the room took on a static cling in the air. "A *week*?"

Larissa rose to her feet, spurred on by the adrenaline in her body, but where could she go? She was hidden under the Nordryggen Mountains, and it would take an army to break into Perle and find

Halla. What had they done to her? Was she still even in Perle? Her throat constricted, and the back of her eyes burned. Larissa hardly registered Anara's hands on her shoulders, shoving her back onto the seat.

"Breathe," Anara snapped. "If you pass out, that won't help Halla. You exhausted your *galdr* and broke through some mystical block in your mind. You're lucky you weren't asleep longer. We're going to get Halla back. I promise, even if I have to storm Perle on my own. But I can't help you if you bring down the mountain on us."

Anara stared pointedly at the soft glow emitting from Larissa's hands. Though she felt her *galdr* building within her, it seemed trapped under her skin. Larissa inhaled, flexing her fingers until the glow vanished. "It's good to know there'll be another set of hands to tear down the wall if it comes to that."

"You could always count on Darien's hands to join in as well."

Larissa blushed, looking away from Anara's smiling face in the vanity mirror. His name fluttered around in her heart like a half-remembered dream of sunshine and a soft ocean breeze.

Anara pulled white strands of hair through her long, thin fingers. "Torsten won't like it in public, but, in private, be Larissa. Maybe that's who the prophecy was about anyway. After all, the Norn made their prophecy with the knowledge of who you would become."

Larissa had never thought of it that way. "Just because I'm Larissa doesn't mean that I don't love you just as much as Lovisa did."

Mischief colored Anara's tone. "I'm sure Darien would like to hear the same."

Hope flooded Larissa's heart and burned through her veins. Just the thought of Darien's smile was enough to set her world on fire. He hadn't given up on her, even when he had remembered their past and she had not. He'd waited, giving her the space she needed. Larissa wished then that Anara's fingers would finish their work quickly.

As if reading her thoughts, Anara smirked, pulling the hair away from Larissa's face, revealing her high cheekbones—more prominent from her recent lack of food. In her own face, Larissa saw her Móðir. She had Queen Stjarna's long white hair and the graceful slope to her nose, but her golden eyes were that of her Faðir.

Larissa's joy at seeing Darien fizzled at the sorrow of thinking of her parents. If she'd expected the return of her memories to solve all her problems, she couldn't have been more wrong. The past was weighed down with both glory and despair, leaving Larissa with a type of double vision resulting in a constant headache. A headache that was not improved by Anara jabbing in pearl studded hair pins to finish the style. It would have been a darling effect if not for how it revealed the thick pale scar that marred her right cheek.

"There's nothing wrong with being scarred," Anara said, her sharp eyes as perceptive as ever. "It shows the warrior you've become. You'll find that most of your people are scarred from Shiko's reign. Your scar will connect you to them in a way your words never could."

Larissa resisted the urge to touch the raised skin. Anara was right; she would display it with pride. She rose from the bench, her strands of loose hair tickling the bare skin on her neck and shoulders. Anara reached down for the finishing touch. The necklace was made of three strands, each longer than the previous and dripping with pearls. The shortest strand hugged tightly against her throat while the longest hung low, settling right above her navel.

Anara eyed the strings. "Do you think Torsten left any pearls untouched in all of the Viðnám?"

But Larissa touched the necklace with hesitant fingers, revering the cool pearls that kissed her skin. "It was my mother's. My father gave it to her as a wedding gift. He said there were so many pearls to remind my mother of all the reasons why he loved her, but even then, he still couldn't fit enough."

"They were wonderful people, Larissa, and they would be proud of you tonight."

She nodded, her throat abruptly too tight and dry to allow her to respond.

Anara squeezed her shoulders. "Time to go fulfill a prophecy, no pressure." Larissa's stilted laugh caught Anara's attention. Her body tensed. "You *did* remember your mother's prophecy when your memories came back, didn't you?"

Larissa bit her lip. "She never told me the full prophecy."

"What?" Shock chased concern across Anara's face. "You don't know the prophecy?"

"She wasn't exactly forthcoming about it," Larissa said in defense. "She was doing everything she could to ignore it, not teach me about it!"

"Then there's no one alive who can tell us what it was?"

Larissa shrugged, but Verðandi's sweet voice called to her from a dream she couldn't remember.

A knock resounded at the door. Anara leaned in close and hissed, "Whatever you do, don't tell Torsten you don't know the full prophecy. The council members will *not* be happy about this."

"What? Why?"

"Loki's knot." Anara pinched her nose. "We're about to start a war based on the hope that you can fulfill a prophecy you were never told."

The severity of Anara's words robbed Larissa's response as did the second knock at the door.

"Come in," Anara said in a louder voice.

At Anara's call, the knocker entered. "Ah, good, you are ready."

Halvor stood in the opened door frame. When Larissa had first met him, masquerading as a physician within the walls of Perle, his clothes had been threadbare. They were replaced now with his own finery and the emblem of the Safír Kingdom etched onto his shoulder noting his position as advisor to the king. His half-moon glasses no longer perched at the edge of his nose, but were pushed up just below his hazel eyes. Though he smiled warmly, his presence washed over Larissa like a bucket of ice. Here was the physical reminder of what was coming, of the deal she'd made to reclaim Halla.

Halvor gestured to two floor-length jackets with large hoods laid across his arm. "King Torsten awaits but requests that you wear these to avoid any curious eyes along the way."

Anara growled, "And ruin the work I just did on Larissa's hair? I don't think so."

Halvor inclined his head toward her. "It's your choice, princess, I'm only sharing what King Torsten expects."

Larissa yanked one of the jackets off his arm. "It's fine."

Once properly hidden, Anara took her time arranging the hood so as to protect Larissa's hair. Then Halvor led them down the winding tunnel paths. Light streamed in from the mouth of the tunnel as Larissa stepped out onto the edged pathway that lined the entire valley. Far below, she made out the shapes of crowds of people moving through the streets all heading in the same direction. Following their movement, Larissa's eyes landed on the tallest building within the valley. Multiple stories tall, it might have been considered a palace if not for its simplicity. Surely, this was their destination.

A larger crowd gathered there, waiting for her.

Larissa breathed deep; they'd waited long enough.

5

Lovisa

Larissa

RUNES DECORATED THE MASSIVE wooden doors. The most frequently carved rune was the Thurisaz, the rune of the Jötnar themselves with its open-ended meanings. Her Móðir and Faðir had taught Larissa all the stories of old, and, of course, Pappa's stories had often centered around the Jötnar and their clashes with the Æsir, but never in her wildest dreams would Larissa think they were still alive. *Ragnarok* had supposedly destroyed them all.

Yet giants and gods still roamed the lands.

Larissa suppressed a sigh. Halla would have loved it all. Halvor moved toward the doors, and Larissa squared her shoulders. Everything Larissa did now was for Halla. It had to be. She would bring her there; Halla would get to see it all herself.

The doors opened into an immense throne room. Gold speckled the black-and-white tiled floors. In one of the thrones sat King Torsten, dressed in his traditional navy and gold. To the side and slightly behind him was a woman dressed just as finely and surrounded by a group of women who looked at Larissa with stark curiosity. But they faded from Larissa's thoughts as her gaze was consumed by the towering figure of the giantess who stood in front of them. Speaker Skaði's deep magenta dress was cut low in both the front and back with slits running up toward the knee on either side. She saw Anara's eyes glance at it in admiration.

"Why couldn't they make me something like that?" Anara hissed in Larissa's ears. "At least her dress allows for movement in a fight."

"Are you expecting to be attacked?" Larissa muttered back, echoing Anara's earlier sentiments.

"Always. How else do you think I've survived this long?"

Larissa's snort died in the back of her throat at the sight of the young man sitting in the second throne. Larissa had never seen Darien look like this, not even as Lovisa. Darien's finery was lined not with his usual silver but with the gold reserved for the Crown Prince. The shadow of a beard clung to his jawline, reminding Larissa of how much time she'd lost to sleep.

Just as Larissa stared at him, Darien seemed to drink in her presence. He'd looked at her that way before, so many years ago, but his expression could make Larissa believe that no time had passed at all, let alone fifty years. As if they could still be what they'd once been. Unlike his father, who rose in slow movement, Darien shot to his feet and bowed in her direction, his mouth curving up at both corners. The temperature in the room rose. Significantly.

"Oh, Kings and Queens," Anara muttered behind her. "Get a grip."

King Torsten nodded in their direction. "Thank you for wearing the hoods, but there is no further need. No one will interrupt us here, and out there, we want the people to recognize you."

He gestured to the side of the throne room where double glass doors led out onto a stone balcony. Beyond the doors, the noise of the crowd rumbled into one indistinguishable and unending buzz. The Viðnám waited.

"That is, if you are truly ready." Torsten's doubtful tone continued. He glanced at the woman and her retinue. "You may go; we will join you shortly."

Inclining her head only slightly, the woman turned. The gold thread on her gown shimmered in the light. Larissa's alarmed gaze caught Darien's look of discomfort. Had King Torsten had taken another queen? Darien's clipped nod was answer enough.

Upon the queen's absence, Torsten's body stiffened. "I have heard the others refer to you as Larissa, but remember that publicly you are known as Lovisa. It is the name that holds the power to move the Viðnám into battle. Do you understand that?"

Larissa pushed down her hood along with her irritation, knowing that Torsten held the power to retrieve Halla. "I understand."

He straightened his collar and tie. "Your job here is to motivate the Viðnám into mobilizing itself into action. You will be able to uphold your part of our bargain, won't you, *Princess Lovisa*?"

"As you are ready to do the same, King Torsten."

From the corner of her eye, Larissa was pleased to see the smirk flitting across Anara's face. Even Speaker Skaði looked content with Larissa's answer. Only Darien and Halvor seemed uncomfortable with the exchange.

"Very well, Princess." King Torsten offered an arm to the Speaker. "We will address the crowd first, and you will join us shortly. They will expect you to speak, but keep it short. Only confirm who you are, and encourage them to follow my lead to victory. Speak nothing of your prophecy; we will discuss it later."

She nodded, her tongue suddenly too dry to speak, grateful to postpone having to confess she knew little about the prophecy. Torsten and Speaker Skaði made their way to the balcony doors. It seemed that the floor was a giant chessboard. The King was making his move, and soon, it would be hers. As the doors closed behind them, Torsten's voice boomed over the rumble of the crowd. "My people, I have assembled you here today—"

Then the doors clicked shut, and Torsten's words reached her as though spoken underwater, jumbled and muffled. Halvor smiled at her encouragingly, but Larissa fought the sickness rising in her throat. After a lifetime of hiding herself, of only speaking of the prophecy in whispers, the whole nation knew her name. In mere moments, she would be expected to stand before these people who didn't know the prophecy any better than she did. They believed wholeheartedly in Lovisa's ability to restore the peace Shiko had destroyed. Yet Larissa's feet were rooted into the stone itself. Who was she to address these people? What did she have to offer them?

"I don't know what to say to them," she whispered to herself.

"Yes, you do." Darien descended the steps. At his approach, Larissa saw two Dariens standing side-by-side. The farm boy who'd protected her in the walls of Perle and the Prince whom she'd fallen in love with. Then the two merged into one, and that old sense of longing rose up again within her. What she would've given to have their reunion not be such a public spectacle. As though sensing the need for privacy, Anara turned to speak with Halvor in a low voice.

Freed from their scrutiny, Larissa moved toward Darien. She couldn't help it. If Anara was right, and there were strings that connected people together, then the thread between them was taut and irresistible. "What if I say something wrong?"

He smiled, shaking his head. "You won't. You want to rescue Halla. Everyone down there has someone they want to rescue. You need to reclaim Perle. Win their hearts now, and they'll follow you into the fire." Darien paused, his fingers searching for something within his pockets. He pulled out a small, smooth pebble and dropped it in Larissa's hands.

She stared at the white stone in wonder, remembering how she and Halla had scoured the riverside for it as a replacement for the pebbles Halla had lost in the fire that destroyed their home. "Where did you find it?"

"Halla must have left it in Helga when we went into Perle."

Larissa ran a finger over its smooth surface, thinking of the family truck she'd left with one of the Viðnám spies. Just one more piece of her peeled away.

Darien cleared his throat. "I'm sorry. It's my fault Halla isn't here, but this way you can have part of her with you."

"It isn't your fault." But the rest of her words stuck like honey in her mouth. She didn't blame Darien, but that didn't change what happened. Halla was gone, and no matter what feelings surfaced, Larissa's full focus had to be on rescuing her. She couldn't allow herself any distractions. And, with the way he looked, Darien was definitely a distraction.

The lining of his jacket caught her eye. "Gold, huh?"

Darien glanced down at his coat. "Faðir has great plans for me, apparently."

"Did you tell him about Aeron?"

Darien nodded, but the pain in his face broke Larissa's resolve. Her fingers brushed over his hand. "I'm sorry."

"Alright, lovebirds"—Anara rejoined them—"time to make our debut."

A smile played on Darien's lips, chasing the sorrow from his eyes. "They're going to love you."

"Indeed." Halvor adjusted his half-moon spectacles. "Prince Darien was correct. They will follow wherever you lead."

Something about his tone caused Larissa to examine the man more carefully. "Is that true for yourself, Halvor? Will you follow me into the fire?"

"For you, Princess, I would venture into Hel's domain if I must cross the goddess herself."

Stunned by his loyalty, Larissa glanced at Darien, who shrugged. He shoved his hands in his pocket and mused, "I've always wondered what it would be like to meet the goddess of death."

Anara snorted. "We might meet her sooner than we'd like if we miss Torsten's cue."

"All too right, Princess." Halvor chuckled. "Let me go and see if they're ready for you."

He slipped through the double glass doors, and Torsten's words floated into the room. ". . . our trials have not passed without reward . . ."

Larissa stared at Anara and Darien, doing her best to ignore the painful absence of Aeron. Their bonds forged in childhood, tested in separation, and strengthened by declarations gave Larissa's feet the capability to move forward. Her mind spun as she tried to formulate what she would say to the people of the Viðnám. Her own people had been halved by Shiko's anger at Lovisa's disappearance. What if her people blamed her for her absence? Hated her?

The sound of the crowd roared again on the other side of the door in response to something Torsten had said. Larissa gripped the pebble tighter. "Is that the entire Viðnám?"

"Not quite," Anara answered, her tone almost bored. "The valley is bursting at the seams. They've called for one member from each household to be present, and even then, it'll be standing room only."

Halvor's face peeked through the opening doors. "It's time."

Forcing her shoulders to release their tension, Larissa strode forward. Darien and Anara flanked each of her sides. She would not descend into the fire alone. Stepping through the doors, Larissa's eyes snatched glimpses of the grand courtyard that sat below the balcony only a single story down. Rays of the sun were disappearing over the cliff sides. Dozens of large, industrial lights glared down upon a courtyard overflowing with hundreds upon hundreds of citizens.

At their approach, an unnatural silence settled on the crowd.

King Torsten faced his people, his voice magnified by the device perched on the stone edge. "Tonight I am joined by three individuals of utmost importance to our future victories over the Empress' reign. May I first reintroduce you to someone who is one of us, a founding member of the Viðnám and its strongest ally, Princess Anara of the Rubin realm."

Anara stepped forward, dipping her head in Torsten's direction before stepping back into the shadows. Her brief appearance was enough to break the dam of the crowd as shouts and exhalations overwhelmed the whispers and murmurs. From her perch, Larissa could see the reactions of many in the crowd. Although hundreds of faces had lit with joy and excitement, Larissa's blood turned cold at the faces of others who turned away in disgust or whose teeth bared in anger and suspicion.

"Princess Anara left us many decades ago on a mission so important, its very purpose was hidden from all."

Larissa peeked at Anara to see a barely concealed eye roll. That was one way to describe Anara's decision to leave the Viðnám after Torsten gave up searching for the Princess and his own son.

"She has returned to us, triumphant in accomplishing much more than we had ever hoped. In her long travels, Anara recovered one that we feared long dead. Years ago, the false Empress took my firstborn son from me. Although we mourn the loss of Prince Aeron, we rejoice in the return of my second." Torsten's voice boomed with triumph. "Citizens of the Safír Kingdom, may I present to you the newly appointed Crown Prince of Safír, the hope of the Safírian bloodline!"

Like waves, shock rippled through the crowd before it was overcome by astonishment and, finally, uncontainable joy. It was easy to tell who belonged to the Safír realm, for their joy was unlike any of the others. Their leader was not childless as they had feared. If they regained their kingdom, they also now had an heir connected intimately to the flow of Ancestral *galdr*. Their kingdom would be secure once more.

Yet even as Darien stepped forward with that crooked smile that caught Larissa's breath, another wave of emotion surged through the crowd. The cheers died out and the whispers grew until the entire valley buzzed. Their eyes turned toward her. Larissa could imagine how she appeared to them: a pale girl whose dress shimmered in the lamplight. No doubt they'd noticed the strands of pearls dripping down and over her gown. King Torsten raised his hand, and at once, all noise ceased.

Larissa fought the urge to wipe her damp hands against the dress, the pebble slippery against her palm. The pearl ring on her finger glowed as though the *galdr* inside of her yearned for release.

"Those of my kingdom, those of the other fallen kingdoms, and those of the Jötnar who so generously welcomed us into your valley: for years, we have waited in the shadows. We have fought impossible battles, and we have lost much. For so long, it appeared the Norn had truly set their faces against us, that even the old gods who survived *Ragnarok* could not be counted on to grant us mercy. It would be a lie to ignore the hopelessness we have battled against."

Solemn expectancy stole through the crowd, leaving them with nothing but silence.

"But today, we are victorious. The Norn have revealed a new twist in the fabric of our lives. People of the Viðnám, may I introduce you to the one destined to dethrone the false Empress, our lost Princess Lovisa of Perle!"

Noise exploded in Larissa's ears, making it impossible to identify every sound that filled the air, encompassing every part of Larissa's being. There were shouts and hurrahs, sobs and screams, stomping feet and clapping hands all mixed into a thunder of applause. Torsten stepped back from the amplifying device and gestured at Larissa to step forward. She didn't miss the warning in his eyes, reminding Larissa that her words now would correspond directly to Halla's rescue or her demise.

Surprised by the even beating of her heart and the emptiness in her mind, her hands rested against the cold stone of the balcony as she looked out into the still-cheering crowd beneath her. Her pearl ring caught the glare of the lights, emphasizing the Dagaz rune carved into its surface—the symbol of a new day, an end and a beginning. It seemed only weeks, not decades, ago that she had looked over her balcony during the Jóltide Festival, watching her people enter into the palace, wishing they knew that she was their princess.

She had dreamed of this recognition. She had craved it with everything inside of her. Looking out over the crowd, though she felt the absence of her parents more than ever before, she was also emboldened by stirrings of vindication. This was where she had always belonged.

As if realizing that she intended to speak, the crowd hushed so quickly they seemed to be holding their breath. A familiar tinge

of panic raced up Larissa's throat, lengthening the silence.

No longer was she looking out at the crowd, but rather she was seeing the faces of Dal and Vern, her adoptive parents, as they had tucked her and Halla into bed at night. Her own Móðir and Faðir as they told her that she would be making her debut to their people. Her heart ached at the memories, and she knew just what to say.

"People of the Viðnám, I am Princess Lovisa, daughter of King Mikkel and Queen Stjarna, granddaughter of Rúna, who first read the runes and taught our ancestors how to access their *galdr* when the world had all but forgotten the gods of our past. King Torsten spoke of your sorrow and your losses. I know that you have suffered for many years. I come to you also scarred by the Empress' hands."

It was impossible to actually see their eyes, but Larissa could have sworn she felt their stares transfer to the scar along her cheek. She was grateful that Anara had pulled her hair back to reveal the wound.

Larissa continued, "I have witnessed the deaths of my parents, the destruction of my people, the theft of my birthright, the loss of those dearest to me."

Halla.

Larissa paused, her throat constricting painfully. A supportive hand pressed against her lower back, and Larissa knew it was Darien. She wanted to lean into him, to let him take this from her. Instead she forced herself to tilt her chin up and continue. The crowd surged forward, desperate to get closer to her. Larissa's heart did not think only of Halla, but also of those whose hearts clung to her every word.

"I am done letting Shiko win." Larissa ignored the way the crowd gasped at the Empress' name. "I am done letting her threaten our lives. Our family and friends, your children, have been enslaved under Shiko's reign, forced to work and suffer under the sentries' abuse. I plan to march on Perle to reclaim what is mine, and I hope that you will join me."

Her declaration was met with utter silence.

Somewhere in the crowd, a baby cried. Heat crept into Larissa's cheeks. Perhaps, the Viðnám were not ready for war. But what would happen to Halla?

She stepped away from the railing.

"Long live the Princess!"

The cry, which had originated somewhere near the front of the crowd, was echoed by a shrill voice far back in the crowd, then immediately picked up by someone near the front and then another and another until the entire crowd chanted in unison. Chanting a name. Her name.

Lovisa. Lovisa. LOVISA.

Dazzled by the turn of events, Larissa turned from the crowd to find King Torsten watching her. She expected ecstatic elation. She had done it. The Viðnám was going to war.

But as the cheers of the crowd swelled to even greater volumes, Torsten's look was not one of joy, but of calculating concentration.

6

Desperate Times

Halla

HALLA STARED AT JUNI open-mouthed. "You really think there's a way out of here?"

"It's a big risk." Juni huffed, readjusting her grip on the large trough they carried between the two of them. Its contents sloshed as they walked. "Pay attention or we'll drop this."

Halla tightened her hold on the metal rim and tilted her head to the side as she breathed.

Sewer duty was just as bad as Halla had feared. It seemed barbaric to have waste buckets instead of plumbing, but Kai explained the *thrœll*'s reasoning. It was a mental war. The waste bucket was just another attack on Halla's humanity. She was a slave, beneath others, as evident by the cold metal in her hands and the appalling scent.

The compound was surrounded by a tall wall, dotted with sentry towers and lined with barbed wire. But at each of the compound's four corners, a trench had been dug into the base of the wall where water flowed out of the compound from underground pipes and into the city's sewer system. It was into this trench that the girls dumped the contents of the trough, which swirled through the bars blocking the hole and into the tunnel that led out through the wall.

Juni stared intently at the bars. "Before I was caught by the *thrœll*, I ran with a group of kids who showed me how to use the sewer system for a quick escape. It's easy because the bars have been so corroded by the water that you can twist them in and out of their drillings."

Halla's bewilderment must have been evident because Juni's voice became even more fervent. "Halla. The bars can be removed. It's how I escaped last time."

"Last time?" Halla nearly shouted. She glanced around quickly, then lowered her voice. "You've been here before?"

Juni nodded, her face tight. "And I escaped before."

Halla's brows tightened in confusion. "Then why are you still here? Why haven't you escaped again?"

"I was caught." Juni touched the bandage around her neck, then winced. "The punishment was . . . severe." Her voice lowered. "I've been wanting to try again ever since I was brought back, but I was scared."

"What did they do to you?" Halla whispered.

Juni wouldn't meet her gaze, but her fingers pulled at the bandage, revealing the skin underneath. Halla's body shuddered as she swallowed the vomit that rose at the sight of the burned and dying skin. There was some type of pattern there, but Halla couldn't make sense of it before Juni replaced the cloth. What kind of injury could cause such a wound?

Halla stared in horror. "If they did that to you before, why would you try it again?"

"We don't deserve to live like this, slaving away, humiliated, waiting for the next beating." Juni rubbed the bruises around the wrist Fenris had grabbed. "And it's not just about me. You can't go to the Empress. You don't have to tell me why, but I know that look in your eyes. It would be a death sentence, wouldn't it?"

Halla didn't know how to answer.

"Besides"—Juni straightened her spine—"this time, I know how not to get caught."

Though Halla's heart swelled in gratitude, her stomach clenched at the danger she proposed. What was worse, to go to the Empress or risk whatever punishment Juni had received? What would happen to Juni if she was caught again? Something worse, no doubt. If only Lara would come, but as the days passed, anxiety and fear had infected Halla's prayers for her sister.

Oblivious to Halla's internal struggle, Juni walked back toward the barracks with the emptied bucket in her hand. "We'll have to wait until there's no moon; we can't be seen."

"Do we tell the others?" Halla asked.

Juni stopped, laying a hand on Halla's shoulder. "We can't. The bigger our group, the more likely we are to get caught."

Juni's words made sense, but Halla's heart remained conflicted. "We at least tell Kai."

Juni snorted. "Smitten, aren't you?"

"No," Halla protested, ignoring the way the tip of her nose heated.

"Fine, but Halla—"

"What?"

"You can't trust Kai."

"Why not?" Halla didn't understand Juni's abrupt seriousness or the way her eyes flickered away.

"He's not—" She stopped.

Halla nearly stomped her foot in frustration. "He's not what, Juni?"

"Look at him," she muttered. "He's not from the South. Even his name gives him away."

Halla's eyebrows raised. "So?"

"Never mind." Juni shook her head as though shaking off an annoying gnat. "We should get back to work."

They moved from barrack to barrack, emptying the waste troughs as they went, allowing Halla to understand the compound better. The barracks had been split by age; some of the children were as old as Larissa, while others, to Halla's horror, were too young to speak. Many of the older children's rotations included the care of toddlers, who flinched at the sound of the *thrœll*'s footsteps.

Night stole over the compound as the children returned to their barracks. On his way out, a *thræll* threw in the bag containing that night's rations, then locked the door behind him. Halla snatched what provisions she could and retreated to her bunk, her mind and stomach churning at the thought of Juni's escape plan. Kai returned first while Juni still scavenged for what could be found. He shocked her by dumping a bruised apple into her lap.

"What's this for?" she asked.

"Eating."

Halla resisted the urge to smack him, but she was already sinking her teeth into the taut skin, enjoying the sugary juice that flowed over her tongue. "I know what an apple is for. I mean why are you giving it to me?"

"No reason." But his eyes wouldn't meet hers.

Halla closed her eyes, enjoying the apple too much to push. "This is almost as sweet as our strawberries."

"Strawberries?"

"My Pappa grows—grew—the best in the commonwealth."

As if sensing her hesitancy, Kai's voice softened. "I'm sorry."

Halla shrugged but kept her eyes closed, remembering the warm sun on her back as she knelt at her Pappa's side during the picking season. How they would carry the strawberries inside, and Halla would help Mamma make jam, taking small spoonfuls when Mamma would pretend to look away. Tears welled under her eyelids.

"You lived on a farm? How did the *thræll* catch you inside the city?"

Halla's eyes snapped open, but there was only curiosity in Kai's face. She bit the inside of her cheek, remembering Juni's warnings. As if summoned by thought, Juni appeared by her side. She cradled her rations in her hands, but her face looked as though it had been set in stone.

Halla reached out to touch her. "Juni, what's wrong?"

"I was talking to the other children marked for the Empress. They overheard the *thræll*. Halla, you're being transferred in three days."

Halla knew her own face mirrored Juni's look of horror, but it was Kai's unnatural calm that distracted Halla from her panic. Understanding made her voice pitch. "You knew, didn't you?"

He picked at his food. "The *thræll* aren't exactly quiet."

"That's why you gave me your apple!" Halla threw it at him. "Don't pity me, Kai! We have a plan; I'm not going anywhere."

Juni shushed her. "Not now. We'll tell him later."

Halla quieted, the sweet flavor of the apple turning bitter in her mouth as Juni's wound peeked from behind the bandage. Halla swallowed her fear. There was no other option. She couldn't wait for Lara, not with a time clock counting down before she would leave Perle entirely. The goddesses would not wait for saving, and neither would she. Her only option was to follow Juni's plan and rescue herself.

7

Dinner Companions

Larissa

LARISSA CLUTCHED HALLA'S PEBBLE in one hand and her dress in the other to keep from falling as she descended the stairs that led out of the throne room. Several military-styled trucks awaited on the deserted street below along with King Torsten, Speaker Skaði, and Anara, but the sounds of the crowd could still be heard in the distance. Lost in thought, Larissa missed the last step and found herself tumbling forward.

"I've got you." Darien grasped her waist from behind, steadying her on the step below. Larissa looked up, determined to control the heat that rushed to her face. Though humor danced in his eyes, his voice was genuine. "You were fantastic."

"If you're quite done congratulating yourselves, we have a banquet to attend." The look on Torsten's face was enough to bring the heat back into Larissa's cheeks. Darien's hands fell away from Larissa as Torsten paused beside them. "You've done well, Lovisa, but that was only your first hurdle. You will need to speak with the high-ranking members of the Viðnám next. Do not speak to them of Halla or the prophecy; speak little, in fact, but enough that they are certain you are Lovisa."

"Faðir," Darien began, his voice rough with emotion. "Larissa won the crowd, and you taught me it's the people's opinion that matters the most."

"*Lovisa* has appealed to the crowd," he corrected, "which represents only a fraction of the Viðnám, might I add. But on a scale of magnitude such as this, she must also convince the generals."

Irritation flashed in Darien's eyes, but it was the surge of *gal-dr* that emanated from Anara that captured Larissa's attention. Anara stared at Torsten with her lips pressed together tightly. A bright-yellow glow colored her eyes as her pupils narrowed to cat-like slits.

"I thought I made it clear that you were to keep your shifting under control while you were here," Torsten snapped.

Anara smiled wide, revealing rows of sharpened teeth. "I think you'll find that I very much have this under control. You might remember that as the Crown Princess of Rubin, I do not answer to you, *King* Torsten, any more than you answer to me."

Speaker Skaði stepped between them. "It is wise for us all to remember that violence between the kingdoms led to our current predicament. While you are the leader of the Viðnám, King Torsten, Princess Anara is correct. Had she control of her kingdom, she would have been crowned Queen by now. She does not owe you her allegiance any more than I do. We must find a way to coexist peacefully; otherwise, this war is lost before it is even begun. Besides, I do enjoy watching her transformations."

Torsten's mouth opened and closed in an undignified manner. "Very well, but for the sake of our cause, *Princess* Anara, I *ask* you to consider refraining from too many *transformations* that might only alienate our allies."

Anara's teeth and eyes returned to normal. "I'll consider it."

King Torsten gestured to the first truck. "We don't tend to use vehicles within the valley; gas is a precious commodity, but Lovisa's presence will make it impossible to reach the banquet hall on foot through the crowd. We'll have to take two trucks."

At his words, the drivers moved to open the back doors in unison. Torsten and Skaði filed into the first truck. Anara approached the second vehicle, muttering to herself. "Like the mighty Thor, we must face the trials wrought for us at the hands of the giant Skrymir."

"Isn't that the story where the cat is actually the serpent?" Larissa asked.

"And the old woman is actually old age itself?" Darien echoed, his eyes twinkling.

Larissa's smile stretched across her face, her mind and body drawn into her past where their conversations had come this easily, but it faded as the smooth pebble in her hand reminded her of Halla.

Noticing, Darien held out his hand. "I can hold it for you. Just through the banquet so you don't lose it."

She *would* look ridiculous walking into the banquet hall with a rock in her hand, and, of course, her dress didn't have pockets, but still she hesitated. Forcing her fingers to unclench, she dropped the pebble into Darien's open palm.

"Darien!" King Torsten called. "Join me."

There would be no argument. That much was clear. Darien tucked the pebble into his pocket, but his gaze lingered. As though of its own accord, his hand reached up to cup Larissa's scarred cheek. "Don't let him get to you. We're one step closer to getting Halla back, and maybe then—"

"Darien!"

He grimaced in comical exaggeration. Pulled by his father's command, Darien walked toward the truck, and the door slammed with obstinate finality.

Anara placed a hand on her hip. "Think Torsten wants to put some space between you two?"

Larissa snorted. "You don't say."

"Come on, let's go before they leave us here."

Navigating the difficulty of their dresses, they slid into the truck. Its cushioned seats rumbled as their truck followed the one ahead of them. The front of the cab was separated by a thick plastic wall from the back, giving them total privacy that Anara seemed all too ready to exploit.

"So what *is* going on between you and Darien?"

Larissa groaned. "Anara . . ."

"Oh come on, you have to remember everything now, right? You two were nauseating to be around, and now you're dancing around each other on tiptoes."

"It's different now." Larissa stopped, her own emotions muddling the words she wanted to say. How could she explain that every time she remembered her life as Lovisa, it threatened to destroy the life she'd built as Larissa? Everything had revolved around keeping Halla safe, but Halla was gone. Before that, Lovisa's life had been about a prophecy that she didn't understand. Now she was an icon for a rebellion she wasn't sure she could win. "I'm different now."

Anara shook her head. "It's like you said: you're Larissa, but only you can decide what that means. The Norn dealt you a rough hand, but you're more than the path they gave you. Like choosing your own name, you can carve your own path."

"And what path is that?"

"It's the same path that led you to gain the support of the Viðnám. It's the path that will lead you to Halla, and then if you choose, it'll lead you to discovering and fulfilling the Norn's prophecy."

"If I choose?" Larissa scoffed, sinking lower in her seat. "I think choice isn't a luxury I can afford."

"Lara, if you choose to save Halla and run, I wouldn't stop you."

Larissa's eyes widened. "You wouldn't?"

"Of course not." Anara smirked. "We both know you never would."

Before Lovisa's memories had come back, it's exactly what Larissa would have done, but now she wasn't so sure. "How do you know?"

"Because I know you wouldn't abandon *them*."

At Anara's pointed glance, Larissa looked out the tinted window. Though the crowd could not see in, Larissa could certainly see them in the lamplight. People who had thronged forward to try and catch a glimpse at the returned royalty. The trucks crawled through the city streets to avoid running anyone over.

Anara leaned against her door. "This is why Torsten seemed unhappy with you after the announcement. You were meant to inspire them to follow *him* into battle, but you made them love you instead. You're their lost Princess, their final hope, and no matter what Torsten does, they will never love him as they love you."

Larissa's eyebrows pinched together. "That doesn't seem fair to Torsten."

"Maybe not." Anara shrugged. "But nothing in war is fair. If I've learned anything since I lost you two, it's that I have to make the most of any advantage I have, fair or not. Just listen."

Lovisa. Lovisa. LOVISA.

The roar of the crowd swelled to a crescendo as the truck passed by, her name echoing from the lips of hundreds. Larissa scanned the crowd, drinking in face after face, memorizing their features as best as she could. They all had someone they loved. They all had someone they'd lost. If she had the power to help, shouldn't she? Fate or choice, this was the path Larissa would follow. She would save Halla, but Larissa wouldn't run. She couldn't.

Her people needed her just as much as Halla did.

The truck lumbered along the crisscrossing streets nestled within the mountains, then crossed through a large gate and into an immense courtyard. The sound of the crowd faded to a dull murmur beyond the perimeter. Larissa's door opened, and she looked into Darien's brilliant sea-blue eyes framed by dark lashes. Tingles of anticipation scattered the rhythm of her heart as she slid her hand into his. There was something incredibly familiar about the shape of his skin, yet accompanied by a strange array of new calluses on both of their hands. It was as if their palms remembered each other but could not make sense of the changes of time.

Stepping onto the cobblestone, Larissa took in the courtyard, which was bathed in the light of the moon that had taken possession of the sky. The runes sewn onto her gown glowed in the moonlight. In the middle of the circular drive was a fountain featuring the sibling goddess Sol and god Mani pulling their chariots carrying the sun and moon across the sky. Ahead of them, King Torsten and Skaði waited—the former with ill-concealed impatience, the latter with her typical self-assured serenity.

"We will enter as one," Torsten explained. "Speaker Skaði, it would be my pleasure to escort you. Darien, you will need to escort both Lovisa and—"

"Just Larissa is fine, Torsten," Anara interjected, adjusting the blood-red garment that hung over her shoulder. "I don't need an escort, and we both know that your war council will be more friendly to Darien if I am not at his side."

Torsten inclined his head, too willing to accept her proposal. "As you wish, Anara."

Though Darien threw an annoyed look toward his father, he offered his arm to Larissa, as he had done for years. All at once, Larissa could see it in her mind, the dozens of events where Darien had escorted her, starting when he was only a boy. The look on Darien's face told Larissa that he was remembering the same thing.

Surrounded by the rebellion, in the home of the giants, with the unknown fate of the Norn hovering over her, Larissa should have felt fear, but when she took Darien's arm, it simply felt like home. They faced the grand ash doors that stood just beyond Torsten and Skaði, upon which two large runes of welcome and hospitality had been inlaid with gold. Anara walked beside them unescorted as they passed through the opening doors.

Dozens of voices bounced off the banquet hall walls. They echoed against vaulted ceilings covered with illustrations that spoke of the old magic—Baldr's mistletoe, Iðunn's golden apples, Hel's ribcage, landscapes encompassing dark forests, and misty mountains containing chaotic wilderness. In the ceiling's center resided a stone well lined with glowing golden runes. Only then did Larissa notice that behind every image and intertwined within them all was the great *Yggdrasil*. Larissa could have stared at it for hours, but the room itself had become unnaturally silent, drawing her attention away from the mural.

The guests had noticed their arrival.

Although everyone bowed to King Torsten, their stares fell to Larissa. Torsten gestured in triumph at the group behind them. "Might I introduce Princess Lovisa, Prince Darien, and Princess Anara."

It was only muscle memory and years of etiquette lessons that prompted Larissa to dip into a deep curtsy. Darien too bowed, and although one might argue what Anara had done was technically a curtsy, it would have been a stretch.

"Let us be seated," King Torsten's voice boomed.

The guests found their seats around the long banquet table with such ease that Larissa wondered if they had been assigned. Servants waited behind each chair, already pouring drinks from the pitchers in their hands. She was guided to a seat closer to the head of the table, where King Torsten resided. On his right sat the Speaker Skaði. On Torsten's left sat Darien, whereas Larissa sat next to Speaker Skaði. Anara took her seat between Darien and another man Larissa did not recognize. At the sight of the man, Anara's face hardened as she turned deliberately away from him.

Not all of the guests were from the kingdoms of Evrópa; many were Jötnar like Skaði. The only physical markers that unified them were their abnormal height and deep amber eyes. Some Jötnar, like the Speaker, had dark skin, darker even than that of the Smaragdians present. Others were paler than herself, and some appeared tanned from the sun, but they all moved with an unearthly cadence.

With relief, Larissa found the dinner companion who sat to her right was none other than Halvor, who winked at her from behind his crescent-moon glasses.

"Well done, Princess," he whispered.

Torsten rose from his seat, a glass in hand. "My most esteemed guests from the kingdoms of Safír, Perle, Smaragd, Rubin, and *Jötunheim*, tonight is a night of celebration." Torsten's voice was the warmest Larissa had heard since he'd first been reunited with Darien. "Tonight marks the turning of the tides. A new thread has been strung on the Norn's great loom. This is the start of a new era in which we will dethrone the False Empress and reclaim our lands, but talk of strategy and war is best discussed in the light of day. Tonight, we drink!"

The guests followed in Torsten's lead in raising a glass and downing the ruby liquid within it. Larissa followed suit. The drink, although chilled, burned her throat the whole way down and left the surprisingly sweet flavor of honey on her tongue. Talk and laughter broke out up and down the grand table.

"Do you like the drink?" Speaker Skaði asked in her melodic tone.

Larissa cleared her throat. "Yes, but I don't think I've ever had it before. What is it?"

"*Kvase*." She smiled around the glass as she took another sip. This close, Larissa could see that her amber eyes were rimmed in the same dark wine-red of the drink. "It is made from the blood of the god Kvasir mixed with the honey of the dwarves."

Larissa's mouth opened, then closed, unsure if the Speaker was serious.

In the seat next to Anara, a man snickered loudly. His dark-brown hair fell in waves touching the top of his collar. He threw back the glass filled with *Kvase* before cocking his gaze in Larissa's direction. "I would tell you not to worry about the dwarves, Princess, but here we sit among giants. Apparently, all the stories of old are true."

Skaði's delicate eyebrows were drawn into disdain for only a moment before she emptied her face of emotion.

"You are the same as you've always been," Anara drawled, not looking at the man.

"It's an honor you remember me." He turned toward Anara. Light danced off the tiny ruby buttons running down his white jacket. " I wasn't sure after such a cold reception, Your Highness."

"I remember you, General Ishaan." Anara flashed him a set of canines that extended past her lips. "I just didn't want to greet you."

"Your tongue is still as sharp as your claws, Your Highness," he returned, baring a smile filled with his own set of sharpened teeth. The servant refilling his glass pulled back in alarm.

Larissa jolted in her seat as the realization sunk in.

"You're a shifter?" Darien leaned forward to look past Anara. Beyond Darien, Torsten's lips turned downward before the king's attention was drawn away by a man who had come to speak with him.

"I am, Prince Darien; perhaps the only Rubinian here, besides Princess Anara, who is able to access our ancestral *galdr*. Of course, my skills are nothing compared to hers. We have missed having your tactical advantages on many missions since you left us, Highness."

"I'm sure you've been just fine." Anara's nostrils flared as she refused to make eye contact no matter how hard General Ishaan tried.

Larissa had never seen Anara look so uncomfortable, and Larissa had seen her when her insides had nearly become her outsides. Nowhere, in either set of memories, could Larissa remember this man. Had Anara met him after Larissa's and Darien's disappearance? One glance at Darien beside her confirmed that he had no recollection of Ishaan either.

A moment of awkward silence pervaded before the arrival of food served on porcelain plates. The normal buzz of conversation rose up once again, but beneath it Larissa felt the stares of the servants, the generals, and even the Jötnar who analyzed her in obvious fascination. Everyone watched her movements, weighing her on the scales within their own minds, measuring her up against the prophecy they'd only ever heard in rumors. Their whispers failed so wholly in their discretion that Larissa wondered if they wanted her to hear them.

"...it's said that she will kill the Empress..."

"...I heard she has *galdr* that's never been seen before..."

"...she's one of the goddesses returned from Hel's realm..."

Larissa focused on her own plate. Let the people think what they would. She needed their support.

"We are so pleased to have you returned to us, Princess Lovisa," came a man's voice from Larissa's right. His face was familiar, but strange. She tried to look underneath the wrinkles at the man he would have been fifty years ago.

"Soren?"

"General Soren now, Your Highness." He inclined his head, his thinning hair more evident at the top. "I represent our people here in the Viðnám." The wrinkled skin around his pale blue eyes creased. "Do you remember me?"

"You were training under my father's advisors." He'd been even younger than Lovisa.

"I was," Soren said, his delight obvious that Larissa had remembered him. "I can't believe I never realized who you were. All those years, the King and Queen claimed you as a ward. They guarded your secret well."

"Perhaps too well," another voice chimed in from the seat next to General Soren. This man stood out from those at the table as severely as the Jötnar, although he was clearly not one of them. His skin was light, but with warmer undertones than Larissa was familiar with. His hair was more than dark; it was the color of pitch. His dress clearly identified him as another general. "How do we know for certain that this is the Princess of Perle?"

"Do you doubt King Tortsten's ability to distinguish fact from fiction?" Anara's voice dripped innocence, but her words were enough to chill those who heard them.

"No, of course not," the man added, his gaze far too hostile to be polite. "Although it is sometimes hard to tell the truth when monsters disguised as friends walk amongst us."

Anara's and Ishaan's faces tightened. Lightning flashed in Darien's eyes. His gaze roved pointedly up and down the man's stature. "Sometimes monsters look just like men, don't they?"

Before he could do more than bluster at Darien's statement, Anara asked, "How would you test her authenticity, General?"

"She could explain where she has been for the past fifty years while her people have bled under the hand of the False Empress."

The table fell silent. Even King Torsten was pulled away from the man with whom he had been engaged in a deep conversation only a moment before. His eyes, like all of those who sat at the table, turned to stare at Larissa.

"And you are?" Larissa asked, more to compose herself than out of actual curiosity.

The man's mouth moved as if he were chewing on something sour; begrudgingly, he tilted his head as if remembering his place. "General Aiko, Your Highness."

"Aiko." Anara twirled the stem of her glass between her fingers. "That's a Diamantian name, isn't it?"

Red splotches crept up the man's cheeks. "I have renounced my commonwealth and the False Empress."

"Naturally"—Anara tilted her head—"but you might want to rethink calling anyone at this table a monster in disguise when you originate from the home of the monstress herself. One might question your loyalties."

The man started to rise.

"*Enough.*"

All faces turned, surprised the sharp voice had not come from King Torsten but rather from Speaker Skaði. Towering over the table, she demanded their attention with a single glare. If Skaði had appeared large before, she was enormous now, her head nearly touching the ceiling. The calm countenance Larissa had grown accustomed to had all but disappeared. Her eyes raged and burned as if on fire.

Galdr poured from her frame, seeping into all in attendance. The only guests that did not flinch from the onslaught were the other Jötnar who watched in comfortable silence, sipping at their *Kvase*.

"Might I remind you that you are all guests under the Jötnar's care? What do we care if you originate from Rubin or Diamant? Are you united against the False Empress, or will you allow yourselves to be destroyed by your own pride as the *Æsir* were on the day of *Ragnarok*?" Skaði's voice rose. "Those haughty gods believed they might rewrite history. They were consumed in fire and water. With their deaths came the destruction of our world, the Separation of our Nations, the reclamation of Ancestral Magic, oh yes, but at what cost?"

King Torsten stood, laying one hand at the Speaker's elbow.

Like a flash of lightning, Skaði turned on the King. All around the table, hands fell to waists where men clasped at their weapons. But instead of attacking, the Speaker quieted, shrinking back into the composure of serenity. As if Skaði's *galdr* had flooded through Larissa's system, every nerve burned a slow but steady fire that raced through her, strengthening her. Her own *galdr* raced to the surface, but something was blocking it, keeping it just under her skin.

Larissa's voice cut the silence. "General Aiko, you want to know where I've been? For the past year, I lived amongst the Safírians, taken in by the farmer Dal and his wife, Vern, and their daughter, Halla. I have witnessed first hand the abuse that you reference and have endured it myself."

Knowing her words would not be enough, Larissa willed her mind to dig into that pit in her stomach where she could feel her *galdr* coiling within her. She pushed past the resistance she felt and opened her hand toward the glass on the table. Like tiny explosions, electricity crackled between her fingers as the glass flew into her palm. She took a long sip of the fiery concoction to settle her nerves, well aware of the eyes that had widened at her nonchalant use of Perlian *galdr* that had not been seen for decades. Setting down the glass, she flicked her fingers, extinguishing the remainder of the glow, but she still had one last card to play. "Before that, I lived amongst the Norn."

True, she couldn't remember most of it, but they didn't need to know that.

Aiko's face paled, as did many others at the mention of the goddesses of fate. Darien smirked into his goblet as Anara grinned openly at Aiko, her teeth bared against his disdain.

"Does that answer satisfy?" Larissa asked.

Although he regained his composure, General Aiko could only nod. The arrival of the first course broke the tension. In time, conversation resumed down the table. Once she was certain no one was looking, Larissa allowed herself a small moment to release the breath she had held tightly in her chest.

This wasn't going to be as easy as she'd thought.

8

Desperate Measures

Halla

Kai stared at Juni and Halla in abject condemnation. "It's a stupid plan."

"This is why I didn't want to invite him." Juni hissed, her face only inches away from Kai's.

The three of them sat on Halla's bunk, doing their best to not wake the other children with their fierce whispers. It had taken forever for the others to fall asleep as Halla chewed at her fingernails until they bled. Only once they were certain they would not be overheard did Juni and Halla tell Kai their plan for escape. Her mind replayed Juni's plan over and over again as they waited to share it with Kai. While Halla had not expected Kai's full enthusiasm, she had not been prepared for his anger.

"You're a *hálfviti* if you really think this will work," Kai continued.

"You're just scared," Juni argued.

Kai ground his teeth. "You *know* what happens to slaves who try to run. Does Halla?"

Juni crossed her arms. "I showed her."

Kai turned disbelieving eyes toward Halla. "And you still agreed to this?"

Halla shrank from his glare.

"What else is she supposed to do?" Juni argued. "Wait and hope the mythical Viðnám chooses to rescue her? She has a better chance waiting for the gods!"

Kai's face went rigid. "If you do this, you'll get more than burned, Juni!"

Juni fumed, staring into Kai's face with enough ferocity that Halla reconsidered their plans. But she couldn't wait for Larissa, not when her transfer was set to take place in less than two days.

"We're going," Juni said. "Are you coming or not?"

In the dark, Halla could only see the silhouette of Kai's arms crossed tightly over his chest. "*Hel's*, Juni, you aren't thinking."

"Let's go, Halla."

Juni jumped to her feet, her dark shadow moving down toward the back of the barrack. The metal paneling had rusted at the bottom, and with enough persistent force, Juni had loosened it in the past twenty-four hours. There would be no replacing the panel after their escape, but if all went according to plan, Juni and Halla would be gone before the gap was noticed. Halla stood, only for Kai's hand to wrap around the crook of her elbow, holding her back.

"Don't go."

Halla stared in shock at Kai's dark silhouette. "I have to; I can't go to Diamant."

"Why?"

"I just can't."

"Does it have to do with that warehouse that collapsed on the day you were taken?"

She bit her cheek.

"Halla, you won't make it. It'll just make things worse for you here, and they won't forgive Juni a second time."

She yanked her arm free. "We have to try."

"You could die."

Halla swallowed, her parents' faces flashing violently before her eyes. "I can't go to the Empress."

Emotion drained from Kai's voice. "You'll regret this."

"Halla, if we're doing this, we have to go," Juni hissed.

She hesitated, but Kai had already turned away. Halla stood torn between the two. Why should he care what she did? He wasn't the one being sent to the Empress in two days. Kai couldn't understand. Her indecision resolved, and Halla scurried down the barrack.

Cold morning air drifted in from the open panel. This was it.

Juni crouched at the opening, her eyes squinting into the darkness and waiting for the change of the sentries. She flicked her hand forward twice. Silent as the stars, she slipped through the hole with Halla on her heels. They ran with their backs against the barrack walls in a crouch that caused Halla's thighs to cramp up. Grateful that Juni was leading in the dark night, Halla could hardly tell one barrack from another.

She stopped so abruptly that Halla collided into her back, causing Juni to hiss as she stumbled forward. Just beyond them was the drainage tunnel and the bars that might lead to their freedom. The tang of sewage water wafted in the air. What stopped them short was not the smell, but rather the empty space between them and the tunnel. There were no further barracks, no bushes, nothing to conceal their flight. Nothing but wide open ground they would have to cross.

Halla's neck tingled as she took in the bandage on Juni's neck. If they were seen, Juni's fate would be Halla's. As for Juni, Halla didn't want to imagine. In the harsh chill of the night, doubts crept into Halla's mind.

But Juni's thin face was set. "I'll go first. Once I'm across, I'll remove the bar that will let us slip through. Then you run as fast and as quietly as you can."

Halla couldn't shake the unease creeping up her throat. They shouldn't do this. Kai was right. Larissa would come; Halla just needed to be patient. She'd already failed Juni once. How could she let Juni risk herself for Halla when Halla hadn't been willing to do the same? She reached out to grab Juni, to tell her they had to return to the barrack before they were caught. Her mouth opened to form the words, her fingers reached out to clasp Juni, but between one breath and another, Juni was gone.

Halla shrank back in the shadows, praying, but never had she felt more alone.

Juni ran with abandon, her head trained forward, refusing to look around her, focused only on the task at hand. Although her feet were swift, it seemed to have taken a ridiculously long time for her to cross the empty space between Halla and the drainage tunnel. Her body became a shadow, consumed by the darkness.

Halla couldn't stand the waiting. She scanned the parameter wall, searching for the white-and-black arm bands that would put an end to their escape, but it was too dark to see anything. Halla could only hope it would be too dark for the *thræll* to see them as well.

The light sound of splashing drew Halla's eyes back toward Juni, though she still could not see the other girl. Halla held her breath.

Please, Frigg, Halla thought, her mind bent feverishly toward the goddess who cared the most for children, *don't let them see us.*

A metallic squeal protested in the darkness. Juni had made it to the bars. There was a short whistle. Juni's signal. The unease in Halla's stomach turned to acid. Fear of being left behind overwhelmed her uncertainty. She leapt from the shadows, straining her short legs to cross the great expanse. She was nearly there. She could see Juni, whose smile stretched across her face as she wordlessly urged Halla to run faster with her hands.

Then Juni's smile vanished. Her hands froze. Blood fled from her face. "Halla, run!"

"Get back here, *skútur*!"

Halla would know Fenris' voice anywhere.

Heavy footsteps landed behind her. Halla imagined Fenris' hot breath on the back of her neck, his hands reaching out like sharp claws of a wolf. But even worse than her imagination was the reality in front of her. Juni squeezed through the gap in the bars.

Indecision strained the furrow of her brows; then, resolute determination chased it away.

Halla reached for her. "Juni!"

Juni slipped away into the tunnel.

Halla's feet slapped the water when large hands wove into what was left of her hair, yanking her back and throwing her against the dirt. The breath left her lungs in one hard swoosh. She rolled to her side, gasping against the emptiness in her chest. Hot tears stung the corners of her eyes.

Juni had abandoned her.

"You stupid *slápr*. I told you not to make me angry," Fenris growled. He grabbed another fistful of hair, dragging her behind him. He turned to face someone Halla couldn't see. "Send someone into the tunnel; bring back the other one."

Halla cried out, her hands clinging to Fenris' wrists, desperate to relieve the pain in her scalp. Rocks and gravel shredded her clothes, sending stinging pain shooting through her nerves. The entire compound had seemingly come to life with noise rising around her, but nothing could compare to the thumping of her blood that pounded in her ears. Adrenaline spiked through her veins, and the air was too thin for her burning lungs.

"Did you really think we wouldn't consider one of you *slápr* trying to use the tunnels? Or that we didn't know how the other one had escaped before?" Mockery and derision laced Fenris' words. "It would never occur to you imbeciles that the weakness in our walls is an intentional opportunity for us to remind you all what happens to those who disobey."

He dragged her toward the middle of the intake grounds, where a large fire had been lit, tended by several of the *thræll*. Halla flinched from the heat of the flames as they crackled as if in laughter. Fenris flung her to the ground. She curled up, tucking her chin to her knees, as if she could make herself disappear, but the world around her was too vivid and brusque to allow her that escape.

Shouts from the *thræll* intermingled with the fire and Halla's own sobs. At the crack of their whips, the barracks emptied and the children gathered like a herd around Halla and the flames. Some of the children who'd been brought in after Halla stared in confusion and fear, but many of the others set their mouths in firm lines, staring at the ground as their eyes worked to conceal their apprehension.

"Move closer," Fenris shouted, grim amusement evident in his words. "I want you all to see what happens to slaves who forget their place."

The snaps of whips overwhelmed any hesitancy as the crowd pushed in closer. Halla buried her face in the dirt, wishing she might choke on the dust that filled her nostrils. She didn't think to stand, or to run.

She had no thoughts of escape, only survival.

Fenris' callused hands grabbed the bare skin on Halla's neck, pulling her to her feet. She choked against his grip, her hands frantically pulling against his. Behind Fenris, someone in the crowd rushed to the front. Halla recognized the messy black hair instantly. But there was nothing Kai could do.

"There is a lesson you *all* must learn." The fire cracked and snapped as if to accentuate Fenris' words. "There is no escape. You are slaves, *skútur* not worthy to be tracked in on the bottom of my boot. Your only purpose in life is to serve the Empress and her decrees. Tonight, I will remind you what happens to those who dare defy our Empress."

Fenris released Halla's throat, shoving her back into the hands of two *thræll* who pulled her arms behind her back. Gasping in air, Halla watched in paralyzed fear as Fenris moved toward the fire and withdrew a long metal rod. The end of the rod had been shaped into a letter Halla did not recognize. Its white glow burned her eyes.

"

This is Thurisaz rune, given to mortals by the giants. Tonight it is a reminder that suffering is the only gift given to those who disobey the Empress."

Juni's rotting skin blurred before Halla's gaze, distorted by her own tears. The sentries forced her head down, exposing the top of her spine.

"Please!" she begged, her body thrashing away from the pain it knew was coming.

Searing pain scorched her skin. Agony ripped through her body as screams tore from her throat. Darkness crowded her vision as she collapsed to the ground.

She was not Iðunn, or Anara, or even Larissa. She was only Halla. A girl with no *galdr*, no hope, and no escape.

ᚾᛁᛘᚱᛋᚾᛁᛘᚱᛋᚾᛁᛘᚱᛋᚾᛁᛘᚱᛋᚾᛁᛘᚱᛋ

Eyes as dark as night, shaded by black hair the color of Anara's feathers, filled Halla's vision. Everything about him was so dark, and yet he was the only bright light in the void Halla had fallen into.

"Come on, storyteller, stay awake."

If Halla could laugh, she might have at the concern in Kai's voice. What did he care? What did anyone care? But she couldn't laugh; all she could focus on was the darkness. And beneath the darkness, Halla could feel the flames.

She dreamed she was back in her family's barn, hiding beneath the trapdoor as the fires set by the *draugr* burned all around her. The fire ate at her side, inching its way up her back, devouring her skin as the flames traveled with greedy fingers until they settled and burrowed into the top of her spine.

She was burning. Halla thrashed against the flames, but she could not move.

"Help me hold her! She's going to make it worse!"

Where had Halla heard that voice? It belonged to a boy with ink-black eyes. Another wave of fire consumed her, burning away thoughts of anything else. This time she dreamed it was the *draugr* whose sharp claws tore down her spine.

"You're going to be okay."

She moaned against the pain, her eyes roving beneath their lids. "Lara!"

"Who's Lara?" the voice asked. "Who's Lara, Halla?"

But Halla had already left the realm of reason. Gods danced across her vision. Frigg looked down upon her in sorrow; she had failed in her duty to protect all children. Loki's mischievous eyes twinkled in delight at Juni's abandonment. Juni had saved herself. Hadn't Halla done the same? The Great Wanderer stroked the head of his raven, all the while examining Halla like some animal he had never yet seen. Curious, yet ultimately unconcerned at her fate.

But more vibrant than any of the gods was a girl with flaming red hair that danced in a breezeless wind. The visions paused, allowing Halla a moment in a serene field where the long grasses tickled her knees. The largest tree she had ever seen stretched from one end of her vision to another. The red-headed child in front of it was even smaller than Halla. She stood on top of the well's stone wall to run her fingers down Halla's back. Halla sighed at her touch, as it left behind a cooling river to soothe the flaming skin.

"It'll be alright, Halla. Sleep."

In the absence of pain, reverence sank in. "Who are you?"

"That's a silly question coming from you, storyteller."

Halla's breath caught. "Verðandi?"

The child-goddess grinned from ear to ear. "Lovisa will know how to find us. We're waiting for you, Halla; we still need you to tell our story."

9

Personal Bias

Anara

Anara analyzed the vein in Torsten's forehead, wondering what it would take for it to actually burst. She leaned back in the seat next to Larissa, yet her body was as tightly wound as a grandfather clock.

"What do you mean, you don't know the prophecy?" Torsten asked through clenched teeth.

Larissa raised her chin. "If you remember my mother, Torsten, you'll remember she didn't like talking about the prophecy. Not even to me."

Torsten's hands clenched upon the table. Beside him, Halvor looked down, his eyes troubled behind his spectacles. Even Speaker Skaði's usual composure was lacking its normal serenity. At his father's side, Darien spun his sapphire ring around his finger, but Anara retained her predatory stillness, waiting to see which way the tide would turn.

Torsten exhaled sharply. "What did she tell you, *exactly*?"

"Exactly?" Larissa shook her head. "Nothing. All I know is what I overheard or inferred over time. The Norn gave my grandmother the gift of the *galdr* but warned her that the peace between kingdoms wouldn't last. Then the Norn prophesied to my mother that I would be the only one who could restore peace, but at a great cost. My mother feared that cost so much that she hid my identity from our people my entire life. That's all I know."

"It's not enough," Torsten muttered, glancing at the four empty chairs at the end of the table. "The council members will be here soon. They will want to be reassured that you can actually defeat Shiko before we risk open war."

Politics, Anara thought bitterly. It was one of the many reasons she'd been glad to leave the Viðnám the first time.

Larissa paled. "You promised if I rallied the Viðnám that you would march on Perle and help me find Halla."

"I'm not a dictator, Lovisa." Torsten sat tall. "The generals represent their people here in the Viðnám. If they are not reassured, they may advocate to not march their people anywhere. Even if I were to force them, would you want unwilling soldiers forced to die for you? Is that the type of Queen you plan to be?"

Darien twisted toward his father. "So, we reassure them without telling them the whole prophecy. We tell them the Norn have sworn Larissa to secrecy."

Anara tapped the ruby pendant that hung around her neck. "They already think Larissa has been living with the Norn for some time, and no one would want to argue against the goddesses of fate. It would work."

Torsten glanced to his left. "Halvor, what do you think?"

Halvor removed his spectacles, wiping them against his shirt. "We'd be lying, Your Majesty. It would be a precarious way to start a war."

"More of an omission than a lie," Speaker Skaði added, her fingers pressed against one another.

The soft thumps of footfalls down the hall sounded in Anara's ears. "Choose quickly, Torsten; the council members are nearly here."

Seconds ticked by; the footsteps grew louder, though Anara knew only she could hear them. Torsten's nostrils flared. "If they ask about the prophecy, I will answer their questions, but Lovisa"—his sharp eyes locked on Larissa—"Norn help you if you are unable to uphold your end of this war."

Anara hissed under her breath just as the knock sounded at the door. The incoming council members took their seats, oblivious to the conflict still lingering in the air. Anara ignored Ishaan, who'd chosen the seat across from her, and met Darien's gaze, her own frustrations reflected in his eyes. Though Larissa accepted the greetings of the generals with a calm voice, Anara noticed the rapid rise and fall of her chest.

"Welcome." Torsten pushed a large map toward the center of the table. "There is no time for pleasantries, so let's get straight to it. Currently, we are situated in the middle of the five kingdoms . . ."

Anara's eyes skimmed over the map she knew from heart, having traveled so much of it. The Viðnám was nestled deep at the center of the map surrounded by the Nordryggen Mountains on all sides—the only reason Anara had not discovered its existence earlier. Diamant, Shiko's commonwealth, resided in the top north segment, but Torsten ignored it along with Smaragd, which lay to the northwest, and Rubin to the northeast. He placed his finger on Perle, which was near the southwesternmost point.

"We will march on Lystheim first," Torsten ordered. "The city of Perle is the least guarded and therefore the easiest to capture. We'll need to locate her Regent swiftly, a man called Hammon. He's ruthless enough to order his men to fight to the death even if it's a losing battle."

Anara knew of Hammon—more specifically of the gallows he used to string up the citizens that displeased him.

"If we depose him early on, we can end the fighting sooner and move the Viðnám within its walls," Torsten continued, walking his fingers to the neighboring commonwealth in the east. "From there, we advance on Safír. We'll have two commonwealths under our control before Shiko is able to send reinforcements from Diamant or Rubin. At that point, we will decide whether to take Smaragd or Rubin next, but the fight north will certainly become more difficult as Shiko realizes the strength of the Viðnám. I anticipate she will send her Regents and *draugrs* to wear us out long before she joins the fighting herself."

"With any luck, the False Empress will not truly see us as a threat at all," Halvor added. "More than likely, she will remain in Diamant until we come to her and wait to strike us down then. She believes herself to be undefeatable."

"That is where Princess Lovisa changes things." Speaker Skaði inclined her head toward Larissa. "The Norn predicted long ago that there would be an end to the peace, but that one would be able to set it right. That one is Princess Lovisa; it is why Shiko burned down half of Perle to try and find her."

"It's war we propose, gentlemen," Torsten finished. "A bloody war, but with every chance of success."

Anara's blood thrummed at the idea. After decades of running, she was ready to hunt, but the council members' faces betrayed their own hesitancy.

General Sture pulled at his large walrus mustache with such force, Anara wasn't sure how it stayed on. "You mean for us to attack? *Now*?"

Anara tilted her head toward the man. "Would you rather hide in the mountains for another few decades, General?"

"Princess Anara," he addressed her, but his darting eyes would not meet her own. "It is not wise to fight unless one is certain of victory."

"If I remember correctly, it was Smaragdians' refusal to fight Shiko the first time that gave her the momentum she needed to claim Evrópa before."

His expression soured. "I believe a good deal of Rubinian *draugr* also assisted in that process."

"Exactly why I'm willing to pay our debts," Anara bit out, ignoring the way Ishaan's lips tightened at her words.

"*Now* is the time," Torsten broke in. "We waited because we didn't believe we could win before. We can now."

"Because of Princess Lovisa?" Ishaan asked. "I'm sorry, but I'm not familiar with the wording of this prophecy. How is she able to kill Shiko when so many others have failed?"

"Because the Norn have said so." Torsten glared around the table. "They have commanded Princess Lovisa to withhold their prophecy for the time being"—he raised his hands at the instant protests—"and I am not one to argue with the goddesses of fate."

An uneasy silence grew as none dared to counter the words of the Norn. Anara took small pleasure in their discomfort.

"Why Perle first?" General Aiko asked, scrutinizing the map. "Surely, if Your Majesty reclaimed Safír first, your people in the city would rush to your side, increasing our armies."

"Are you insinuating that the people of Perle wouldn't do the same for their lost Princess?" General Soren demanded, a vein bulging in his neck.

"Of course not," Aiko answered with a wave of his hand. "But Perle is the weakest of the commonwealths; there is no tactical advantage to reclaiming a city filled with half-starved citizens. Many will be unfit for war."

"General Aiko is not wrong, tactically speaking," Ishaan agreed.

Halvor lowered his glasses, wiping them against his sleeve. "Generals. I, too, eagerly wish to reclaim Safír, to see if my family still lives, but sometimes there is more to our choices than personal wishes and tactics."

Aiko scoffed. "But—"

Anara growled; she would rather go up against another *draugr* than listen to old men bicker for another moment. "We're wasting time. Perle might be the weakest in numbers, but it is also the least defended. If that is not reason enough, General Aiko, King Torsten has made this promise to Princess Lovisa, and he can't go back on it now."

Torsten's face tightened. "I am well aware of our agreement, Princess Anara."

"I hate to say it." Aiko's well-oiled voice grated against Anara's ears. "Though I feel someone must for the sake of the Viðnám. Perhaps the Princess might consider releasing King Torsten from the agreement. Surely, Princess Lovisa must see that reclaiming a city filled with able fighters must take precedence over any personal bias."

"You overstep, General." Darien's irritation was ill-concealed.

Though Aiko bowed his head, Anara heard the words he whispered against his chest. "Hardly any whiskers on his face, yet he scolds me."

Larissa rose silently without show, but it was enough to silence the room. She flattened her palms on the table. "I am reclaiming Perle. My mind won't be changed. If you have a problem with that, I will go myself with whoever will join me."

Anara grinned openly in delight at Larissa's threat. If she were to go, it was clear that the Viðnám would be split in half, as many would follow her.

"Your people are ready, Highness," General Soren chimed.

"The Jötnar will stand with the Princess, of course," Speaker Skaði's voice added serenely.

"As will we all." King Torsten's voice was tight, silencing any of Aiko's protestations. Anara didn't doubt Torsten would have upheld his end of the bargain, but it was clear he did not appreciate the corner Larissa had backed him into. "That is my final decision. All we have left to discuss is how."

"Shiko's neglect of Lystheim will work to our advantage," Halvor said, pulling the map toward him and scratching out the numbers and locations of the sentries within the three rings of the cities. "The Outer Wall is our biggest obstacle."

"Explosives?" General Soren asked.

Halvor shook his head. "We don't have enough. We could blast through the Second Wall, but the Outer Wall is thicker and made of stronger material."

"So a small team, then?" Darien asked.

The king's advisor smiled at him. "Exactly, Prince. A small team would be able to get within the Wall unnoticed. They would need to disable the main gates before any of the sentries could trigger a lockdown, which would fortify the city and prolong any attack.

With the gates open, the next wave could march in without resistance."

"The goal is a swift battle," Torsten added. "We can't waste time or men on a drawn-out siege."

General Aiko nodded. "But how will they get in?"

"Produce Day," Anara, Larissa, and Darien answered in unison.

Darien leaned back, waving for Larissa to continue. "The gates will already be opened. Trucks will be coming and going from the walls. We might even contact some farmers and stow away beneath their produce."

"We?" Torsten asked.

"We," Anara confirmed, already loving the idea. Her skin itched with excitement. "Lovisa, Darien, and I have experience entering Perle unnoticed. No one else has our level of *galdr*. We would need an additional three or four members to help us subdue the sentries at the Wall, but it could be done as long as a first wave was waiting to join us at our signal."

The generals did not respond, but rather waited for the King's reaction. Torsten tugged at his beard, his eyes lingering on his son. "This is a job that could be done by many in the Viðnám without risking three lines of Ancestral Blood."

"Your Majesty," General Aiko spoke in measured tones. "Surely, if Princess Lovisa is meant to kill Empress Shiko, this will not be an impossibility for her."

"It would give the people hope to see their lost Princess leading the charge," General Sture added, smoothing the tips of his mustache.

Anara scoffed, but quietly enough that she was not heard. Subtlety was not the generals' strong suit. Their support of Larissa's plan was nothing less than a test of her courage and skill. While worry seeped out of the lines on Soren's face, Ishaan watched with mild interest.

"They are my people, Your Majesty." Larissa's voice was calm, gentle even, but there was no mistaking the certainty with which she spoke. "This is my responsibility."

Anara nearly howled in delight. This was the Princess she had always known Lovisa could be.

"Where the Princess goes, I go," Darien continued.

"As do I," Anara finished, before Torsten could speak the words that so clearly burned the tip of his tongue.

Torsten's hand fell from his beard. "And should the Empress have her War Dog waiting for you to return?"

Anara's hand involuntarily splayed over the scar that stretched across her abdomen—a result of the last time they'd fought against Calder.

Darien's voice was unyielding. "He won't stand in our way."

"Your armies will be right behind them, Your Majesty." Speaker Skaði folded her long, manicured fingers on the table. "The risk is minimal. When the people hear that their Princesses and Prince are leading the path for them, it will only embolden them for the fight. I believe this is an acceptable choice."

Torsten dipped his head. "It's decided then, but you're not going alone. Halvor, you will accompany them and serve as advisor and ambassador, particularly to the farmers we will try and recruit along the way."

"Yes, Your Majesty. Might I recommend Haki and Jari?" Halvor asked. "They have run more trucks in and out of Perle without suspicion than anyone else."

"An excellent idea."

For once, Anara agreed with Torsten. The twins had acted as double agents within Lystheim, posing as sentries while helping runaways leave the city. Anara hadn't seen Haki since he'd led Darien, Larissa, and herself through the tunnels into the Viðnám. He and his brother had been instrumental in getting them out of Perle—though Anara struggled to remember most of it, having been unconscious for the majority of their rescue. They would be helpful, particularly Haki, who looked nearly giant himself.

In her peripheral vision, Anara caught Ishaan's shift in posture too late. He lifted his hand. "I volunteer myself, Your Majesty. If my Queen is going, I must go to protect her."

Anara didn't hide the growl that rumbled in her chest. "You're not needed."

Anara caught the shared glance of confusion between Larissa and Darien but didn't bother to address it. Her gaze hardened on her old advisor, who glared at her in return. No doubt, he too was replaying the conversation they'd had before she'd left the Viðnám. Anara's stomach twisted as she remembered his accusations.

Torsten eyed them in contemplation. "General Ishaan is not as powerful as you, Princess Anara, but he is still strong. We can't afford any personal bias to affect the success of this mission. General Ishaan will join your team."

Anara's fingers transformed into claws that scraped into the underside of the table before she could restrain herself.

Loki's Knot, she thought.

10

Money at Midnight

Halla

"Wake up, storyteller."

The grit around Halla's eyes flaked upon their forced opening. She was back in the barrack, back on her bunk. The light filtering in through the skylights was fading. Juni's bed next to her was empty, and the sight of it nearly rivaled the pain of the burn on Halla's spine.

"Drink."

Halla obeyed without hesitation, her parched tongue aching for water. It was only after she had sated her thirst that she realized who held the bottle to her lips.

Kai sat beside her, his black hair pushed away from his face as his gaze hovered over her neck. Halla raised a hand, her fingers briefly brushing against the bandage before her hand was caught away in Kai's long fingers.

"Don't touch it. You don't want it to get infected."

Her hand lingered in his for a moment. Then Kai returned the bottle to her lips. She took it from him and swallowed several more mouthfuls. There was a distinct fuzziness in her mind, and she couldn't quite place the time of day.

"How long was I asleep?"

"A full night and day."

That helped explain the hollow feeling in her stomach.

"You were right."

"I usually am. What was I right about this time?"

"About getting caught."

He looked down. "I didn't want to be."

Halla sat up, wincing from the pain. The rest of the children in the barrack were crowding around the bags of food that had been thrown in, scrounging about for the most edible items. Yet even in their frenzy, they looked more subdued than before.

Halla clenched the thin blanket beneath her, steadying herself enough to ask, "Where's Juni?"

"Gone."

She stopped breathing. "You mean—did they—"

"She's not dead," Kai hurried to say. "She got away."

"What?" Halla's heart thumped painfully, but beneath the pain, there was joy. "How? Fenris said he knew about the tunnels; he said he used them as bait to make a lesson out of slaves."

"The *thræll* were focused on you. In the chaos, she got out." Kai's lips twitched. "Fenris wasn't happy; they sent a search party, but they haven't found her yet."

Too stunned to say anything, Halla only nodded.

"I'll go see if I can find us any food, or what passes as food here."

Halla watched him go, but she couldn't quite summon enough energy to care about what food he might bring back. He returned with a selection of crumbling bread and canned vegetables. Halla grabbed one at random, flinching again at the pain that laced down her spine. Fenris had chosen his spot well. Every movement hurt. Kai munched at the food in his hands, hardly looking in her direction.

Halla forced herself to swallow several spoonfuls of what the can claimed were peas before setting it down. "Why are you helping me?"

"Someone has to."

"Not for much longer," Halla whispered. "Tomorrow I'll go to the Empress."

"Would it really be so bad?"

"Yes."

Silence permeated the space between them. "Can you tell me why?"

Halla ran her finger around the edge of the can.

"Who's Lara?"

Halla flinched, the edge of the can slicing against her finger. She sucked at the small cut, then asked, "What?"

"You called for her while you were . . ." Kai crossed his arms over his chest to indicate Halla's comatose state.

"She's my sister."

Kai's eyes darted to those around them as though checking on their privacy. He leaned in close to Halla's ear. "Is she with the Viðnám?"

Halla jerked away, then whimpered at the pain her sudden movement caused.

"I saw your face when Juni mentioned them. Is that why you can't go to the Empress?"

Halla pulled her knees into her chest. "I don't know where she is."

"Do you know how to find them?"

Though she knew full well who he meant, Halla asked, "Who?"

"The Viðnám?" He moved toward her. Halla started at the sudden intensity in Kai's eyes. "If we could get out of here, could you find them?"

"Oh no, I'm not trying that again. My sister will come for me."

Kai's eyes dulled over. The corners of his lips fell. "No one is coming for us, Halla."

It was the absence of pain in Kai's voice that made Halla realize just how deeply he felt the truth of his words. But Halla didn't feel them, wouldn't allow herself to believe them. Verðandi had all but promised Halla she would see Larissa again. Even though the dream was beginning to fade into her subconsciousness, Halla clung to it. Pappa always taught Halla that the Norn stood apart from the events of the world, watching, recording, weaving the fates, but remaining outside of it. Yet Verðandi had spoken to Halla directly.

We're waiting for you, Halla; we still need you to tell our story.

The Norn needed her? Perhaps it was just a fantasy in her mind after all.

The other children sat quietly in their bunks, gnawing at their rations with fear written in every movement. They were a reflection of herself: broken. Halla had lost. Tomorrow she would be shipped to the Empress. She couldn't help the Norn, she couldn't even help herself, but there was one thing she could do. She glanced over at Kai, who seemed to already know what Halla was thinking.

He jerked his head in their direction. "Looks like they could use a story."

It took no time for the children to gather once Halla made it clear she was ready to share a story. They needed something hopeful. *She* needed something hopeful, and she knew just what story to share.

"Once upon a time there was a beautiful goddess named Iðunn. At her fingertips, flowers blossomed, vines grew, trees bore fruit, and the *Æsir* were granted immortality." Halla paused for dramatic effect, as her Pappa had done so often when telling this tale.

She wove her words in the air, the images playing out before her eyes. Lovely Iðunn had been kidnapped by the Trickster Loki for the giant Thjazi, who wished to rob the *Æsir* of their fruit of immortality. While she spoke, Halla's strength returned and fear fled. Under the soprano of her voice, she could have sworn that she heard Pappa's baritone leading her through the story, as though he sat beside her. Halla's heart hurt her for a moment, thinking of her Pappa, but she pushed it aside and reached for the story instead. She would make one difference though, a slight rewrite from the original story.

". . . Freed from his clutches, Iðunn escaped Thrymheim and traveled the nine realms until she returned to her family in Asgard.

The Trickster Loki was punished for his weaknesses, and Iðunn remained in her garden of golden apples until the day of *Ragnarok*."

At first the children remained, spellbound by Halla's voice before they realized her story had ended. Reluctantly, they filed back to their bunks, settling in a peace Halla had not known since she'd arrived. Only Kai remained, his back against the barrack wall. His hands rested against his knees. The flickering moonlight caused a shadow to appear like a black stone against his fingers before it shifted and disappeared.

"Nice story, but I was always taught that Iðunn had to be rescued by Loki."

Halla blushed, not having expected anyone to notice the change she'd made. "Never. Iðunn rescued herself; everyone knows that."

"If you say so."

"How do you know all these stories? Who taught you, Kai?"

In the dark, she couldn't see him well, but she could feel the way he shifted on the bunk before answering. "My mother."

"Do you miss her?"

He scoffed. "No. She doesn't miss me; why should I miss her?"

"Your father?"

"Never knew him."

"An older brother? Sister?"

"Let's just say no one is looking for me."

Halla's mind wandered to Lara, Mamma, and Pappa. She had taken them for granted. What would it have been to be like Kai, whose family did not care if he lived or died? She pushed herself back against the wall of the barrack, sitting shoulder-to-shoulder with Kai. It was easier to ask her questions when she wasn't looking at him.

"How did they catch you?"

"Oh, they didn't," Kai spat bitterly. "My mother sold me."

Halla's jaw dropped open.

"Don't look at me like that."

She quickly closed her jaw. Halla nudged his foot with her own. "You're wrong, you know, about no one coming for us. My sister will come, and when she does, you can come with us too."

Kai sucked in a quick breath. Halla wasn't sure what had made her say it, but she couldn't take it back if she wanted to. Kai had no one else, and everyone deserved to have someone. Halla could have remained there in comfortable silence all night.

The barrack door slammed open. A dozen *thræll* poured in, lights flashing in their hands as they shouted at the children to stand and present themselves for inspection. Halla blinked against the lights, her body frozen in fear. Kai pushed Halla to her feet before falling in line beside his own bunk. Fenris walked in behind the others, his hands folded behind his back, but he was not the last to enter. Behind Fenris, a man entered without a light in his hand or a gun at his side. He was not a *thræll* or a sentry or anything Halla had ever seen before.

The man wore a long white robe with the hood pushed back to reveal a bald head covered entirely with runes. The skin exposed at his neck and hands revealed similar runic tattoos as well. He strode in with a purpose, his eyes scanning the children that trembled before their bunks. His gaze roved over Halla. She quickly averted her eyes to the ground, but it was too late.

"Her," he said, his finger outstretched in her direction.

Fenris' lips curled back in a barely concealed snarl. "She's not for sale."

The tattooed man lowered his arm, turning to face Fenris. So quickly that Halla barely noticed it, the man pressed a bundle of money into Fenris' open hand. He leaned back and smiled. "You would not deny the gods what they have asked for, would you?"

At Fenris' calculating expression, another *thræll* moved to whisper in his ear. "You have marked her for the Empress—"

"Find a replacement," he snapped, shoving the money in his pocket. "Who are we to deny the gods?"

The *thrœll* yanked Halla forward, clasping the metal restraints around her wrists. Her lips trembled, but fear silenced her voice. She had received a reprieve from the Empress, but what on Evrópa did it mean that she had been asked for by the gods?

She turned panicked eyes on Kai, but he was watching the tattooed man who stared at him in return. The man's head cocked to one side as though he was trying to decide something. "Well, aren't you a long way from home?" He glanced back toward Fenris. "How much?"

Hope grew like an unwatered weed that perhaps the man would buy Kai too. Perhaps, Halla wouldn't be alone.

The number Fenris offered was high, too high.

To her surprise, the man withdrew the amount with ease, stuffing it into Fenris' hand once more. Staring at the money, Fenris opened his mouth to speak but then closed it again as though he had thought better of questioning it.

The *thrœll* clasped restraints around Kai's wrists and added a chain that connected him to Halla. The other end of the chain he gave to the tattooed man. With a firm tug, the man pulled them along with him. The other children watched, their eyes wide and round. Halla lifted her chin, knowing it was what Iðunn would do. She would not appear weak. As she passed by Fenris, the *thrœll* stepped before her.

"Be careful, little girl," he said with a deep chuckle. "I've heard those who upset the gods are offered as sacrifices to the giants."

Another tug on her wrists compelled Halla forward. She kept her eyes on Kai's back as they ventured out into the night, bound by their wrists and, perhaps, by fate herself.

11

Shocks and Summons

Darien

IT'D BEEN DAYS SINCE the war council, yet Darien had been unable to speak with Larissa in private since then. They'd only met in councils, straightening out the details, going over the plan minute by minute, allowing for every possibility. They'd discussed how long it would take for the Viðnám to mobilize. Every able-bodied person reported for their position, waiting on orders from their generals. Others—their families, the wounded, and the weak—packed their belongings. If all went according to plan, the majority of the Viðnám would be moving into Perle by the end of the week. It was a momentous task, and perhaps that was why Torsten took every opportunity to speak or train with Darien.

Darien bowed his head beneath the weight of his father's mental attack.

"Focus, Darien," Torsten ordered.

They faced off in a private room devoid of all furniture apart from some mats piled neatly in the corner. They'd gone back and forth for hours. Sometimes Darien would attempt to control Torsten with his *galdr*, and sometimes he would try to defend himself. When their brains tired, their hands fell to their swords. Perhaps his father was doing his best to prepare him, but Darien's lack of freedom made him wonder if their prolonged training sessions had something to do with keeping him away from a certain Princess as well.

"You can't let anyone slip through your mental wall. Without it, you're as good as dead." Torsten had dispensed with his formal jacket and crown but retained his air of regality nonetheless. His gaze burrowed into Darien, and the pressure in Darien's mind increased. Yet even as the stabbing pains grew worse, Darien knew his father was holding back.

Mentally, he focused on building his wall, brick by brick, cementing the layers against Torsten's intrusion. It was training he had received in his youth, and Darien pulled from those memories to defend himself. His ring finger grew warm as he used the sapphire on his hand to channel the *galdr* from within. In his mind's eye, he pictured the rune etched into that sapphire—Laguz, Njord's own rune, curved like a shepherd's hook. So focused on channeling his *galdr*, Darien hardly noticed his father drawing his sword until the blade rested at his collarbone.

"Dead," Torsten said.

Darien raised his hands in surrender, but the distraction had decimated his walls, allowing his father entry into his mind. His body stiffened under his father's will. It was over.

Torsten lowered his sword and released his hold on Darien's mind. "You have to be present mentally *and* physically, Darien. I don't understand why this is so hard. Aeron always—"

Torsten stopped, and Darien swallowed against the painful lump that had solidified in his throat. What was there to say? He wasn't Aeron? His father already knew that.

"Go to the range. We'll speak again before your departure."

"Faðir," Darien called to his retreating back. "At the last meeting, you said we would meet with the farmers to see if we could win them to our side and smuggle us through the walls."

"Yes?"

"You didn't say what we would do if they disagreed."

Torsten turned, a raised eyebrow the sign of his confusion. "Then you commandeer their trucks and hold them as war prisoners until we can determine their loyalty."

His father departed the room, the conversation apparently closed. Strategically, Darien knew the plan was logical, but it caused a sharp contrast between the father of his memories, who'd often chosen to see the best in people, and the man that now led the Viðnám. Even worse, he couldn't stop thinking of Aagen and Jon and of the other farmers who might not be willing to risk their families for strangers, no matter who they claimed to be. Then, of course, there was the persistent voice in his mind that would not leave. It nagged at him at the most inopportune moments, calling him a fraud in his gold-lined jacket that should have been Aeron's.

It was enough to make him want to put a fist through the wall. Instead, he threw open the door, following his feet as they took him to where he was ordered to go. Although Torsten demanded that Darien train with his ancestral weapon, even he could acknowledge the advantages of a gun in a war. Darien paid special attention to the markers on the tunnel walls. Speaker Skaði constantly reminded him how easy it would be to get lost within the mountain.

He breathed a sigh of relief when he found the mouth of the tunnel that overlooked the Viðnám. As always, the sight filled him with hope. Though the Jötnar preferred to reside within the mountain itself, the people of the Viðnám had built their homes within the valley, cradled between the mountains. From his vantage point, Darien could see and hear the bustle of the city as families prepared for what was coming. Their plan seemed impossible, but so had the presence of giants only weeks ago.

Finding the steps that lined the canyon walls, Darien descended, invigorated by the sun on his skin. The shooting range was near the cliffside, both as a safety precaution and as a courtesy to those who lived in the valley. Following the loud pops to the range, Darien was more than pleasantly surprised by the familiar white braid hanging down Larissa's back as she faced away from him, pulling the trigger again and again. She'd ditched the fancy evening gown and looked more like the farm girl he'd met on Produce Day only weeks ago, with a leather jacket zipped up tight against the cool valley breeze. She was more beautiful each time Darien saw her.

He stood back, waiting until she lowered the hand gun and removed the earmuffs, letting them hang around her neck. She switched the mechanism that brought her target to her, showing the scattered shots within the abdomen of the practice silhouette.

"Nice," he called out.

She turned, a smile tugging at her lips. "Darien."

The sound of her voice was all it took for Darien to appreciate how utterly alone they were. He wasn't sure where the instructor of the course had gone off to; Darien was only glad that he was gone. In the past, being with Lovisa had been as easy as breathing, but after fifty years apart, Larissa looked at him with hesitancy that caused him to pause.

Larissa clicked the switch again, sending her target back out on the range. "Come to practice?"

His tongue unstuck from his mouth. "Faðir's orders."

Larissa's shoulders tightened, but she nodded and offered him her gun. "Not sure Torsten would want you here if he knew I was here."

Ah. That explained her caution. He held the gun loosely in his hand, making no move toward the target. "Has he said something to you?"

"Not in so many words, but he's made his feelings about us spending time together clear."

He shrugged. "He accepted it before; he'll get used to it again."

"You weren't the Crown Prince before," she muttered.

"That doesn't have to change anything—"

"It could mean trouble with Torsten."

Darien reached for her arm. "You're worth the trouble. I missed you."

Her gaze softened. "I missed you too, Dar."

It was the way she said his name that drew him toward her with undeniable force. He reached for her, but Larissa's eyes flashed around.

"Not here," she said, but she didn't move away. "I need Torsten's support, especially until I get Halla back."

"He won't go back on his word," Darien promised. "We'll get Halla. We'll reclaim Perle."

"You make it sound so easy." Larissa's hands fidgeted at her sides, a faint glow surrounding her fingertips. "I'm . . . struggling with my *galdr*. It didn't used to be like this; I used to be stronger."

"It's the same for me when I'm training as well. I think our minds remember, but our bodies need time."

"We don't have time." Larissa shoved her hands in her pockets. "I shouldn't be here. I should have left for Halla days ago. Every day that I'm here is a day that she waits for me. I'm tired of playing Princess. I'm ready to go get my sister."

As if fed by the agitation in her voice, the glow increased from Larissa's hands. She caught his gaze and raised her hands in front of her face. To Darien's surprise, they shook.

She groaned. "And I can't stop them from doing *that*. When I reach for my *galdr*, it feels like there's a flood waiting to be unleashed, but I can't use it for more than parlor tricks. I know the Viðnám needs me. I know what I'm doing here is important, but Halla is important too. What are they doing to *her*?"

Small crackles of energy snapped between her fingers. Without thought, Darien set the gun on the bench and reached out to take her hands in his. An electric current shocked his fingers, but he held on tight despite the discomfort. Besides, the physical sensation was nothing compared to what was running through his heart.

"It's okay, Lov, look at me." Darien waited until Larissa's golden eyes met his own. He stared into them, breathing slow and steady until Larissa's breathing matched his rhythm. "We're going to get Halla back. I swear it on the *Æsir*. We *will* get her back."

Though her hands clasped his with enough strength to hurt, she nodded. As the glow subsided from her fingers, the shadows beneath Larissa's eyes became more pronounced.

"When was the last time you slept?" he asked.

She shrugged. "Last night, I think."

"You think?"

"The *mara* keep me awake."

Darien didn't need to ask. *Mara*—those creatures responsible for nightmares—had plagued Darien's sleep nearly every night after his fight with his brother, sending him visions of Aeron accusing Darien of taking his place while Calder smirked from the shadows.

He tucked her hair behind her ears, letting his fingers linger on her cheek. "You can tell me about them, if you want to."

Larissa's breath shook as she inhaled. "It's Verðandi."

Darien's fingers froze on her face. After Larissa had unlocked the block in her mind, she'd shared with Darien and Anara what she remembered of her father's murder at Shiko's hands and her mother's own sacrifice. Queen Stjarna had poured out all of her *galdr* into Verðandi—the youngest of the Norn—who in turn had used it to hide Larissa and Darien in time itself. It was a debt Darien could never repay. "What does she want?"

"She wants me to come to her."

"Do you think she could tell you the rest of the prophecy?"

"Probably." Larissa looked away; Darien's hand fell from her face. "But I have to get Halla back first. Everything else can wait. It has to."

Everything? Did she mean him too? The end of Larissa's braid fluttered in the wind, tickling the bare skin of Darien's arm. Gunpowder lingered in the air, but Darien smelled cherry blossoms from his memories of the Jóltide Festival. As though suddenly aware of their closeness, Larissa's eyes widened, but she didn't move away. It was the encouragement Darien needed. Maybe, just maybe, they could go back to who they were before.

"Larissa, I—"

"Darien, I—"

They laughed, perhaps more nervously than they would have in the past.

"Am I interrupting something?" Anara's bored voice came from behind him.

Larissa stepped back, tugging at her jacket sleeves. Darien half turned his head toward the other girl. "You have the absolute worst timing, do you know that?"

Anara swaggered over, her ruby pendant winking from behind her tan leather jacket. The old one had been irreparably damaged by the *draugr* and Anara's own blood, but this new one looked similar enough. "Oh, don't let me stop you. I just came to let Larissa know we're being summoned by Speaker Skaði."

"The Speaker?" Larissa asked. "What does she want with me?"

"All three of us, actually. I was supposed to find Darien next, but his inability to stay away from you saved me the effort."

Darien could've strangled Anara, but to be honest, he wasn't confident he could take her in a fair fight. Instead, he let his sigh contain the full breadth of his irritation. Anara only smiled in his direction.

He passed the gun back to Larissa, who stowed it in her holster, revealing Halla's pebble peeking out from her pocket. A pang of guilt followed by a shot of fear worked its way through Darien's gut. He sent up a silent prayer. Halla had been his responsibility, and he would make it right. Then he would continue this conversation with Larissa; she would know that the last fifty years had done nothing to change his love for her.

Darien cracked his neck. "Let's go see what the giants want."

12

Galdr

Larissa

THE LOW RUMBLE OF the crowd was ever-present in the background. Though the armored truck was comfortable on the inside, Larissa found herself missing Helga with an unmatched ferocity. As they drove through the valley, her mind wandered back to the feel of Darien's hand on her own. Since she'd woken, she'd been floundering, adrift at sea, and he was the shoreline, a place for her to find refuge from the current that threatened to consume her. Or at least, he had been.

Torsten's opinion on the matter was clear. Darien wasn't a second-born Prince anymore. He was the Crown Prince, and with that came responsibilities Larissa and Darien had ignored their entire youth, when Aeron had been the barrier between Darien and their father. Between the duties of the crown and Halla's rescue, now was not the time for Larissa to linger on whatever emotions Darien stirred within her. That was easier said than done when Darien's side was pressed against her own, when he smelled of fresh clothes and sunlight.

The ride was shorter than Larissa expected as they took the path around the outside rim of the city instead of passing through. The truck's measured slowing drew Larissa's attention to a large mansion built into the side of the mountain. On its steps, Speaker Skaði waited, her dark skin glowing under the strong sun. Beside her stood another Jötunn who contrasted Skaði in nearly every way. His long white hair blew around his waist, though his pale skin showed no wrinkles. Only their heights and eyes shared similarities. They tilted their heads in greeting as Larissa, Darien, and Anara exited the truck and made their way to the mansion's front steps.

"Welcome." The Speaker led them inside to a large office near the front doors. Books lined the walls from ceiling to floor. A desk sat near the back wall, and several couches and chairs were arranged in a pleasing pattern to fill in the rest of the space. Skaði gestured at the furniture, taking her own place behind the desk. "Make yourselves at home."

Larissa perched on the couch nearest to her, feeling anything but at home. There was a certain alienness to the Jötnar that couldn't be erased by hospitality and good manners. She took comfort in Darien's presence as he settled beside her and in Anara's watchful gaze.

"I have been waiting for an opportunity to speak with you three," Skaði began, "but it has not been easy to seek a private audience."

Anara leaned against the bookshelf near the door. "Shouldn't it be? After all, isn't this your valley?"

Skaði glanced at the white-haired giant and laughed. "My valley? Hardly."

"But aren't you the Speaker?" Larissa asked. "Don't you rule over your people?"

"We do not recognize royalty amongst my people. We have no governance, no authority. One might say we live beyond the borders of rule and order; it is part of why the *Æsir* disdained us in the past. With the arrival of the Viðnám, we found it necessary to unify our voices through one individual. We needed a Speaker. I wield no authority over the Jötnar; they wield it over me, as they always have."

Larissa shook her head. There was still something she didn't understand. "You've lived in this valley since *Ragnarok*. How'd we not know you were here? My grandmother traveled every inch of Evrópa in establishing the five kingdoms."

"Queen Rúna knew of our existence, but we are getting a bit ahead of ourselves and I do not want to neglect my company." She nodded to the white-haired giant beside her. "This is Eluf."

Larissa dipped her head in acknowledgment, her question burning a hole through her tongue. "Why did you summon us?"

"You don't know the prophecy the Norn gave your mother, and you have yet to regain access to your full *galdr*—"

Larissa's mouth gaped open. "How did you—"

"Our ears are everywhere within these mountains. We can help you, but we ask for a favor in return."

Larissa hesitated, seeing the similar wariness on Darien's and Anara's faces as well. "What's the favor?"

"When the world burned and the Norn saved a fragment of mankind, we Jötnar saved ourselves. We've always been more in tune with our *galdr* than your ancestors, but we were never able to wield it properly until Rúna shared the knowledge of the runes that she gathered from the Norn."

Eluf raised his eyes upward. "The *Æsir* enjoyed hoarding their secrets, but look where it got them."

Larissa was grateful that Darien at least looked as confused as she did by this turn of conversation, but Anara's eyes narrowed.

"Our kind was not welcome outside of our valley," Skaði continued. "Rúna made that clear once she discovered what we could do. The other kingdoms would have been jealous of our connection to *galdr*. She thought it best we remain separated, and we have never been ones for the rules of royalty."

"What do you mean, your connection to *galdr*?" Anara asked, an edge to her voice.

Skaði folded her long hands on the table. "Our *galdr* is not like yours, with only one rune to give us strength. The *Æsir* practiced eighteen types of *galdr*. The Norn granted mankind only five of them. You may know this already, but what you don't know is that most Jötnar are able to wield more than one *galdr*. We are not restricted to bloodlines. King Torsten is aware of this, but none others."

Larissa swallowed, attempting to comprehend what the Speaker was saying. *Galdr* had been uncommon fifty years ago, limited mainly to the royal families. Shiko had made it even rarer by eliminating the monarchies. If Larissa understood correctly, then the Jötnar were the most powerful beings that roamed Evrópa besides the gods themselves. As if Anara understood the implications as well, she pushed off the wall, moving to stand defensively beside Larissa and Darien.

Larissa clenched her glowing hands. "Why are you telling us this?"

Skaði looked at the giant standing beside her. "Eluf is one of the most talented of the Jötnar, possessing several types of *galdr*, including yours, Princess. He can teach you how to channel your *galdr*, and I can help you discover the secrets of your prophecy."

"In return for what, exactly?" Anara asked, suspicion underlying her tone.

"When the world is reborn at the end of the False Empress' reign, my people will no longer be a secret. We will need a place in the new world. What better choice than to strengthen our alliance now? We only ask that you keep the training between you and Eluf a secret. What he teaches you is not meant for all to hear."

"Our secrecy. That's all you want?" Larissa asked, her mind racing to understand the implications of Skaði's proposal.

"Indeed." Speaker Skaði crossed her legs, leaning back in her seat. "And a promise to remember who your friends are once you ascend to your throne."

"Friends?" Anara scoffed. "So, as our *friends*, will you be joining us when it comes to outright war? Or will you continue to hide in this valley just like you did when Shiko brutalized kingdom after kingdom?"

As though the wolf Sköll really had swallowed the sun, an unrelenting chill permeated the room in response to Anara's accusation. Speaker Skaði's expression of politeness did not waver, but there was a layer of steel underneath it. "Do you know what happened the last time Jötnar went to war?"

Anara held her gaze, matching steel for steel. "*Ragnarok*."

"Precisely. When the Jötnar go to war, the world crumbles. If you see us in battle, it may be the last thing you see."

Anara shook her head. "I don't believe that."

Eluf eyed her in disdain, his presence larger than before. "Then pray to those dead gods we never have to test your disbelief."

"And what's to stop you from turning on us?" Anara moved toward the giant, her head tilted back to challenge his gaze. "With your *galdr*, you could destroy us all. Why should we trust you?"

Beside Larissa, Darien's hand twitched toward his sword. The weight of her gun against her hip did little to reassure Larissa. It was as Anara said: they'd have no chance if the Jötnar were truly as powerful as they implied.

"Peace." Speaker Skaði's voice was like a spell that softened the stillness of the air, bringing back warmth and light. "As we told Torsten, we do not desire the power and rule that is so enticing to you mortals. Jötnar have two natural instincts that war within us—chaos and serenity. In the decades before *Ragnarok*, we gave ourselves over to chaos. It nearly destroyed us. If we were to give ourselves over to it once more, I fear we would not survive. We seek contentment and serenity—an alliance—in exchange for our help." She turned to Larissa. "Will you accept our offer?"

Four faces stared, waiting for her answer. Though Anara's brow was pulled in apprehension, Darien appeared more thoughtful than frightened. Larissa breathed in, knowing she could not ask them to make this decision for her.

She stood, offering her hand to the Speaker. "Yes, I accept."

Skaði rose. "Then we have no time to waste."

She grasped Larissa's forearm, turning her palm to face the sky. Her curved nails dug into Larissa's skin. Darien's sword scraped against his scabbard and Anara growled, but Larissa could not see them. Her legs went weak, and darkness consumed her vision as she felt separated from the physical world around her.

ᚾᛁᛗᚱᛋᚾᛁᛗᚱᛋᚾᛁᛗᚱᛋᚾᛁᛗᚱᛋᚾᛁᛗᚱᛋ

Within the void, there was only Larissa and the Speaker, surrounded by rushing winds that sought to tear her from Skaði's grasp. The giantess shouted in an old language that raised the goosebumps on Larissa's arms. Galdr and power encompassed them, pressing down on Larissa, squashing the air from her lungs. If not for the giantess' grip, Larissa would've been pressed into the ground itself. A high soprano voice answered back, scolding, but the words were jumbled by the wind.

Skaði's grasp on Larissa tightened as she shouted once more, and light tore through the darkness. There came the sound of crashing waves and a scream so terrible it cut through Larissa's soul. But just as suddenly, the ground from beneath them disappeared and Larissa screamed into the wind, falling with the giantess plummeting right beside her.

ᚾᛁᛗᚱᛋᚾᛁᛗᚱᛋᚾᛁᛗᚱᛋᚾᛁᛗᚱᛋᚾᛁᛗᚱᛋ

Larissa gasped, satisfying her begging lungs, only to find herself back in the study once again. Skaði's grip on her arm weakened. The giantess fell back into her chair, though with a soft grace. At her side, Eluf stood with glowing hands raised. Looking behind her, Larissa saw Anara and Darien both struggling to move against Eluf's *galdr*. She recognized it immediately; he was manipulating the energy in the air around them, condensing it to hold them captive.

"Stop!" she cried, throwing up her own hands to combat it, but there was no need.

Eluf lowered his arms. Darien slid between Larissa and the desk while Anara's hands transformed to claws that she dug into the wood, letting it splinter beneath her.

Larissa lowered her shaking hands. "What just happened?"

"Explain yourself!" Darien demanded, his sword pointed at Skaði's throat.

"The Norn are not the only ones with prophetic abilities." Skaði opened her eyes, and Larissa gasped. The red rims around her irises had devoured the amber color. "I attempted to see what the Norn had seen, but they blocked me. They want to speak with you directly, Larissa."

"Great, thanks so much for all your help," Anara bit out, sarcasm heavy in her voice. "We'll be leaving now."

Larissa ignored Anara's hand on her arm, held captive by Skaði's guarded expression. "You saw something else though, didn't you?"

The speaker pressed her palms together, touching her dark fingers against her chin. "There is loss in your future, and if you are not careful, it will destroy you."

Halla. Crippling fear rose in Larissa's chest. She stumbled forward, clinging to Darien's arm for support. "Who?"

Skaði shook her head. "I do not know. I was not allowed to see."

Eluf placed his hand on Skaði's shoulder. The intimacy of the gesture shocked Larissa enough that she listened to his words. "Loss can change not only a person's path, but their soul as well. You need look no further than the False Empress to know this. You must be careful to not allow your loss to corrupt you, Larissa. Your *galdr* is powerful and must be controlled, or you will succumb to the same chaos and madness that took the Empress."

"What?" she whispered in horror. "I'm not Shiko. I can barely access my *galdr* at all."

"I can help you with that." Eluf moved around the desk, but Darien blocked his way. The Jötunn raised his hands to show a faint glow around his pale fingers. "If you will allow me to uphold our end of the bargain."

Larissa nodded at Darien, who let Eluf pass, his long white hair flowing behind him. Ignoring Anara's growls, Eluf lifted Larissa's hands, unbothered by the sparks that flew between her fingertips.

"Energy manipulation is about control," he said. "Safírians rely on constructing and deconstructing defenses around a mind for their persuasion. Rubinians are naturally fluid in *galdr*, allowing it to shape their form. Diamantians use their imagination to summon a false reality. But Perlians, and Smaragdians to some degree, need utter control to maintain and grow their *galdr*. For those of us who manipulate energy, our possibilities are nearly endless. We can move it, harden it, wield it to some degree—"

"I know all this," Larissa snapped. "My Móðir taught me well. My mind remembers"—her eyes flicked to Darien—"but my body doesn't."

"Who is in control of your body, then?" Eluf asked.

"I am, but—"

"Then be in control." Sparks flew between Eluf's fingers, stinging where they fell on Larissa's hands.

"Let her go," Anara snarled.

"No, I'm fine." Larissa winced, but didn't move. She could feel Eluf's *galdr*. It pulsated through his hands, almost as if he were trying to impart it to her. "What are you doing?"

"Our *galdr* is not only about control; it is about cycles. Like the way blood flows through your veins, pumping through your heart and back out again, you must allow your *galdr* to do the same. I can show you how by cycling my *galdr* through you."

"Are you crazy? You want to transfer your *galdr* to me?"

"Like everything else, *galdr* is energy." Eluf spoke calmly, but the red around his eyes increased, eating away at the amber color. "I will give enough so that you understand what I mean, but I will reclaim what is mine."

Before she could resist, Larissa felt the shift in her hands. They'd stung under Eluf's touch moments ago, but now they burned. The sensation started in her fingertips; then, the fire sank deep into her palms. Past her wrists, the fire gained in speed, spreading up her arms and shooting straight for her heart.

Larissa couldn't speak if she'd wanted to. Though unpleasant, the experience wasn't painful. It was more like tiny sparks running concurrently in the vessels under her skin as Eluf's *galdr* spread from her heart, reaching down to her toes and cycling back again. Beneath it, Larissa sensed something different, a candle to Eluf's inferno. It was her *galdr*, rousing from where it slept in the pit of her stomach. As if called, it uncoiled itself, following Eluf's *galdr* as it cycled once more through Larissa's body. She was no longer burning, but rather, her whole self thrummed with warmth.

Only then did she realize Eluf had let go of her hands. She could no longer feel his *galdr* at all, but she sensed her own more potently than she ever had before. The pearl ring on her finger nearly hummed in delight. Tears stung at the corners of her eyes. "How did you do that?"

"I told you, I cycled—"

"No." Larissa's voice broke. "How did you do that and *live*?"

Eluf shared a confused glance with Skaði that was echoed on Darien and Anara's faces as well. The image of her mother pouring out her *galdr* into Verðandi played over and over again in her mind. "My mother did that, and it killed her."

Speaker Skaði fixed Larissa with an inquisitive stare. "What did Queen Stjarna do?"

Larissa wrapped her arms around her chest; the warmth of her *galdr* faded. "Shiko had killed my father. Darien had been injured. Shiko's soldiers were breaking down the door to kill us when my mother summoned Verðandi and asked her to hide us. The goddess demanded payment. My mother did what Eluf just did. She poured her *galdr* into Verðandi, but it killed her."

Shock was Skaði's only response.

Even Eluf looked shaken. "I only sent a fraction of my *galdr*, and I called it back. *Galdr* feeds on our lives; it's as vital to us as blood.

Queen Stjarna must have given every ounce of her power for it to kill her."

"But why would a goddess need *galdr*?" Darien asked, his hand on Larissa's shoulder. "Don't they have enough?"

"A question for the goddess," Skaði murmured. Then, louder, "After you reclaim Perle and find your sister, you must answer the Norn's call. They will have answers. They will offer guidance and insight. Only, be careful. The Norn, like the gods, are not to be trusted."

"But the giants are?" Larissa hadn't meant for the question to come out like a challenge.

"Trust only yourself, Lovisa." She inclined her head to Anara and Darien. "And those you love."

13

Unabsolved Sin

Anara

ANARA CRACKED HER KNUCKLES, then rotated her neck until she heard the satisfying crunch.

Gods, giants . . . What's next, will the dragons return? she thought, walking a step behind Larissa and Darien. They were returning to the truck that awaited them outside the Speaker's house. Though their meeting had not been publicized, Larissa's guards were holding back a small crowd that had gathered to see their lost Princess. At Larissa's presence, they surged forward, but upon catching sight of Anara, they paused in their tracks.

Their whispered voices were crystal clear to Anara's sensitive ears.

" . . . the shifter-Queen . . ."

"*Draugr*, more likely . . ."

A scratchy, high-pitched call drew Anara's gaze to the sky, where a red-tailed hawk circled above them. Her lips tightened as the hawk dove. She remained unmoved even as the hawk's feathers blurred, and its form shifted the instant before it touched the ground.

Ishaan bowed. "Your Highness."

Darien and Larissa turned in surprise, their hands on their weapons before they registered Ishaan's face. Even the crowd shrank further back from the presence of a second shifter.

Anara crossed her arms. "What do you want?"

Ishaan bowed to Darien and Larissa. "All arrangements have been made. We are to pack up our items tonight and rest for an early departure tomorrow morning."

Eager anticipation displaced Anara's displeasure at seeing Ishaan. At last, it was time to leave. But even in her excitement, Anara could not ignore Ishaan's pointed look. Whatever else he'd come to say, it was clear he wanted to say it in private.

One of the guards approached. "Your Highnesses, we must leave before the crowd grows any larger."

Larissa nodded, her mind no doubt still occupied by the conversation with the giants. She followed Darien into the truck, but Anara remained.

"I'll follow on my own," she called out.

"Your Highness," the guard said. "The crowd—"

"Won't want anything to do with me. They'll follow as soon as you leave. I have my own way of getting back."

As if registering the truth of her words, the guard nodded and shut the door. In the tiniest gap before it closed, Anara caught Larissa's inquisitive face. Anara knew she would have questions later.

Just as she'd predicted, the moment the truck departed, the crowd dispersed, some following it while others returned to their homes. Few remained, lingering just across the street, their hard eyes glaring at Anara and Ishaan. One man stood and crossed his arms, hostility oozing from his body.

The General's eyes lingered on the man in the distance. Ishaan's lip curled. "Someone should teach him some respect."

"And give him even more reason to distrust Rubinians?" she sighed. "Ignore him, and ask me whatever it is you wanted to ask."

Before Ishaan could ask anything, several other men joined the first on the street, stalking toward Anara. Their hands were curled into fists. Ishaan moved to stand in front of Anara, but she only snorted. She'd dealt with men like this before.

"What do you want?" she asked the largest man who assuredly was the leader, her voice bored and detached.

"You should leave." The largest man pushed back his jacket, revealing a gun at his side. "We know what you are, *draugr*, and we'll put you down like the stray you are—"

Ishaan's clawed hand wrapped around his throat before the words had died on the man's lips. Blood dripped down the man's neck as he gasped for air, pulling uselessly against Ishaan's grasp. Behind him, his friends reached for their guns but froze as a snarl ripped from Anara's chest.

"Only one of you has committed an offense punishable by death," she growled. "Think carefully before your next move."

Like dogs with their tails tucked between their legs, the rest of the men fled, not daring to look back at the one still in Ishaan's grasp.

With a huff, Anara returned to the problem at hand. "General Ishaan, let him breathe and take him to Torsten for his punishment."

"I can kill him just as easily here," Ishaan argued, tightening his hand until the man's eyes rolled back in his head. "Then I can dispose of the others as well. I can still smell them."

"Do as I command," she ordered, her growl returning. "And tell Torsten I only require imprisonment. Then he can serve on the front lines of the battle. Fate can decide what to do with him from there."

After a second, Ishaan snarled, then let the unconscious man fall to the ground. "And if fate decides he lives?"

"Then he lives. I won't be his executioner. I won't allow his actions to force me to become the monster he thinks I am."

Ishaan shook his head, his eyes revealing the bitter words his tongue held captive.

"What did you want, Ishaan? I need to prepare for my departure."

A rumble penetrated Ishaan's composure. "That is what I wanted to discuss. We march for Perle, and then for Safír. The council then wants to reclaim Smaragd, and only then will they consider mounting an attack on Rubin."

"Besides Diamant, Rubin is the most defended." Irritation leaked through Anara's voice. "It makes sense to wait until the Viðnám is at its strongest to attack."

A tick of annoyance pulsed in Ishaan's cheek. "All due respect, Your Highness, that's only part of the reason."

"You don't say?" Anara tilted her head in mock surprise. "I'm not an idiot, General. I know full well that the Viðnám would much rather burn down Rubin than reclaim it at all."

"Then why won't you listen to me? I was to be your advisor; let me advise you. Fight for Rubin, for *our* people, in these ridiculous council meetings instead of serving under the other monarchs." Ishaan's voice hardly concealed his bitterness. "Why won't you fight for our people, but you'll defend trash like this?" He kicked the body at his feet.

"I won't argue this with you again." Anara's voice went deathly cold. "And you will not disrespect me by assuming that I am not fighting for *my* people."

Ishaan pursed his lips but bowed, his body stiff with reluctance. "Then I will see you on the road, Highness."

"I will send guards to help you with the body." In a twist, Anara's body shifted into the raven that soared over the valley without a backward glance, but not even flight could cool her burning heart. It was always the same. People would always hate Rubin for what they'd done in allowing the Empress to corrupt their bodies and *galdr* to serve her purposes. Ishaan, always so focused on restoring Rubin to its former glory, would never admit to the sins staining the soul of their kingdom. Nor would he wonder as Anara did, if their sins could truly be redeemed.

14

Property and Companions

Halla

Sunbeams hedged over the horizon; light flickered over the sleeping city, but the sun couldn't rise fast enough for Halla. It'd been hours since Kai and Halla had been loaded into the transport truck. Though the bed was covered with thick canvas sheeting, Halla's only source of warmth had been Kai, who still slumbered next to her. How he'd been able to sleep in the cold was incomprehensible to Halla, who had shivered all night.

Perhaps it wasn't just the cold, but the unknowing that kept her awake. The tattooed man had left them under the watch of a sentry to make arrangements in the city, but that was all Halla had overheard.

She touched her wrists where her amulets of Frigg and Eir used to reside. The *thræll* had taken them from her upon her capture. As it so often did, her mind turned to Larissa. There was no proof, but Halla knew with all her heart that Larissa had made it to the Viðnám. With the same assurance, Halla knew that Larissa would come, but she couldn't come soon enough.

At the sound of approaching footsteps, Halla bolted upright, then groaned as the blunt pains of agony shot down the back of her neck and spine.

Kai stirred and looked her over once. "You shouldn't move so quickly."

"Oh, really?" Halla hissed through gritted teeth.

Kai rolled his eyes and neck, cracking the bones and setting Halla's teeth on edge. His nonchalant attitude was both reassuring and irritating. The truck door opened, followed by the sudden turn of the engine. Then they were moving again toward an unknown destination. Unable to see through the thick canvas surrounding them, Halla closed her eyes, imaging the city as she had first seen it.

Toward the Outer Wall, there were many warehouses, like the one in which they'd fought off the *draugr* and Calder. The further in they went, the more the city turned from industrial to residential, but the houses near the rim looked desolate and damaged, nothing at all like Halla had imagined them to be. Though the exteriors of the buildings improved the closer they got to the Second Wall, Halla couldn't stand the lack of space. Every building was pushed up against the next, built on top of one another with only thin alleys separating them. Though she'd dreamed for so long about exploring the city within the Walls, it paled in comparison to the beauty of her farm.

But thinking of her farm made her think of Pappa and Mamma and Tucker. She pulled her knees in tight to her chest and stared at the shadows that the sun cast alongside the canvas.

Kai watched her. "You okay?"

"We don't know who we're being sold to or where we're going. Doesn't that bother you?"

He shrugged. "Can it be any worse than being shipped to the Empress?"

He had a point.

The noise of the city increased as its citizens came alive with the light of the day. Even now that Halla was in the city, she was still apart from it, not one of them.

"Who do you think the man is?" she asked.

"The one covered in runes? One of the Hoorg. Someone high up, too, with all those tattoos."

"The what?" she asked, certain she'd misheard him.

"The Hoorg," he repeated more slowly. "They worship the gods."

"Don't we all?"

"Not like them. They're practitioners of the runes."

Halla gasped. "They have *galdr*?"

He paused. "How do you know what *galdr* is?"

"My Pappa told me stories." Halla's words raced over one an-other.

"Hmph." Kai's narrowed eyes revealed how little he believed her answer. "But no, they don't practice *galdr*. Only those with Ancestral Blood can do that. I mean, I guess maybe some of them might, but most of them don't."

"Then what do they do?"

"Supposedly, they're the voices of the gods. Their worship is what keeps the gods alive and willing to intercede on our behalf. They offer sacrifices, burn incense, you know"—he shrugged his shoulders—"stuff."

Halla gulped. "Sacrifices?"

"Not human." He grinned. "At least, not that I know of."

The transport slowed to a stop. The rumble of idling engines intermingled with shouts from sentries. Kai looked up as if he could see through the canvas. "We must be at the Second Wall."

Despite herself, a strange sort of giddiness eased its way into Halla's mind. "What's beyond the Second Wall?"

"The Court of the Aristocracy. It's where all the upper-class citizens live. They're usually favorites of the Regent or families of the Empress' generals. It's also where the Hoorg's main temple is."

The cranking of a gate squealed uncomfortably against Halla's ears. Then the truck jerked beneath her. Kai swayed as the truck moved on. "Halla, is there something you should tell me?"

"What do you mean?"

He shrugged, but the intensity behind his eyes spoke volumes. "You showed up in the barracks the day after something major happened in the city. Something related to the Viðnám, where your sister may be hiding. You know about *galdr*, but not about basic city layout. I can't help you if I don't know how."

"I don't know why you're helping me at all."

He didn't offer an explanation.

Halla didn't know how to break the silence. She resisted the urge to touch the bandage that covered her burn; the movement reminded her of Juni. Her skin throbbed constantly, but underneath the soreness was a tight, stingy feeling. She did her best to keep her head forward, but even when she stayed still, the pain was her constant companion.

By the time the truck stopped again, Halla's stomach was protesting loudly. Her hunger was quickly stifled by fear as the zipper to the canvas slid open. The tattooed man beckoned them forward.

Kai stood first, awkwardly offering Halla his bound hands to help her up. Maneuvering around the restraints, Halla's fingers grasped his and stepped out of the truck and onto the street. Her mouth fell open, and her feet froze. She could not have moved if she wanted to; her eyes were too busy taking in the sights of a world she had never known existed.

The Court of the Aristocracy looked nothing like the city within the outer section. From the smooth paved streets, to the groomed lawns, to the mansions with stone walls and glass windows, to the fountain that gurgled in the courtyard, every portion of the Court was properly spaced and designed. Though the transport had stopped in front of one mansion, Halla could see another further down the lane. Unlike the outer city, in which the buildings had been pressed together with disinterested care, there was space here to breathe. The smell of the sewers was gone, replaced by roses that grew all along the drive. A butterfly fluttered from petal to petal in idyllic serenity. Halla could have stayed and watched it all day, but the unyielding tug on her wrists would not be denied as she was dragged toward the back of a red-brick mansion with massive columns lining the porch that wrapped around the house.

Despite the pain in her neck, Halla's head swiveled from side-to-side, her eyes drinking in the sights. *This* was what she had imagined from the city. Far off in the distance, behind yet another wall, Halla could discern the top towers of the palace. The sight of them sent a thrill through Halla's heart. That had been Lara's home once, and, Halla had to believe, it would be hers again one day.

Arriving at the back door, the tattooed man pressed his finger against a button that sent a clanging response throughout the house. In mere seconds, the door opened, revealing a tall man in a crisp suit and tie. He peered down his particularly long nose at the children, wrinkles creasing around his eyes.

The tattooed man extended the length of the chain that bound Halla and Kai. "Brought for your master, a gift of the gods, in exchange for his recent generosity to their temple."

"Remove the chain, Brother Gorthr, but leave the restraints and the key." The man's voice sounded overly formal to Halla. "My master thanks the gods for their gift."

Brother Gorthr removed the chain and vanished back toward the front of the house. Halla had not been fond of the man, but his absence brought further uncertainty.

The man in the suit twitched his thin mustache. "I am Hovmester, steward of this home. It is my duty to keep charge of and maintain order among its various lower inhabitants. You will follow me."

Halla spared one last glance at the beautiful garden. No doubt Iðunn's own garden looked similar.

"Do not think of running. It will only end poorly for you." Hovmester sneered at the bandage on her neck. "Though perhaps, you've already learned that."

Heat rushed to Halla's cheeks as she stepped inside the doorframe. If the exterior had been refined, it was nothing compared to the luxury within the home. The marbled floor led down a hall decorated with gold-embossed lights that never flickered like they had back on Halla's farm. Her bare feet slapped uncomfortably loudly as they made their way toward the end of the hall where two doors waited.

"You"—Hovmester looked at Kai and pointed at the left door—"will enter through here. And you"—he glared at Halla and motioned to the other door—"will go here. I cannot allow the family to come across either of you in your current state. The others will instruct you on your tasks."

With effective swiftness, Hovmester turned the key in each of their restraints. Halla rubbed the skin around her wrists. She looked to Kai, but he was already heading toward his door. Though she feared leaving him, the look on Hovmester's face allowed no room for argument. She bowed her head and entered through the door.

ᚾᛁᛞᛗᛚᛋᚾᛁᛞᛗᛚᛋᚾᛁᛞᛗᛚᛋᚾᛁᛞᛗᛚᛋᚾᛁᛞᛗᛚᛋ

HALLA QUICKLY LEARNED THE difference between servants and slaves. Servants were paid, and although it was a low position, a servant still maintained an air of freedom and worth.

A slave like Halla, on the other hand, was property.

The short, hard-eyed mistress of the servants' quarters had reinforced this by stripping Halla and pushing her into a tub of water before it turned warm. The bandage on her neck slid free in the soapy water and earned a look of disgust from the mistress. She'd dressed Halla in a simple uniform of pants and a long shirt, then assigned Halla to another woman. The pressed apron around the second woman's waist distinguished her as a servant rather than a slave. As Halla shadowed her out of the room, she looked toward the door where Kai had disappeared.

She stopped, hesitant in her words. "I came with someone else. Do you know where he is?"

The maid pursed her dark lips, tucking a stray brown hair behind her ear and smoothing out her bun. "Male slaves work outdoors. Best not to concern yourself with anyone but yourself. Come girl, there's work to be done."

Reprimanded, Halla tucked her chin to her chest and scurried after the maid, who didn't even ask Halla's name. Perhaps that was intentional; property didn't have names. She shivered as cool air scraped across her revealed brand.

But even her growing isolation couldn't shake Halla's awe as she wound through the mansion. The main house was far more elegant than the servants' quarters had been. The only artwork she'd ever seen had been Mamma's drawings in Pappa's storybook, but even she could recognize the paintings on the walls were superior in every way.

As Halla heeded every instruction the maid ordered—making beds, gathering soiled clothes, emptying the trash from the bustling kitchen, restocking logs in fireplaces—she only grew more aware of the insignificance of her farm that had been her whole life. And of the discrepancies between the aristocracy and the farmers outside the walls.

The only glaring lack of the home was in its occupants until Halla realized that the maid was intentionally steering them away from any potential run-ins. After days confined to a small barrack, Halla's legs and back tired quickly of the work, but she was determined to keep pace. The only nagging concern on her mind was Kai.

"This is the library," the maid explained, bringing Halla's mind back to the present and pushing through the giant oak doors inlaid with the runic symbols of the gods. Halla resisted the urge to reach out and touch them, but instead accepted the feathered duster the maid handed her. Worry creased the lines around her eyes. "Every book must be dusted, but the master does not like us to be in his study long. Do this quickly."

The maid set about her task without further explanation. Halla's fingers found the nearest book and plucked it from the shelf, removing the dust underneath. Without meaning to, she flipped through the pages, the words greeting her like familiar friends in a strange place. She'd never seen so many books in one place.

Though Halla tried to move quickly, her fingers paused again and again to stray through the pages of the books. She wasn't sure how much time had passed when a familiar story greeted her from the pages. She'd only just begun to read about the formation of the five kingdoms when the book was snatched from her hands.

"That doesn't belong to you," a harsh voice said.

An open palm cracked against her face, sending her crashing to the ground. The pain in her face was doubled by the pain in her neck. A man towered over where she lay, stunned, on the ground. His blond hair was buzzed short, and authority emanated from his posture. He turned a threatening finger on the maid. "You, maid, explain yourself."

The woman's trembling voice came from behind Halla. "She is new, sir; she did not listen to my instructions."

Halla flinched as the man stepped over her toward the maid. "Then it is *your* fault for not keeping her in line."

There was a sharp crack followed by the woman's muffled cry. Halla dared not move. The master of the house—he could not be anyone else—turned back to Halla. His dark green eyes were flat and empty, a strange contrast to the angry twist of his lips. "I would say a whipping might teach you, but your brand tells me you're not the type to learn."

Halla trembled, closing her eyes as her tongue raced behind closed lips, uttering prayers to the gods.

"Father?"

A soft voice came from the door, inviting Halla to open her eyes. Standing frozen in the doorway, the girl looked to be around Halla's age, though significantly taller. Her pale pink dress was several shades darker than her fair skin. With a bow perched atop her platinum curls, the girl looked as though she'd stepped out of the artwork that hung on the walls. But her face was beautiful, open and sweet with kind eyes. They were the exact same shade as those of the master of the house, but hers were alive with compassion.

"What's wrong?" she asked.

"Nothing to concern yourself with, my darling." The change in his tone was astonishing. It was as though he'd become an entirely different person capable of compassion and rationality.

But the girl looked at the book lying on the ground beside Halla. Her eyes brightened as she picked it up. "Ah, thank you for finding my book."

Halla gaped at her, unsure of what to say.

"You sent her in here?" he asked, doubt coloring his tone.

"Of course I did. I needed the book for my lessons. I saw Hovmester bring her and the boy this morning. I figured she was my gift. You always give the best gifts. Thank you, Father." The girl fluttered forward, pressing on the tips of her toes to kiss her father's cheek. She motioned toward Halla. "Come along."

Halla looked to the maid for guidance but the woman was studiously looking at the floor. With no other choice, Halla rose to her feet, keeping her head bowed as she passed the master and followed the daughter into the hall.

"Walk behind me, not beside me," the girl whispered when Halla caught up. "You'll get in trouble."

Halla fell in step. They passed through many floor-level rooms and ascended the grand staircase that gracefully curled up onto the second floor. The girl led Halla down the hall, then into a spacious room. Crossing the threshold, Halla suppressed a gasp. Decorated in lace and flowers, the room was fit for a Princess. With an elegance beyond her years, the girl sat herself at a tea table by the tall window that looked out into the back gardens.

"I'm Saessae." She spoke her words around her smile, adding a slight lilt to the end of her sentences. "But around the others you'll have to call me Miss Saessae. You *are* new here, aren't you? Where did you come from? Who is the boy who came with you? What's it like outside the Second Wall? What—"

Halla opened her mouth but found the words wouldn't come out even if Saessae stopped talking long enough to allow her to answer, which she never did. Halla's feet had yet to find their solid ground in this new place, her brand *burned*, and her ears were still ringing from the master's blow, making it nearly impossible to wrap her mind around the questions Saessae continued to fire in her direction.

As if reading Halla's thoughts, Saessae paused mid-question. "Sorry, that was too much." She took a breath, the perfect image of composure. "Let's just start with your name."

"H-halla," she stammered.

"Where did you come from?"

Halla bit her cheek. "I was taken by the *thræll* in the Outer Wall."

The delightful look vanished from Saessae's face. "I don't like the *thræll*. I'm sorry they took you, but I'm glad you're here."

"Why?" The word fell out of her mouth before it could be stopped.

Saessae plopped her chin into her palm. "It's boring since Mother's death. There's no one to talk to. Everyone is too scared of my father." She paused. "He isn't kind anymore."

Whether it was the sense of shared loneliness or shared grief, Halla couldn't resist lowering the barriers around her heart. "Is that why you helped me?"

"I helped you because you needed it." She shrugged. "Besides, I've been asking my father for a companion for months. I figured I might as well use the situation to my advantage."

"A companion?"

"He wouldn't like that term. A personal slave is what he would call you, but I'd much rather you were my friend." There was a hesitancy in her statement as though she feared Halla's rejection instead of the other way around.

"Oh." Halla stumbled over her words. "Of course, it's just . . ."

"Yes?" she urged.

Halla's fingers played with the seam of her shirt. "I came here with someone, and I just want to know if he's alright."

"The boy, right? Father keeps the male slaves outside mostly." She glanced over her shoulder and out the window. "But I know of a way that you could talk with him."

"Really?" Hope sprouted in her chest.

A surprising glint of mischief glinted from Saessae's eyes. "We'll have to be sneaky. We'll wait until after my father has gone to sleep, in the darkest part of the night."

Halla hesitated. Saessae had saved Halla from her father's brutality, but even so, the burn on the back of her neck ached a warning. Still, if this was the only way to check on Kai . . . "Let's do it."

15

Giftless Children

Darien

Darien's mother cultivated a beautiful garden on the cliff-side next to their palace. Darien spent months pruning the plants alongside her as Aeron trained under their father's command. But it was a rare day when Aeron was just as free as Darien to sit on the edge of the cliff that overlooked the ocean waves crashing on the jagged rocks below. Aeron let his legs dangle over the cliff, leaning back on his hands as he closed his eyes with his face turned toward the sun.

Darien nudged his shoulder. "So what cosmic event allowed me to be blessed by your presence, brother? It's not often you step out of those oh-so-important council meetings."

The tiniest slit opened Aeron's right eye at Darien's tone. "Not all of us get to play with the flowers all day."

"It's a difficult life I lead." Darien twirled a carnation between his fingers before tucking it behind his ear. "How's it going, really?"

"The meetings are boring."

"What?" Darien's shock was genuine. "You, the Crown Prince of, what did you call us, the-greatest-kingdom-in-Evrópa, is admitting that sitting in a room with a bunch of Faðir's stodgy old advisors is actually boring?"

"If you tell Faðir I said that, I'll push you off this cliff myself."

Darien laughed. "Like you could take me."

Whatever Aeron might have responded died on frozen lips. His skin turned pale and cold as the frivolity drained from his face. Darien watched in horror as Aeron's face aged and sharpened with *cruelty. Calder's smile settled into a smirk as his eyes sparked with life. "You were plotting against me even then, weren't you, brother?"*

Calder's palms flattened against Darien's chest, shoving him off the cliff and sending his body plummeting through the air. Sharp rocks pierced his skin—

Darien's body froze, suspended at the moment of his own impalement. Paralyzed by the pain, Darien could only stare at the red-headed child who walked toward him on the raging waters. Power and light radiated from her skin as her hair curled around her face. A tidal wave rose behind her.

"Verðandi?" he asked, a tremor in his voice.

"I can save you." Verðandi's soprano voice rang even over the roar of the rising waters. "Convince Larissa to come to us. She must know the truth, and so must you."

Then the wave fell, crashing against the cliff and consuming them both.

ᚾᛁᛜᛂᛋᚾᛁᛜᛂᛋᚾᛁᛜᛂᛋᚾᛁᛜᛂᛋᚾᛁᛜᛂᛋ

Darien stood in front of his father's study, his eyes heavy with sleep. Not even the sun had woken, and the mountain tunnels were colder than ever. Darien knocked, the ghost of Aeron and the memory of Calder's voice haunting him, but it was Verðandi's demand that coiled in his stomach like a serpent waiting to strike.

"Enter." Torsten's voice traveled through the thick wood.

He entered, his royal garb replaced with farmhand clothes—all a part of the charade they were about to embark upon. He stood at attention, feeling the weight of his ancestral sword on his hip and the gun resting on the opposing side. Larissa, Anara, and the others were already waiting for him at the cargo truck, but his father had summoned him. So here he was.

"Faðir." Darien nodded, folding his hands behind his back.

Torsten rose from his desk. "I'll keep this brief—I know the others are waiting—but I want to make myself clear."

Darien waited, careful to clear his face of his growing apprehension.

"Princess Lovisa is critical to the Viðnám's success, but she can never be more to you than your ally. Whatever childish infatuation you had when you were younger cannot exist any longer. You are the Crown Prince, and when we reclaim our kingdom, we cannot risk the curse of the giftless children."

Darien stood speechless at Torsten's direct order. Though he'd suspected his father's feelings, Darien hadn't anticipated such blunt callousness. "Faðir, we don't even know if giftless children are real—"

Torsten's brows lowered dangerously. "And you would risk your kingdom on the hope that they're not?"

Darien clenched his fists, hating the supposed curse that had haunted his steps. When the Norn had given Rúna the power of the gods, they'd supposedly warned her that a child born from a mixed union would be robbed of the *galdr* of either parent, if the child survived at all. It was this curse that struck fear amongst the monarchies that their *galdr* could be lost and their kingdoms weakened because of it.

"The *galdr* within our people is weak enough as it is," Torsten continued, barely containing the anger in his tone. "Shiko targeted the royal families and even far-off relatives in an attempt to eradicate all *galdr* apart from her own. It's imperative we strengthen the bloodlines of each kingdom once we re-establish them. Otherwise, we may as well go back to how humanity existed after *Ragnarok*, killing each other over scraps of the world."

Darien stepped toward his father. "I don't believe it. Our world is more established than after *Ragnarok*; it's not the same. Besides, I'm not the only one left with Safírian *galdr*."

"Then who else, Darien?" Torsten thundered. "Your brother, the traitor? You can't hide your responsibilities behind Aeron anymore. He is gone, and you must rise to your position."

Darien held his father's gaze in a silent battle of wills.

"Did you know I nearly died in the escape when Safír fell?" Torsten finally asked. At Darien's shocked face, he laughed without mirth. "Of course you didn't. You weren't there. You were in Perle, with Lovisa."

Darien heard the accusation as clearly as if his father had shouted it.

"Your mother died, though. Aeron was dead, or at least, I thought he was, and you vanished without a trace. Those of us who survived banded together. Then we found the Jötnar, and they gave us a place to grow and flourish. But in our safety, a new danger was brought to the forefront of the people's minds. What would happen if I were to die? For all I knew, Shiko had already ended the Perlian line. I couldn't allow her to end mine as well."

Torsten sat at his desk and stared not at his son, but through him, as though Darien was not there at all. "I didn't want a new wife. I still mourned for Meya, my love. I didn't want new children when my last had been ripped from me. But my people needed me to find a new wife. The Viðnám needed me to have heirs. Who would lead them if I fell? The Jötnar? No, the Viðnám needed certainty in the future. So I married again, but the gods refused to grant me more heirs."

Darien thought of the woman he'd seen only on occasion. She stood in the shadows, surrounded by her court, but forgotten by her husband once she'd proven to be an unsuccessful solution. Darien couldn't even remember her name.

Torsten refocused on Darien. "Then you returned, practically from the dead. With Aeron gone, you are the heir. Not only to the throne, but to our bloodline. You cannot forget that."

Darien's blood burned not on behalf of Larissa, but for himself. Why couldn't his father see that Darien was trying? "You think I don't know that? You think I don't care about our people?"

"It is more than just caring for them. We must sacrifice ourselves for them. Their needs are our own. Our bloodline protects them—"

"But it didn't!" Darien interrupted, slamming his palms on his father's desk. "For centuries, the kingdoms separated themselves from one another for the sake of our bloodlines, but in the end our separation only aided in our destruction. Look at the Viðnám! This is proof that we don't have to be separate any more. We can mix our kingdoms and our people—"

"To what end?" Torsten thundered, rising to his feet. "So that we can live in hiding? So that you can pursue Lovisa? You hate that I might sacrifice your happiness for the sake of our people, but you would sacrifice our people for the sake of one girl?"

Yes, I would, he wanted to shout, but even as his heart demanded it, his mind rebelled. Could he really put himself before his entire kingdom? The thought alone was enough to tame Darien's temper.

Torsten adjusted his collar, seemingly taking Darien's silence as a concession. "Remember, Darien: even as you walk from this room, as you travel to Perle, you are not alone. People are watching, trying to determine whether our line is strong. I trust you to not shame me."

Darien's gut tightened, but he didn't speak. It would only make things worse.

Torsten rose to his feet. "We'll discuss this further after we reclaim Perle Go; our armies will set out by nightfall behind you. Make sure the gate is open by the time the first wave arrives."

Darien turned, but stopped at his father's voice.

"One last thing. If the Empress' War Dog is there, be sure to put him down."

Darien nodded curtly, but Torsten was already absorbed in the papers on his desk. He strode across the room, shoving the door open before his lungs burst from unspoken words. The door closed, just as Darien pounded the bottom of his fist into the wall.

"Darien!"

Larissa stepped into the light. Dressed in all black combat gear, she'd been nearly invisible in the shadows before. She reached for his hand, turning it over and prodding at his fingers. "At least nothing is broken; why would you do that?"

Darien leaned against the wall, enjoying the feel of her fingers caressing his hand. "Had to be done," he muttered.

"Because *clearly* the wall deserved it."

"Something like that."

Her gaze shifted at his tone from examining his hand to analyzing his face. She let Darien's hand fall back to his side. "Your father?"

"We don't need to talk about it." Darien flexed his stinging hand. "Come on, I'm sure the others are waiting. Let's go get Halla."

"You make it sound so easy. Get Halla. Reclaim Perle."

Darien shrugged. "Add in a couple giants and the goddesses of Fate messing with our sleep, it's practically foolproof."

"Well, that's good, since so many of the council members seem to think we're fools."

Darien's voice turned serious. "We'll prove them wrong. They'll see."

"Wait"—her feet slowed—"did you say *our* sleep?"

Darien hadn't meant to mention it. "New dream. Same message."

"For a goddess with an eternity to live, Verðandi could learn some patience."

Snorting in agreement, Darien followed Larissa through the winding tunnels and down the long flights of steps to the loading bay, where a large transport truck awaited them. Anara stood to the side, speaking with Halvor and blatantly ignoring General Ishaan. Darien's irritation, calmed by Larissa's presence, resumed at the sight of the shifter who watched Anara from nearby. Though he knew Anara certainly didn't need any help, Darien was more than happy to knock the general on the ground if he said anything impertinent to Anara.

The twins, Haki and Jari, walked around the truck, finalizing their inspection. Though their faces were nearly identical with matching buzzed hair, Darien could tell them apart instantly. Haki stood near the engine, his enormous frame making the truck look small in comparison. His sentry's uniform pulled tight across his chest and arms. Long scars peeked out from under his rolled up sleeves from where Anara had attacked him—before she'd known he was on their side. He smiled and bowed upon noticing Darien and Larissa.

His twin, Jari, nodded and eyed them warily. He'd not been welcoming when last they'd met. At Darien's and Larissa's arrival, the group quieted as the weight of what they were about to attempt settled over them.

"For Halla." Anara's words echoed in the large space.

At Darien's side, Larissa smiled, her feet moving toward the truck. "For Halla, and for Perle."

Darien's strained smile hid the apprehension that Verðandi's dream had rooted in his chest.

16

Ghost Stories

Larissa

THE GIANT ASH TREE *stood before her, blocking out the sun and sky and casting half of the clearing in shadow. At the base of the tree, standing between the three massive roots, the small goddess beckoned Larissa forward. Her feet carried her of their own accord, having walked this path before. Larissa couldn't have stopped them if she tried. And she had tried, in so many past dreams.*

"You called?" she asked, resignation seeping through her words.

"Didn't you miss me?" Verðandi asked, all smiles as she hopped up onto the rim of the stone well. "You used to spend so much time with me."

Larissa sighed, never knowing how to respond to the child-goddess who nearly radiated with massive amounts of galdr and yet seemed so delicate. "I need sleep, Verðandi."

The goddess nodded serenely. "Halla's waiting for you."

Larissa stiffened. "Is she alright?" Larissa's eyes glanced at the shimmering surface of the well. "Have you seen her?"

Verðandi giggled and gestured Larissa forward with her hands. "See for yourself."

As eager as Larissa was to see Halla, her steps forward were tentative. She hadn't forgotten the last time she'd looked into the well, before she'd remembered her past, and been consumed by the light within. But the temptation of seeing Halla overrode her caution.

Grasping the cold stones, Larissa peered into the swirling waters that settled onto a familiar face. Although the image only captured a portion of the girl's face, the rest shrouded in darkness, Larissa would have recognized Halla's freckled nose anywhere. A sharp gasp escaped her lips at the sight of Halla's hair, cut short around her ears and neck. The water rippled, and she was gone.

"No," Larissa cried, "bring her back!"

Verðandi knelt on the sides of the well and dipped a small hand into the waters, stilling them at her touch until the surface shimmered like a mirror. Larissa stared, willing Halla to reappear. Only her reflection stared back, but there was something wrong with it. Larissa's eyes darkened, her face narrowed, and her white hair turned coal black. Empress Shiko glared back at her from within the well. Larissa's shaking hand touched her cheek, and the reflection did the same.

"Stop it," Larissa snapped, but she couldn't look away.

Shiko's reflection sank into the waters, replaced by images of a city laid out before her with canals of water and overflowing trees winding through the buildings that glowed with light. There was a palace set in the middle of the city, surrounded by gardens and ponds. The curved architecture of the building was familiar, and an old memory spoke to Larissa.

"Why are you showing me Smaragd?" Larissa asked.

"Once you have Halla, once you have your kingdom, you must come to us," Verðandi ordered.

"I don't know how to find you."

"That is why you must travel to Smaragd. Someone there will show you the way."

Larissa nearly groaned in frustration. "Why can't you just show me the way? Why can't you just tell me whatever it is you need to say?"

Verðandi let her fingers dance. The images changed rapidly at her touch: Darien's face, then Anara's, then more faces she did not recognize flashed across the surface of the water. "It is not only your thread that must intertwine with ours."

Larissa swayed as the cargo truck rumbled beneath her. Her body protested against the hard wooden bench, but at least the truck bed was covered by a large canvas roof protecting her skin from the sun. It'd been hours since they left the Viðnám—hours since Larissa's latest vision, but she couldn't shake the images from the well. She'd wanted to talk to Darien, but privacy was not a luxury they had.

While Haki and Jari took turns driving toward Lystheim, Halvor, Darien, and Larissa rode along in the back. Halvor sat on the opposing bench with his head tucked into his chest. Anara and Ishaan scouted the road from the skies, though Ishaan would occasionally be forced to rest alongside the others. His *galdr* was not as expansive as Anara's, who remained airborne throughout the day. There had been little talk at the beginning—reviewing their plan—but conversation had died out, leaving only the hum of the truck.

Even without talking, Larissa was hyper aware of Darien's presence. He sat beside her with his eyes closed and his head leaned back against the canvas covering. His shallow beard clung to his sharp jawline, and a black curl fell over his eyes. She could see the pulse beneath the muscles in his neck.

"Like what you see?" Darien asked, the brilliant blue peeking through one of his eyes.

The blush colored Larissa's cheeks, but flapping wings saved her from responding as Anara soared into the truck bed through the rear opening. She shed her transformation and landed on her feet with the ruby sparkling at her neck. The truck slowed beneath them.

Halvor raised his head, pushing back his crescent shaped glasses. "Why are we pulling off the main road?"

"We're well inside Perlian territory," Anara explained. "The nearest farm is only a couple miles out."

Another set of flapping wings announced Ishaan's return to the group, which tightened Anara's entire posture. Curiosity and concern rose up within Larissa at Anara's response. She intended to find out exactly why Anara seemed to hate the other shifter.

"Night will fall in an hour," Anara continued as the cargo truck crawled to a stop beneath them. "It's best for us to rest here tonight and wait until we know the first wave of the Viðnám is closer before approaching the farmers."

"We should go now, your Highnesses," Ishaan countered. "It gives us the time to meet with more potential allies."

"And if we have farmers opposed to the plan?" Anara didn't hide the scorn in her voice.

A vein throbbed in Ishaan's forehead. "We commandeer their trucks and hold them until we depart for the Outer Wall as King Torsten decided."

"And if we have more farmers against our plan than for it, General?" Anara snapped. "There are not enough of us to manage multiple farms. We would risk detection of an Empress sympathizer getting past us and reporting us to the sentries."

"Not if we tie them up. Knock them out. Incapacitate them however we see necessary."

"We are not *incapacitating* innocent families against their will." Darien's voice was as tight as Anara's.

"We'll wait here for the night," Halvor announced. "Princess Anara is correct. We'll approach the farmers tomorrow, and only enough to get us inside the Wall without detection. No more. We're not recruiting soldiers."

Ishaan ground his teeth. "Then I will make sure the area is secure."

At that, he took flight, his wings nearly clipping Haki's head as the twins rounded the back of the cargo truck. Halvor relayed their plans, and the twins hurried to set up camp further within the trees. Halvor hopped down after them, but Larissa grabbed Darien's and Anara's arms before they could follow.

"Anara, who is Ishaan?" she asked once the others had walked outside of earshot.

Anara's eyebrows raised with exaggerated innocence. "General of Rubin, remember?"

"She means who is he to *you*?" Darien asked, crossing his arms and moving next to Larissa to block the tailgate of the truck.

Anara smirked, as if amused. "I've beaten *draugr*s before you know? I can get past you two without even shifting."

"Probably," Larissa agreed. "And we can't make you tell us anything, but we'd like to know just how much we should hate this guy."

"What?" she asked.

"On a scale of putting dirt in his coffee"—Darien mimicked sprinkling something in an imaginary cup—"or dropping him in the ocean as a sacrifice to Jörmungandr?"

"Didn't Jörmungandr die during *Ragnarok*?" Anara asked.

"You're kind of missing the point," Darien argued.

"The point is," Larissa cut in, "we're your friends, and you can tell us."

Anara shrugged, sitting on the bench. "I never liked him, even when we were kids."

"Kids?" Darien interrupted. "He looks old enough to be your father."

"He's younger than me actually," she said with a smirk, "but my *galdr* is stronger. Are you forgetting that I wasn't frozen in time with you for fifty years?"

Darien shifted. "Oh, right."

If Larissa was being honest, she'd often forgotten it as well. Anara looked only a few years older than herself, a side effect of her constant use of *galdr* that slowed the aging of her physical body.

"He was rude and arrogant. His family had *galdr* due to some marriages within the royal bloodline further back in his family tree. He thought that made him better than everyone else who didn't have *galdr*." Anara shook her head. "When we first joined the Viðnám, he and I were the only remaining shifters that we knew of that hadn't been tainted by Shiko's curse. At first, it was a relief to not be alone, but as time passed, he became ruthless, power-hungry, and cruel. He took the missions I wouldn't because there was no line he wouldn't cross."

Larissa noticed the way Darien's face tightened. Did he wonder what missions Torsten had approved that Anara had denied?

Anara fiddled with the ruby pendant around her neck. "He sees himself as my advisor, as his ancestors were for my father, and makes it clear regularly that I am failing my people. A better Queen would put her own people first. A better Queen would not serve another Queen."

"That's ridiculous," Larissa spluttered. "You don't serve me."

"You asked who he is," Anara repeated. "He is the ghost of Rubin, sent to haunt me until I pay for my people's sins in siding with Shiko and restore them to their former glory."

Larissa leaned over, her hand on Anara's arm. "We will."

"Will we?" Anara's gaze pinned Darien where he sat. "Do you think your father honestly cares if we reclaim Rubin? Wouldn't it be easier to burn it to the ground on the march to Diamant?"

"That's not going to happen," Darien argued, nodding his head at Larissa. "We wouldn't let that happen. We'll help you save your people too."

"If we even deserve it," she muttered. "Maybe the gods have cursed my bloodline to destruction."

Larissa tightened her grip on Anara's arm. "I don't believe that, and neither do you."

She patted Larissa's hand, then stood. "We'll see."

ᚾᛁᛒᛚᛋ᛫ᚾᛁᛒᛚᛋ᛫ᚾᛁᛒᛚᛋ᛫ᚾᛁᛒᛚᛋ᛫ᚾᛁᛒᛚᛋ᛫

DINNER WAS EATEN AROUND the fire that chased away the chill of fall. Ishaan had returned from his scouting, having noted the ten closest farms to choose from. As Halvor laid out the plans for which farms they would approach first, Larissa found herself retreating inward.

Halla.

Larissa held the image of her sister within her mind's eye, drawing strength from the knowledge she would find Halla soon. The memory of Halla's cut hair gnawed at her, filling her with apprehension. A tingling sensation crawled across Larissa's palms, and she knew, without looking, that they were glowing.

Before they'd left, Eluf had sent her a message, instructing her to practice her circulation to gain better control of her *galdr*. Larissa did so now, imagining the heat at the tips of her fingers expanding into her palms, then her wrists.

Everything is made up of energy, her mother had once taught her. *Imagine if energy had substance. Imagine you could feel it.*

Larissa's eyes burned at her mother's voice.

Our galdr *allows us to manipulate even the unseen,* she'd once said, *but you must have faith in the unseen or you will never master it or yourself.*

With her mother's voice lingering in her ears, Larissa moved the heat through her body until she swore she could feel it in the tips of her hair. As it receded back to her hands, Larissa knew the glow was gone.

Darien's voice cut through her concentration. "Halvor, you said before in the council meetings, you hoped to find your family alive in Safír?"

Halvor pushed up his crescent-moon glasses. "I've been searching for years. When Shiko took control, I was separated from my sister in the chaos. I thought she was dead until recent reports proved not only is she alive, but she also cares for her grandchild. A boy. Marinos." Halvor's eyes and tone softened on the name.

"We'll find them, Halvor," Darien promised.

The man sighed deeply. "We must focus on Perle first. Then, perhaps, if the Norn favor us, we will make it to Safír."

"We'll make it," Haki promised, tearing a large bite from the jerky in his hands and winking at Anara. "We've got three monarchs of old on our side. We're already favored."

"Not that I'm complaining," Anara said, leaning back on her hands, "but how did two sentries end up joining the Viðnám?"

Larissa raised her head in time to catch the glances Haki and Jari shared with one another. There was hesitancy in the larger brother's eyes and anger in the smaller brother's. Jari's fingers rubbed at a medallion that hung from his neck. The light of the flames glared off the metal, revealing the eight tridents emanating from the Helm of Awe. It was an old symbol for protection and power.

Jari's eyes flicked in Larissa's direction before he huddled over the cup in his hands. "Our story is not suitable for current company."

All hands stilled on cups and plates. Larissa set down her own meal. "If you're afraid of offending me, you don't need to be."

"It's not that," Haki tried to reassure. "There are more encouraging stories to tell before a battle."

Larissa met the smaller twin's eyes. "Jari, you can tell me."

"Very well, Princess." Jari turned toward her, ignoring Haki's hand on his arm. "The day Perle fell, the day you disappeared, Empress Shiko thought you might still be hidden somewhere within the palace, and so she burned it to the ground with the servants still inside."

Nausea rose in Larissa's throat, even Anara looked unsettled on the other side of the fire.

"She had her armies seal up the doors and windows. My grandfather was burned alive because Shiko was searching for you." Jari's voice grew harder with each word. "My grandmother was pregnant with my mother as she watched the palace crumble to ash. She fled to one of the nearby houses and hid herself. Many who stayed behind were imprisoned, but they were the lucky ones. If anyone ran and was recovered, they were executed without trial for treason. Their bodies were left on display for months as a warning to those who remained."

He paused, but Larissa didn't know what to say. In the crackle of the burning logs, she swore she could hear the screams of the Perlians—her people trapped in her palace—who paid for *her* disappearance. The smoke of the fire was thick in her nostrils.

But Jari was not done, nor was he responding to Haki's attempt to stop him.

"After that, the Empress enacted her one-child policy. In the case of twins, she gives the mother the choice of who she gets to keep and who she has to sacrifice into the Empress' service. My mother could not choose, so she hid me, the second-born, for years, telling everyone that she had lost me in delivery while registering my brother as her only child. I was discovered when I was eight years old. My mother was executed for her treachery. In front of both of us."

Jari's voice caught. Even Haki looked sick at the memory, his eyes narrowed in anger and pain. Jari cleared his throat. "My brother and I were enlisted to serve the Empress, to be hated by those around us for the actions we were forced to commit. We were never given a choice to be anything else, not until the Viðnám."

Jari's tale was met with silence, the kind that lingered in the soul.

"I'm sorry," Larissa whispered, shaking her head.

"It wasn't your fault," Haki started, but Jari clenched his jaw, clearly in disagreement with his brother.

"Your story," Halvor interrupted, "reminds us why we fight and the hope that our returned monarchs bring to their people."

Larissa looked down, unable to swallow around the lump in her throat. Darien's hand rested between her shoulder blades, but his comfort barely dented the pool of grief and guilt that engulfed

Larissa. She hadn't chosen to be hidden by the Norn or to leave her people at Shiko's mercy, but that didn't change the facts. Her absence had caused her people nothing but hardship.

And judging by the look on Jari's face as he glared down at the fire, studiously ignoring her, it would take more than pretty apologies to regain the trust of her people.

17

If Only Tonight

Darien

PACKING UP THE CARGO truck had taken little to no time, leaving Darien with a lack of purpose as they all waited for Anara and Ishaan to return from their scouting mission. They were meant to visit the farms in their vicinity and report back which farmers might seem most sympathetic to the Viðnám's cause.

Darien drummed his fingers on the log next to the ashes of last night's fire. Halvor sat near him, peering through his spectacles over the map of Perle once again. The twins were checking the truck, if for no better reason than to occupy their time. Larissa paced nearby. Though she'd wished Darien a good morning, she'd seem preoccupied and unwilling to meet his gaze. He could only attribute it to nerves.

"Couldn't Haki and Jari drive us through the Wall?" Darien asked. "They're still dressed like sentries."

Larissa stopped pacing.

"Nowhere for us to hide in the back," Halvor answered without looking up.

"He could say we're prisoners."

"No good either. They've been gone too long; by now I'm sure their absences have been reported. If they were recognized at the Wall, we'd lose the element of surprise. Be patient. Princess Anara will return shortly."

Larissa's pacing resumed. Darien rose, moving away from the road and back toward the trees. He tapped Larissa on the elbow. "Walk with me?"

She nodded, but still her eyes would not meet his. They went far enough to escape Halvor's eyes and ears.

"What's wrong?" Darien asked.

"I knew it was bad, but I didn't know—" Larissa stopped, shaking her head. "What happened to Jari and Haki, to the Perlians, it's my fault."

"How is that your fault?"

"She was searching for me. Shiko punished them because I wasn't there."

He reached for her, his hands on her arms. "We never knew your mother was planning to send us to the Norn. We had no control over the situation. You can't blame yourself."

"What about before then? How often did we focus on our own wants, our own worries, that we all missed what Shiko was planning?"

He shook his head. "We were kids, Lov."

"I was the Crown Princess, Darien. I was a descendant of Rúna and possessor of Ancestral Magic. I should've taken my mother more seriously when she spoke about the prophecy; I should've pushed her to explain so that I would know what I'm supposed to do to fix everything, but I didn't. I was too focused on the day she would present me to our people." She breathed in sharply. "I was too focused on you."

Darien's stomach squeezed at the memory of her hand in his, the low laugh that only he got to hear. "On me?"

"So much of my life was a lie meant to protect me, but you . . ." She paused, her lips pulling into a reluctant smile. "You were real. And when I was with you, I got to be real too. When I was with you, I didn't care about prophecies or even my throne, I just cared about you."

"And I just cared about you. Why are you making it sound like that's a bad thing?"

"Your father would get so mad at you, even then. He said your duty was to the Safírians and not to me."

Darien cradled her face in his hands and ran his thumb along her scarred cheek. Blood pumped through his heart in a way that was almost painful. "He was wrong."

Looking pained, she pulled away from his touch. "Maybe he was right."

Darien worked his jaw, hurt making his words harsh. "What do you mean?"

"Do you remember the day before Aeron left to defend Smaragd?"

Bitterness seeped in Darien's stomach, crawling up his throat.

"Aeron wanted you to go with him. You didn't want him to leave without you, but you didn't go with him because of me. If you'd gone, maybe things would be different. Maybe Aeron wouldn't be—"

Calder, Darien's thoughts finished. "Or maybe I would've turned out just like him, captured by Shiko's armies."

"We lost focus on our people. We were too focused on each other."

Darien ran a hand through his hair. "What are you saying?"

She took a deep breath, seeming to steel herself. "There's so much at stake, more than just rescuing Halla. These are our people, Darien, and they've been waiting for us for fifty years. They need us, and we can't allow ourselves to become distracted."

"Is that what I am?" Pain lay thick on his words. "A distraction?"

"No, but—" She sighed, struggling to speak. "You're the Crown Prince now, Darien. It changes things. Your first duty has to be to your people, just as mine must be to my people. We don't have the luxury of putting our desires first anymore."

Unwanted truth rang in her words. It was the same truth his father had tried to instill in him, and yet hearing it from Larissa made all the difference. She was fighting for her people, even as she fought for her sister. What was Darien fighting for?

Her, he thought. It'd been enough before. When he was younger, he'd been content to support Aeron as he prepared for the crown, to encourage Lovisa that her people would love her, to be a friend to Anara who needed nothing but his friendship. But now . . .

He'd all but given up on Aeron, convinced Calder had killed whatever part of Aeron remained. If Aeron was truly gone, Darien would have to do whatever he could for his people; but in his heart, he wasn't sure what that would entail, let alone if he would have the strength to sacrifice whatever it took.

If she could fight for her people and Halla, couldn't he fight for his people and Larissa? "If this is about me taking the Crown—" he started.

"Your Highnesses, I—oh." Halvor paused mid-step, having nearly bumped into them and looking up from the map still held in his hand while he adjusted his glasses with the other. "I don't mean to intrude, but Princess Anara and General Ishaan have returned."

Darien bit his tongue, resisting the urge to send the older man away. But Halla was too important; Perle was too important. Was this what his life would consist of from now? Ignoring his heart in favor of duty? "We're coming."

Halvor nodded, quickly heading back the way he'd come.

Darien grabbed Larissa's hand before she could follow. "We'll talk more later. Our people are important, but so are we."

He let her hand fall, but she remained transfixed where she stood, staring at him as though she wanted to say something. At the sound of Anara's voice, she turned back toward the road, leaving Darien no choice but to follow. The others huddled around Anara where she pored over a map she'd unrolled on top of the hood of the cargo truck. Halvor drew an X on top of one of the nearest farms.

"—not that one." Anara pointed at the X Halvor had just drawn. "He's ancient, and unkind to his farmhands. He might turn us in if he thought it would earn him a free month's rations. We should visit the farms more to the south." At their approach,

Anara looked up. A grin stretched across her face. "Ready to start a rebellion?"

ᚾᛁᛈᛏᛋᚾᛁᛈᛏᛋᚾᛁᛈᛏᛋᚾᛁᛈᛏᛋᚾᛁᛈᛏᛋ

OF THE FIRST THREE farms they visited, two families agreed to help their smaller group infiltrate the Wall with little need for persuasion. Regardless of the farmers' enthusiasm, Haki and Jari each remained with one of the families to ensure there would be no betrayal of their plans. As the sun slid toward the horizon, exhaustion set into Darien's bones. The third farmer was proving to be less willing than the others.

"The Viðnám is already on its way," Havlor reassured the farmer and his wife. "There will be no repercussions from the Regent for aiding us. The Perle Princess will restore her kingdom to what it once was."

The family huddled together in their kitchen. The woman held a small boy in her arms, and an older girl cowered behind her father's legs. Anara had chosen them for the presence of the second-born the farmer attempted to pass off as belonging to one of his farm hands, but it seemed only to backfire. Darien couldn't blame him for his wariness.

"I can't risk my family for a Princess I don't even know exists." The man's voice was firm. "You should leave."

Larissa stiffened beside Darien, hanging back as Halvor had instructed her to do. No one knew what the Perle Princess looked like, and Halvor had wanted to keep it a secret as long as possible. She tightened her arms across her chest, though Darien knew she wanted to intervene.

"Then you leave us no other choice." Ishaan's voice was a growl as he stepped forward. His eyes darkened in a way that Darien associated with Anara's transformations.

Darien's hand reached for his sword, but Anara was already there, blocking Ishaan's path to the family. "Stop."

It was one word, but the power behind was enough to send a chill down Darien's spine.

Ishaan's growl deepened. "King Torsten ordered that any resisting families be placed under arrest until we were finished with the mission."

Larissa pushed off from the wall. "But these are not King Torsten's people."

She strode forward and pulled back her hood, revealing her braided hair the color of starlight, her golden eyes, and the thick scar running from her cheek to her ear. Even in such simple clothes, Larissa emanated authority as she never had before. She moved to stand between Ishaan and the farmer's family. "These are *my* people, General, and if you lay so much as one finger on this family, I will deal with you myself."

His eyes narrowed, and no one could miss the snarl that rumbled in the back of his throat, but he inclined his head. Darien smirked from his place near the front door, releasing his grip on his sword, content to watch Larissa put the shifter in his place.

"Are you the Princess?" came a small voice.

Larissa knelt, facing the girl who hid behind her father's legs, and held out a hand. Glowing sparks crackled between her fingers. Though the girl clapped in delight, the farmer and his wife gasped before falling to their knees.

Larissa's face paled. "Please stand. As my friends told you, we will reclaim Perle tomorrow, but we need trucks and drivers that are familiar to the sentries to get us through the Wall. Will you help us?"

It was the mother who replied with a waver in her voice. "Your Highness, we want to help, but we have our own children to think of. Please understand."

Only Darien noticed the look of hurt and guilt that flashed in Larissa's eyes. She tilted her chin up, and the vulnerability was gone. "I understand. We won't force your help, but we will stay here with you to make sure no one else is alerted to our plans. Where are your farm hands?"

"They went to their own homes for the night, about a mile north."

"Then we'll be sure to be gone before the sun has risen."

"Princess," Halvor said. "We were supposed to have at least three—"

"It will have to be enough, Halvor. I won't force my people into any more danger."

"Thank you, Your Highness." The mother breathed a sigh of relief.

The father's tongue finally unraveled. "You are welcome to stay in our home. It isn't much, but we can relocate to the barn—"

"*We'll* stay in the barn," Larissa interrupted. Her voice brokered no argument.

The father pulled his wife and children closer to him. "Thank you, Princess. We may not be brave enough to oppose the Empress, but we are hopeful that you will."

All eyes swiveled at the slam of a door as Ishaan stormed through the threshold.

Halvor hesitated before bowing his head in Larissa's direction. "I will send Ishaan to alert Haki and Jari to our situation. I will remain in the house to keep watch. You three may as well head to the barn and rest."

Before they could leave, the small girl dashed between her father's legs and tugged at Larissa's leg. Surprise flickered across her face as Larissa knelt and turned her ear to the girl. Although the parents had rushed forward, they paused as the girl whispered something in Larissa's ear that was too soft for Darien to catch.

Larissa's eyes shone as she blinked rapidly against the wetness. She reached out a hand and tugged gently at the girl's hair as Darien had seen her do to Halla. "Of course."

Then she stood, and the little girl was taken into her father's arms. Larissa turned, leaving Darien and Anara no other choice but to follow her to the barn while Halvor stayed behind. As they crossed the field to the barn, Darien's eyes searched and failed to find Ishaan. Perhaps the Rubinian had shifted. Whatever the reason, Darien was grateful for the man's absence.

The inside of the barn was warmer than the cool night, although not by much. Most of the stalls were empty apart from a horse, two pigs, and some chickens. With doleful eyes, the animals watched the trio cross the hay-strewn floor and climb the ladder up into the loft above.

"That was quite the show of force in there, Lara," Anara said. "I like it."

Darien couldn't have agreed more.

"You mean, you think it's about time," Larissa countered.

"Something like that." Anara settled into the hay, throwing her arms behind her head. "Rest up. Tomorrow we change the world."

Darien chuckled. "No pressure."

"Oh, *all* the pressure. That's what makes it fun."

Larissa settled into the hay. "I'm glad you're on our side."

"As you should be," came Anara's smug reply.

Though Darien could tell the moment Anara drifted off to sleep, no doubt exhausted from her near-constant transformations, he lay awake. His mind was a tumult of chaotic and disorganized thoughts. Beside him, Larissa tossed and turned. Minutes went by, and sleep eluded them both.

With a sudden creak, the loft floor protested as Larissa bolted upright. Darien forced his breath to come and go in even rhythms as he watched her crawl across the floor and descend the ladder. She disappeared into the shadows, slipping through the barn door and into the night. Darien sat up, suddenly aware that Anara was staring at him.

"Don't look at me." Anara yawned, turning over to her other side. "I'm not going to follow her."

Darien's mouth twitched up as he shoved on his boots then slid down the rungs of the ladder. Passing a chicken that rustled in frustration, Darien escaped out into the night air. Although he could not see Larissa, he could sense her. He might not have Anara's keen animalistic instincts, but he could feel Larissa's radiating *galdr* from a nearby cabbage field.

She stood with her back toward him and her hands outstretched. Golden crackles of electricity sparked between her fingers as she raised them higher still. Pebbles and stones rose up, hovering in the air around her. Darien watched, suddenly struck by the memory of the first time she had shown him her *galdr*. He was as amazed by her now as he had been then, yet their earlier conversation made him hesitate to approach her when he wouldn't have before.

We can't allow ourselves to become distracted, she'd said.

But she *was* distracting; how could he pretend otherwise? The way her brows knit together with concentration as she flipped her long, pale braid behind her back and raised glowing hands to the sky. The way she tightened her eyes as crackles of energy sparked between her fingers.

He cleared his throat. "Practicing?"

The rocks clattered together to the ground as Larissa spun to face him. "Darien."

"Sorry, I didn't mean to startle you."

"It's okay." She wrapped her arms close to her chest. "I couldn't sleep."

"Want to talk about it?"

She hesitated, and Darien wondered if she was replaying their earlier conversation the same way he was. Was she rethinking what she'd said?

"They don't believe I can protect them," she whispered. "That's why they wouldn't help us. They don't think I can do it."

Darien measured his words in the same way that he measured his steps toward her. "You'll prove them wrong. And once they realize that you mean what you say, they will follow you."

Sparks flew between her fingertips, and a stone flew up into her hand. "Do you remember the first time I learned to do this?"

Darien chuckled. "Aeron was so mad. He said it gave you an unfair advantage whenever we would skip rocks across the lake." A smile tugged her lips and lifted Darien's expression along with her own. All he'd ever wanted was to make her happy. "What did the girl say to you? Back in the house?"

"She thanked me for not hurting her parents or her little brother." Larissa's smile disappeared; her hand clenched around the pebble, her voice breaking along with her composure. "That's all these people know, pain and suffering; they're surprised when they receive compassion. How am I supposed to fix this? Darien—"

He rushed to her, sweeping her into his arms. She did not resist, cradling her head in his neck as if he could shield her from the cruelty of Shiko's reign. He held her more tightly until the trembling in her arms softened. In that moment, she fit in his arms just as perfectly as she had years and years ago. She smelled of dirt and hay, but he didn't mind. If only she would stay in his embrace.

But the moment ended when Larissa pushed herself away. "We can't, Darien. Tomorrow we'll reveal to all of Evrópa that we have returned. Even if everything goes according to plan, even if we find Halla and reclaim Perle, we still have the other commonwealths. I still have to face Shiko. And even if we're successful there, we have our responsibilities to our people. We can't let anything distract us from them."

He was ready to argue. There had to be a way they could serve their people without losing each other. But he stopped at the sight of her tense shoulders and the look of set determination on her face. Her focus was Halla. Her focus was Perle. Now wasn't the time to discuss anything else, no matter what they both felt.

She didn't need a love; she needed her friend.

He chewed on his words before finally saying. "If that's what you want. But if everything is going to change tomorrow, then

we can have tonight.”

Her brows pushed down over golden eyes. “What do you mean?”

With a grand flourish, he gestured to the cabbage patch around them. “Princess Larissa of Perle, would you do me the honor of joining me to stare at the stars?”

“You can’t be serious.”

“Why not?” he asked, his arms still outstretched. “As you said, our world may end tomorrow, or we may start a very long and difficult journey. Why can’t we just be a farm hand and a farm girl enjoying the beautiful night sky?” He settled, patting the ground beside him.

Seemingly against her will, her lips curved up. “You really want to just sit here and look at the stars?”

“Yep. If you can see them past my stunningly good looks, that is.”

He was pleased to see her loosen the tightness in her shoulders and roll her eyes, as Lovisa had done so often in the past. Larissa lay beside him, and though Darien kept what distance he could, he couldn’t stop looking at her. He would freeze this moment in his memory, because when it was over, it would be morning. Morning would bring tomorrow.

Tomorrow would bring uncertainty, violence, and maybe even death.

Tomorrow, they would once again be forced into the roles the Norn had seen fit to bestow upon them. Darien would still be the Crown Prince, and Larissa would still be the lost princess of the prophecy, with all the duties and restrictions that those titles entailed.

Tomorrow, they would be separated by their own paths.

But tonight, for this moment, they could simply be.

18

Stone Steps and Barn Ladders

Halla

"Keep up, Halla!" Saessae called after Halla stopped yet again.

But Halla couldn't stop gawking at the shops that lined the cobblestone streets. It was one thing for jewelry to shine, but Halla couldn't understand how even the clothes shimmered in the sunlight. The clothes were forgotten at the smell of freshly baked pastries coming from an open door. Halla peeked her head in, just quickly enough to catch sight of the strawberry-and-cream cake sitting on the counter. Drool gathered in her mouth, but the sweet melody of a song turned her head in another direction. She couldn't see anyone playing an instrument and only then realized it was floating from a speaker within a shop. The sight of her reflection contrasted against a black wig displayed in the next window sent Halla scurrying after Saessae. The world of the aristocracy was entirely different from the world she'd grown up in.

At first, Halla hadn't known how she would pass the time waiting for night when she could go and check on Kai, but Saessae had the perfect distraction. She accompanied the other girl down the streets of the Court of the Aristocracy, always several steps behind. Though she was careful to keep her eyes down as they passed other high-ranking members of the city, Halla drank in as much of her surroundings as she could.

The only thing that dampened her spirits was the metal bracelets biting into her wrists. Slaves were not allowed outside their master's home without them.

Throughout the inner section of the city, the icons of Vör—the goddess of wisdom—were more prominent than those in the outer section. Though Halla had most often seen the statues of Vör as an elderly woman blindfolded, here she was represented in her youth, her eyes staring at Halla with the blindfold hanging from her open palms. It wasn't only Vör but also Njörðr, Týr, Iðunn, Hel, and even Loki that decorated their path.

"Saessae," Halla whispered. "Why are there so many more statues here than in the outer city?"

Saessae lifted her gloved hand, pointing slightly at the simple yet elegant building erected at the end of the lane. It was built with three sections of triangular rooftops on top of each other. The stone steps bore painted golden runes that led up to the doors.

"What *is* it?" Halla asked.

Saessae spared a glance that Halla was beginning to recognize whenever she asked a question she should know the answer to if she'd grown up in the city. "It's the temple of the Hoorg."

Halla's mouth parted, remembering the little Kai had told her. The man with the runic tattoos—Brother Gorthr—belonged to the Hoorg. Halla shivered. Kai may have reassured her they did not perform human sacrifices, but she had no desire to test his accuracy. She bowed her head as several aristocrats exited the building, waiting until they'd passed to ask Saessae, "Why are we here?"

"Worship." Saessae's voice wobbled. "It's something I would do with my mother."

Halla nearly reached out to comfort her, but the throbbing on her neck was enough to still her hand. On padded footsteps, she followed Saessae into the cool dimness of the temple. There were even more statues within than without. Though Halla had grown up praying to the gods, there was something unsettling about the sculptures. There was no kindness in Iðunn's face. Hel sneered in satisfaction. Týr threatened all who passed by with the chains that had once bound Fenrir.

In the center of the temple, a gnarled tree stretched for the high ceilings. Its roots cocooned into thick coils near the base and broke the tile surrounding it. Figures in brown robes strode here and there, but Halla's anxiety peaked at the sight of a familiar man dressed in long white robes and tattooed with runes.

"Brother Gorthr," Saessae greeted the man with obvious familiarity.

"A delight to see you, Miss Saessae." He inclined his head, but his eyes strayed to Halla. "The gods have caused our paths to cross again."

Before Halla could figure out if she was meant to respond, Saessae spoke. "Thank you for bringing me Halla. The gods are generous."

"Only to those who serve faithfully. Perhaps one day you will join us in our worship."

Saessae's eyes glimmered, but her lips turned downward. "I don't think my father would approve."

"No one can deny the gods." He spoke lightly, but Halla shivered at what felt like a threat beneath the man's words, drawing his attention. "Your new slave—"

"Companion," Saessae corrected.

His gaze flickered to the metal bracelets on Halla's wrists. "Your new companion has not been purified. She ought to remain outside while you conduct your worship."

"Of course, Brother Gorthr. Wait for me outside, Halla, and don't talk to anyone."

There was no unkindness in Saessae's command, and Halla slid out without complaint, grateful for the sun that chased away the shadows of the temple. She moved to the side of the building behind the bushes to avoid the aristocrats that passed through the entrance. In the sudden silence, Halla realized how alone she was. She hadn't been alone since Fenris had captured her. She wore no chains; only her branding and bracelets marked her for what she was.

For the wildest moment, Halla imagined running down the cobblestone street, never stopping until she found her way out of the city and back to Larissa. Her neck tingled, and she nearly cried out at the remembered pain of the hot iron against her skin. She shook where she stood, knowing she'd never make it past the Second Wall. Besides, she couldn't leave without Kai.

She leaned against the wall of the temple, sliding down to rest against it, hidden from those that passed just on the other side of the foliage. A butterfly fluttered from petal to petal on the flowers in front of her. Halla dipped her chin to her knees.

"Sister Wren, what is troubling you?"

Halla stiffened at the deep voice just beyond the bushes.

"Nothing," a high voice squeaked.

Pacing footsteps crunched the leaves on the ground. Through branches and leaves, Halla caught sight of the brown robes of the Hoorg's members. Hidden as she was, they could not see her, but she could hear them.

"Sister, tell me."

The pacing stopped. "I can't sleep. I see the city, but in my dreams, Perle burns. And we burn with her."

"If that is the will of the gods—"

"I must speak with Regent Hammon and warn him—"

"No." The voice was firm. "Brother Gorthr has warned us to keep our visions to ourselves for now."

"But, we serve Regent Hamm—"

"We do not serve Regent Hammon," a new voice interrupted. Halla recognized it immediately as Brother Gorthr.

She leaned in toward the bushes, peering through the gaps between the foliage to see the speakers bow at Gorthr's arrival. Their folded hands were decorated in similar runes to his. Halla didn't understand. What was the point of the runes if they couldn't wield *galdr*?

"Remember, Sister Wren," said Gorhr, "we serve the gods. Let's go and discuss this vision of yours. Brother Brunnen, please escort Sister Wren to my office."

The taller of the two led the smaller away, but Gorthr remained. He stepped closer to the bushes where Halla hid, holding her breath until her lungs ached for mercy and her body trembled. She pulled at her metal bracelets, hoping the pain would chase away the fear.

"I know you're there," he said.

Halla inhaled sharply, springing to her feet. Before she could escape, his hand clasped around her elbow, yanking her through the bushes to his side.

"Let me go," she spat through her teeth, hissing at the pain in her neck.

"Be still, or I'll call for a sentry."

The threat was evident even in the calmness of his voice. Halla stilled instantly, but she couldn't help the tremors that coursed through her. Though she knew she shouldn't, Halla's eyes followed the trail of runes that peeked out of the man's collar and wound up and around his head.

His dark eyes narrowed. "Why would the gods be interested in you?"

"What are you talking about?" Halla resisted the urge to pull away, feeling Gorthr's nails scraping her skin.

"I was sent a note to collect you from the barracks and bring you into the city from one of the gods' trusted. There are hundreds of unlucky children in those barracks." He lowered his face to hers, seeming to seek out the secrets of her soul. "What makes you so special?"

"Nothing!" she squeaked. "There's nothing special about me!" As she said the words, Halla deflated. It was the truth. If she'd been born like Larissa or Anara, she wouldn't be so helpless. The thought drove the fight from her body.

"Halla!" Saessae's faint call came from the front of the temple.

Gorthr released her elbow, straightening his spine. "I very much doubt that. We'll see what the gods have planned for you."

Though Saessae called again, Halla's feet were cemented by the ominous undertones in his words.

"Your mistress calls. Run along. I'm sure we'll see one another again soon."

As if Gorthr's words had commanded the ground to release her feet, Halla ran.

As Halla rounded the temple's corner, she knew she'd been gone too long. Apprehension and uncertainty marred Saessae's heart-shaped face. "Where were you?"

"I—" Halla's words died in her throat. Though Saessae had been kind, Halla could practically hear Larissa screaming at her to not trust others so easily. Besides, there was something about the tattooed man that made Halla's mouth seal shut. "I was waiting on the side of the temple. I didn't want to get in the way."

"Oh." Relief washed over Saessae's face. "We'd better get back if you want to see your friend tonight."

"Right." Halla followed several steps behind Saessae as they walked away from the temple. Though she tried, Halla couldn't resist looking back at the temple that loomed in the distance where Gorthr stood on the steps, watching her walk away.

ᚾᛁᛪᛏᛋᚾᛁᛪᛏᛋᚾᛁᛪᛏᛋᚾᛁᛪᛏᛋᚾᛁᛪᛏᛋ

SAESSAE HAD THE SPIRIT and ingenuity of a second-born, Halla decided as she shadowed the girl through the darkened hallways on bare feet only hours later. Just as Halla had fallen into bed, Saessae had appeared, whispering for her to take off her shoes and follow if she wanted to see Kai. Reassured by the other maids' soft snores in their shared space, Halla didn't hesitate.

Kai had cared for her when no one else did; she just needed to see that he was alright. She was honor-bound. It had nothing to do with the fact that she missed him. Nothing at all.

Though she did her best to keep track of Saessae's chosen path, Halla was hopelessly lost when Saessae sneaked past the door that Halla had thought led to the back of the property. "Isn't that the way?"

Saessae shook her head and whispered, "All the doors have wires that trigger an alarm after dark. We have to get out unnoticed."

They entered the kitchens, which were quiet and cold without its normal occupants. Halla couldn't help but turn in a wide circle as she took in the granite countertops and the porcelain sink that hadn't cracked like the one at home. A large island sat in the middle, large enough that Halla could live there comfortably with more than enough room to spare. There was even a small, sleek television that looked nothing like her family's dusty, broken box tucked away in the corner of a counter. Saessae tugged on her hand, pulling her to the cabinets that lined the far wall.

In the farthest corner of the room, she pulled open the cabinet door and removed the towels stacked neatly inside. She emptied the cabinet, which seemed shallower than it should have been, revealing another door behind the first. Saessae giggled. "*This* is how we get out."

Halla grinned. Saessae definitely had the spirit of a second-born. On hands and knees, Halla squeezed through the narrow pathway after Saessae.

"Why is this here?" she whispered.

"All of the mansions have a secret tunnel," Saessae explained. "Some even have two."

Though smaller than the other girl, Halla's hips grazed each side of the passage. Once outside, they scurried across the smooth stone porch. The cold night breeze raised goosebumps on Halla's skin but soothed the constant irritation hovering at the back of her neck. They kept to the shadows of the well-groomed bushes as they made their way to a large barn. Though in Halla's opinion, the word *barn* was incorrect. The building in front of her was big enough to encompass her farmhouse, barn, and personal garden. It housed the animals, but also the male slaves.

Upon reaching the building, Saessae pressed her back against the wood, her eyes reflecting the brilliance of the moon. Above them, a window was cracked, no doubt allowing air to ventilate the barn. She knelt on one knee and placed her hands together, clearly offering Halla a boost up. "He'll be on the second floor. Good luck."

"You're not coming?"

"Someone has to keep watch. You have five minutes; make them count." Saessae's tone was uncharacteristically serious. "I wouldn't want to lose my companion before I get to know her."

Five minutes. Halla placed one foot in Saessae's hands and lunged for the windowsill. With Saessae's extra boost, Halla was halfway through the window. Another shove, and she had to stop herself from tumbling inside. Her descent was less graceful than she would have liked, but at least the hay broke her fall.

Raising her head, she came face-to-face with the mournful eyes of a cow that questioned her intrusion. Halla stroked its neck, murmuring excuses as she inched around the enormous creature. Though guided by snores, it took Halla longer than she wanted to find the ladder that led to the loft. She ascended into pitch blackness and stood frozen at the top of the ladder, unsure how to proceed, how to find Kai, knowing that her minutes were quickly ticking by.

Not knowing what else to do, she whispered. "Kai?"

Someone very near her feet stirred. "Halla? Please tell me that's not you."

Halla crouched, feeling Kai's legs near her feet. It made sense that as the newest slave, he would be placed at the edge of the loft, farther from the warmth of the other bodies. She moved closer to his face so that her whisper was hardly an exhale. "You could at least pretend you're happy to see me."

"I can't *see* anything," he hissed, his words blowing air into her face. "What in Hel's name were you thinking? Are you trying to get yourself killed?"

"I wanted to make sure you were okay."

Even in the dark, Halla felt Kai stiffen. "You risked another punishment just to make sure I was *okay*?"

Halla fought the urge to cross her arms. "Yes, but I can see that was a mistake."

Kai's hand grabbed the crook of Halla's arm before she could leave. "That was . . . kind of you. No one's done anything like that for me before. Stupid, but kind."

Halla ignored the insult, choosing instead to accept the compliment.

"How did you get out of the house?"

"There's a secret exit in the kitchen. Saessae showed me."

"Another slave?"

"Not technically . . ."

"Then who?"

Halla bit her cheek, knowing Kai wouldn't like the answer.

He sighed, loud enough that Halla nearly jumped. "She's the master's daughter, isn't she? What is it with you and who you choose for friends?"

"I chose you, didn't I?"

"That just proves my point."

At a sudden snore, Halla's comeback died on her lips. They both stilled, waiting as the man farther off readjusted, and his breathing fell back into a steady rhythm.

"So, are you okay?" she asked.

"I'm okay. Are you?"

The phantom touch of Gorthr's hand on her arm sent a shiver across her skin.

Kai's hand rubbed the goosebumps on her arm. "Are you cold?"

"Saessae took me by the temple today." Kai's hand stopped moving at Halla's words. "There was a man there, named Gorthr. It was the same man who brought us here."

"Avoid that temple and all of the Hoorg."

No duh, she thought, but only said, "I should go. Saessae said not to take longer than five minutes."

"Then go. Only, Halla . . ."

Halla paused, one foot on the ladder. "Yes?"

"Thank you. For checking on me."

Halla was grateful for the darkness that hid the way her nose and cheeks burned. "You're welcome."

"Just don't do it again, okay? I'm not worth it."

He turned away before Halla could respond. She dropped down the ladder and darted back across the barn until she found the cow's stall. The Norn must have been smiling, for Halla found a stool used for milking and positioned it directly under the windowsill. Though the effort took more than before, she was just able to push herself through the window where Saessae waited on the other side to pull her through.

"Your boy okay?"

Halla flushed. "He's not mine, but yes."

"Good, let's go."

The mansion loomed in front of them. Halla felt more trepidation in returning to the house than fleeing from it. Swallowing against the fear, she followed Saessae across the porch, through the cabinet passage, and into the kitchen. With silent hands, they stuffed the towels back in the cabinet and turned to leave.

But approaching footsteps froze them where they stood.

Saessae recovered first, shoving Halla in the pantry and closing the door after squishing herself inside as well. The door had just clicked when the kitchen lights flickered on. Warped from either age or time, the seam between the pantry door and frame was almost an inch in width, allowing Halla a thin layer of sight into the kitchen to watch as the master of the house drew a bottle from the counter and gulped down half its contents while turning on the small TV that sat on the counter. The sudden noise grated against Halla's nerves. Shaking with fear, she was grateful when Saessae clasped her hand.

Light poured from the screen, nothing like the static that Pappa had at times been able to coax from their old TV before it had passed into a peaceful death. The colors were stark and vibrant. Halla felt as though the images on the screen might actually step through the glass and appear in real life, yet Saessae was completely unimpressed. It was only another reminder of the differences between those within the Second Wall and those beyond.

Halla pressed her face against the door, mesmerized by the woman who stared through the screen almost as if she could see Halla watching from the other side of the glass. The woman was beautiful, but there was something terrible in her expression. Her coloring, not unlike Kai's, was so different from what Halla was used to in the south. Her stark black hair was pulled into a clean bun, and a crown of diamonds dripped around her head. A deep blush spread across her fair skin.

". . . we must protect what we have created. I, your Empress, challenge each of you to be mindful of those around you."

Hel's icy fingers trailed down Halla's spine. *This* was the Empress?

Halla's entire body pushed against the door, desperate to see more than the crack allowed. The woman on the small screen was older, yes, but by no means old. She looked even younger than Mamma had. Of course, Halla remembered, that must have been due to the Empress' use of *galdr* that preserved her body and slowed her aging. The woman's tone compelled Halla to listen. There was authentic concern for her people in her voice, ringing true above a steel foundation.

The woman never blinked her angular eyes that peered through the screen like a predator stalking its prey. "Even now, your neighbors, your slaves might plot against you. It is your duty to protect our shining nation or else let it plunge into darkness and bring upon us another *Ragnarok*."

With her final warning, the Empress vanished, replaced by a man with graying streaks in his dark hair. Though the gray spoke to advanced years, the man's face was hard and attentive. Stripes of ranking decorated the right shoulder of his well-pressed suit. Halla could recognize her own ignorance in many ways, but in this one, her Pappa's reminders served her well. The black stripe embossed in the Isa rune was enough to represent his position as Regent of Perle.

His voice was deep, and an undercurrent of anger coursed through it. "Your Empress has protected you tirelessly for the past five decades, but it is our job, *your* job, to repay her kindness in turn, lest you find yourself on the wrong side of history. Our illustrious commonwealth is only tolerated by the Empress' good graces. Those who would dare defile our Empress have a place reserved for them in my gallows, but those loyal enough to report will be rewarded—"

The master of the house harrumphed, drowning more of the bottle as he watched the screen in mild disinterest. With a final click, he turned it off and set down the empty bottle. Halla could only see parts of him as he walked back and forth, perhaps searching for another bottle. His hand reached for the pantry.

Saessae pulled Halla away from the door, as if she could shield Halla with her own body. But Halla knew no manner of sweet talking would get her out of this one. She would be punished. Severely. Her lips formed the prayers of memory and repetition. The back of her neck burned.

The master stopped. Through the crack, Halla could see the master's palm shaking. He noticed it as well and frowned at the offending appendage in disgust. Seeming to reconsider, he lifted the empty bottle in his other hand. So slowly that it seemed the master might be toying with Halla, he withdrew his hand, turned off the light, left the bottle on the counter, and shuffled out of the room.

Saessae's hot exhale settled on the back of Halla's neck. It itched in discomfort, but Halla remained unmoved. What if it was some kind of trap? She waited, but seconds dragged into indefinite minutes.

Finally, Saessae nudged her from behind. "Let's go."

Blissful uneventfulness greeted them in the hallways as Saessae returned Halla to her quarters before sneaking away with the promise to see her in the morning. Halla climbed into her bed, weary to her bones despite the adrenaline coursing through her veins. Though she swore she'd never be able to sleep, it came swiftly.

The Empress' face and voice followed Halla into her nightmares, accompanied by Brother Gorthr watching from the shadows.

19

Unnatural

Anara

THE TREES OF THE *Myrkviðr Forest crowded in, blurring every-thing in Anara's vision. Even in her wolf form, she could not see the sun, but was lost in shadow. Though the growl started in her chest, when she opened her jaw, nothing came out. She was voiceless.*

It was the muteness that alerted Anara to the presence of her dream. Only in dreams could she be silenced.

She prowled through the trees, searching for the child-goddess no doubt behind the mental intrusion. A flick of flame-like hair flashed from behind the trees. Anara pounced but found nothing in the deep mud. A girlish giggle broke the silence of the trees. Again, Anara opened her mouth, but no sound could be heard.

Loki's knot, *she cursed.* Get out of my head.

Just beyond the trees nearest to her, something twinkled from the ground. A pile of emeralds glared up at her from the dirt. In the interval between seconds, Verðandi appeared, scooping the gems from the ground and holding them out like an offering for Anara to smell. The tang of incense flooded her nostrils.

Trust him, *Verðandi said.* Don't keep me waiting.

ᚾᛁᛉᛏᛋᚾᛁᛉᛏᛋᚾᛁᛉᛏᛋᚾᛁᛉᛏᛋᚾᛁᛉᛏᛋ

ANARA STIRRED IN HER bed of hay, allowing the soft, earthy scents to cleanse out the sharp odor of her dream. She rubbed her temples as though she could chase away the headache the dream had left. Though her parents had taught her a certain reverence for the gods, Anara silently cursed the smallest of the Norn who'd stolen the peace from her sleep as she rose in search of Darien and Larissa.

She found them asleep in the cabbage field with their hands intertwined and Larissa's head resting against Darien's side. Anara hesitated in waking them, knowing that her presence alone would shatter the solace they'd found in each other. Not to mention the latest prompting of the Norn, who were clearly running out of patience.

She cleared her throat. "It's time."

Their bodies tensed at the sound of her voice. Darien's eyes went to Larissa, but Larissa sprang to her feet. Instantly alert and focused on Anara, she missed the way Darien clenched the hand that once held hers.

"They're waiting for us." Anara gestured toward the farmhouse where she could smell pancakes burning on the stove.

The three crossed the field in the darkness of the early morning. Inside, the farmer and his family sat at a table, upon which lay a meager breakfast. Halvor joined them, though he'd put little on his plate. At the trio's entrance, the family rose from their seats and bowed.

Larissa paused. "Oh, please don't do that."

"Your Highness, we would be honored to share this meal with you before you go." The farmer pulled out a chair at the head of the table for Larissa.

"We know it isn't much," the wife continued. "But you are welcome to everything we have."

Anara could already hear the protests on Larissa's and Darien's lips, but she was never one to turn down a free meal. She sat next to the daughter and slid a pancake onto her plate. After taking a bite, Anara smiled at the girl. "Delicious."

The girl stood on her chair to smooth Anara's long strands of black hair. Her tiny fingers reached out to touch the golden ring in Anara's nose. "It's so pretty."

"Benia," the mother scolded.

Anara took another bite. "She's alright."

As if encouraged by her tone, the girl, Benia, sat herself on Anara's lap, more to Anara's surprise than anyone else's. It had been years, possibly decades, since Anara had experienced the trust of a child. At least, without the paranoia of parents who feared that Anara might change into a *draugr* and devour their child whole. But once the parents realized Anara did not mind Benia's presence, they turned back to serving up plates for a reluctant Larissa and Darien. Benia continued to munch on the bread clutched between her small palms.

"The other farmers are on their way as we speak," Halvor explained. "General Ishaan is leading them here."

Benia stilled in Anara's lap. She turned her head to whisper. "Is that the man who wanted to hurt my daddy?"

Anara bent her head so that her whisper would not interrupt the others' conversation. "I won't let him hurt your family."

"Mama says he can change into animals." There was wonder in the child's voice, but also fear. "She said he's unnatural. What does unnatural mean?"

The sweet syrup of the pancake turned bitter. *Unnatural.* "It means that he doesn't belong. Now shh, I need to listen."

Of course, Anara had been listening the whole time, but she feared further questions from Benia. She wanted to enjoy the current state of acceptance from this farmer and his family, even if it was based in ignorance. At some point, their small son took up residence at Anara's feet, playing with some stuffed bear. Anara grabbed one of the dry pancakes from the table and passed it to the boy below, who smiled in thanks.

"Each of us will hide in produce trucks driven by one of the farmers," Halvor was saying. "We'll have to leave the cargo truck here for the time being. It would draw too much attention. We must reclaim the Outer Wall without letting any sentries past us to warn the interior levels of the commonwealth." Halvor's eyes carried unspoken meaning. "We can't allow news to spread to the wrong people."

Calder.

From the corner of her eyes, Anara caught the tightening of Darien's face and the rigid set of his shoulders. Though she'd heard what he'd told Torsten, Anara doubted whether Darien would be able to kill his brother if the time came. Her heartstrings twisted at the thought of Aeron but hardened at the twang of pain that resonated from the scar that stretched across her abdomen. If Darien couldn't put Calder down, she would.

The hum of nearby engines grew into a roar, which could only mean the arrival of the other farmers. Anara's excitement for battle turned to unease as her ears picked up more than two promised engines. If these weren't their promised trucks, they could only be sentries. She stood, handing Benia back to her mother.

"Halvor, there are more than two trucks coming up the road."

Understanding sank in as the room's occupants jumped to their feet. Anara was at the window, her eyes the strongest of any but stronger still when she used her *galdr*. A familiar surge of power redirected toward her eyes. The world around her crystalized in minute detail. Down the road, Anara could make out five trucks bumbling down the dirt path, but they were not sentry vehicles as she'd feared. They were ordinary pickup trucks, packed and ready for Produce Day. At the front of the line, Haki and Jari leaned out of the back of the truck. High above them, Anara spotted Ishaan circling.

She breathed a sigh of relief. "It's alright. It looks like we have more support than we thought."

A tiny gasp drew her gaze down at Benia, who had sat beneath her and pointed into Anara's face. "Your eyes are yellow."

Anara blinked away the transformation, but the damage was done. The mother raced forward, snatching her child and retreating several feet away from Anara, who had not moved. The farmer too grabbed his son, a kitchen knife held tightly in his hand.

Silence reigned in the farmhouse. Benia peeked at Anara from behind her mother's protective arms. Anara rose slowly for their sake. "I'll go and greet the others."

Halvor's explanations filled the silence even as the screen of the front door slammed behind Anara. She pounded down the porch steps, steadying her breath. It wouldn't matter what explanations he gave. The family's fear ran too deep. She heard the door open and close again and the swift footsteps behind her. By the smell, she knew it was Larissa who laid her hand on Anara's shoulder.

"I'm sorry."

Anara exhaled, her breath visible against the cold air. The fear of others was not her responsibility, not her guilt. She would not carry it. She had enough guilt as it was. "I'm fine."

The screen door opened again. Darien and Halvor joined them as the approaching trucks screeched to a halt. Down the line, farmers disembarked from their vehicles. Haki and Jari stood at the front of the line, looking well pleased with themselves, particularly Jari. Ishaan shifted in the air, landing on his feet.

"We brought a few more men," he said.

"Yes, I can see that, General," Anara remarked dryly. "How many of them did you force?"

Thunder clouded Ishaan's brows. The red of his face contrasted against his graying sideburns. Before he could answer, another man, a farmer, stepped forward.

"Every man here came willingly. We believe in our Princess." His eyes narrowed on Larissa. He kneeled, mimicked by the dozen of men behind him.

Anara frowned. "Who are you? How do you know she is the Princess?"

"I am Kelby, Highness. I was sent a dream from the gods. They showed me the truth—"

Anara met Larissa's and Darien's eyes, knowing they thought the same thing. *Norn.*

"—and instructed me to find more farmers who would do anything to remove Regent Hammon from Perle. With your guards' permission, I gathered as many as I could throughout the night. More would have wanted to come."

"They will have their chance," Haki said, cracking his knuckles. "When the main force of the Viðnám arrives, they can join them."

At his words, a cheer rose up from amongst the farmers.

Halvor clapped his hands together. "Enough talk. Which trucks have room for stowaways? Princess Lovisa, Prince Darien, Haki, Jari, and myself will need to be hidden."

"It would be an honor, Your Highness," Kelby volunteered for Larissa while other farmers spoke up, offering room in their trucks.

"Princess Anara. General Ishaan. I take it you two will remain in the sky and keep watch?" Halvor asked.

Anara smiled. "My wings weren't meant for small spaces."

"I follow my Queen," Ishaan responded.

Though Anara did not want his company, she could see the wisdom in having him in the sky, if only to draw the attention away from herself.

"Then it is settled," Halvor said.

At his word, farmers scrambled to create hidden crevices in the trucks for their stowaways. Seeing the looks of discomfort as Larissa and Darien crawled into their hiding places only reminded Anara of how grateful she was for her own wings and the open sky. Her *galdr* surged as she burst out of her skin, shedding the shackles of the earth and taking flight into the air.

From the window of the farmhouse, Benia's mouth fell and her eyes widened at Anara's transformation, but then Benia was gone and out of sight along with the guilt and regrets that plagued Anara's human consciousness. Not even Verðandi's dreams and demands could catch her in the air. Her black feathers gleamed in the sunlight, and she cawed in pure ecstasy at the rush of wind beneath her wings.

After decades of hunting and being hunted, Anara was ready for war.

Part Two

Einvaldi

The rule of man *is determined*
By the generosity of the gods
But the life of a man is determined
By the whims of the Fates.

-Urðr, *Book of the Past*

20

The Outer Wall

Larissa

Halla. Halla. Halla.

Larissa's sister's name acted as a talisman against the claustrophobia as she rode in the back of Kelby's truck. It was more than just the boxes pressed up against her back; it was the memories of her recent trip into Perle and its disastrous consequences that threatened to break Larissa's composure.

To distract herself, she reviewed their objectives. Infiltrate Perle. Disable the gates. Subdue the sentries. Wait for the Viðnám's second wave. Remove Regent Hammon from power. Find Halla. Find Halla.

Halla. Halla. Halla.

Muffled by boxes but loud enough to pierce the din, Anara's caw broke through Larissa's repetitions. The Wall was in sight.

The truck's deceleration contrasted sharply against the blood racing through Larissa's veins. Her truck had taken the lead of their convoy. Darien hid in the truck behind her, but all five trucks would need to clear the gates before they could attack. The elements of surprise and shock would allow them to conquer the Intake Yard before reinforcements could be summoned.

The simplicity of their plan did not calm Larissa's race of emotions. Fear. Hope. She wasn't sure which was strongest, only that they battled each other in her soul. Larissa focused on cycling her *galdr* through her body, letting it consume her thoughts. She had to be steady. They had to keep the gates open, or the Viðnám's intended invasion would turn into a drawn-out siege. Larissa's fingers grazed the grip of her gun, hoping that Halvor's estimations of the sentries manning the Intake Yard had been correct. If there were truly so few, Larissa might not have to draw her weapon.

After what seemed like hundreds of pauses and jolts in the truck bed, the trucks approached the gate. Sentries' voices sounded as they walked around the truck, inspecting the produce that hid Larissa.

One's muffled voice passed through the crates. "Follow the previous truck into the unloading area. Once you are finished, you may collect your family's rations."

The truck rumbled forward for only a short time before it stopped altogether, but Larissa was not free until the others made it inside as well. For this reason, Larissa had been packed into the farthest corner of the truck bed; but with every box that was removed, her adrenaline grew.

"The last truck was just cleared," she heard Kelby murmur close to her hiding space. "Get ready, Princess."

Larissa gripped the gun so hard it hurt. Her *galdr* warmed her stomach, spreading through her limbs and lighting every nerve on fire.

For my people.

She was ready.

For Halla.

Kelby removed the final box blocking her escape. *Shock and surprise*, Larissa reminded herself. Kelby pulled her to her feet. At the end of the truck, one of the laborers gaped at her with an open mouth and wide eyes. Nothing about Larissa, from her heavy work boots to the silvery scar that stretched back into her braided hair, would suggest royalty, but even he could not miss the golden auras surrounding her hands.

Anara cawed above in delight as Darien, Haki, Jari, and Halvor rose from their own confines. The farmers, laborers, and slaves froze, their mouths open in shock. Some of the slaves were only children, marked by their bracelets and frenzied whispering at the sight of Larissa, but their presence nearly undermined Larissa's composure. She scanned them quickly, assuring herself that Halla was not among them.

The sentry nearest Larissa took notice first and pointed his gun at her. "Where did you come from? Get down from there!"

She raised one hand slowly, catching their stares with the golden electricity that glowed and crackled between her fingers.

"I am Princess Lovisa, the true ruler of the Perle Kingdom. This is your only opportunity to lay down your weapons."

Several of the sentries balked, their hands shifting on their weapons. The other farmers and slaves stepped back at Larissa's demonstration.

"And I'm Óðinn, king of the gods," the sentry heckled, seemingly unfazed by Larissa's show of *galdr*. "Regent Hammon can put your little light show to shame."

She flexed her fingers. Pebbles and rocks around the Intake Yard rose, trembling in the air. She knew that this was her one chance to prevent any violence. "I don't want to hurt you. You are my people. This is your last chance to stand down."

Though the sentry's face tightened, he pointed his gun straight at Larissa's heart. His finger curled against the trigger. "Get down from there, or I'll kill you where you stand."

An eerie calm cooled the fire in Larissa's stomach.

The sentry never saw the raven that swooped down. Nor did he see the raven shift into a young woman who tackled him to the ground with surprising grace as she removed the weapon from his hands. By the time he looked up, his own weapon was trained between his eyes.

Anara's hand held steady. "You should listen to your Princess."

"Shifter," the man hissed. Then louder, "Kill the shifter!"

As if broken from a trance, the other sentries reached for their weapons. Larissa flung her arms forward, palms out, pelting the rocks in the direction of the sentries, who dropped their weapons to cover their faces. A shot rang out, and a sentry lay dead at

Anara's feet, but the bullet had not come from her gun. General Ishaan was already turning his weapon on the next nearest sentry.

Then there was only chaos.

Darien and the others jumped from their truck beds, joining the melee that kicked up a dust cloud all around them. Slaves hid behind trucks while farm hands rallied to Larissa's side. She ducked as a gunshot rang out then flung herself from the truck bed onto the sentry nearest her, knocking the gun clean out of his hand. They rolled across the dirt, each trying to gain the upper hand.

Larissa cried out as the sentry twisted her braid around his hand and pulled her to the ground. He landed on top of her, pinning her arms beneath his knees and wrapping his hands against her throat until the world spun.

The noise of the fighting grew louder; no one could see her. She could not see them either, but she could see the gun that lay on the ground only a few feet away. Focusing her mind, her hand flexed as a glow encompassed her fingers. Before the sentry could realize what she was doing, the gun flew straight into the man's temple with enough force that he fell to the ground beside her and did not get up again. A thin trail of blood trickled from the side of his eye.

Clambering to her hands and knees, she took great gulps of air, noting the way the man's chest rose and fell. She hadn't killed him, but she could have. The thought shook her.

"Larissa!"

Darien's hand landed on her back.

"I'm fine," she choked out, raising her eyes to look at him.

"I was across the bay; I tried to get here." He glanced at the un-moving sentry beside them. "Looks like you did just fine without me."

"Oh yeah," she huffed, accepting his hand as he helped her to her feet "Just fine."

With her breath returning, she looked around the bay. The other farmers who knew nothing about their plan had joined them, wielding only their fists. Even some of the bay workers had engaged in the fight, while others fled or hid behind trucks. As quickly as it had started, the fight was over. Haki and Jari tied up the unconscious or wounded sentries.

"Traitors," one man spat in disgust. "It doesn't surprise me that Haki would turn, but you, Jari?"

"I never turned," he retorted. "I never served the False Empress."

In wolf form, Anara herded more sentries toward them. They trembled at the sight of her lips curled back in a snarl. Even the sentry closest to Jari clamped his mouth at her approach. Halvor tended to Kelby, who had a nasty hole in his leg. But where was Ishaan?

A great grinding noise met her ears.

"The gates!" Darien shouted.

But it wasn't the iron gates still hanging open that concerned Larissa. It was the enormous, solid stone walls sliding out from within the Outer Wall, pushing toward each other slowly. Halvor had warned them about this fail-safe. If those walls were to close, it would take nothing short of explosives to bring down the wall.

Larissa's gaze snapped up to the top level of the Outer Wall, upon which sat the guard tower. She could only make out the shape of the man inside operating the machinery. Ishaan was already on top of the wall, running toward the tower, but he would never make it before the walls slammed shut. Larissa ran toward the narrowing gap, placing herself between the great rock walls and spreading out her arms toward each. Hot *galdr* raced down her arms and gathered at her fingertips, just waiting for her to direct it.

Larissa closed her eyes, trusting that Darien would protect her from any attack. The walls inched ever closer, but she shifted her mind's eye to the space between them, imagining the empty air solidifying into a brick wall, unyielding and unbreakable. Her fingers flexed of their own accord as she directed all of her energy into that empty space, solidifying it, strengthening it, creating a barrier against the encroaching stone. She felt the moment the walls hit her *galdr*.

It was as if someone had reached down into her lungs, stealing all the air from her body. The walls shuddered in protest as the gears grinded against one another in frustration, but they stopped all the same.

Immediately, her fingers trembled.

"You can do this, Lara," Darien stood with his back pressed against hers.

The shaking in her fingers traveled to her wrists, then to her arms. Her shoulders ached against the strain. The walls themselves shivered in anticipation of their freedom as her *galdr* weakened. What was Ishaan doing up there?

In her mind, Queen Stjarna approached, her eyes alight with pride. *You are stronger than you know, Lovisa.*

The memory gave her strength to hold on.

Far above, Larissa registered the scream just before she felt the thump on the ground in front of her. Simultaneously, the pressure from the walls vanished entirely. With a final heave, Larissa shoved the stone walls back on their tracks, shattering the iron gates from their hinges.

The Viðnám had a clear path. Larissa's arms fell as her body swayed, and her eyes fluttered open.

The body that lay on the ground in front of her made her wish she had kept her eyes shut. She turned, too quickly, away from the sentry's corpse, falling into Darien's open arms that held her close. She breathed him in, drowning in his familiarity, closing her eyes as the shakes worked their way through her body. She hadn't experienced the after-shakes since she had first started her training with her *galdr*.

Your galdr *is not a bottomless pit, Lovisa,* her mother had warned when Lovisa was thirteen years old. *If you push too far, it will take everything from you and burn you up from the inside out. These shakes are to remind you of your limitations, to warn you of your hubris.*

"Larissa, did you hear me?"

Reluctantly, she raised her head from Darien's chest to look up into his face.

"We did it. Look."

He was right; the fighting was over. Besides the men that Ishaan had killed, it appeared that the rest of the sentries had been subdued without further deaths. They sat huddled on the ground under Haki's supervision. Beside him, Jari turned to meet Larissa's gaze. For the first time, the hatred in his expression had lessened. His gaze traveled beyond her to where the broken gates lay. There was something in his expression that Larissa had never seen before. An almost grudging respect.

"Your Highness!" Halvor called out from the other side of the bay. Anara stood beside him, along with many of the farmers and laborers who had joined the fight. Even Kelby was back on his feet, though leaning heavily against a truck. A hawk soared down from the wall before transforming into Ishaan, who landed next to Halvor.

Larissa noticed how the farmers stepped away from his presence.

She and Darien moved to join the group. At her arrival, the men moved aside bowing low as she passed.

"Your Highness."

"My Princess."

Larissa nodded at the men as she passed by them but was saved from having to give a speech by Halvor's words.

"We've secured the Outer Wall and entrance into the rest of the city, but make no mistake, we are not done yet. Ishaan, the second wave waits behind the tree line. Go and tell them to advance." There was a flutter of wings, and Ishaan was gone. "Anara, can you fly over the city and see if anyone has noticed our arrival?"

She nodded, but before transforming, she turned to Larissa. "I'll keep an eye out for Halla as well."

Then she too was gone, riding the wind.

Halvor adjusted his spectacles. "We'll remain here and keep the Wall secured until King Torsten arrives—"

A keening sob rose from behind one of the farmer's trucks. They turned to the noise. A group of children wearing the metal bracelets of slavery knelt huddled in a circle. In the midst of their circle, a body lay face down on the ground with short blonde hair covering her face. Larissa's breath caught at the bullet wound in the girl's tiny body. She fell to her knees beside the other children, turning the girl over with shaking fingers.

Relief was quickly followed by heavy, painful guilt. The girl wasn't Halla, but she was someone's child, and she was dead. Somewhere in the fighting, a stray bullet had found an unintended victim. Darien's mouth was pressed into a hard line at the sight of the girl. Even Halvor looked unsettled. Larissa reached out, closing her eyes and muttering a prayer.

Over the weeping of the children came the rumble of dozens of trucks, and then the war cry of hundreds of voices filled the air. Larissa looked over her shoulder to see the Viðnám's second wave racing toward the Wall, but there was no joy in her heart. Only fear. With their arrival, the battle would continue into the main city of Perle. People would die. Children would die. What would happen if Halla got caught in the crossfire? What had she done?

"Halvor," Larissa called. "Where would Halla be?"

"The barracks, if she hasn't been sold—"

"Where are the barracks?"

"Your Highness, the plan was for us to search for your sister after the battle—"

Larissa turned to the slaves still circled around the girl on the ground. She raised her hands and clenched her fingers. All at once, their metal bracelets fell from their wrists, clattering into the dirt. "I'm sorry for your friend. I need to find someone before the same thing happens to her. Where are the barracks?"

The oldest of the children stared at Larissa, rubbing his chafed wrists. He couldn't be more than fourteen. "In the East Sector of the city, near the Second Wall."

"Thank you." She rose to her feet. The Viðnám's second wave had nearly arrived. "Halvor, see to it that these children are protected."

"What are you going to do?"

But Larissa's feet were moving before Halvor could stop her. She could hear Darien following right behind her. She knew they both should wait; they had a duty to wait for King Torsten and stick to the plan. But her duty to Halla was stronger. She had to get to the barracks before Halla could become more collateral damage, and if Halla had been sold, then gods help the *thrœll* that withheld what Larissa needed to know.

She ran through the winding, narrow streets, passing the industrial section of the city, always veering to the east. Cables hung between the houses, many cracked from the sun. In the distance, Larissa swore she could see the destroyed warehouse from her last visit. Memories of the last time she'd fled this city combined with memories of her past overwhelmed her. Ghosts of what had been called out to her from the streets, but she couldn't stop, couldn't wait to understand her double vision. She could only keep moving. An unyielding hand tugged her hard, pulling her into an alleyway.

"Darien, what—"

His hand covered her mouth as he pushed her up against the wall. His gaze strained against the mouth of the alley. A sentry rushed past them, unaware of their presence, hurrying toward the Outer Wall.

Releasing a sigh, Darien removed his hand from Larissa's mouth and placed it on the wall behind her. He offered her a crooked grin. "Sorry about that."

Even in the shadows of the alley, the intensity behind his eyes stopped Larissa from moving out from under his arm.

A cough drew their attention away from one another toward the end of the alley, where Anara had landed in a flurry of feathers. "You do know a war is going on, don't you?"

Larissa pushed away from the wall, separating herself from Darien. "I'm going after Halla."

"So naturally, the two of you ran off without any backup?"

"Naturally." Darien grinned.

"Not entirely without backup," came Haki's deep voice.

All three turned toward the mouth of the alley where the twins stood.

"I thought I smelled you two," Anara said.

"What are you doing?" Larissa asked.

"We followed you. We know this city better than anyone else," Haki explained. "We know where the barracks are."

"We can get you there quickly," Jari added. "And back into the fight."

"Thank you, Jari," Larissa said.

The tall man nodded in her direction just as a shrill ringing split the air. Larissa covered her ears with her hands, but it did little to alleviate the pain. Anara grimaced, baring her teeth at the sky.

"What is that?" Darien shouted.

Jari drew his gun. "The city's alarm. They know we're here."

21

Passageways

Halla

Saessae twirled before the mirror. "What do you think?"

Halla smiled, resisting the urge to touch the beautiful dress that the master had given his daughter. He'd ordered Halla to help Saessae with the twenty-four buttons that lined the back. Its short-flared skirts swayed with Saessae's inability to remain still, and Halla shoved down her jealousy. "It's beautiful, Miss Saessae."

"Oh, stop that, Father isn't here." But Saessae's playful demeanor changed to thoughtful. "Halla, has your hair always been this short?"

Halla's fingers brushed against the rugged edges. It took her longer than she liked to answer. "The *þræll* cut it."

Saessae pulled Halla over to her large vanity, sitting the smaller girl on the bench before it. She rifled through the drawers until she withdrew a small lavender bow. With hands gentler than Halla had become accustomed to, Saessae brushed Halla's hair, then using the bow, she pinned back a small portion of it.

Halla stared at her in the mirror, desperate to hold back the tears that threatened to spill. "Why are you being kind to me?"

"My mother believed in the gods like everyone else, but she loved Baldr the most. He was kind and generous, which was why Loki wanted him dead. My mother used to say that every act of kindness is a sacrifice to Baldr. And with it, we can undo the damage that Loki did when killing Baldr." Saessae lowered the brush. "I don't know if that's true, but when I'm kind, I feel like my mom is with me again."

In the echo of Saessae's touch, Halla felt the ghost of her Mamma's hands. Tears blurred Halla's vision. "Thank you."

Saessae's smile was back. "Besides, now we both have something pretty."

Reluctantly, Halla removed the bow from her hair. "I can't wear it. If your father sees it—"

"I know." Saessae's hands wrapped around Halla's, encasing the bow in both of their fingers. "But I still want you to have it. So you know that you're not alone."

Halla relented, gently pushing the bow into her pocket, but not so deep as to crease it. A light knock sounded at the door. Hovmester entered, folding his hands behind his back and sticking his nose in the air. The house steward's gaze was as hard and uncompromising as it had been the first day Halla arrived.

"Miss Saessae, it's time for your lessons," he announced.

"I'm ready. Come, Halla."

"Your father expects you alone, Miss Saessae. The girl is to work in the kitchens today."

Halla glared at the ground, but the burn on her neck locked her words behind her lips. Saessae tossed an apologetic look on her way out of the room. Halla started after her. Perhaps if she was lucky, she could sneak something better to eat than the hardly edible leftovers she'd been given the night before.

Hovmester blocked her path. He eyed her like something distasteful he'd found on the bottom of his shoe. "You will remember your place. I will see to that."

Halla resisted the urge to stick out her tongue. "I didn't do anything wrong."

Hovmester's eyes narrowed. Before Halla could guess at his intentions, he leaned forward, snatching the bow from Halla's pocket. "This is Miss Saessae's bow, you little thief."

Halla cried out as his hand grasped her upper arm. "She gave it to me! Ask her!"

But Hovmester dragged her down the hallway, ignoring Halla's protests. "Let's see what the master thinks about that."

Her nails dug into his arms as he yanked her down the grand staircase. A sudden and all-encompassing ringing blared around them, stopping them short of the final steps. It wasn't coming from inside the house, Halla could tell that much.

Hovmester's mouth gaped like that of a fish caught on a line. He stuttered under his breath. "Someone's breached the walls."

Lara!

Indecision halted Halla's limbs even as her mind cried out at her to run. Still stunned, Hovmester loosened his fingers, and Halla's resolve strengthened. She *was* Iðunn, and she would not cower before mere mortals.

With all the might that her small body possessed, Halla kicked at Hovmester's shins. In his surprise and pain, the old man cried out and let her go, but the incessant ringing of the bells drowned his protests.

Halla fled to the kitchens, unsurprised to find them empty even as something boiled over on the stovetop. No doubt the staff had been driven out from the unrelenting alarm. Thanking the gods, Halla ripped open the cabinet in the corner and threw out the towels that lay in her path to freedom.

Just as she touched the hidden door, a hand fell on her shoulder, yanking her back. Hovmester dragged her away from the cabinet, his gnarled fingers digging into her shoulder. Halla screamed, even as her insults mingled with the ringing that would not stop.

Hovmester's grip on her shoulder slackened. He looked at her with an odd, unseeing gaze on his face, then slumped to the floor. Saessae stood behind him with a cast iron pan hanging from her gloved hands. Though terror at what she'd done flooded her face, she shouted, "Go, Halla!"

Halla reached for her hand. "Come with me!"

Saessae dropped the pan, backing away in fear. "I can't. I have to stay with my father."

As though summoned by her words, the master's voice rang out just beyond the kitchen. "Saessae!"

"Go, Halla, before he finds you." Saessae darted away.

Halla didn't wait for the door to stop swinging. She squeezed her body through the gap in the cabinet and ran across the gardens and field as fast as her feet would carry her.

Two paths lay before her. One led to the street and possibly her freedom. It was the road Anara would have chosen, Larissa would have chosen, Juni would have chosen. But there was another path leading to the barn that Halla barreled toward without hesitation. She could not leave without Kai.

Halla ran in through the open door, her eyes darting from figure to figure. Many covered their ears against the onslaught of the bells, but there, running toward her as if he'd been waiting, was Kai. He grabbed her hand in his and, without words, pulled her out of the barn, out of the fields, onto the street.

In the distance, the Second Wall loomed, growing ever closer as they ran toward it. Joining the sounds of the bells came the voices, coming from the outer section of the city. Smoke gathered on the horizon.

Someone's breached the walls, Hovmester had said.

Halla's legs burned as she pumped them faster, keeping pace with Kai. She knew exactly who had breached the wall.

Larissa was coming.

The thought fueled her, enough that she didn't complain when Kai's sprint turned into a prolonged run. The street leading to the Second Wall became incredibly crowded, to the point that Halla didn't understand why she and Kai hadn't been stopped. Even without their metal bracelets, their clothes, their hair, and the bandage on the back of her neck all screamed slaves. Whether it was because the sentries were so focused on flooding toward the gates of the Second Wall or because the citizens were too astonished at what was happening or perhaps even interference of the gods themselves, no one looked twice at two fleeing children.

As more people crowded their path to the Second Wall, Kai pulled Halla off onto a side street. They knelt behind shrubbery bushes in someone's personal garden. The fresh floral scent contrasted strangely with the rising shouts and the heavy tread of the sentries' boots.

"We have to get on the other side of that wall," Halla said, clutching the stitch in her side.

Kai worked to slow his breathing. "We don't know what's on the other side."

"My sister is there; I know it."

Kai's eyes narrowed. "How are you so sure? You don't even know if she reached the Viðnám or if they'd allow her to fight with them."

Halla smiled. "Trust me, she'll be at the front."

Confusion drew his brow even tighter.

"There has to be a way to get past the sentries, right? And past the wall?" Halla asked.

"There's a way, but it'll be dangerous."

"More dangerous than waiting here to be caught?"

"Fair point." Kai bounced on his toes. "Follow me."

He ran at a crouch toward the Second Wall. Halla followed in a similar position. They weren't running toward the wall, but rather parallel to it. She would have questioned Kai further, but she couldn't risk being overheard as they passed under open windows and crouched through gardens. They could be recaptured any minute. As they ran, the beautiful, well-kept lawns faded into concrete and stone. There were fewer roses here and more barrack-shaped buildings pushed up right along the Wall.

Kai stopped, shoving Halla down behind the building they'd nearly rounded. Thudding footsteps approached; then, a unit of sentries ran by.

"... it's the Viðnám ..."

"... the sentry said they used magic ..."

"... Princess Lovisa ..."

Halla's insides squirmed with the onslaught of emotions. Fear of discovery. Excitement that Larissa was there. Hope that she was right. She looked at Kai but found only doubt lingering in the crease between his eyebrows. He pointed at the nearest sentry barrack. "We go through there."

"You want us to go *into* the barrack?" Halla squealed. "Do you want us to get caught?"

"Yes, I ran all this way so we could get a bit of exercise before being locked up again." He rolled his eyes. "There's a passageway through the Second Wall. It's so sentries can get out and flank any enemy that attempts to penetrate the main gate."

"How do you know that?"

"Like I told Juni, I *listen*. Most people are just particularly unobservant." He looked again at the barrack. "It should be empty at this point. Everyone's gone to the fight, but I'm going to go in first and make sure it's clear. You stay here."

Halla grasped his arm as he moved to stand. "What? You can't go in there alone. What if there are sentries?"

He shrugged. "Then you hide and see if your sister gets through the wall."

"Kai—"

But he'd already reclaimed his arm and started running across the street, slipping into the barrack without hesitation. Halla dared to breathe. Time dragged on. Had there been sentries after all? Was Kai hiding from them now or had he already been captured? Or worse, had Kai found the passageway but determined it was safer to go alone than to come back for Halla? But no, Kai wouldn't do that.

Would he?

So wrapped up in her thoughts, Halla nearly missed the hand stuck out of a barrack window. A boy's hand, waving for her to hurry.

Leaping to her feet, Halla raced across the street. She ignored the fearful part of her that hesitated to reach for the door and threw herself inside the barrack. Kai was waiting, a finger over his mouth.

"I don't think anyone is here," he whispered, "but we're better off quiet."

The barrack was far larger than the slave barracks, the beds thicker and longer. Kai led her past the beds, then through an area with tables set up for eating. At the end of the long building was another door for the bathroom. Halla looked around for the sign of another exit, anything. Panic set in. "Kai?"

But Kai was thinking, his face screwed up with effort. "Come on."

He grabbed her hand again and pulled her into the bathroom with him. There in the corner was another door labeled supplies, but Kai was already pulling on its handle. There were no toiletries but a dark, gaping mouth with a concrete floor and stone walls.

Kai smirked. "Told you."

He pulled her forward, and the tunnel consumed them.

22

To the Wall

Darien

"Release them." Darien's words dripped *galdr*, his voice cutting through the ever-present ringing of the bells. His eyes drilled into the soul of the *thræll*. The man stood so close that Darien could see the reflection of his own eyes, and the ring of blue around his pupil intensified as the *galdr* pulsed through his bones. Under Darien's influence, the *thræll* turned and unlocked the barrack doors. Larissa pushed past him to slide into the last barrack.

"Wait here and cuff your hands together," Darien ordered, just as he had with every other *thræll* they had come across. Then he too slipped through the barrack door, doing his best to ignore the ringing of the bells.

Whatever the Viðnám was doing, the sentries of Perle had taken notice. If the Viðnám was following the plan, the second wave should be well on their way to the Second Wall, but success would depend on what reinforcements Regent Hammon had sent from the inner rings of the city.

Larissa scanned the children with frantic eyes, her lips tightening in despair. Darien did a similar scan, but Halla wasn't there. She drew in a shaky breath, addressing the children on the bunks that shrank from her presence. "You're safe now; we're here to help."

"Come on," Darien said, keeping his voice as gentle as he could. "Let's get you out of here."

"You mean it?" the boy closest to them asked.

The children in the other barracks had acted much the same way. The older ones had been even more suspicious. The youngest hadn't understood what was happening at all. But at each barrack they had unlocked, they convinced the children that they were being rescued. Suspicion turned to disbelief that changed to shock that transformed finally into a giddy excitement.

"I mean it." He threw open the door, gesturing for the children to pass through.

Larissa remained rooted in the middle of the barrack as the children left, her shoulders tense and her hands curled into fists. "She isn't here."

Darien's own fear and fury rose up. "Let's go find out where they sent her."

Chaos greeted him outside. All of the *thræll* had been rounded up, bound, gagged, and thrown together against the eastern gate. Many of them still wore dazed looks caused by Darien's *galdr*, while others were beginning to regain their own thoughts. These glared at the ground, their eyes brimming with anger as they gnashed against their gags. Jari stood guard over those, not hesitating to use the heel of his boot if any of the *thræll* got too wiggly.

Meanwhile, Anara and Haki were doing their best to corral children of every age. Many of the children first looked at Haki with fear in their eyes, but as the gentle half-giant spoke soft words and bounced three of the crying toddlers in his arms, the others warmed up to him, soon pulling on his legs. Anara grouped the children, assigning older teenagers to the younger ones and instructing them on how to get to the Outer Wall. The Viðnám's third wave would keep them safe until the city had been reclaimed.

As they approached the *thræll*, Darien's gaze locked onto the man near the front with an angular face and a wide mouth that reminded Darien of a muzzle. Even with his mouth gagged, the man's eyes shouted insults and threats. From his defiant posture and the stripes on his shoulder, it was clear he was in charge.

Darien pointed at the man. "We need to talk to him, Jari."

The ex-sentry nodded, hauling the man to his feet and shoving him toward Darien. A large welt on the back of his head still bled. He must have been one of the *thræll* who fought when they first arrived.

Darien ripped the gag from his mouth. "There was a young girl named Halla. Where did she go?"

The man snarled, his mouth twisting. "Why would I tell you anything?"

"Where is my sister?" Larissa snapped. Electricity seemed to condense the air around her body.

Darien knew it was her *galdr*; he also knew it would be better for all involved if she did not lose control of it now. She might need it later. He pushed the air out through his teeth, his gaze locking onto the unfeeling gray eyes of the man in front of him. "Tell me where you sold her."

A vein bulged at the man's temples. "Bite me."

The pocket of *galdr* inside Darien's mind burned and enlarged as Darien dived into it, forcing his way into the thoughts of the *thræll* before him. It had not been easy to find a way into the other *thræll*'s minds until he'd realized what motivated them. For most it was power, for some it was fear, but neither seemed to unlock the mind of the man who stood snarling at him. Darien could tell Larissa was losing her patience.

"Your sister? Hmm." The man licked his lips. "Little blonde thing?"

Darien's body went rigid as Larissa's *galdr* pulsed through the air. The next moment, Darien was shoved aside as Larissa's hands wrapped around the man's neck. "What did you do to her?"

The man choked on his laugh. "Taught her a lesson."

Sparks flew from Larissa's fingers, scorching the man's neck. He stopped laughing, not from the pain, but because Darien had found a way in. It wasn't power or fear that motivated the man. It was the thrill he got from causing pain.

At his sudden silence, Larissa dropped her hands, her face flushed as she stepped away, making room for Darien to strengthen his mental connection. It wasn't a connection he wanted to hold for long. The darkness in the man's mind threatened to swallow Darien whole with images of torture and brutality that Darien knew he could never unsee.

"Tell me your name," he commanded, trying to gauge the control he had over the man's mind.

"Fenris," the *thræll* spat. His eyes widened at his mouth's betrayal.

"Fenris, like the wolf?" Darien rolled his eyes, doubting his parents would have given him that name. "Answer my questions or you'll end up like your namesake. Where's Halla?"

Fenris' mouth trembled. His eyes bulged as the redness under his skin burned brighter and brighter. Darien could feel him resisting his influence as no one ever had before. He had been trained, but by whom? Forcing his mind not to wander, Darien directed all of his *galdr* into cracking the safe of this man's mind.

A man's mind is his haven, his father had once taught him. *You should never enter it without permission unless absolutely necessary.* Darien wasn't sure his father would say the same now, but even if he would, Darien was certain this was one of those times. He pushed harder, even as his own head throbbed in pain.

Halla's face flashed in the man's eyes, dragged forward by Darien's insistence, but there was something wrong about the image. Her hair was shorn, and the skin on the back of her neck was ragged and burned.

Fear for Halla drove Darien to press harder than he ever had. Harder than he should have. "What did you do? Tell me where she is!"

Darien felt the strain of his *galdr* on Fenris' mind, like an elastic band stretched too tight. Fenris' eyes widened as blood dripped from his nose. A giggle burst from his lips. "Too late. You're too late."

Darien dove further, trying to make sense of the images in Fenris' mind. There was a bonfire, and Halla was screaming. Darien's stomach clenched, and he resisted the urge to vomit.

The elastic band in Fenris' mind snapped. His eyes rolled behind his head. "Court of the Aristocracy. Gift for the gods." He slumped to the ground.

Darien stumbled at the rush of *galdr* that fled his body. Fenris twitched at Darien's feet, his eyes open but unseeing as he mumbled incoherently to himself.

The mind can only handle so much before it breaks, his father had once said.

Darien's nausea rose. What had he done? Jari dragged Fenris' body toward the other *thrall* who stared at Darien in terror. Anara and Larissa crowded around Darien.

"Darien. Darien." Larissa shook his shoulders.

Had he broken Fenris' mind? Visions from the slaver's memory still played before Darien's eyes.

"You okay?" Larissa's voice cut through.

Darien shook his head, driving away the images, trying to ignore the gibberish that still poured from Fenris' mouth. He'd done what he needed to do for Halla's sake. Darien owed her that much. "I'm fine."

"The Court of the Aristocracy is behind the Second Wall," Anara said, joining them.

Larissa groaned. "It'll take too long to get to the Second Wall on foot."

"Why go on foot?" Darien jerked a thumb toward the outer perimeter of the compound where several transport trucks sat before a gate. As Larissa moved toward them, Darien's eyes caught on the other *thrall*, who stared at their fallen leader in shock. "What about *them*?"

"Haki and Jari are going to lock them in one of their own barracks." Anara answered.

"We can't wait for them," Larissa argued. "We need to go now before Halla is moved again."

"I know." Anara laid her hand on Larissa's shoulder. "They'll meet us at the Second Wall; it's where the Viðnám is heading too."

Larissa nodded, even as she started toward the trucks on the northwest exit. Anara tapped Darien's arm.

"You're both getting stronger, but make sure you don't push yourselves too hard. You know the price. I'll scout ahead," she said before transforming into a flurry of feathers.

"Maybe you should take your own advice," Darien shouted to the raven in the sky. Anara only cawed in response.

Feet pounding against the dirt, Darien raced after Larissa, joining her in the truck. He reached for the keys left on the dash. Snorting at the *thræll*'s lack of security, Darien drove straight through the gate, which clanged violently after their departure. With his eyes on Anara flying up ahead, they raced through the streets, hardly bothering to slow at turns. The truck was large and loud enough that people jumped out of its way long before they heard the horn.

Though the slave barracks were situated well within the city, Larissa's knuckles whitened against the door handle as minute after minute passed by. Driving became more precarious as the streets grew more crowded. Citizens fled through the streets, toward the Outer Wall. Gunfire could be heard off in the distance. The Second Wall loomed ever closer up ahead.

With a sharp caw, Anara flung out her wings, letting the air catch her body as the truck raced past her. Having lost his guide, Darien slammed on the brakes. "What is she doing?"

Then Anara flew in through the open window, transforming as she did so and squeezing herself in between Larissa and Darien. "We're nearly at the Second Wall. So is the Viðnám, but Regent Hammon sent quite the welcome team to greet them."

"You could see them?" Darien asked, wondering if his father was near.

"They're only about a mile to the west. We'll need to head that way and rejoin the Viðnám." Anara raised her hands against Larissa's protest. "Our best chance of getting Halla back is to get past the Second Wall. To do that, we'll need the Viðnám."

Darien avoided the crowd of fleeing citizens, taking a sharp left. The muted sounds of a battle crystalized until Darien could make out shots and shouts, screams and charges. The Viðnám had to be close, along with Regent Hammon's reinforcements. Although his anxiety to find Halla rose with every passing minute, Darien could not help but think of his father. "Sounds like they're putting up more of a fight than we anticipated."

"Don't worry." When Anara grinned, it was feral and wild. "We're winning."

Darien pressed his foot down; the streets were emptier here. He didn't need Anara's directions now. The Second Wall loomed over the tops of the buildings, a blot on the sky itself. Anara stiffened, her head turning toward the open window.

"Brace yourselves," Larissa advised as Darien turned the next corner.

The street emptied them out into a wide open area that stretched as far as Darien could see. Beyond that empty space was the Second Wall. All along the Wall, the Viðnám fought with sentries. Near the front of the line, Larissa could see King Torsten and Halvor dueled with two Kafteinns, though neither were Calder. The other generals from the War Council led their own groups of men and women against the sentries. General Ishaan, sometimes a man, sometimes a beast, defeated three sentries at once. Farmers from the loading bay led a wave of citizens against a group of sentries, holding nothing but rocks or their own closed fists. Several farmers fell under the gunfire before the sentries were overwhelmed by the sheer number of bodies crashing down upon them.

Darien's eyes scanned the fight once, twice, three times, relieved to find no *draugrs*. He cut the engine; he could go no further without risking the lives of the Viðnám as well. His hand gravitated toward his gun, as did Larissa's. Beyond the fighting lay the gates to the Court of the Aristocracy, and beyond that gate was Halla. Darien knew Larissa would fight every sentry herself if that was what it took, and he was determined to fight right at her side.

Without a word, they leapt from the truck, throwing themselves into the fray.

23

Catch and Release

Halla

Halla's bare feet slapped against cold, damp ground. Though she shivered, the back of her neck burned. Kai was a relentless force, moving her forward through the thick walls that surrounded them. Halla had never thought about the thickness of the wall that separated the Court of the Aristocracy from the outer section of the city until she ran through it. She was convinced that the darkness would last forever. As it was, it ended with a dull thud as Halla nearly slammed into Kai's sudden stop.

"Hel's bells," Kai cursed, and he sniffed, almost as though he had a cold. "Found the exit."

"Do you think the barracks are empty on this side?"

"Should be." Kai sniffed again. "Everyone should be out to fight at this point."

Light filtered through the door Kai pushed open. Halla gasped at the sigh of blood trickling from his nose. "Kai!"

"I'm fine," he snapped, but blood rose to his cheeks. "I found the door with my face, that's all."

Halla bit her cheek, knowing whatever she would say would only embarrass him further.

The tunnel deposited them into yet another bathroom. Halla swallowed as Kai opened the door, her breath held as she waited for someone to catch them. Kai looked around, pinching his nose with one hand and gesturing Halla forward with the other. In silence, they made their way through the barrack, passing the rows of empty beds. Only this time, Halla noticed the empty walls where guns and other weapons were obviously held. Gunshots rang out in the near distance.

Larissa.

Fear overwhelmed her hope now. Her sister would be in the battle. Larissa would be in the midst of it, because of Halla. But fear made her brave.

She passed Kai and opened the door that welcomed her back to the Outer City. No longer muffled by walls, the shouts of the battle increased. Kai stood beside her, momentarily blinded by the light and noise.

Halla adjusted first with just enough time to notice the two sentries standing in the street staring at Halla in surprise. "What—"

"Run, Kai!"

He grabbed Halla's hand—it was slick with blood——but even if he hadn't been pulling Halla along, Kai's short legs were no match for the sentries.

"Stop! We're not going to hurt you."

A giant hand fell on Halla's shoulder, brushing against her brand. She flinched, thrashing against the sentry's grip. Her small hands had little effect against the man's massive frame. To her left, Kai was in a similar state. Although his captor was significantly smaller than her own, Kai was no match for the man that held him in the air if only to stop Kai's flailing punches.

"Whoa, easy there," the sentry barked.

"Halla!" Kai cried out. "Let her go!"

"Halla?" the bear of a man holding her echoed. "Are you Halla? Your sister is looking for you."

Halla's hands froze in midair. "You know my sister?"

"Yes." As if sensing that Halla would no longer try to flee, he released her.

"Is she here?" she asked, her head swiveling from side-to-side as though Lara would appear out of thin air.

"She is." His smile transformed his face, and for a minute, Halla forgot that he was a sentry, but only for a moment.

She stepped back. "Why are you dressed like that?"

"We're spies for the Viðnám, but we're on your side. Your sister has been searching for you everywhere. We went to the compound first, but you weren't there."

Unfiltered glee raced through Halla's veins as she turned toward Kai. "I *told* you she would come for me!"

At some unspoken communication between the two men, the thinner one released Kai's hands. It was only then Halla realized the men were twins. Kai rubbed at his wrists with a hooded expression. "How can we trust you?"

"We're not shooting you on sight," said the thinner man.

The larger one shot him a glance. "Don't scare them, Jari."

"I'm not scared," Halla corrected. "Where's my sister? Can you take us to her?"

"We got split up, but I'm sure Princess Lovisa is at the Second Wall with the King and the rest of the Viðnám. We can escort you there."

Halla's exuberance was punctured by Kai's strangled voice. "Princess Lovisa is your *sister*?"

Heat flooded into the tip of Halla's nose. "Well, yeah."

"That's something someone might tell a person," he blurted out.

Jari's impatient sigh cut off Halla's retort. "Pick up the girl, Haki. She won't be able to keep up with us. Can you run, boy?"

"My name is Kai, and yes, I can run."

"Come on, Halla, hop on." Haki crouched, turning his back to Halla so she could scramble up and loop her arms around his neck. She did her best to ignore the pain that spread from the tip of her spine. Before she was properly settled, the twins were running, Kai following close behind.

The sounds of fighting increased. Around them, Halla watched as Perlians either hid themselves away in their homes or flooded the street, running toward the Second Wall. Some paused when they saw Haki and Jari, but when the sentries ignored them, they too ignored the sentries.

Up ahead, Halla could see the back of a crowd and the gate of the Wall. Somewhere in the chaos, she knew Larissa waited.

24

Perle

Larissa

Everything was in disarray.

With Anara and Darien in tow, Larissa shoved her way through the crowd toward the Second Wall. The sentries formed lines in front of the gates, forcing the Viðnám's organized march to dissolve into tumult. Near the front, King Torsten fought, more often now with his sword than with his gun. The close quarters of the fighting had all but eliminated gunplay, aside from the most reckless combatants who didn't care whom they hit. Larissa pushed through the rebels, drawing nearer to where the sentries and Viðnám collided. Anara disarmed those who came too close, but Larissa could see how she restrained herself, disabling instead of killing.

"Watch yourself!" Darien called out, lifting his sword to shield against the knife of a sentry that had emerged from the lines.

Larissa raised her hands, releasing a bit of the *galdr* that was demanding satisfaction. It sent the sentry flying through the air until his body was lost in the fray.

Both Anara and Darien stared at Larissa with wide eyes.

"What?" she asked.

Darien chuckled. "Remind me not to get on your bad side."

Larissa's smile was brief as her eyes roamed over the pandemonium. The spit in Larissa's mouth turned sour at the sight of gallows standing fifty feet tall beside the gates.

"Push forward!" came Torsten's cry.

The wave of bodies around Larissa surged toward the gate, breaking through the lines of the sentries who were outnumbered three to one. Random shots popped off, and more bodies fell to the ground. Larissa stumbled over one, forcing herself to not look, but she felt the warm spray of blood that coated her face. To her right, General Soren led a flank of men firing their own guns in response. The sentries fell back, their bodies pressed up against the gallows and the gate. One by one, those that remained raised their hands in surrender. Larissa shoved her way to the front of the crowd, followed by Darien and Anara, where Torsten wiped his bloody sword on the shirt of a nearby fallen man and slid it back into his scabbard.

"Lay down your weapons, and you do not need to die," he ordered the sentries.

"Who dares defy the Regent of Perle?" The question came from the man atop the gallows' stage. Larissa hadn't even seen him arrive. He wore a military suit, yet his guns remained in their holsters. He sneered down at the Viðnám, glaring particularly at Torsten.

Torsten stepped toward him. "Hammon, your men are defeated. Accept your defeat and save what lives are left."

Unexpected resentment stirred inside Larissa at the sight of the man who abused *her* people from his position of stolen authority.

"Who dares defy the Empress of Evrópa?" Hammon demanded.

"I am King Torsten of the Safír Kingdom, and on behalf of the Perlian people, I reclaim this commonwealth from the False Empress."

At his words, the Viðnám cheered.

A sneer stretched across Regent Hammon's face. "I see no king, and there is no longer any Safír Kingdom. I see a *vámr* begging for scraps from the table of its master."

The Viðnám rustled at the word, gripping their weapons more tightly; the crowd surged forward, revealing how it had grown in size. Many of the Perlians had joined the Viðnám. They stood weaponless apart from the determination in their eyes. King Torsten raised his hand to still his men.

"Can we not discuss this matter like gentlemen? You are outnumbered; there is no hope of you defeating our forces today. Surrender, for the sake of the rest of your men and of the aristocratic families beyond this wall. Otherwise, we will have no choice but to kill and burn as necessary."

Larissa's stomach clenched. That was not the deal. Perle did not deserve to burn any further.

"You are not Perlian," Regent Hammon spoke, his words brimming with contempt. "The people will never rally to you. You have no right to rule here." Beyond the gate came the sound of marching boots. "Did you really think this was the only army that I had?"

Sentries poured through the gate of the Second Wall, their weapons trained on the Viðnám rebels who gripped their own weapons more tightly in response. Larissa paled as the reinforcements supported Hammon's forces, adding to the men standing around the base of the gallows. The Viðnám could still win, but it would be a bloodbath.

King Torsten's face settled into resolved determination. His hand reached for his sword, but just as suddenly, it froze. Disbelief and anger passed over his face.

"My Lord?" Halvor asked.

Torsten's response came out haltingly through his strained jaw. "He will—not release—my hand."

Veins on the King's hand popped against the pressure as he strained to remove his sword from its scabbard. Understanding dawned on Halvor's face at the same moment that Larissa realized the truth.

Regent Hammon was manipulating energy. Not only did he possess *galdr*, he possessed *Perlian galdr*.

"Release—me," Torsten commanded.

Regent Hammon laughed. "I am the rightful Regent of this commonwealth. Only those of Perlian blood could challenge me. Bow before me, and I'll let your pathetic army live."

Darien adjusted the grip on his sword. The sound of Hammon's laugh grated against Larissa's ears. Her blood boiled at the thought of someone with Perlian ancestral power willingly serving under the Empress. She scanned his face, but there was no familiarity there. He must have been born after her disappearance.

Anara shifted in her stance, readying herself for the kill. Even if she took out Hammon, it would only set off more fighting, more death. There'd been too much bloodshed on her streets already; Larissa had to do something before the city was bathed in the gore of her people.

Larissa stepped out from among the Viðnám's rebels, who grinned with wild abandon as they recognized their Princess. The Perlians who had joined the battle pointed and stared, fierce whispers breaking out. Darien and Anara flanked her as they emerged from the crowd, poised for the attack but waiting, as if understanding Larissa's desire to stop the conflict before it could begin again.

The sentries aimed their weapons at Larissa as she placed herself directly in between the Regent and King Torsten. Hammon's brows narrowed, in distaste instead of anger.

"I am Princess Lovisa, the rightful ruler of Perle, and I challenge you."

The hush of the crowd fell like thunder in her ears.

On the stage of the gallows, the Regent's eyes widened a fraction before narrowing in distaste at Larissa. The nooses hung behind him, ever ready for their next victims, swaying in the soft breeze.

"Princess Lovisa is a legend," Hammon sneered. "A myth perpetuated by the weak and traitorous."

Larissa raised her hand, upon which shone the pearl ring, the emblem of her royalty. She could only pray to the gods that her hand would not shake before this man as she felt the weight of her nation's eyes upon her. Golden sparks singed her fingers as power emanated from her. The sentries nearest her stepped back as it washed over them.

"I *am* Princess Lovisa," she repeated, her voice steadier than her heart. "I'm not here to bargain with you, Hammon. I am here to take back what is mine."

"That is—"

"I speak instead to those of you who stand guard," Larissa continued, cutting off Hammon's protest. Her eyes were no longer on the Regent, but rather on the rows of sentries that stood around him, protecting him. She thought back to what Jari had told her.

My brother and I were both enlisted to serve the Empress, to be hated by those around us for the actions we were forced to commit. We were never given a choice to be anything else.

Many of the sentries stared in hatred or passivity, but for some, there was a glimmer of curiosity in their eyes.

"Some of you chose this path. Maybe it was the only choice available to you, maybe your family owed the Empress a debt. Maybe you had no choice at all. I know that some of you may even blame me for who you are and what you have done in order to survive. The people of Perle support me because they are tired of feeling powerless. You think you have power now, but I want to offer you something you've never had. A real *choice*."

Several sentries shifted on their feet, readjusting their weapons, but they made no move to attack. Hammon, his *galdr* still holding Torsten at bay, glared down at Larissa with hatred in his eyes.

"She's no princess," he spat. "Kill her!"

Torsten's sword slid several inches from its scabbard, and Hammon returned his glare to the King, keeping the energy around him condensed and pressed in against Torsten's form. The sentries shifted, and Viðnám rebels alike shifted, but none attacked. As though compelled, they waited like a bated breath to hear what Larissa would say next.

"Hammon will tell you there is no choice. He will order you to guard him with your very lives even though you have no chance of defeating us all. He will tell you it is your duty to the Empress to die for him, but it is *your* life on the line, not his. This is *your* choice. You can fight us, or join us, or walk away. I will not enslave you as the False Empress has, but I cannot allow you to enslave my people, our people, any longer. What choice will you make?"

The wind whispered amongst the vast crowds.

"Attack her or hang!" Hammon's harsh voice broke the silence.

The sentries' eyes were on one another, waiting and watching to see what choice their fellows would make. Near the front of the line, a young man—a boy, really—with a shock of fiery red hair met her eyes. They were only feet away from one another. He holstered the gun that seemed too large for his hand.

"I will serve my Princess."

A thrill of joy raced down Larissa's spine, but a second too late, her eyes caught the movement as the sentry behind the boy raised his own gun.

"No!" she cried, flinging her *galdr* out, calling his gun to her hand, but she was too late. The shot rang out, piercing through the boy who collapsed to the ground in front of her just as the gun landed in her palm.

The shot released the crowd like a cork springing from a bottle. Larissa fell to her knees beside the boy, who clutched at his bleeding chest, his lashes fluttering over half-closed eyes. She took one look at the wound and knew there was nothing she could do.

Behind them, Larissa heard a growl and the cling of steel as Anara and Darien defended her from attacks, but they could only last for so long. Whatever restraint Anara had exhibited before vanished in a sea of blood. Perlian blood that Larissa had failed to save.

Another pair of hands entered her vision. "I'll take him, Princess."

It was a sentry. Tears streamed down the man's face that looked far too similar to the dead boy's to be a coincidence. Larissa's head jerked in the mimic of a nod as she rose to her feet. All around her, the flailing of arms and bodies crowded her vision, but there, on top of the gallows, Hammon fled, firing shots into the crowd, his hold on Torsten gone.

Larissa's skin burned with the force of *galdr* inside her veins, growing with every second. She pushed through the crowd, scorching those who came too close. Where she passed, yelps of pain followed, but she could not tell if they were from allies or enemies. She knew if she turned, Darien and Anara would be behind her, engaged in one altercation or another, but she didn't have time to wait. She had to get to Hammon before he fled.

If he escaped, it would only prolong the battle. It would only delay her search for Halla and put others at risk. She needed to end this now.

Larissa broke through the crowd at the base of the gallows. She took the steps two at a time until she reached the stage and raised the sentry's gun at the Regent's retreating form. "It's over, Hammon. Call them off, surrender."

The Regent turned slowly to face her, his empty hands up in a show of surrender. He carried no weapon save for the pearl rings he wore upon multiple fingers—a tactic those with lesser *galdr* would employ to better help channel their power. His fingers tensed, and the sentry's gun was ripped from Larissa's fingers to where it clattered across the deck, falling into one of the empty square holes beneath the dangling noose, leaving her hands just as empty. Her gun pressed against her side, but there was no chance to reach for it.

Static danced in the air as he turned his *galdr* on her, but she reached out to counteract with *galdr* of her own. She could feel how he sought to freeze her limbs, to immobilize her where she stood, but he had greatly underestimated the power building within her. Larissa trembled once before throwing off his restraints and tightening her grip on the energy surrounding his body. She envisioned every particle of it as if it were tree sap, clinging to his skin, binding him until his face went red with the effort of trying to escape.

With her free hand, she removed her gun from her waistband, raising it level with the man before her.

He snorted like a bull as he attempted and failed to shake the *galdr*. "Release me."

"Renounce your claim to Perle, and tell your men to stop fighting," she countered, not bothering to wipe at the bead of sweat that rolled down her forehead.

"Never."

Larissa's arms shook as the *galdr* took its toll. She should shoot him and be done with it, but he was unarmed. He wasn't attacking. It would be wrong. Wouldn't it?

No doubt, King Torsten would have shot him by now.

But what kind of ruler would that make her if this was her first act as Queen-to-be? Would she be just like Shiko, killing those who were weaker than her because it was the simplest solution?

They remained frozen in the silent battle of wills as Larissa held Hammon perfectly still, even as the gun shook in her hand.

"Lara!" Darien's footsteps thudded across the platform. "It's okay. It's over."

Larissa's eyes strayed to the crowd. Darien was right. Though few still fought, most of the sentries had surrendered to the Viðnám. King Torsten and Halvor were heading in their direction, no doubt to take Hammon captive as their prisoner. Larissa released her breath, lowering the gun.

Too late, she realized she'd also lessened the restraints she'd placed around Hammon. Movement flickered from the corner of her eyes. She turned back, registering the gun in his hand, the way his finger flexed toward the trigger, the muzzle pointed not at her, but at Darien.

"No!"

With a snarl, she raised her hands to shove Darien out of the way, allowing what remained of her *galdr* to surge through every fiber of her being. The force of it pushed him across the stage just as the bullet passed by, but the wave of *galdr* could not be contained. It barreled across the wooden deck, slamming into Hammon with all the force of a tidal wave, lifting him from his feet and hurling him against the Second Wall. The crack of his head against the stones resounded in the silence. Then his body thudded to the platform beneath the gallows.

Larissa stared at the blood pooling around Hammon's body. She'd killed him. Darien rose to his feet, his hands falling onto Larissa's shoulders, checking her over for any bullet holes, but the wound was not in her body. It was in her mind.

That crack of Hammon's body played over and over again.

Her breath was harsh in her own ears. *She'd* killed him, without hesitation. Did she even regret it? Viðnám, Perlian, sentry alike stared at Hammon's body where it lay. Larissa had only ever killed a *draugr*, but the *draugr* had not looked so human in death.

Hammon was a monster, she told herself, but the pit in her stomach remained as she stared at the broken body that resembled so many of the others that littered the streets of her kingdom.

King Torsten ascended the steps, followed closely by Anara. His voice boomed over the crowd, "Hammon is dead. Lay down your weapons or meet the same fate."

With frantic obedience, sentries raised their hands, dropping guns and knives which members of the Viðnám hurriedly removed from their reach. Larissa could hardly bear the way the sentries gaped at her. In hate. In *fear*. As if *she* was the monster.

"Long live the Queen!"

Larissa's eyes snapped toward the voice, shocked to find Jari who looked at her with approval. Then the entirety of the Viðnám was screaming the same chant, screaming her name, but her ears had gone deaf. Even her battered heart flopped in joy.

Standing next to Jari, Larissa saw the familiar freckled face.

Halla! her heart screamed as she jumped from the stage, pushing through the crowd. Halla ran to her, her small hands shoving her way through the bodies. The sisters collided, falling to their knees as they locked each other in an embrace.

Larissa wept, not caring who saw or what they thought as she clung to her sister. Based on the wetness on her shoulder, Larissa guessed that Halla was crying also, her face buried in Larissa's neck. As if disconnected from her heart, her mind made note of her sister's shorn hair and the burn at her neck that Larissa was careful not to touch. She would hunt down whoever had done these things, but her heart shushed such thoughts, reveling in the warmth of her sister.

There'd been enough blood, too much blood, to let thoughts of vengeance override the pure relief that flooded through her.

Only after the chanting of her name stopped did Larissa reluctantly release her hold on Halla, though she kept her sister's hand in her own even as she stood. All around her, the Viðnám and Perlian citizens bowed to one knee, one hand over their heart and another reaching out toward Larissa in acceptance of their lost Princess.

She could have wept again.

A tug on Larissa's braid broke her attention.

Halla grinned up at her with shimmering green eyes that reminded Larissa so much of her mother. "I knew you could do it!"

And when Halla looked at her with such admiration, Larissa could nearly forget the blood she'd shed to save her sister. Nearly forget Shiko's retaliation that was sure to come.

25

Prisoners of War

Darien

WITH HAMMON'S DEATH, BREACHING the Second Wall had been all too easy. The Viðnám swarmed in, but Torsten had kept Darien back along with Larissa and Halla. There was no need for them to go house to house, dragging out the generals, aristocratic families, and remaining sentries, his father said. Their men would see to that.

Torsten waited in the open courtyard near the wall as aristocrats and generals were brought to kneel before him. Unbeholden to Torsten's command, Anara had darted off through the streets of the Court of the Aristocracy with abandon. Though Darien never doubted her safety, he scanned the city streets for her return.

"Lara, this is Kai." Halla's soft voice came from Darien's left. She gestured to a young boy that Darien hadn't noticed before. His clothes shouted "slave," but there was nothing else remarkable about him. Perhaps that was why Darien hadn't noticed him. He tried to commit to memory the boy's lanky form and angular eyes that darted away from Darien's inspection.

"He helped me when we were in the barracks," Halla continued, looking at Larissa.

Larissa squeezed Halla tight against her side. "Thank you, Kai; I'm in your debt."

Darien raised an eyebrow at Larissa, noting the odd tone in her voice, but she didn't respond to his questioning gaze. Kai nodded at Larissa in respect before looking away again. Was he scared of her? After Hammon's death, many citizens, though in awe of their returned Princess, were giving her a wide berth. Their words were far kinder than those of the men being brought to kneel before Torsten. Their whispers rose, targeting the Princess that stood to Darien's left.

" . . . she killed Hammon . . ."

" . . . she used *galdr* like it was nothing . . ."

" . . . broke the Outer Wall on her own . . ."

" . . . she'll kill us all . . ."

The stiffening in Larissa's posture was all it took for Darien to know that she heard the accusations too. She turned her back on their whispers and brushed aside the hair at the back of Halla's neck, examining the burn beneath it. Her jaw clenched several times before opening. "What happened?"

But their attention was diverted by a man in uniform being pushed toward the courtyard. He swore loudly as Anara shoved him from behind, keeping a firm grasp on the man twice her size. She pushed him to the cobblestone ground and bared her teeth in his face. At the sight of her fangs, the general paled, his mouth opening and closing without sound. Giving him a satisfied look, Anara left him under Haki's and Jari's supervision.

Seeing Darien, Anara walked in his direction. "The palace is ours."

Though she'd spoken to Darien, Torsten responded. "Casualties?"

"No more than what it took to get here; the sentries surrendered once they knew that Hammon was dead."

Darien's unease increased, not at the thought of casualties, but at the growing number of families that were being rounded up in the courtyard. Dazed, confused children were forced to sit beside their parents, who stared at the ground in burning silence.

Larissa looked on in concern though she, too, was trying to hide it. Even Anara's lips were pressed into a thin line at the sight of the toddler who clung to her mother's neck, but it was Halla who bounced with worry. The boy, Kai, whispered in Halla's ear, but she shook her head in anguish. Darien leaned toward her, his eyes avoiding the branding that made his stomach clench and his hands yearn for something to hit.

"What's wrong, kiddo?"

Halla clutched a small lavender bow so tightly that the fabric crumpled in her fingers.

Darien knelt, his face on the same level as her own. "You can tell me."

"What are they going to do to them?"

Darien didn't need to look at Halla's gaze to know she was asking about the aristocratic families. He hesitated. A quick glance up revealed Larissa's concerned expression as well. "I'll find out," he said to them both.

Torsten barked orders as more aristocrats were forced to kneel in the courtyard. Even through his stern countenance, triumph shone through his eyes.

"Faðir," Darien said, using the honorific to soften the interruption as he approached.

Torsten beamed at his son. "We've done it. Before you know it, we'll be reclaiming Safír as well. Our people will rejoice just as the Perlians did today."

Warmth encased his stomach and traveled through his body at the thought. *Our people,* his father had said. Darien had heard the words so many times, and yet they had never mattered to him quite as they did in that moment. *He* could free his people, just as Larissa had done. All of his life, he'd looked up to Aeron, knowing it would be his job to support his brother, grateful the kingdom would never rest on his shoulders. But Darien felt it then, the overwhelming desire to free his people. It was a burn he'd never felt before.

But the burn was doused by the sight of those kneeling behind his father. "Why are we gathering the households of the aristocracy?"

"The generals will be put on trial and imprisoned or executed according to their crimes."

"And their families?" Larissa asked, having joined Torsten and Darien with Halla at her side.

Torsten frowned. "All who served the Empress will be imprisoned until their loyalties can be tested."

Darien's forehead furrowed. "What about the children—"

"Saessae!" Halla cried out, her body turned toward a young girl added to the kneeling crowd. Larissa's grip held Halla back from flinging herself toward the girl with shell-shocked eyes. Her mouth formed Halla's name. Halla tugged at Larissa's arm. "Saessae wouldn't hurt anyone. She isn't loyal to the Empress. We can trust her."

Larissa turned toward Torsten and crossed her arms. "Release the child."

Torsten's jaw clenched. "No."

Darien glanced around, grateful no one noticed the standoff occurring in the midst of them. Only Halvor, who stood to the side determinedly looking in another direction, could hear the argument.

Larissa caved first. "These are my people, Torsten."

"These are my soldiers, Lovisa. Do you want us to leave and see what happens?" Torsten sighed, releasing some of the tension from his body. "You must trust me, Lovisa. I am doing what is best for you and your people. I won't harm anyone who doesn't deserve it."

"But you'll imprison infants and children?"

"This is war. You don't even know this child. You have no idea what she is capable of. Let's say that I release her. What's to stop her from running off or communicating with those sympathetic to the Empress and informing them of what happened here today?"

"Who's to say Hammon hasn't already sent informants before the battle?" Larissa argued.

"Can you trust her? This girl you've never met? These children were bred on love for the Empress. They've nursed on it from their birth. It is all they've ever known."

Looking over the crowd of captives, Darien saw what his father meant. While some of the children looked on in fear or shock, many glared at Torsten and Larissa with hatred. Some even caught his gaze and tilted their chins in defiance, reflecting the anger on their parents' faces.

"It's not right. Darien, tell him—" Larissa's voice stopped, noticing the look on his face. "You don't agree with him, do you?"

"If Halla says she trusts the girl, then I trust her, but the rest of them . . ." Darien gestured. "Look at them, Lara. They're your people, but they might not accept that yet."

Larissa stepped back, and it took everything for Darien to not recant his words. The look of approval on his father's face only made it worse. "*Faðir*, will it really hurt to release one child?"

The approval lessened but did not vanish. Darien knew his father, knew the frustrations that passed behind his calm eyes as he weighed out the cost of acquiescing to Larissa's request. "If it means that much to you, Princess, but the girl will serve under supervision."

"As a slave?" Halla squeaked.

"No," Darien spoke quickly, resting a hand on Halla's shoulder. "No, that's not what he meant. Right?"

Halvor stepped back into the discussion. "The palace will need servants, your majesty. Why not send her to work in the kitchens? Others within the Viðnám will be able to monitor her closely there. See that she doesn't harm anyone"—he glanced down at Halla, his face softening—"and that no harm comes to her."

"An acceptable proposition," Torsten agreed. "Unless you have any further objections, Princess Lovisa?"

Just as Darien could read his father, he could read Larissa with even more ease. It was the right choice, the only choice, but it was a choice Larissa had been backed into. Something she didn't appreciate. "You can't keep the other children imprisoned indefinitely."

"As long as it takes, but no longer," Torsten promised, which Darien knew was not much of a promise at all.

Without waiting for his father's approval, Darien waded through the bodies, ignoring the animosity pointed in his direction. The ring on his finger was enough to identify who he was and the role he played in their demise. He approached Saessae, ignoring the way her father struggled to his feet only to be shoved back down by one of the Viðnám. He offered a hand to the girl who trembled on the ground. Her fear wasn't unlike that which he'd seen in the eyes of the slaves he'd freed from the barracks. Darien shoved the image away. Those children had been victims of the Empress. Abused by those in power. It wasn't the same.

"Come on, Halla's waiting."

At Halla's name, the girl took Darien's hand, though her eyes remained wary. Her father struggled again and shouted around the gag in his mouth as Darien led Saessae through the captives. Reaching the edge, he released her hand just as she raced toward Halla.

"Halla, I don't understand." The girl's perfect curls bounced in distress. "What's happening? Who are these people?"

"It's okay." Halla held Saessae's hands. "The Viðnám reclaimed Perle. Princess Lovisa will make everything right now."

Incredulity flooded her face. "What do you mean, *right*? Halla, they've destroyed Perle, just look at it."

Smoke drifted throughout the city where fights had broken out. Even now the Viðnám was still working to put out small skirmishes through the outer section where sentries attempted to flee.

"No. The Viðnám want to get rid of the Empress. They want to bring back the peace we had before."

"Peace?" Anger flooded her voice. "Does this look like *peace* to you Halla?" She glanced at Larissa, shivering as she looked away. "They're saying *she* killed Hammon. In cold blood."

"He would have killed Darien—"

Saessae's voice rose in hysterics. "She'll kill all of us!"

Larissa's cheeks reddened, but she remained by her sister's side. Halla looked at Saessae; disbelief coloring her face. "No, Saessae, you're safe—"

"And my father?"

"You said yourself he wasn't a kind man!"

"That doesn't mean I want him dead! I thought you were my friend." She yanked her hands out of Halla's grasp. "I want to go back to my father."

Larissa's shocked face was nothing compared to Halla's, but Torsten only looked on as if it were all too predictable. Motioning to a sentry near him, Torsten ordered the girl taken back to her father. She left without another glance in Halla's direction. In between blinks, Darien caught sight of the lavender bow in Halla's hand that she crumpled and shoved into her pocket. He watched Larissa guide Halla away from the growing crowd, whispering to her as they walked.

Torsten caught Darien's eye. "There is a time and place for mercy. You'll learn one day." He clapped his hand on Darien's shoulder, then moved on to instruct the guards on what to do with the prisoners.

Darien's gaze followed Saessae as she sat beside her father. With her head bowed against the sun, she looked more like the children from the slave barracks than ever, a victim in a war she had no part in.

26

Ballroom Tension

Larissa

AT THE BALCONY'S STONE edge, Larissa watched as all of Perle, from the front courtyard of the palace all the way to the Outer Wall, buzzed with action and purpose. It brought back memories of the time before, when Perle had not been stained by blood but illuminated by winter lights that danced amongst the stars as the land took its well-earned rest. The Smaragdians loved their forest just as fiercely as the Safirians loved the ocean. The Rubinians celebrated the eruption of their sea volcanoes, and the Diamantians found solace in their white-capped mountains. But for Perlians, it was fertile soil and a bountiful harvest they enjoyed the most. She could hear the melody played at every Cherry Picking festival, soft and whimsical, so different from the chants she'd heard at the festivals in Rubin.

Four days had passed since the reclamation of Perle. Four days since the remaining sentries and aristocrats had either pledged themselves to Princess Lovisa and the Viðnám or been imprisoned while hurling insults at Lovisa. Four days since the rest of the *thræll* had been imprisoned for their actions and their slaves freed. It would take weeks, if not months, to sort out the innocence and guilt of each man, woman, and child, but by the end of four days, Perle had been returned to royal blood by royal hands.

Hands that gripped the stone with so much force, Larissa was surprised the balcony did not crack beneath her fingers.

The hum of the city was constant, inescapable even, as Larissa stood so far apart from it. On the far horizon, specks of trucks passed in and out of the Outer Wall as the rest of the Viðnám arrived. With Perle's population so severely diminished by Shiko's violence, King Torsten had argued it made more sense to bring the Viðnám to Perle rather than keep them in the Nordryggen Mountains. Yet even with the supposed room for the extra population, the city was bursting at its seams. The Viðnám would need to build on their momentum and move quickly to reclaim the Safír commonwealth to the east before the Perlians began to resent the Viðnám's invasion. All of this was a worry for another day, Larissa had been told.

Tonight was for celebration.

Perhaps that was the true reason Larissa felt panic clawing its way up her throat and why she wore the golden gown and silk slippers when she would rather be in her jeans and boots. An attendant had left her only moments before, assisting Larissa with the gown that put all others to shame. The summer-hued fabric was unlike anything Larissa had ever seen, even in the days before Shiko's betrayal. She wasn't sure where Torsten had found it. The front lace of the gown clung high against her neck while the back dipped dangerously low. Pearls encased in gold chains hung in semicircles, the metal kissing the bare skin of her back and arms. Intricate braids that tickled her shoulders were woven into her hair. Her mother's necklace had been brought from the mountains, and Larissa found comfort in stroking the pearls.

"You look beautiful." Halla's voice was filled with awe as she touched the front of Larissa's gown.

Larissa couldn't help but chuckle. "You don't have to sound so surprised."

"I mean, this is the first time I've seen you out of your boots. Plus, you've been covered in blood recently."

Larissa's laughter died in her throat. She heard the crack of Hammon's body against the wall. Hammon had deserved death, but how many deaths would Larissa be responsible for by the end of the war? Breathing past the memory, she turned to her sister.

Halla grinned at her, the twinkle of mischief in her eyes as she twirled around so that Larissa could take in the full picture. Halla's gown was lavender with long sleeves and a knee-length skirt that billowed with every turn. If she had wings, Larissa might have mistaken her for a fairy.

Her sister's laughter was a balm to Larissa's conflicted soul. Halla radiated sheer joy, taking true advantage of all the benefits Larissa's royalty had allotted her. Yet even as Halla twirled and giggled, the scar at the back of her neck winked at Larissa beneath Halla's short hair, reminding her of everything Halla had endured.

After the battle, Larissa had brought Halla to the best physicians within the Viðnám. They'd treated her burn with dwarf cornel nectar, closing the wound and removing the blossoming infection, but it had left a silvery scar that would never go away. The first night of their reunion, the sisters had stayed up long enough to greet the sun the next morning. When Halla spoke of Fenris and the barracks, Larissa felt immense satisfaction in knowing that the man had been left mentally broken after Darien's *galdr*. He would spend the remainder of his worthless life drooling behind bars. When they talked about Juni and Saessae, Halla cried. Larissa could only hold her as the tears her sister had held on to for so long wore themselves out.

But Halla wasn't crying anymore, not as she twirled and admired her outfit in the full-length mirror leaning against the wall. Larissa choked down the surge of emotions, willing herself to remain in the present. "You look beautiful too, *bebe*."

Although Halla wrinkled her nose at the endearment, Larissa could see the pleasure she took from the compliment. "I can't believe I get to go to a ball tonight!"

Of course Halla was excited about the ball, whereas Larissa could only think of the coronation. As the sole survivor of her bloodline, Larissa was Queen, or near enough. All that remained was her coronation and the weaving of her threads into the *Tæpəstris Friðarsamningu*. The Tapestry of Peace, first given by the Norn and destroyed by Shiko during the Great *Hrun*, was far out of Larissa's reach, but the crown was not. It was a technicality that Torsten claimed needed to be rectified immediately if Larissa was to hold authority over Perle when Shiko's army came for them. Halvor estimated they would have a week before Shiko learned of Perle's loss.

Anara disagreed. Shiko had spies everywhere. Even now, someone could be reporting that Lovisa had returned. Perhaps Calder was already on his way.

Larissa shook off her foreboding. "You'll be the prettiest girl there, more beautiful than Freya herself."

"You shouldn't say that," Halla said, the smile falling from her face. "You might anger the gods."

Look at our world, she thought. *The gods are already angry.*

But she said, "Freya will understand."

A knock at the door prevented Halla's response. Anara slipped in, her presence demanding their attention. The blood-red gown clung to her neck but left her arms bare. The hemline dripped to the floor, transforming from red to nearly black with slits on either side of her long tan legs. Around her wrists were two bands connected to the sheer fabric of the dress that rose like wings when she raised her arms. Rubies adorned her head, ears, throat, and wrists.

Despite it all, she plopped herself on the bed and smiled at Halla. "You look lovely."

Halla beamed.

"Are you aware that someone's waiting for you down the hall?" Anara jerked her chin toward the door. "The guards won't let him pass."

"Kai," Halla nearly shouted. "I told him to meet me here. Is that okay, Lara?"

Larissa forced her smile to hold. "It's fine. Why don't you go join him, Halla? Anara and I'll be with you in a minute."

Halla bounded through the door.

"Still full of energy, I see." Anara's voice was dry.

"Thank the Norn," Larissa muttered, wondering if they actually deserved her thanks.

"You don't like him."

Larissa raised her eyebrows. "Like who?"

"The boy. Kai."

Anara wasn't wrong. The dark-haired boy had stuck by Halla's side as often as possible, staring at Larissa with disbelief. Though Halla vouched for him, Larissa couldn't help the distrust she felt every time she noticed his dark eyes watching her only to flit away before she could catch his gaze.

"Is it because he is Diamantian?" Anara asked.

Larissa's sharp inhale was loud even in her own ears. "So I'm right."

"I looked into it like you asked me. His appearance certainly fits, but his records with the *thræll* are spotty at best. It appears his own family sold him into slavery. How he ended up so far south in Perle is unclear."

His own family, Larissa thought, a twinge of pity undermining her distrust.

"It isn't his fault," Anara commented.

"What isn't?"

"Where he was born. It isn't his fault. People look at me and they see Rubin. There's distrust. When they realize I'm a shifter, there's fear and hatred. I can't help who I am, and neither can the boy. He stuck by Halla when no one else did; that should be enough."

Larissa's cheeks heated, thinking of the way the farmer's family had reacted to Anara after learning she was a Rubinian and the pain that had flashed in Anara's eyes. Here she was doing the same thing to Kai. "You're right."

"Of course, I'm right." Anara rose, smoothing the dress. "That being said, I'll keep an eye on him. There are some gaps in his history I would love to fill. Are you ready?"

It was like whiplash, trying to keep up with Anara's train of thought. Larissa's mind switched back to what lay beyond the door. First there would be the celebration ball. Although all Perle and the Viðnám had been invited to attend, Larissa knew the festivities would bleed into the streets and homes of the city. The palace and its grounds could only hold so many. Torsten claimed it was the release the city needed.

After the ball would come the coronation. Larissa would officially be Queen.

"As ready as I'll ever be," she responded, but the lack of sleep laced her voice with exhaustion.

Anara noticed. "More dreams?"

"Verðandi grows impatient," was all Larissa would say. "I'll have no choice soon but to see what she wants from me."

"Well, you won't have to go alone—but first, the crown."

As a girl, Larissa had dreamed of this day, but it wasn't happening quite as she'd expected. Though Anara didn't say a word, Larissa knew she understood. With Rubin under control of one of Shiko's regents, Anara was an unofficial Queen herself. Larissa vowed silently that she would see Anara restored to her rightful place. If anyone deserved to rule, after everything she had gone through, it was Anara.

Halla and Kai waited for them in the hall. Tonight, Kai had been outfitted with new clothes, although not as fine as the royals'. He pulled at the black collar in discomfort, stopping quickly when he noticed Larissa's approach.

Anara was right that Larissa judged him in part due to his origin, but there was something else. It was the way he watched her out of the corner of his eyes, the slight pause and tensing of his posture whenever she entered the room. At first, Larissa chalked it up to him feeling awkward in the presence of royalty, but he didn't react the same way to Anara's and Darien's presence.

"Ready?" Larissa asked, determined to put her prejudice behind her.

Halla beamed. "Ready!"

The four wound their way through the palace halls and stairs. Although the original had been burned down, it appeared the new palace had been constructed as a replica of the old. Ghosts of Larissa's past haunted her at every turn. She ignored the sound of gunfire and her father's anxious voice calling her name.

A hand settled on her shoulder for a moment. Larissa met Anara's eyes. They seemed to whisper, *I hear it too.*

It was a relief when the sound of music and laughter swelled, crowding out the other memories in Larissa's mind. They arrived at an outer chamber that concealed them from the ballroom, where hundreds of guests awaited their arrival. At the doors leading into the ballroom stood King Torsten with Darien at his side. Larissa paused. Darien's eyes drank in her image before locking on her face. His expression wasn't just adoration, but admiration. Could he see the same thing in her own eyes?

Darien's suit was dyed in the signature blue of his kingdom. The gold accents representing his new title as Crown Prince were like a slap in the face, reminding Larissa of obstacles that separated them no matter how he felt.

No matter how *she* felt.

"Could your attendant do nothing for your face?" King Torsten's question raked harshly against Larissa's ears. His eyes locked on the scar cut across Larissa's right cheek.

Larissa smiled, letting her grin pull against the scar. "Even if she could, I would've asked her not to. Would you cover up the scar if it was on your face and not mine?"

Kai snorted in surprise, but thankfully, Torsten did not hear it or see how Halla elbowed Kai sharply in the ribs. He tended to ignore them both. Instead, the King turned away, pulling at his gloves. "No matter. It's time."

It was only then that Larissa noticed the woman standing behind him. So this was the second-wife Darien had told her about. Her face, though beautiful, held no expression. Larissa couldn't remember if Torsten had ever said her name. Larissa moved toward her, if only to introduce herself, when the trumpets on the other side of the door resounded, drawing the music and laughter to a hushed whisper.

Through the opening glass doors, Halvor's voice could be heard. "Announcing King Torsten and Queen Einsa of the Safír Kingdom, Crown Prince Darien of the Safír Kingdom, Crown Princess Anara of the Rubin Kingdom, and Crown Princess Lovisa of the Perle Kingdom."

With each of their names, they walked through the threshold, standing at the top of a gigantic staircase before descending. Although Halla's and Kai's names had not been called, Larissa walked in with her arm linked through her sister's. Kai followed like a shadow down the steps.

A mixture of Viðnám and Perlians waited for them below. The Jötnar had chosen to remain in the Nordryggen mountains with Torsten's full support. The longer their alliance remained a secret from Shiko, the greater the advantage.

Larissa followed King Torsten's lead as he passed through the crowd to the end of the ballroom where five thrones waited. The center throne was unlike the others, in both size and adornment. Torsten took the seat on the right of it, with Einsa taking the seat beside her husband's. Darien and Anara took the seats on the left. As this was Larissa's kingdom, the largest, ornate seat belonged to her.

She paused before it, her breath caught in her throat. She could nearly feel the spirits of her mother and father standing behind her. Blinking away the tears, Larissa took her place.

A cheer from the crowd rose, and the music resumed. Though King Torsten had outlined how the evening would proceed from here, Larissa found herself lost in the music and the lights. In all her life, even before Shiko's betrayal, she'd never been the center of such a celebration. Around the room, tables laden with every type of food were overflowing. The floor filled quickly with dancing people whose laughter spoke of freedom and security. Larissa's smile only grew larger when she spotted Halla dragging Kai over to one of the dessert tables. Meanwhile, those who wished to speak with royalty were already forming lines.

"Princess Lovisa, it is an honor to stand before you once again. I knew you could do it." General Soren bowed before her, the gold in his sash gleaming under the bright lights.

"I'm glad to see you. I wanted to thank you for the way you led your men from the front during the siege. Not all generals would have done that."

Soren's face reddened. "It was my pleasure, Your Highness; I would have done anything to free our kingdom from the False Empress."

Before General Soren could speak further, the next person in line shoved forward, vying for a moment with the Perle Princess. King Torsten had warned Larissa that much of this night would be spent addressing the crowds, generals and officers as well as common folk. Everyone would want a moment with her, even just to introduce themselves. Larissa forced herself to smile and nod, to listen and respond when necessary. She had always hated the formal small talk that accompanied the festivals her parents had thrown every year, but she would not allow that irritation to show itself now.

Name after name was introduced, and face after face appeared and was replaced by the next one in the queue. Larissa did her best to remember each but knew she was failing miserably in that regard. To her right, King Torsten remained just as inundated as Larissa, yet he never seemed to tire. Even Queen Einsa looked amicable as she nodded at General Aiko. Larissa forced what she hoped was a neutral expression before turning to greet the next person.

"May I have your first dance?" Darien stood in front of her with one hand extended and a lopsided smile on his face. He leaned in close enough that no one else could hear and added, "Your rescuer has arrived."

With a smile that finally felt genuine, Larissa grasped his hand, ignoring a pointed look from King Torsten, and followed Darien across the hall. "Your timing couldn't have been better."

"You did look a bit like a wrung-out cloth."

She swooned in mocked exaggeration. "Just what every girl wants to hear."

"A very beautiful wrung-out cloth," he amended.

Larissa's laughter rang out across the tiled floor. Darien could always make her laugh.

"I'll take it you've forgiven me?" he asked.

They hadn't spoken in the last days about what had taken place with the children of the Perlian aristocrats, or how Darien had sided with his father. Larissa sobered, thinking of Saessae. "You were right."

"I'm sorry, can you say that again? I don't think you've ever said that to me."

"Well, don't get used to it," she grumbled as he led her to the middle of the floor. She took her place across from him, hearing the first stirrings of music. "I don't know if I remember how to do this."

"You can't blame your memory loss for this one, Lov," Darien chuckled. "You never were a good dancer."

"Maybe I just needed a better partner," she teased, but her retort was cut short as his hand found her waist and her fingertips touched the hair at the base of his collar.

The music swelled, and Darien pulled her closer to him in step with the music. Larissa's eyes darted to the staring crowd. As the steps took them to the edge of the dance floor, their words floated to her ears.

". . . killed Hammon without touching him . . ."

". . . he had it coming, he would've killed us all . . ."

". . . what's to stop her from killing someone else . . ."

Darien's lips brushed against her ear. "Ignore them."

"They think I'm a monster." Beneath the smiling faces of the crowd, Larissa swore she could see the fear in their eyes.

"No they don't. They haven't seen anyone this powerful—"

"—since Shiko."

"It's not the same thing, Lov; don't do that to yourself." He spun her, then pulled her in closer. "Come on, fretting only makes you a worse dancer, and we've got a crowd to impress." Darien's fingers cupped Larissa's chin, pulling her face away from the crowd until his face swallowed up her vision. His thumb caressed the skin just beneath her lip. "Ignore them. Look at me."

There were a million reasons why Larissa shouldn't have decreased the space between them, but she couldn't remember a single one as she moved closer to Darien. Then she was lost, adrift in his sea-blue eyes. The other dancers, the onlookers, even King Torsten faded away. For all of Larissa's jesting, Darien was an excellent lead. With ease and poise that betrayed the hours spent practicing, Darien led her across the floor, gliding, twirling, and dipping Larissa when spurred on by the music. Their bodies remembered the rhythm, the steps they had practiced in their youth, but Larissa's heart beat erratically as she tried to catch her breath. All the while, Darien smiled, his heart fully on display, etched in every fiber of his being.

It was one of the things Larissa loved about him.

Too late, Larissa saw in Darien's eyes the way her own emotions were written so clearly on her face. The music slowed, along with their movements. Darien's fingers brushed the scar at her face, pushing back the hair that had fallen free. "My father was wrong, by the way. You're more beautiful with the scar."

Larissa went warm all over. Her fingers brushed against the edges of his hair, yearning to tangle themselves within his curls. "You're growing your hair out."

He chuckled, but it was too low and intimate for humor. "Crown Prince obligations."

"Oh, I didn't realize. Is the beard a part of those obligations?" Her fingers trailed to the scruff forming on his cheeks. "It suits you."

"You suit me."

The music died.

"Darien—"

His lopsided grin was back. "No distractions, I know. I think I'm starting to understand." He bowed low, kissing the knuckles of her hand and sending a tingle up Larissa's arm. "Why don't we check on Halla?"

He was offering her an out, a way to regain her composure, but Larissa didn't want it. She wanted the music to continue. She wanted to spend more time in his arms. But the kingdom was watching; Torsten was watching. "Probably a good idea."

Ignoring the way her fingers missed his company, Larissa searched for Halla, locating her standing off to the side of the ballroom with Kai. Halla's mouth moved without pause, her eyes round and wide as she took in every inch of the ballroom. Beside her, Kai looked around at whatever Halla pointed out, his eyes hidden at times by dark hair that fell over his face. Larissa had told Anara she would try harder where Kai was concerned. What better a time to start than the present?

Halla, seeing her sister approaching from across the room, waved Larissa down. "Lara, you have to try this!"

Larissa lifted the pink beverage from her hand, leaning in low to whisper, "Remember, it's Lovisa in public, Halla."

"Oops, right."

Darien eyed the drink in Larissa's hand. "What've you got there, kiddo?"

"I don't know, but it's so good!"

Hesitantly, Larissa sipped, then forced herself to swallow, grateful she hadn't gulped it down. The best she could say for it was that it tasted pink. "Your sweet tooth is really disgusting, you know that?"

"Give it back, then," she said, snatching the drink away. "Kai thinks it's good, don't you?"

Kai shrugged, not meeting their eyes. "Sure."

Larissa laughed as Halla shoved Kai's arm. "Some friend you are! You're supposed to take my side."

"Princess Lovisa," a deep voice said.

Larissa repressed the urge to sigh at the interruption. She had known that the moment she stopped moving, there would be more faces that wanted her attention. Larissa replastered her polite smile and turned to the voice.

The sight of the white-robed man halted the words on Larissa's tongue. But it was more than just the oddity of the runes that snaked up his neck; it was the way Halla's body had gone rigid with tension. Even Kai mirrored her posture. As if in response, Darien moved in front of them, blocking them from the man's sight.

But he had already noticed Halla, and a slow smile crept up his face. "Hello again. It appears I was right about the gods having more in store for you."

Larissa's hand went to her waist before remembering she'd left her gun in her room. "Who are you and how do you know my sister?"

"I am Brother Gorthr, your Majesty. I last saw—your sister, did you say?—on the steps of the city temple."

A slight nod from Halla confirmed his words. "He's the one who bought me from Fenris."

Hot *galdr* scalded Larissa's veins. Her hands burned and glowed. "You treated my sister like cattle."

"Careful," Darien whispered as several of the nearby crowd turned at Larissa's raised voice.

"Ah, Brother Gorthr," Torsten called, joining their group. At the sight of Darien and Larissa's defensive stances, he raised his eyebrows. "Is something wrong?"

Brother Gorthr inclined his head to the king. "I was just introducing myself to our long-lost Princess, but I'm afraid I may have made a bad first impression."

"I thought all slavers had been imprisoned," Larissa spat out, careful to conceal the shaking in her hands. "He bought and sold Halla. What is he doing here?"

Brother Gorthr clucked his tongue. "I never sold her. She was given as a gift—"

"A person can't be *given* as anything," Larissa snapped.

Torsten's face darkened. "Brother Gorthr is an upstanding member of upper society and a pillar in the religious community. He is no more a slaver than Halvor. If we arrested every person who'd ever bought or transferred a slave within the city, we'd have no one left. Besides, Brother Gorthr has offered to house all the children of convicted war criminals in the temple so that they do not have to remain imprisoned any longer than necessary. I thought at least that would please you."

Larissa glanced at Darien, but his look only confirmed her own unease. Even so, there was little else she could do as Torsten's frown deepened into a scowl. "Thank you, Your Majesty," she bit out, "for thinking of the children."

"They are most safe in my care. Some were most eager to come," Brother Gorthr added, looking at Halla, "like your friend Saessae."

"Is she alright?" Halla blurted out, though remaining behind Larissa.

"Shaken up by the changes in her life, of course, but she is just fine. She will adjust and come to realize just what a blessing it is from the gods to have our Princess returned to us."

Larissa ignored the praise. A loud gong rang out through the hall.

"Ah, it is time." King Torsten's voice boomed over the noise of the crowd. "The coronation will now commence in the Hall of *Konungr*."

At his words, the crowd spilled toward the opened doors, pouring out of the ballroom. Halvor approached the king's side, drawing him into a conversation. In the commotion, Brother Gorthr leaned toward Larissa. "Your Highness, you must not keep the Norn waiting any longer."

Larissa stepped away as though his words had burned, but Brother Gorthr was already gone, carried away in the tide of the crowd. Darien leaned toward her. "What did he say?"

Torsten patted Halvor on the shoulder, turning once more to Larissa. "Let us move on to the Hall."

Larissa shot Darien an apologetic look. She would explain later. Larissa couldn't worry about Brother Gorthr or the Norn right then. As the gong rang out again, it summoned her. Her people were waiting for their Queen.

27

Uninvited Guests

Anara

Anara's line of guests had been much shorter than Larissa's. Shorter than any of the other monarchs' lines, in fact. Few dared to speak one-on-one with the Crown Princess of all shifters. Sitting in the banquet hall only reminded Anara of why she preferred her years of solitude to the regality of royal life. There were advantages, however, to being least liked. With all eyes on Darien and Larissa dancing, Anara escaped onto one of the various outside balconies. She breathed in the night air, resisting the urge to shift into a raven and feel the freedom rustle through her silky feathers.

Inevitably, her peace did not last long.

"They'll never accept us." General Ishaan stood at the door, half-concealed by shadow. The ruby on his thumb shimmered as it caught the light from inside. "No matter what we do for them, we'll always be shifters."

"People fear what they don't understand," she responded with more confidence than she felt. "Eventually, they'll understand; then, they won't fear."

He scoffed. "Do you really believe that, or is that just what you tell yourself as you risk your life for every ungrateful person in that room?"

Anara ignored him.

"Doesn't it bother you?" he hissed. "You've given everything for them to have their kingdom back, and they hate you for who you are."

"Not all of them," Anara said.

"You're the Crown Princess of the Rubinians. Why do you spend all of your time serving Lovisa? Why won't you fight for *our* kingdom? *Our* people?"

"You're right; I *am* the Crown Princess. What makes you think you have any right to speak to me this way, *General*?"

He bowed stiffly. "I was trained to serve under your father, to advise him and then you when your time came."

But Anara didn't want to talk about her father. "What about you, Ishaan? Why do you serve King Torsten?"

Ishaan shrugged. "Power. Status. Revenge against Shiko. Same as you."

"Not the same as me," Anara snapped. "I don't serve anyone; Lovisa is my friend. One day, I will fight for my kingdom."

"When?"

"When our debts are paid."

He bared his teeth. "Rubin wasn't the only kingdom to willingly serve Shiko. Smaragd—"

"Smaragd surrendered and lay down for Shiko to trample over like we all knew they would, but Rubin?" Anara scoffed. "We were the strongest. We were the most courageous, and apparently, we were also the most prideful. If any kingdom stood a chance against Shiko, it was Rubin, but our people gave that up and leapt at a chance for more power, and look what it did to them!"

Ishaan's lined face was stone cold. "Would you have your people pay for that mistake forever?

"My people," Anara spat, "twisted their bodies—their souls—to serve the Empress. Rubin will be the last commonwealth to be reclaimed after we pay for the consequences of their sins."

"And of those innocent within the city?"

Anara gritted her teeth. This was always Ishaan's final barb. "What would you have me do? I can't reclaim Rubin on my own; we need allies—"

Anara's head snapped toward the balcony door at the faint scent of rotting flesh. She growled deep in her chest.

Ishaan stood alert. "What is it?"

Anara pushed through the double glass doors. Inside the banquet hall, the crowds were emptying into the corridor that would lead them to the Hall of *Konungr* for Larissa's coronation ceremony. A familiar tickle ran across Anara's skin as the transformation morphed her nose into a snout. She sniffed the air, but the smell was gone, as if it had never existed in the first place. Only the strong scent of burning incense remained.

Ishaan stood next to her, a similar look of frustration on his face. "Did you smell something?"

"Anara! There you are; we're about to start!" Darien waved her down as he approached, but his hand froze in the air. "What's wrong?"

"I smelled a *draugr* outside, but the scent is gone," Anara answered, cutting off Ishaan's exclamation. "We should join the others in the Hall."

Darien's hand wrapped around the hilt of his sword. "We need to tell Larissa and my father."

"And stop the coronation?" she asked as trumpets sounded from the other room. "What would that accomplish? It's better if we continue as planned and watch for the *draugr*, if it's still here at all. It might already have left to report to Shiko."

Anara walked briskly across the ballroom floor and down the halls, wishing she had worn something with more traction than satin slippers. No matter. If it came down to a fight, she wouldn't remain in those slippers for long. Larissa waited for them in a back room nestled behind the Hall of *Konungr*, looking up in relief while Torsten scowled at their disheveled appearance.

"Where have you been?" Torsten waved his hand. "Never mind. The two of you, get into your places. General Ishaan, please take your place."

Ishaan nodded, but as he passed, he whispered low enough that only Anara would hear. "I'll see what I can smell."

Darien stared hard at Anara, his insistent look prompting her to explain to the others.

"Is everything alright?" Larissa asked.

"Anara smelled a *draugr* in the ballroom," Darien answered, his arms crossed.

"Subtle, Darien," Anara muttered, then, in a louder voice, "It was gone before I could investigate further."

"You think you smelled a *draugr*?" King Torsten demanded. "Here?"

Larissa's eyes widened; her fists clenched the golden fabric at her thighs. "Halla. She's in the crowd. I have to go to her."

"No," Torsten argued, his hand grabbing her arm. "We are about to begin the coronation. There may not be a *draugr* here at all."

"And if there is?" Larissa shot back, yanking her arm from his grasp. "That's my sister out there!"

"And this is your kingdom, your people," Torsten hissed. "*If* there is a *draugr*, then its main purpose is surely to spy and report back to Shiko, making it even more important that we solidify your claim to the throne as soon as possible."

"He's right," Anara cut in. "Ishaan is already in the crowd hunting. Darien and I will watch the crowd from the stage. We'll keep Halla close, Larissa."

Though she still looked poised to run, Larissa asked, "You'll protect her?"

"With our lives," Darien promised, ignoring the look his father sent him.

Larissa lifted her skirts in her hands. "Then let's get out there."

Inhaling deeply, Anara led the way out of the back room and onto the stage that had been prepared. The long hall was overflowing with an audience. Though the pews were packed, even more people crowded the side aisles and stood in the back of the room. They spoke in loud whispers that only grew in excitement at the sight of Anara and Darien. Their voices echoed off the high stone ceilings and marbled floors. Anara took her place on the left of the throne, her eyes scanning the crowd.

Ishaan prowled along the perimeter of the population, but he shook his head when he spotted Anara's questioning glance. Darien took his spot on the right side of the stage, merely a foot away from where Halla and Kai sat in the front row of the Hall. He leaned down and motioned to Halla to whisper in her ears. Though Anara couldn't hear his words over the crowd, she watched the color drain from Halla's face, causing the girl's freckles to stand out in sharp relief. Kai's frown deepened as he looked around the room, yet there was no fear in his face, only apprehension. Anara had sympathized with him from the start, recognizing the way people looked at him in distaste, but his bravery made her like him even more.

Already waiting center stage was Halvor, who held the crown of Perle in his hands, having found it in one of Hammon's vast treasuries. The delicate gold band was interwoven in braids and accentuated with pearls that glistened like raindrops. Behind Halvor, General Soren stood, proudly carrying a bowl of liquid kohl in a ceramic bowl.

As the door to the back room opened again, the entirety of the crowd silenced. King Torsten entered first, a gold crown embedded with sapphire stones resting on his head. At the sight of the King, the crowd rose to their feet. Then came Larissa.

Her eyes darted around the room, resting on Halla, who beamed at the sight of her sister. Larissa looked to Anara, but Anara only shook her head in response to Larissa's raised brows. There was no trace of the scent in the room. Reassured, Larissa strode toward the center stage. Larissa's golden dress swirled around her legs as she knelt before General Soren.

The old Perlian dipped two fingers into the kohl before dragging a finger down the center of Larissa's face, starting at her forehead and ending just at the brow. Then came another line of paint from her lower lip to her chin. A horizontal bar across the bridge of her nose and cheeks joined the rest. As Soren continued his design, he spoke in the ancient language of a people long dead. Few beyond the royalty knew of the language, fewer understood it, but Anara remembered her lessons well.

As General Soren listed the duties of the Crown, he wound oaths that would bound Larissa to her people. It was a contract between the Queen and her citizens, as binding as any marriage, a covenant of servitude and protection.

Pride swelled in Anara's heart, pushing out the anxiety and frustrations that had lived there for so long. As children, Lovisa and Anara had played many pretend games in which Lovisa was finally able to claim her title, but they had never imagined it would be like this. It felt wrong somehow, to continue forward without the Tapestry of Peace. Generations of monarchs had woven their lineage into the enormous tapestry before Shiko had destroyed it on the night of her betrayal, and no mortal could duplicate what the Norn had fashioned.

With the facial design finished and the ancient oaths recited, General Soren stepped back, allowing King Torsten to take his place.

"Princess Lovisa of Perle, do you swear to protect the people of this land?"

Anara watched Larissa's throat constrict as she gulped before answering. "I do."

"Do you swear to put the needs of your people before your own?"

Her eyes darted to Darien. "I do."

"Do you swear to maintain and uphold order and prosperity within Perle?"

"I do."

Torsten beckoned Halvor forward, removing the crown from where it sat on its cushion. "And do you, Princess Lovisa, swear to fight against the False Empress for the sake of your people until she is removed from power?"

Anara stiffened. The very blood in her veins rebelled against the rotten smell that leaked into the air. Before Larissa could respond, a cackle broke the tension, so violent that it shattered the reverent silence as if it were glass. The sound echoed off the cathedral walls, bouncing off the high ceilings, but Anara had no difficulty locating its source.

A woman stood in the middle of the crowd, a blue gown cascading around her legs. Although her head was bowed, her shoulders trembled with every laugh that hissed through her lips. Stinging tingles raced over Anara's skin in preparation for the change that it knew was coming. Darien descended the stage, his sword drawn, his body shielding Halla's. Larissa rose to her feet.

The woman raised her head, locking her manic gaze on Larissa. There was no color in her pupilless eyes.

"The Empress knows what you have done." At the sound of her raspy voice, the crowd cowered in fear. The woman screeched in a painful imitation of a laugh. Someone whimpered.

A hawk dove toward the woman's neck, its sharp beak only an inch from her soft skin before the woman's hand shot up. But it was not a hand at all; rather a black, scaled claw dug its nails into Ishaan's wing. "I have no quarrel with you, brother; be gone."

With an effortless fling of her hand, the body of the hawk thumped against the castle wall.

Screams rose from the crowd as hundreds of spectators fled, pushing at one another, trampling each other in their desperation to flee. In the middle of the room, the woman's body broke, bending over backward as scales covered her skin and horns sprouted from her head.

"Loki's knot," Anara cursed.

She leapt from the stage, her body transforming mid-jump, and landed on all four paws. The *draugr* straightened its body, towering over those who stood too close. Wings sprouted from its back, clipping those who had been unable to escape in time, splattering the ground with blood. Before it could attack further, Anara threw herself at the *draugr*, her large claws catching on its scales, rolling with it to the floor, pinning it beneath her enormous body.

The monster screeched, and Anara's ears flattened against her head in her best attempt to block out its debilitating effects. It took one look at Anara, its eyes narrowing in distaste.

"Your Highness." The *draugr*'s words were distorted by the shape of its lolling tongue. "*You* I have a quarrel with. You're supposed to be dead!"

The force of its push was enough to fling Anara into one of the side pews. The *draugr* rose, swiping a claw toward Anara's underbelly where her scar was still noticeably visible. A hair's breadth from contact, the *draugr* froze, its claws suspended in the air. The creature's eyes widened in disbelief as they locked onto Larissa, who stood at the end of the aisle, her hands held out toward the *draugr* as golden light sparked between her fingers.

Already sweat beaded on Larissa's brow; she would not be able to hold the creature forever. Anara regained her footing, backing out of reach; her stomach clenched remembering the last time sharp claws had torn it open.

"You never should have returned, little Princess," the monster taunted Larissa, a shudder running through its massive wings. "You can't hold me forever."

"She doesn't have to." Darien edged toward the monster, his sword drawn.

Anara padded on large, silent paws, paralleling Darien's steps so that he advanced the front of the *draugr* while she approached from behind. Although the *draugr*'s body remained fixed in place by Larissa's *galdr*, its eyes followed Anara as long as possible, snarls rising from its lips. Anara's gaze locked on Darien, who nodded in her direction. They would attack together while Larissa kept the monster immobilized.

"Wait," came the command.

King Torsten stood at the base of the coronation stage. Although the hall had nearly emptied apart from the soldiers who stood at the exits to ensure that the creature could not escape, General Soren and Halvor had remained at the King's side. Torsten strode down the aisle, his own weapon drawn.

"Why did she send you?" King Torsten demanded. "Shiko would have known you couldn't succeed on your own. What is her message?"

"Succeed?" The monster cackled. "I have succeeded; look at what has become of your precious coronation. As for her message, she has none. My Empress does not lower herself to deal with the scum. I was not sent by her. I was sent by *him*."

King Torsten paled.

A beat passed before Darien spoke up. "*Calder* sent you?"

The *draugr* bared its teeth in a poor resemblance of a smile at the sound of Larissa's gasp. "Your brother says hello."

Anara sensed the moment the *draugr* broke from Larissa's hold. It pounced from where it stood, its sharp claws making quick work of throwing Halvor and Soren from its path. Their bodies crumpled to heaps in the aisles. The soldiers nearest rushed to their sides, checking the slight rise and fall of their chests—the only sign of life. Several more surrounded Torsten, who only raised his sword to block the *draugr*'s attack.

Darien and Anara leapt into the fray, each attacking the sinews that connected a wing to the *draugr*'s body. Anara snapped her powerful jaws on the joint. The King parried each swipe of the creature's claws with his own sword, and the sound of its nails scratching the blade sent shudders down Anara's fur. As she choked on bitter blood, Anara gave one last tug and ripped the wing from the monster's back. At the same time, Darien sliced through the other wing.

The screech that fled the *draugr*'s throat sent Anara to the floor. She pressed her massive paws against her ears, whimpering against the sound that ricocheted in her brain. King Torsten and Darien cradled their heads in their hands, kneeling on the ground. Just to the side of the stage, Kai leaned over Halla, his hands covering her ears. Soldiers writhed from the pain of it.

Where was Larissa?

A gunshot rang out, silencing the screech as the *draugr* clawed at the hole in its neck.

Larissa stood on the stage, one of the guard's guns held firmly in her hands. Sensing his chance, King Torsten rose, swinging his sword in a sharp arc as the *draugr* fell to its knees. The blade swept cleanly through muscle and bone, decapitating the creature before the light in its eyes had died.

Shuddering, Anara released her hold on her *galdr*, willing her form to return to normal. She tried not to look at the creature at her feet, tried not to think of the person, the woman, the Rubinian it had once been. Or the fact that her own people wanted her dead. Or how her stomach ached with pain that would not go away.

She stepped over the broken and bloody wing, scanning the destruction and catching her reflection in the crown that lay at Larissa's feet.

As if feeling Anara's gaze, Larissa scooped up the crown. Her lips twisted as she descended from the stage. Grasping Halla, she pulled her sister tightly against her chest before approaching Torsten and Darien. Soldiers worked on reviving Halvor and General Soren. Even Ishaan, having returned to his human form, limped toward them and ignored the blood dripping down from the wound in his head. His face twisted in disgust when he saw the dead creature.

Torsten covered his nose. "How did it mask its smell?"

Ishaan knelt, pulling something from the creature's neck that Anara had missed during the fight. It was a thin black chain. A pendant hung on it, engraved with sharp lines unlike any Anara had seen in her studies. The faint smell of incense clung to it. Ishaan handed it to Anara. "I'm assuming this had something to do with it."

"If Shiko has a new way of masking her assassins, we'll need to counter it." Anara scratched at the metal, but it revealed no secrets. "Though this may have more to do with Calder than the Empress."

Larissa handed the crown back to Torsten, never letting go of Halla or the gun in her other hand. "Either way, if Calder is back, the coronation will have to wait."

28

Flight

Larissa

Within hours, the palace had been locked down, the guests sent home, and the city scoured and secured. The guards who had heard of Calder's identity were sworn to secrecy. While Halvor and General Soren were sent to the physicians to check for any lasting damage, Ishaan had refused treatment.

"Someone needs to make sure the *draugr* was alone," was all Ishaan said before leaving the palace.

King Torsten, Larissa, Darien, Anara, and Halla gathered in another chamber to discuss the corrupt Prince. Torsten attempted to dismiss Halla, but Larissa was adamant in refusing him. She would not let Halla out of her sight, not now, but she was surprised that Torsten either didn't notice or chose not to acknowledge Halla's shadow as Kai followed her into the room.

Larissa didn't wait for Torsten to speak. "I have to leave."

Darien may have inherited Torsten's eyes, but Torsten had retained all of his stubbornness and suspicion. "Explain yourself."

"The Norn have sent me dreams. Not just me, but Darien and Anara too. They're calling me to them, and in return, they'll tell me the full prophecy of how to defeat Shiko."

Torsten's clasped hands tightened as he shot his son a questioning glance. Apparently, Darien had not told him about the dreams. Torsten glared at Larissa. "You would leave your people right after reclaiming your kingdom and without your crown?"

"My people are safe. I'll appoint General Soren as Regent during my leave. The Viðnám is more motivated than ever to advance east to Safír. I've done what you asked of me. I've upheld my end of the bargain, and I'll keep fighting with the Viðnám, but what is the point of us reclaiming the kingdoms if I don't know how to defeat Shiko?"

He sighed deeply. "I suppose in a few weeks, after we reclaim Safír—"

"That won't work," Larissa argued. "Verðandi told me to start in Smaragd. I have to get there before Calder or Shiko send reinforcements from the North and block my path."

"If the Norn told you to go to Smaragd, we'll go there after Safír, but you are needed here with the Viðnám. My answer is no. You must wait until the timing is right."

Larissa crossed her arms, her skin rubbing against the smooth satin of her gown that she had not yet had time to change. "I'm not asking for your permission, I'm making you aware of my decision."

His eyes narrowed in anger.

Trying to hold onto some semblance of respect, Larissa said, "I'm not your subject, Torsten. When it comes to the Viðnám, I'll yield to your authority every time, but this is about me. The Norn are the ones who gave Rúna the prophecy that started this whole mess. We can't hope to succeed without that knowledge. Calder's *draugr* already invaded our safety only days after re-claiming Perle! We need more information."

"Faðir, Larissa is right," Darien interjected. "We have to go."

Anger pulled Torsten's brows down over lowered eyes. "I might be able to concede that *Lovisa* must go and speak to the Norn, but *you* and Anara are needed here. I will send a host of guards to accompany her. Besides, Lovisa proved tonight that she can defend herself." It would have sounded like a compliment if not for Torsten's patronizing tone.

"And leave her at Calder's mercy?" Anara scoffed. "What if he's waiting for her on the road? You know Larissa is our most important asset in removing Shiko from power."

"Which is why she should stay here until we can bring the force of the Viðnám behind her."

"But she is also being summoned by the Norn," Anara continued. "That can't be ignored."

"She's not the only one being summoned," Darien's voice was as unyielding as his father's. "We have to go with her. The Norn have sent us the dreams as well."

Father and son stared at one another, a silent yet visible battle clear in their eyes. Larissa tried to ignore the pang of guilt that built in her stomach. It wasn't her fault the Norn continued to plague her with dreams, or that her mother hadn't told her more of the prophecy in her youth. It wasn't her fault that she had to leave her people—again. Or that Calder's presence and the Norn's insistence necessitated Darien and Anara's accompaniment. And yet, she hated the tension between Darien and his father.

"This is your choice, then?" King Torsten asked, his voice tight with anger. "You will choose her over your own people? Again?"

"I'm choosing *both*," Darien said. "Our people deserve to be free, but what about what Larissa said? Why free them if we can't guarantee this freedom? Let us go to the Norn. We'll get our answers and meet you at Safír. We'll reclaim our kingdom with the knowledge to actually keep it safe."

Pride swelled in Larissa's heart. Darien had never wanted the throne, but Larissa could see the beginnings of a just ruler in him, as long as he was given time. Even if that meant there would be no future for them. Larissa refused to allow her mind to travel that road any further. Instead, she focused on the way Torsten analyzed his son, confident that he would see the wisdom in Darien's words when he would not accept them from her.

King Torsten sighed. "The Norn returned the wrong son."

An audible gasp escaped Larissa's lips at the same time a growl ripped from Anara's chest. Halla, who had slumped over in her seat, straightened, her eyes widened in alarm. The only emotion on Kai's face could be found in his raised eyebrows.

Darien breathed slowly, nodding his head as though he'd expected nothing else. "I returned myself. And in case you forgot, Aeron made his choice. I may not be the son that you wish was standing before you, but I'm all you have left."

"I can't order Lovisa or Anara to remain, but I am your father and King. You are not to leave."

Larissa rose from her seat before Darien's rebellious look could give him away. "Then there is nothing left to say, King Torsten."

Larissa led Halla into the hallway, accompanied by Anara and Kai. Through the open door, Larissa watched as Darien moved toward his father, as though he would say something; then, the heavy door swung shut, blocking him from her view. Would he try to convince his father or had he seen the futility in such actions?

"Lara, are you okay?" Halla touched her arm. "You're shaking."

Larissa didn't answer, couldn't answer. She wasn't afraid. She was angry, obvious by the way her *galdr* burned her insides and snapped between her fingers in short bursts of static energy. She said nothing but pulled her arm away, careful not to let her *galdr* hurt Halla as it had once before. The group made their way in absolute silence to Larissa's room.

Outside the door, Anara pulled on Kai's shoulder. "Let's give the sisters a moment."

From the look in Anara's eyes, it was clear she knew exactly what Larissa planned to do. Larissa nodded in appreciation, closing the door behind her and Halla. She yanked the dress from her body, letting the gown cascade to the floor in a rumpled heap. In no time at all, Larissa washed the paint from her face, dressed in the clothes she'd used to sneak into Perle, and replaced her satin slippers with worn-out work boots. Halla fluttered around her, looking more like a fairy than ever.

"So, what's the plan?"

"I'm answering the Norn's call." Larissa shoved her gun into the holster at her side and started undoing the intricate braids around her face. "You need to stay here where it's safe."

"So safe that a *draugr* attacked us?" Halla crossed her arms. "Besides, you're not the only one the Norn are calling."

Larissa's fingers froze in her hair. "What?"

Halla removed her own lavender gown and changed into something less conspicuous. Her slow movements grated against Larissa's taut nerves, but Halla seemed to be working up the courage to tell her something.

"I didn't tell you, because I didn't know how you'd react. When they—burned—me . . ." Halla stumbled over the words. "Verðandi was the one who took away the pain. She told me to come to her and that you would know how to find her."

Larissa sank to her bed, groaning into her hands. Taking Halla was *not* part of her plan.

"Halla, Smaragd is under Shiko's control. I know nothing of the Regent there. I could be leading you straight into danger."

"We shouldn't be separated. Bad things happen when we're separated." Halla bent down to retrieve a jacket from the ground, and Larissa's throat clogged at the sight of the scar at the base of her neck.

A soft knock at the door was followed by Anara sliding through the small gap. She raised an eyebrow at the bickering sisters. "So, we're still going then?"

"I'm not going to sit here and do what Torsten tells me when the Norn have the answers."

"Never doubted you for a minute." Anara revealed the two bags slung across her back. Clearly, she'd done more than wait in the hall. She grabbed the empty bag and tossed it to Larissa, who only just managed to catch it. "Put your stuff in there."

Larissa shoved in extra clothes. "Then why were you so quiet with Torsten? Why—?"

"—didn't I say anything?" Anara finished for Larissa. "I knew there was no point in arguing with him when we were going to do what needed to be done."

"Better to ask forgiveness than permission?" Halla offered.

Anara grinned. "I don't really ask for either."

Halla glanced at the door. "Where's Kai?"

"Grabbing his own bag; I figured you'd be coming with us and would want him to come along too."

Halla threw herself around Anara's waist, but only Larissa noticed how Anara winced, touching her stomach when Halla let go. Minutes trickled by as Larissa packed the bag with clothes for herself and Halla. Her gaze slid to the door more often than she'd care to admit, wondering if Darien was still with his father.

Someone knocked, and the door opened. Kai stepped in with a bag slung over his shoulder. As though uncomfortable with the stares in his direction, he closed the door and leaned against the shadows on the wall.

"Now we wait for Darien," Anara said.

"How will he know where to find us?" Halla asked.

Anara looked at Larissa. "He'll look for Larissa."

They didn't wait much longer before there was a knock at the door again. Darien had changed out of his finery. He strapped his sword and gun to his dark gear, clothes meant for movement.

His presence alone was a balm to Larissa's anxiety. "Darien! I didn't know if Torsten would let you come."

"I told him I wouldn't." His eyes held hers with palpable intensity. "But nothing could keep me from going with you, Lov."

Kai leaned toward Halla and whispered, "Didn't you say they're supposed to be some kind of secret? They're pretty obvious."

"Only to anyone with eyes." Anara's dry remark let Kai know he wasn't as quiet as he thought.

Another knock sounded at the door. Darien laid his hand on his sword, but Anara rose, swaggering to the door. "Relax, I sent a message to arrange our departure."

Astonishment flooded Larissa to see Jari standing on the other side of the opened door. He bowed to Anara. "It's ready. Bay Three. We'll take your bags. You're too noticeable with them."

Grabbing the bag from Anara, Jari handed it over to Haki, who waited at his side. As if noting the confused looks, Anara explained, "I asked Jari and Haki to prepare a truck for us. We'll be out of the city before Torsten knows we're gone."

"Do you really think he'd try to stop us?" Larissa asked.

Anara side-eyed Darien. "He might try to stop some of us."

"Don't walk as a group or all at once," Jari warned. "There's too many of you."

"Jari," Larissa called before he could leave. "Thank you. I know what it looks like, that I'm leaving my people. Again . . ."

His eyes met hers and he bowed, not the forced movements he'd made before, but a genuine bow that caught Larissa by surprise. "You kept your word, Princess. You freed your people. I believe you will come back."

His belief was a promise in Larissa's heart, a vow that she would not, could not break. She would come back. The twins left without another word, though Haki smiled at her even buried beneath their bags.

"I'll take Halla and Kai with me," Anara said. "Give us five minutes, then follow us down to the bays. Take the servants' stairs in case Torsten goes looking for Darien."

Then they were gone.

Awkwardness pervaded the room as Larissa watched Darien rock on his heels. She moved toward him, conscious of the anger he was trying to hide.

She laid her hand on his arm. "Your father was wrong to say what he did."

"Is he?" he muttered. "Look at everything he's accomplished. He survived Shiko's execution of the royal families. When he thought he'd lost his entire family, he didn't break—he founded the Viðnám. He's been undermining Shiko every day. If my father thinks I am the wrong son to have returned, then I am."

"No, you're not," Larissa grabbed his arm more tightly. "Your father *did* break. Look at him, Darien. He's not the same; he had to become someone different to survive, just like we did. But this person he's become can't recognize how incredible you are. Don't you doubt yourself, Prince Darien of Safír."

As though drawn by an irresistible force, Darien closed the gap between them, wrapping his arms around her. It had been days since their night watching the stars, but Larissa fell back into that moment as easily as if she had never left. She wanted to tell Darien that he didn't need to come with her, that he could stay with his father and serve his people, but she was terrified that if she said so, he would do it. And she wanted him to be with her.

"Thank you for coming with me," was all she could say.

"Of course, but Larissa . . ."

Her heart sputtered at the way his voice trailed off. "Yes?"

"I'll get you to the Norn safely, but if you have to stay there, if there's another obstacle—" He struggled to find the words. "My people need me like yours do. My father will march on Safír in a week. I have to be there. I have to be a part of it. If I really am going to rule one day, I could never look my people in the eyes if I hadn't been a part of their liberation."

Larissa swallowed, understanding every word he said. Darien was hers, but only for a time. Then he would go. He would have to go.

She stepped back. "After the Norn explain the prophecy, I'll go with you to Safír. I want to help you like you've always helped me. But if I can't, if you have to leave, I understand." She couldn't distract him from his responsibilities.

No distractions. Her words came back like a slap in the face.

Darien nodded, more to himself than to her. "It all depends on the Norn, doesn't it? Does it ever feel like they're playing a game and we're just the pieces?"

"More and more each day."

Darien reached back, pulling up his large hood and shading his face. Larissa mirrored his movement. He tugged the right side, shielding her scar. "We should go. It's probably been long enough."

But Larissa moved to the desk in her room, rummaging through the drawers until she found a piece of paper and a pencil. Quickly, she drafted the note leaving General Soren as acting Regent over Perle while she was gone. At least this way, Torsten's hold over Perle would be influenced by one of their own even in Larissa's absence.

"Okay, I'm ready."

As Larissa followed Darien down the halls that led to the servants' stairs, memories assailed her in waves. They'd done this before, she realized. Escaped hand in hand down the stairs, past the servants' confused looks. Only then, they'd been escaping lessons and lectures, off to find Anara and Aeron to lounge by the lake or stroll through the city. How time had changed everything.

The last set of stairs exited out the side of the palace. They only had to cross the expansive grounds to reach the royal mews, stables that had been renovated over time to stall not horses but the royal vehicles. In the third bay, Anara waited in the driver's seat while Halla and Kai leaned out the sides of the truck bed. Larissa could have laughed at the sight of the familiar rusted blue pickup.

As Anara turned the key, Helga greeted Larissa with a loud grumble. Larissa ran her hand along the passenger door's peeling paint. She pulled herself up, scooting in next to Anara to make room for Darien. "How?"

Anara shifted Helga into gear. "Apparently the Viðnám brought her to Perle; she was too old to be of use in the battle. Haki thought you might like to see her again; plus, no one would expect the Princess of Perle to be in this old contraption."

"Don't worry." Larissa rubbed the dash, feeling Helga's familiar vibration under her hand. "She'll get us where we need to go."

29

A Plan, Sort Of

Darien

THE LATE EVENING DRONED on as Darien followed Anara's feathered shape in the sky, yet his soul still warred within him.

The Norn returned the wrong son.

Shame so potent it was nearly physical burned his skin, and underneath that was the lingering fear that his father's forgiveness had run dry. Perhaps this decision would be the final blow to their already shattered relationship. With every mile Darien drove further from Perle, the guilt settled more deeply in his stomach. He could hear his father railing at him for abandoning his people because of Lovisa. His father would never understand that it was only in watching Larissa rally her people that Darien had realized his own desire to champion *his* people. His father's impossible standards would never have convinced him of Safír's need, but Larissa's example and selflessness had.

Ever since Larissa had reclaimed Perle, Darien had dreamed of Safír, of her sandy beaches and sparkling horizons. The smell of the Safírian ocean shoreline wafted through his memories, stirring his longing to turn around and drive straight home. He could nearly taste the whitebait fish he and his mother would fry on lazy days.

Fond memories mingled with the plans he had for Safír's future. Darien would reclaim his commonwealth and restore it to the kingdom it once was. Then he would stand at the cliffside upon which his palace stood and watch the waves crash against the rocks below, letting the sound of the ocean fill him with peace. His father would stand beside him, finally pleased, maybe even settle his hand on Darien's shoulder and look at him the same way he'd look at Aeron. With pride, instead of displeasure.

So strong was the image in his mind that Darien could nearly smell the salt of the shoreline that lay miles away. In the passenger seat, Larissa shifted in her sleep, drawing Darien back to the present. She'd shoved her jacket up against the window as a makeshift pillow, muttering something about asking the Norn for directions. Strands of white hair fluttered in her soft exhales. The vulnerability in her face was enough to undermine Darien's composure. He understood now what she meant about no distractions, about how their focus needed to be on their people. He even agreed to a certain extent, yet here he was, driving away from his kingdom.

For her.

He reminded himself there was no point in reclaiming any of the commonwealths if they could not ultimately overthrow Shiko. But that was only part of Darien's reasoning.

Life had been easier when he'd only cared about Larissa, when the fate of his people hadn't rested on his shoulders. He'd been so shielded by Aeron's presence, who thrived under the weight of their father's expectations. Darien nearly wished that Aeron was there but recanted the thought immediately. There was no Aeron, only Calder, and the longer Calder believed they were in Perle, the safer they would remain.

Calder. His blood simmered at the thought of the brother his father wished he would be. Darien's fingers tightened around the wheel as he forced his foot to hold even on the gas. It would do no good to take out his frustrations on Helga. The old girl probably would break down in protest. Plus, any sudden increase in speed was sure to rock Halla and Kai where they sat in the bed of the truck.

Larissa stirred, muttering incomprehensibly in her sleep. Her eyes fluttered open and caught Darien staring at her. Even with her hair plastered to one side of her face, she looked beautiful.

She stretched, cracking her neck. "How long was I asleep?"

"A couple of hours. The Norn have anything to say?"

Larissa nodded. "She told me to speak with Kiah."

Darien blew out a sharp breath. "Kiah's alive?"

Older than the other royal offspring of their generation, Princess Kiah of the Smaragd kingdom hadn't truly been a part of their intimate group, but she'd been friendly enough. Kiah had been expecting her first child just as Shiko plunged their nation into war. It was Kiah who had written to Aeron begging for assistance in the Smaragd kingdom. When word had come that Aeron was dead due to Smaragd's surrender, Darien had always assumed that Shiko had killed Kiah and her unborn child as well. It appeared he was wrong.

"Verðandi said Kiah can show us how to reach her."

"Do you think Anara knew that Kiah was alive?" Darien asked.

"Let's find out."

Darien honked the horn loudly enough for Anara to notice, then pulled the truck over, noticing that the trees around him had grown thicker and larger. They must be nearing the Myrkviðr Forest, which marked the border between Perle and Smaragd.

Banging resounded against the cab's ceiling, and Halla's voice came through the open window from the truck bed. "Are we stopping here?"

Larissa leaned out the passenger window. "Not yet, sit tight!"

Anara glided down, shifting in midair and landing on her feet beside the driver's open window.

Darien wasted no time. "You knew Kiah was alive?"

As they always did when discussing Smaragd, Anara's lips tightened. "Yes."

"And you didn't tell us?" Larissa asked.

"There's been a lot going on; it didn't matter that the coward princess survived."

Larissa sighed in exasperation. "Well, it matters now. The Norn want us to see her."

Anara swore. "You can't be serious. It's bad enough to go to Smaragd at all—Shiko's sentries will be everywhere. But to go into the heart of the city itself?" She rubbed at her temple. "The gods and their games."

"Why though?" Darien asked. "Do they want us to get caught?"

"It would make their game more interesting, wouldn't it? But no." Anara sighed. "The Myrkviðr Forest has always had its connections to the Norn, and no one knows these trees better than Kiah. It's only . . ."

"What?" Darien prompted as Anara's voice drifted.

"Verðandi visited my dreams the night before we took back Perle."

"That's why you weren't surprised when I told you we had to go to Smaragd," Larissa interrupted.

"Right, but in my dreams, she said to trust *him*, not her."

"Him who?" Darien asked.

Anara growled. "If I knew, we wouldn't be having this conversation; I'd have already found him and gotten my answers. We'll start with Kiah and figure it out from there."

"But how are we going to speak with her?" Larissa asked. "We don't even know where she is. What if she's in prison? Finding her could take days."

"No, it won't." Anara hesitated. "She's the Regent of Smaragd."

"What?" The word escaped Darien's lips before he could pull it back. The last he'd heard, Shiko had slaughtered the entire Smaragdian royal bloodline.

Anara's fingers rubbed slow circles in her temples. "Look, let's find a place to stop tonight and figure out our plan. We can't just stay parked on the side of the main road. That's asking for trouble."

With a flurry of feathers, Anara was gone, circling back in the sky.

"Do you ever get the feeling that Anara doesn't like the Smaragdians?" Darien asked in mock innocence.

"What gave it away? Her look of disgust whenever they're mentioned?" Larissa answered in similar faked curiosity.

"I was thinking more about how she calls them cowardly every chance she gets."

Larissa's head fell back against the headrest. "This is just going to make it more complicated."

The pressure built behind Darien's eyes as he pulled onto the darkening road. It wasn't just the sun's descent that affected the light, but also the thick forest around them. Growing up, Darien had heard the stories of Myrkviðr Forest. Every mythical creature had its origins in the forest's soil and its birthplace in the Gadofass Falls. It was said that the very trees, rocks, and animals all emanated their own *vættir*, or spirit. One could never be too careful around still bodies of water or silent trees. While the loud trees were joyous, the quiet trees were angry.

"Myrkviðr Forest," Larissa muttered, wrapping her arms around her chest as she shifted away from the window.

"Sure, you can decapitate a *draugr* but you're scared of a few ghost stories."

Larissa rolled her eyes. "Like the forest doesn't give you the creeps."

Darien laughed, but he had to admit, there was something about the trees that unsettled him. Like an internal alarm alerting him to some danger that never came. "I'm sure Halla is loving this."

Larissa groaned. "She's still bitter she missed the home of the Jötnar."

"We'll take her back to the valley, after all this is over."

Larissa stilled, and Darien realized a moment too late why.

We'll.

The word held the implications of a future they might not have.

After a moment of silence, she asked, "Are we doing the right thing?"

Going to Smaragd? Leaving Perle? Suppressing their feelings for one another? Darien wasn't sure which she meant. He took the safest option. "The Norn know the prophecy. Your people are safe with General Soren, and we'll return to my people soon. We can't help them if we don't know what we're up against. Knowledge is power."

She pulled her knees up to her chest. "I know; you're right."

"Tell me a story."

As Darien had intended, shock chased the melancholy from Larissa's face. "What?"

"You always knew the best stories when we were kids. I've been driving all day, and I need help staying awake."

She crossed her arms and smirked. "The constant threat of capture and execution doesn't do the trick for you?"

He grinned for a second and shrugged. "After so long, it becomes the same-old-same-old. Come on, Lov, please?"

She softened, as she always did when he used her old nickname. "You know all of my stories."

"What about something Dal taught you?"

Larissa hesitated. Darien kicked himself mentally for bringing up her deceased adoptive father.

"Okay," she said finally. "I know one. Do you see that constellation over to the right?"

He located the cluster of five stars barely visible in the dimming light. "Yes."

"That is Aurvandil the Valiant. Dal called him the saddest of the stars. Aurvandil left his wife to help a friend on a quest, but on the way home, he fell into the icy river. Unable to save Aurvandil, his friend returned to Aurvandil's wife and told her that Aurvandil chose not to pass into the afterlife. Instead, he became a star so that he might watch over her for the rest of her days. She was comforted every time she walked under the night sky, but when Aurvandil's wife died of old age and passed into the afterlife, Aurvandil remained in the sky. The lovers were forever separated."

After a beat of silence, Darien barked out a laugh. "Not *quite* what I was thinking when I asked for a story. Would it kill you to share one with a happy ending?"

She threw her hands in the air in exasperation. "Tell your own story, then! It's the gods; none of their stories have happy endings!" But her own laughter let him know she wasn't serious.

Darien's eyes grew heavier as the shadows lengthened across the road. He hoped Anara would find a place to stop soon.

Larissa's fingers played with the edge of her sleeve. "Do you think Halla is okay back there with Kai?"

Darien's eyes caught on the rear view mirror. He could catch a glimpse of Halla leaning on the side of the truck bed, staring into the forest around them. "Why wouldn't she be?"

"What do you think about him?"

"I don't really know him, besides the obvious."

"That he's from Diamant." Larissa's voice was too light, too forced.

"That bothers you?"

"Doesn't it bother you?" she asked.

"He isn't Shiko, Lara."

"I know." Frustration crept into her voice. "But I see him, and I see *her*."

Shiko. The Empress. "That's hardly fair on him."

She slumped against the door frame. "I know; I'm working on it."

Anara cawed, catching a low draft of wind and drifting toward the side of the road. There was a slight gap between the thick line, but Darien could only go so far before the forest provided no allowance for Helga's bulky frame. Though the stretches of road between commonwealths were often abandoned, it would only take one sentry's vehicle to cause a spectacle. He could only hope they weren't looking too closely at the forest.

Larissa threw open her door before he'd come to a complete stop, no doubt wanting to stretch her legs. Darien moved more slowly, his body stiff from a day's worth of driving, and shoved open Helga's door, joining Anara and Larissa at the back of the truck bed where Halla and Kai waited for them.

Halla stared at Kai, her eyebrows pinched together in concern, but there wasn't time for Darien to investigate, Anara was already arguing with Larissa.

"—no," Larissa was saying. "There is no way you are going *alone* into Smaragd. What if something goes wrong? We'll never know."

"Larissa, I've done missions like this a hundred times before. Nothing will go wrong if it's just me. No one will even know I'm there."

Larissa snorted. "Except for Kiah. How did she become Regent anyhow? Shiko murdered her parents!"

"Kiah was given a choice," Anara said. "She swore her loyalty to the Empress and enslaved her people for her own survival."

"And her child's," added Kai.

They all turned to the boy, who had uttered the words seemingly without intending to be heard. He traced the grooves of the open tailgate, unwilling to meet even Halla's eyes.

But Darien's mind was already moving past this. "*Did* her child survive?"

"Apparently so." Anara waved a hand at the question. "No doubt he's just as spineless as the rest of his people."

Darien shared a look with Larissa. Smaragd and Rubin had never exactly agreed on their philosophies, but the war had only made their division more distinct. Darien hedged his next question carefully. "Anara, do you think you're the best person to go?"

"What's that supposed to mean?" Her words were deadly cool.

"Only, we need information from Kiah, and ideally, we're not planning to torture it out of her." When Anara didn't respond, Darien said more forcibly. "Because torture is *bad*, remember?"

Anara rolled her eyes but released her crossed arms. "Yes, yes, torture is bad." She examined her lengthening nails that curved into claws. "But a lot comes before torture."

"Anara!" Larissa cried in exasperation.

"Kidding! Mostly." Her nails shrank, but the mischievous grin remained on her face. "I'll get in and out with none but Kiah the wiser."

"She turned on her own people for her survival. What makes you think she won't turn on you?" Larissa asked.

"It's not a matter of loyalty. Kiah won't reveal my presence if she doesn't have to."

"Why, because you're so charming?" Darien asked.

"Because of her pacifism. She won't want to cause a scene or bring Shiko's attention to Smaragd. She'll give me what I want as long as I leave. She'll want my presence to remain a secret more than myself. She's Smaragdian."

Anara's words rang true, and although he didn't love the idea of her going in alone, it would be far less conspicuous than them traveling as a group. Larissa kicked a rock at the ground. "I still don't like it."

"We've got another half a day's worth of driving for you to come up with something else," Anara offered. "But if not, that's the plan. The sooner we're heading back to Safír to meet with the Viðnám, the better."

On that, Darien couldn't agree more.

"So, camp then?" Halla offered.

"I'd rather not," Larissa interrupted. "Anara's right, and without much tree cover here, we'd be better off to keep moving."

Darien resisted the urge to groan as the burn behind his eyes reminded him of his exhaustion. It would take driving through the night and then some to reach Smaragd.

Though he made no sound, Anara shot him a side glance. "You're dead tired. Larissa can drive. I can spot ahead, but my owl form won't hold as long as my raven. I'll have to rest more. We'll be taking a risk."

"We're taking a risk anyways," Kai muttered. Halla nudged him, looking more annoyed than perhaps his comment warranted.

Darien scratched at the scruff on his face, his mind ticking off their objectives one by one. Drive to Smaragd without being seen by sentries. Sneak Anara inside. Retrieve directions from Kiah. Find the Norn. Avoid alerting Calder to their location. Rendezvous with the Viðnám in Safír. Find a way to stay with Larissa. And then there was just the little complication of overthrowing an Empress who had demolished centuries of peace.

He let his hands drop in surrender. "Well, it's a plan. Not a good one, but we've had worse."

Larissa's lips turned up in a flash, and Darien wondered if she was thinking of the disastrous summer carnival of her thirteenth birthday too. He caught himself before he could speak again.

No distractions.

But as Larissa walked away, Darien's eyes trailed after her. He wasn't fooling anyone. Least of all himself.

30

Books and Weapons

BY THE TIME THE sun shone on Anara's wings, they'd entered the heart of Smaragd territory. The city of Treheim was only a few miles away. For a people whose ancestral *galdr* was the ability to heal, their decision to side with Shiko had harmed so many.

Anara swerved in the sky, directing Larissa to hide Helga in the close-knit trees on the side of the road. She dove through the branches and landed with a muffled thump in the back of the truck bed just as Helga came to a stop.

Though Kai jumped at her appearance, Halla smiled. "Anara! Finally, someone I can actually talk to."

Halla's words were clearly pointed at the dark-haired boy who refused to look her way.

Kai threw his hands in the air. "I don't even know what you're mad about!"

"Ugh, boys!" Halla leaned back against Helga's side, not bothering to respond further.

Interesting, Anara thought. She huddled next to Halla and grabbed the blanket that covered the smaller girl's legs. "Scoot over; it's freezing up there."

Halla scooted and covered them both.

"Everything alright back here?" Anara asked.

"Fine," Halla answered shortly.

The tailgate of the truck shuddered open as Larissa unlatched the lock. Following her heightened sense of smell, Anara kicked the large black jug filled with gas toward Darien as he walked into sight.

"Might as well fill her up for the return journey. We're only a few miles out from the city. Any closer and we're asking for someone to notice us. If all goes well, I'll be back before sundown. Unless Larissa came up with a better plan?"

The look on Larissa's face was enough of an answer. With a deep yawn, Darien snatched up the jug, walking around to Helga's side.

"We just what? Wait here and hope no one spots us?" Fear and exhaustion made Larissa's voice harsh. Anara had heard her use the same tone with Halla more than once.

"Pretty much, and if someone *does* spot you, you hightail it out of here as if you were the moon that Fenrir was chasing." Anara's lips twitched, then stilled at the way Halla's body stiffened beside her. With her head tilted down, Anara caught the silvery scar peeking out from beneath Halla's hair that Fenris had branded her with. "Oh, Halla, I'm sorry. I wasn't thinking."

"It's okay." But as Halla pulled her knees into her chest, Anara cursed her sharp tongue that often spoke thoughts better left unsaid.

Though Kai looked as though he wanted to say something, the boy did manage to hold *his* tongue.

Having finished fueling Helga, Darien laid an arm on Anara's shoulder. "One addendum to your plan. If you're not back by sundown, we're coming in after you."

"Don't be ridiculous. If I don't make it out, there's no way you're making it in."

Darien shrugged. "You searched for us for decades. We wouldn't be here without you. It's a risk we'd be willing to take."

Anara shook her head in exasperation that was only partly real. "Guess I better make it back before sundown for *your* sake then."

Feathers sprouted from her pores as her body shrank. With a final caw, Anara shimmied off the blanket and winged over the treetops. Flying had always proven an excellent distraction from the realities of life, but as Helga shrank and then disappeared from her view altogether, Anara's disquiet grew. She would be quick, she promised herself. It wasn't like the last time she'd been separated from Larissa and Darien. They would still be there when she returned. But Anara's wings burned as she flapped harder, determined to make it back before sundown.

ᚾᛁᛉᛏᛋᚾᛁᛉᛏᛋᚾᛁᛉᛏᛋᚾᛁᛉᛏᛋᚾᛁᛉᛏᛋ

ANARA DRIFTED TOWARD THE luminous city, overgrown with trees that refused to be tamed by the Empress' mandated walls. Even Treheim's Outer Wall was harder to make out from the air with the abundance of flora growing on the streets and on rooftops. Smaragd had clearly flourished under the Empress' reign, its people's pacifism granting them security at the cost of their freedom. A draft of wind carried Anara closer to the city.

Like Lystheim in Perle, Treheim was built of three levels, progressively getting larger the further they stretched from the center. Unlike Lystheim, which was built on a hill, Treheim was entirely flat and consumed in green.

Anara flapped her wings, fighting the exhaustion that had always seemed to plague her whenever she visited Treheim. She wondered if it was her own aversion to Smaragd that made her so eager to leave, but even as a child, she'd been uncomfortable in visiting the Myrkviðr Forest and the kingdom within. There was something about the forest that dulled her senses, making her feel off-balanced. She ruffled her feathers, attempting to dislodge the fog settling in her mind.

By the time she reached the palace in the innermost circle, Anara's wings burned with the effort, but she could hardly afford to rest then. She circled around, stopping on balconies to stare into windows, until she found what she was looking for.

Princess Kiah, or *Regent* Kiah now, sat in her office with her back toward her open window. Anara didn't need to see her face to know it was her. She resisted the urge to fly in and peck at the woman's perfectly styled curls. Not hard enough to do severe damage, of course, but enough to bring her discomfort for several days.

Darien's words stopped her. She was there to make friends, not enemies. If ravens could sigh, she would have.

She wondered if it might be better to skip Kiah entirely and search instead for the library she'd once heard about from a Smaragdian refugee. Perhaps it would hold clues to the Norn's location. Anara hadn't mentioned her backup plan to the others, knowing the Norn had told Larissa to seek out Kiah first.

Ugh, gods. Resistance flooded her thoughts.

With one hand, Kiah rifled through papers on her desk; with the other, she scratched under the chin of the large skogkatt lounging in her lap. The forest cats were bountiful in Smaragd; just another reason Anara hated to visit. Due to their larger-than-normal size, skogkatts deluded themselves into a false sense of ferocity which had left Anara on the wrong end of many pouncing incidents as a young child.

Anara landed on the balcony and tucked in her wings, letting out a warning caw as the skogkatt in Kiah's lap leapt up to the desk to stare at the bird. Though there was no one else in the spacious room, Kiah's shoulders stiffened. Anara swooped from the balcony, through the window frame and landed in her human form before Kiah, her feet muted on the thick carpets.

The skogkatt hissed, laying its ears flat against its head. Anara hissed back.

Kiah rose from her desk in equal measures of alarm and peace as her eyes widened. Her fingers soothed the skogkatt as they ran down the cat's spine. Anara's irritation increased at the sight of the woman's obvious health. Kiah's vivid green dress complimented her bare, dark arms and shoulders. The emerald ring on her finger sparkled with her slow movements, a reminder of the power of the gods that lay within her blood. Her face, though aged beyond Anara's with lines that creased her eyes, still held the youth associated with the frequent use of *galdr*. Yet even with that power, she'd still chosen to roll over and play lapdog to the deranged Empress. Anara ground her teeth, but the knowing look in Kiah's eyes told Anara she wasn't hiding her dislike nearly as much as she thought she was.

"Anara," she said, her tone conversational, as though they were old friends speaking over tea. "What are you doing here?"

"Not surprised to see me alive?"

Kiah's lips twitched. "There were rumors. Besides, you've always been a survivor."

"No thanks to you." The words cracked over her tongue before Anara could stop them.

"Have a seat." Kiah gestured to the chair across from her as she sat back down, laying her palms flat on the desk before her. Even her nails were manicured. Anara nearly growled at the sight of such luxury and peace. How many deaths could have been prevented if Smaragd had held their ground? But no, Anara's nails had been bathed in blood while Kiah had sat atop her tower.

"Why are you here?" Kiah asked again, an edge of steel now laced into her words. "I hardly think you need me to remind you what would happen if any of the sentries caught you here."

Anara snorted. "A mess for you to clean up while I fly away free."

Kiah raised an eyebrow, unamused. "What's to stop me from calling my own guards?"

"Spare me the empty threats. We both know if you did that, I'd still get away, and you'd bring Shiko's attention to your city. How many of your people would become collateral damage as she searched for my whereabouts?"

Anara breathed in as Kiah's lips tightened; her ears tingled as they sharpened into points, and tufts of fur erupted along the edges. Kiah wasn't stupid enough to reveal Anara, but that didn't mean Anara wanted any unwelcome surprises either. Anara turned slightly as the curtains on the far end of the room rustled in the wind. She breathed deep, smelling something floral and woodsy, but it was all overwhelmed by the incense that burned on Kiah's desk. They were alone.

"What do you want?" Kiah asked.

"I need you to tell me where I can find the Norn."

Kiah's fingers tapped the desk. "Never took you as one to rely on the gods, Anara."

"I'm not," she admitted easily enough.

"Then why?"

"Does it matter?"

"Not particularly." Kiah shrugged. "I never could understand you, even when you were a girl. So much violence with Rubinians. I'm not surprised where it led your people."

Growling, Anara slammed her own palms onto the desk, her claws scratching the wood beneath her. The skogkatt hissed again, leaping from the desk and disappearing behind the curtain. "And where did your *pacifism* get your people? Your son will never wear his crown, and your husband—"

"Enough." Though quiet, the one word held enough strength to surprise even Anara.

Anara ran her tongue along her teeth before she spoke again. "Tell me what I need to know, and I'll leave. Trust me, I don't want to remain here any longer than you want me here."

Kiah leaned back in her chair, folding her delicate hands in her lap. She shook her head, her short, spiraled hair bouncing with the movement. "I can't help you, Anara. Our people don't take sides. I won't alert the Empress to your presence—you're right, I don't want her here—but I can't help you find what you seek."

"Can't or won't?" Anara sneered. "Never mind, it's the same thing to you, isn't it, *Regent* Kiah?"

Anara knew she should stay, try and persuade Kiah, but there was no point. A Smaragdian would only ever see their own needs. Anara let her nails sink into the desk further, contemplating whether the threat of violence would compel Kiah to help them, but Darien's annoying reminder played over in her mind. They weren't Shiko. They had to do things differently, or there was no point in doing them at all.

Anara turned, not toward the window to leave, but rather toward the door.

"Where are you going?" Panic entered Kiah's voice.

But Anara was already sliding out into the hallway. Kiah might not be willing to share her secrets, but Anara knew where she could find the answers regardless. The Library of Seiðrbók was Smaragd's greatest treasure. Though no doubt it had been ransacked by the Empress, Anara knew what Shiko did not. During her travels, she'd overheard a Smaragdian runaway speaking about a hidden subterranean level under the library that contained the Smaragdian historical texts. Before they'd left the Viðnám, Anara had confirmed with General Sture that there was indeed such a place. If there was something written about the Norn, Anara was sure to find it there.

Spurred on by her resentment of Kiah's inability to choose a side, Anara shifted, allowing her wings to guide her through the halls. She ignored the looks of the aristocracy, winging into yet another hallway before the servants could decide whether or not they ought to get a broom to shoo her outside. Anara found the stone steps that led to the lower levels and, confident she was alone, shifted back into her human form.

The unguarded library doors surrendered easily under her touch, and Anara slid between them. She wrinkled her nose as the smell of a warm metallic blanket with a twinge of old paper washed over her. Underneath the library's odor, she caught the same scent of incense that seemed to have followed her from Kiah's office.

She weaved between bookshelves, avoiding the librarians and meager bibliophiles. Though perhaps she needn't have bothered, as they all were consumed in the pages of the books they held to their faces. Two women in particular discussed a line in one of the books, each commenting on how the author could have improved the passage. The rows of shelves led on until Anara lost sight of the entrance. It was nearly impressive how much literature Smaragd had collected and even retained over the years.

Nearly, she thought. *It would be more impressive if they valued people as much as their precious books.*

In the farthest corner, where Anara could no longer hear the library's other occupants, she stopped. The rich, earthy scent was stronger here, and the air was a few degrees cooler. The entrance to the subterranean level had to be near. Her hands trailed along the spines of the books. The pads of her fingers pressed into books in a methodical fashion, knowing the trigger had to be near.

Her fingers stilled at the quiet patter of footsteps heading her way. With less patience, she pressed into the spines that nearly cracked under the pressure.

Come on, come on. Where is it?

The footsteps grew louder, though their owner was still hidden by the shelves. The overwhelming scent of incense wafted toward her along with something undeniably male.

Distracted, her fingers knocked a book from the shelf. The sharp tang of the underground greeted her senses. A small cylindrical latch presented itself in the gap caused by the missing book. When she turned it, the mechanisms behind the wall clanked in response.

A gap, so thin that even Anara's advanced sight almost missed it, appeared at the end of the shelf. As the approaching footsteps grew in volume, she pressed her body through the opening that widened incrementally around her. Once through, she leaned against the wall, feeling it latch back into place.

She exhaled, not in relief, but in reluctant awe.

The only light in the small cellar was a lamp sitting on a table in the center of the room. All four walls were covered in floor-to-ceiling shelves, which was not all that remarkable apart from the books that sat upon them. There were books on the creation of the cosmos; the first humans; the *Æsir*-Vanir War, followed closely by their joint war against the Jötnar; and stories of Óðinn's lost eye and Sif's golden hair. Anara's fingers hesitated over the blood-red book titled *The Binding of Fenrir*. Beside it was a book about *Ragnarok* and the Rising.

Anara pulled the tattered leather book from the shelf, knowing by *Yggdrasil* on the cover that it was the book she was searching for. She fanned through the pages, her eyes scanning for the right words. She paused at the illustration of the Norn sitting in *Yggdrasil* with the well wrapped in roots at its base.

The Norn, concealed in shadows, were only recognizable by their fiery red hair. Their names shouted at her from the page as the story told of how the Norn had given the power of the gods to humans to ensure their survival post-*Ragnarok*. Rúna, Larissa's grandmother, even made an appearance in the story, but when she left and later returned to humanity, there was nothing about where she'd come from.

No landmarks, no directions. Nothing that would help them get to the Norn.

Dust billowed from the pages as Anara slammed the book in frustration. Though she scrutinized the other titles on the wall, she knew none of them would tell her what she needed to know. The Norn had protected their secrets too carefully.

"What's the point of sending us to Smaragd?" Anara asked herself, pacing the length of the miniscule room. She lifted her head toward the ceiling. "Why not just tell us how to come to you?"

As expected, there was no answer. Anara growled in frustration. It was the sudden breeze in the stagnant room that cooled her temper.

Someone else was coming through the passage.

Anara pressed her back against the shelves, so that whoever it was would have to push past her to get inside. The same smell of incense assailed her nose so forcefully that she nearly sneezed. The shadow of a man slipped into the room. Before he could notice her, Anara whirled on him, slamming her full strength into the man who'd dare pursue her. She shoved him up against the bookshelf, hearing the wall click once again as it settled into place and locking

the two of them inside. She was as trapped as he, but those were odds that Anara could appreciate.

Bracing her forearm against his throat to prevent him from shouting for help, she hissed, "If you value your life, you'll forget you ever saw me."

To her surprise, the man smiled. He was annoyingly tall, tall enough that he was able to stare down at her when many others were not. As he was caught in the shadows, Anara could only make out his dark skin, emerald eyes, and the flash of his brilliant white teeth.

"And yet, I'm the only one of us who is armed," he said.

Anara growled low in the back of her throat, her teeth elongated into fangs as her fingernails transformed into claws that scraped his throat. "I'm always armed."

At that, his smile vanished, but a look of wary fascination replaced it. "So it's true. You're really a shifter. I didn't think any of you still existed. Besides the *draugr*, of course."

"You followed me because you were *curious*?" Anara scoffed. "Idiot."

"I followed you because I can help you." His eyes narrowed. "Though you're making it extremely difficult so far."

Anara narrowed her eyes, keeping the pressure against his throat. Her ears flicked toward the secret entry, but from the silence on the other side, it seemed no one had heard their scuffle. "You're Smaragdian. What help could you possibly offer me?"

He eyed her arm, raising his hands in surrender. "Do you mind?"

Anara pushed harder. "I do, actually. Tell me whatever it is you have to say before I get bored enough to finish what I started."

Anger replaced fascination in his eyes. "Typical Rubinian. Straight to violence."

"Typical Smaragdian, straight to deflection. If you have something to say, say it."

He worked his jaw. "I can take you to the Norn."

Anara nearly dropped her arm in surprise, but she forced her body to hold steady. "Why would I want to go to the Norn?"

"Isn't that what you asked Regent Kiah for?"

"How do you know that? Who are you?"

There was something familiar about the shape of his nose and the fullness of his lips. She shifted her body, letting more of the lamp light coat his face. The light caught on the small emerald hoops and studs lining his ears, their shape and coloring so similar to the ring on Kiah's hand and identical to the emeralds she'd seen in the dream Verðandi had sent.

"I'm Masai," he said.

Loki's knot. Anara had assumed that Kiah's child had lived, but she'd never come into contact with him, and she certainly hadn't expected him to look like *that.* As if he could read her thoughts, a smug smile crept up his face. She dropped her arm, stepping away from him as Masai rubbed at his neck.

"How did you know I was here?" Anara asked.

He raised an eyebrow, amusement back in his eyes now that he could breathe properly. "You didn't think my mother wouldn't have a way of alerting me to danger in our own home, did you?"

The fluttering curtain in Kiah's office and the sharp smell of incense came back to Anara. It was the same smell that coated Masai's dark skin. Anara assumed it had been from Kiah's desk, but her eyes narrowed at the realization. Had Masai been hiding behind the curtain and listening to their conversation? Had the Smaragdians found a way to mask their scent? It was clever, for a city filled with soft-hands, anyway.

"How do you know how to find the Norn?"

"Every Smaragdian royal learns the story."

"Haven't you heard? There is no Smaragdian royalty, only regent-puppets under the Empress' command."

Masai crossed his arms, but he leaned back against the bookshelf, unruffled by Anara's insult. "The Norn said you wouldn't like me."

Goosebumps raced down Anara's arms. "What did you say?"

"The Norn," he said slowly, his voice patronizing. "I assume you've heard of them."

Anara's hands twitched. "Start speaking or I'll rip your throat out."

"As fun as that sounds, it's not necessary. The Norn told me you were coming and said you would need directions on how to find them. The moment you left my mother's office, I followed you to pass on the Norn's message."

"I'm surprised a Smaragdian would help a Rubinian."

He shrugged. "You don't exactly argue with the gods."

"You also don't have to follow them blindly," she said half-heartedly, but her mind was already running in a different direction. Was Masai the reason the Norn had forced this little detour into Smaragd? Still, Anara didn't know him and certainly couldn't trust him. She would hear his message and leave him to the Norn and their dreams. "Give me the directions."

"Not so fast. The Norn said I'm supposed to go with you."

At that, laughter bubbled out of her mouth before she could stop it. "You? A soft-handed Smaragdian wants to rough it in the Myrkviðr Forest in search of the goddesses of fate?"

Masai's lips tightened. "In case you haven't noticed, all of Treheim is encased in the forest."

"Have you ever left your precious city?"

Masai shifted. "No."

Anara smirked. "That's what I thought."

"You take me with you, and I'll take you to the Norn. Or you leave without me and figure it out on your own. Up to you." Masai folded his arms, matching Anara's posture.

Her eyes trailed his face. If he'd been born soon after the fall of Smaragd, he had to be nearly fifty years old, yet he didn't even look thirty. Anara paused. If his *galdr* was strong enough to stunt his aging, it would come in handy—if she accepted his offer, that is.

"Why?" Anara asked again. "Dreams from the Norn aside, why?"

Masai held Anara's glare. Something in her expression must have made him realize only honesty would work. He uncrossed his arms. "My people deserve better than this."

Anara shook her head, already regretting her decision, but they were out of options, and she was out of time. Verðandi's command rang in Anara's ears: *trust him*. Unlikely, but if this was the way to find the Norn, she would let him accompany them. Besides, if she didn't return to the others soon, she risked Larissa coming in after her with a foolhardy plan and a besotted Safírian.

"Fine, you can come. But if I catch so much as a hint that you're leading us in the wrong way, I'll put you down myself. Do you understand?"

Masai only smiled at the threat. "I'd like to see you try."

31

An Encounter

Halla

HALLA DUG THE TOE of her shoe into the loose dirt, burrowing deeper and deeper until nearly half of her shoe was covered in soil. Her fingers splayed out on the damp bark of the thick root she sat on. Everything about that place felt alive. The birds called to one another from branches, some kind of furry animal had crossed Halla's path only moments ago, and even the trees seemed to hum in anticipation. The entire commonwealth of Smaragd was *alive*. Halla breathed deeply, soaking in the serenity their relative silence offered.

"She should be back by now. We shouldn't have let her go." Her sister's voice traveled through the trees, which wasn't hard for it to do, as Larissa had forbidden Halla to walk too far.

"Since when do we *let* Anara do anything?" Darien asked, his voice dry with humor.

Halla snorted, in full agreement with Darien. Anara would do what Anara would do, and she would be fine. She was like Freyja in that way, strong and courageous and impulsive.

"What are you snorting at?" Kai settled down beside Halla, his feet sticking out far past her own. Drat her own lack of height. It made her feel like a child, though of course, Larissa would only remind her that she was one. But she didn't want to be reminded, not when she was sitting next to Kai. Besides, she was still angry at him.

"What?" he prodded. "You're still not talking to me?"

"Sucks, doesn't it?" she muttered.

She glanced up as if she could see through the thick canopy of branches. A persistent tingle ran across her skin at the sight of the Myrkviðr Forest all around her. Stories of these trees tumbled around in her brain. But even more distracting than the mythical forest of the gods was the annoyingly aloof boy who hadn't spoken more than a handful of sentences since they'd left Perle.

Sure, he'd listen as Halla gushed about the stories her Pappa told her, but as time wore on and Halla's throat grew sore, she expected Kai to pick up the conversation. They were finally free to speak, but no matter how Halla poked or prodded, he'd revealed very little of his personal life, erecting a barrier between them without even trying. Not only that, but there was a certain gloomy element to his expression that Halla couldn't understand. Didn't he realize that they were living out one of the greatest stories that would be told to future generations?

"I don't understand why you're mad at me."

Halla flicked the dirt off her shoe. How annoying of a *boy* could he be? The only thing stopping Halla from yelling at Kai outright had been the mumbles she'd caught from his sleep. Though the sleeping bag and his own slumber had garbled most of the words. Halla had only heard a few of the phrases.

"...can't go ... not safe," he muttered. "Don't send me."

Halla's heart softened at the memory of his nightmares. She had them too, though hers often featured the burning heat of the iron and the reverberating voice of the Norn who called to her to come and find them.

Kai waved a hand in front of her face. "Hello? Skogkatt got your tongue?"

Halla considered edging around the topic but decided to adopt Anara's technique instead. Straight to the point. "What's wrong with you?"

He leaned away, his brow furrowed into a tight *v*. "Nothing. What's wrong with *you*?"

"You've barely said a word to me since we left Perle."

"I listened!"

"That's not the same thing," Halla protested. "You won't tell me anything about you!"

He crossed his arms, kicked a stone at his foot, and glanced at the overhanging canopy. "This forest always freaked me out."

Curiosity lessened Halla's irritation. "You've been here before?"

Alarm flickered across his face before it was replaced with detachment. "I passed through after I was sold into slavery."

"From Diamant, right?"

Though his expression remained impassive, his eyes had grown wary. "Who told you that?"

"No one," she answered honestly. It hadn't been a single person, but rather a murmur that followed Kai's presence the moment he and Halla had set foot in the Perlian palace. "Why didn't you tell me?"

"Does it really matter?"

"It matters to *me*." Maybe this was the heart of Halla's anger. Hadn't he trusted her like she trusted him?

Kai stood. "Why? So you can look at me like Juni did? Or turn on me like Saessae did to you?"

Halla's mouth dropped, speechless at the wounds his words inflicted.

He looked down into his hands. "I shouldn't have said that."

Halla breathed deeply; something about the forest cushioned the blow of his words. "I don't care that you're from Diamant. Is that why you've been so weird?"

"Part of it," he admitted.

"But?"

"But what?"

"I'm not an idiot, Kai," she snapped. An unfortunate thought rooted in her mind. "What is it? Is it me? Do you wish you hadn't come?" *Will you leave me like Juni and Saessae?*

"It might have been better if I hadn't come," he said.

Halla bit her cheek, hating the way tears burned the back of her eyes, but she held her breath, refusing to let the tears fall.

"I just mean—" Kai's tired voice sharpened. "Are you crying?"

"No." Halla sniffed.

"Halla, I didn't mean because of *you*. There's a whole war about to implode. What if this plan goes wrong? What if we're making a mistake?" Kai huffed. "What if bringing *me* was the mistake?"

"Because you're Diamantian? No one is going to see you. Besides, I like having you around."

He shrugged, but the tips of his ears burned red. "I like being around too."

With Kai talking again, Halla summoned the courage to ask, "What is Diamant like?"

"Very cold," he said slowly, his fingers picking at the root beneath them. "But the mountains are beautiful. In the winter, when the lights dance across the sky, you forget the cold. In the summer, the sun never sleeps."

"Never?"

"Never. We have to put shades on all the windows, and even then, it's hard to sleep."

"Do you miss it?"

Kai quieted. "I miss parts of it. I miss the Ice Lantern festival and sticky rice cakes. I miss my brother."

"You have a brother? Is that why your parents sold you? To protect him?" Halla's stomach turned at the thought. "Why didn't he stop them?"

"He didn't know," Kai whispered defensively. "My mother did it when he was away. He wouldn't have let her go through with it."

Halla fidgeted, pulling her jacket hood closer around her ears. "Why didn't he come for you?"

He grinned again, but there was no mirth in his expression. "Not every sibling can be a lost Princess, Halla."

Heat rose in her cheeks. "He must miss you. We'll find him, Kai. Just like we found Larissa. I'll help you find your brother."

His smile vanished. "It would probably be better if we didn't. What else do you want to know?"

Halla paused, resisting the urge to ask more about his family, but she sensed that topic had closed. Her cheeks blushed at her next question. "How old are you?"

"Fourteen, almost fifteen, I think. I didn't keep track in the barracks."

Only a year older than herself, maybe two at most.

"You seem . . ." Halla struggled for the words. "Older."

"My brother said I was born a grumpy old man."

The faint rumbling of an engine in the distance cut off Halla's laughter. The sound grew louder at incredible speed. Halla recognized it immediately. A sentry's armored truck was approaching. She leapt to her feet and, followed by Kai, raced toward Helga.

Larissa intercepted them at the forest's edge. With one glance, she silenced Halla's questions and drew even Kai into obedience as she ushered them back into the woods. Soon they were all crouching low behind the giant roots that snaked in and out of the ground. They were far enough to not be seen from the road, but close enough to see Darien where he fiddled with one of Helga's back tires.

"Lara, what about Dar—"

"Shh," Larissa hushed her, pulling Halla down closer to the ground.

Halla clamped her mouth shut as the armored vehicle drew into sight. The doors flew open on both sides of the truck as two men jumped out and approached Darien. Though their weapons were not drawn, their hands hovered above them. A third silhouette waited in the truck.

"Kings and Queens," Lara cursed, shifting her body beneath her. "We thought there would only be two."

Halla understood then as Darien gestured toward the tire, his explanations of getting stuck in the mud floating to where they hid. Though one of the sentries stooped to look at the tire, the other gazed into the trees, his feet pulling him in Halla's direction. Darien noticed it too.

He turned on the sentry closest to him, and even from their distance, Halla could hear the silky tone that coated Darien's words, convincing the other sentry that he was too tired to continue, that he needed sleep. The only problem was, the other sentry heard his command as well.

Watching his fellow sentry fall to the ground, the man backed away from Darien, reaching for his gun. "What—?"

Darien lunged forward, catching the man's wrist in his hands. Both men slammed against Helga's side in the struggle for his weapon then fell to wrestle over it on the ground. The third silhouette threw open his door, pulling the handgun from his waist.

Larissa launched to her feet, followed by Halla and Kai. A gunshot rang out as Larissa's hands slammed against Halla's back, shoving her to the ground so fast that dirt went up her nose. The bullet splintered the tree trunk behind her. Halla snorted out dirt, catching Kai's wide eyes as he took in the damaged tree. Larissa's hands were still on his and Halla's backs, pressing them down and out of range. Larissa glared at the third sentry, who half-hid behind the hood of their armored truck.

Larissa flung herself forward, lifting her hands to deflect the other bullets the man sent her way. Darien stood over the second sentry, who lay limp on the ground, holding the man's own weapon in his hands. Awe filled Halla at the sight of her sister approaching the third sentry, deflecting bullet after bullet into the ground with a solid shield of pure energy. Not even the sharp caw of a raven could distract Halla.

The man was nearly within Larissa's reach when his fingers slid from the gun. A dazed expression froze his face before he slumped over the hood of the truck, then slid to the ground.

Anara stood behind him, the butt of a pistol still held aloft in her hands. She raised her eyebrows in Larissa's direction. "Throwing a party without me, huh?"

Larissa huffed. "Oh yeah, can't you see all the fun we're having?"

Anara stepped around the truck, ignoring the three unconscious sentries that lay on the ground. "This is exactly why I can't leave you two alone; you always get into trouble."

"Hey," Darien protested, brushing the dirt from his clothing. "We had it completely under control."

"Sure." Anara peered at Halla and Kai, still lying on the ground hidden by the trees. "Totally under control."

Halla rose to her feet, brushing off the leaves from her clothes, then flinched at the soft touch in her hair.

Kai pulled back his hand. "Sorry, there was a bug."

Halla shivered at the squirming insect between his fingers. "Ugh, thanks."

"Did Kiah tell you how to find the Norn?" Darien asked as Halla and Kai approached the group.

Anara brushed back a stray strand of ink-black hair. "Well, not exactly—"

Another motor sounded, rapidly drawing closer.

Larissa swore under her breath. "*Another* one?"

Darien gripped the gun in his hand more firmly. Kai stepped in front of Halla, his body shielding her from the view of the street. But Anara laid a hand on Larissa's shoulder. "It's okay; I know this one."

A motorcycle roared its greeting as its rider pulled up alongside them.

"A friend of yours?" Larissa asked.

"I wouldn't call him that." Anara crossed her arms. "Let's call him a lead instead."

"A lead?" Darien asked. He lowered the gun but kept it unholstered. "To what?"

"The Norn, supposedly."

The rider skidded to a stop and hopped off in one graceful movement. He was tall, taller than any of them, with dark skin and thick black hair cropped short against his head. Though he wore travel clothes like the rest of them, both of his ears were studded with emeralds. Halla thought he looked like one of the old forest gods draped in green and gold.

"You couldn't wait for me?" he asked.

Anara snickered. "I thought you said your bike could keep up."

"Not when you take off as a wolf through the trees." Anger flitted across his face as he leaned down next to the sentries. "What did you do to them?"

"What did *we* do?" Larissa asked, incredulity in her voice. "*They* attacked *us*. Who are you? Anara, who is this?"

Anara sighed. "Princess Lovisa, Prince Darien, meet Masai, the rightful Prince of the Smaragdian kingdom."

32

Peace and Protection

Larissa

LARISSA PINCHED THE BRIDGE of her nose, counting out her breaths as Masai went from sentry to sentry, checking their vital signs. In concise words, Anara explained how Kiah refused her request, but that Masai had offered his help, prompted by the Norn.

"But to bring him with us? Couldn't he just have given us the directions instead?" Larissa hissed at Anara.

"Trust me, I asked. You need to find the Norn. Darien needs to get back to Safír. We don't have the time to argue this."

"How can we trust him?"

"I never said we could."

"How did you even get him out of the city without him being noticed?"

"You know I can hear you, right?" Masai knelt beside one of the sentries who lay on the dirt. "And I'm the Regent's son. I can go wherever I please."

Anara crossed her arms. "Must be nice to be in such a place of privilege."

He scowled at her but returned his attention to the sentry that Anara had knocked out with his own gun. Blood trickled from beneath his hair. Masai spoke softly under his breath, then Larissa watched in amazement as the broken skin on the sentry's head knitted itself together. Halla's breath of astonishment was accompanied by a soft "wow." Even Kai seemed moderately impressed, though it was always difficult to tell. His eyes were quick to hide his emotions.

"You do realize these men work for the Empress?" Anara drawled.

Masai rose. "You do realize not all of these men were given the choice."

Anara waved her hand. "Everyone has a choice besides rolling over and playing dead."

As though sensing the incoming danger, Darien stepped between them. "If you're on their side, then why are you here?"

Masai looked at Darien, the anger in his face abating. "I never said I was on their side. I just don't want to see innocents hurt."

Anara leaned against Helga's side door. "Then your mother should have put up a better fight."

Darien threw her a look that so clearly said *that's not helping* that Anara smiled and raised her hands in surrender. He turned back to Masai. "Why are you willing to help us find the Norn if your mother isn't?"

Larissa caught the tightening of his stubbled jaw and the way Masai flexed his hands at his side. "My mother is protecting our people as best she can. I'm doing the same thing."

"What do you mean?" Larissa asked.

As if noticing her for the first time, Masai let his eyes linger on the scar on her face. "There've been rumors about the lost Perlian Princess for decades, of course, but never anything concrete. What was the point in fighting a war you knew you couldn't win? But things changed after what you did in Perle."

A pit grew in Larissa's stomach. "How do you know about that?"

Anara eyed Masai. "The Empress disabled all forms of communication."

The Smaragdian shook his head. "Not amongst the Regents. She allows a single radio frequency to be opened between herself and the Regents. It's primarily so that she can communicate with them, but Hammon broke protocol when your rebellion attacked. He sent a message to all of the other commonwealths warning them you were in the city. When my mother didn't hear from him again, she assumed the Viðnám had been successful."

Darien's face paled, Larissa resisted the urge to steady him. If the other Regents already knew, then so would Calder. And so would Regent Omiros of Safír. The Empress would send more than just sentries to greet the Viðnám in Safír. Their timeline had shrunk even further.

"Fine," Larissa said. It didn't matter if they couldn't trust him. He had directions, and apparently the approval of the Norn, so that had to be enough. "But if we doubt your sincerity for even a moment, we won't hesitate to do whatever needs to be done."

Masai chuckled, a deep throaty chuckle. "And here I thought you were supposed to be the princess of peace."

"Do you know what peace comes from?" Anara asked sweetly. "War."

Masai frowned but turned toward Darien, perhaps sensing that he was the most amenable of the group. "We should go. My mother didn't exactly know I was leaving."

"Great," Anara mumbled. "Now she's going to think I kidnapped you."

Masai raised an eyebrow, looking down at Anara from his towering height. "As if you could, little wolf."

Before Larissa could blink, Anara had shoved Masai up against Helga's side. "Call me that again, and you'll find out just how big my bite can be."

Larissa groaned. "Enough, both of you. Load up."

Halla and Kai scrambled up into Helga's tailgate while Darien wedged his way in between Masai and Anara. With a smirk, Masai walked away and mounted his bike, the engine roaring to life under his touch.

Anara watched him go in distaste. "I'll keep watch from above. If Calder's known about Perle all this time, his *draugrs* could've picked up our scent outside the city. He could be closer than we realized."

Energy crackled between Larissa's fingers at the thought of Calder finding them with Halla. She'd just gotten her sister back. She wouldn't lose her again. Indecision and guilt rumbled in her stomach. "I never should've let Halla come."

Anara shook her head. "Too late for that kind of thinking. Halla would've hidden in the truck anyway. One way or another, we would have found ourselves on the same path. Let Calder chase us; this time, we'll be ready."

With a feral grin, Anara shifted, darting off toward the sky on black feathered wings. Larissa breathed deeply, forcing the *galdr* to fade from her hands. Anara was right. Even if Calder did find them, it would be different than last time. *They* were different. She hopped in Helga's cab beside Darien, but her eyes held onto the rearview mirror long after they left the unconscious sentries behind.

ᚾᛁᛪᛏᛋᚾᛁᛪᛏᛋᚾᛁᛪᛏᛋᚾᛁᛪᛏᛋᚾᛁᛪᛏᛋ

"WE'RE NOT GOING NORTH anymore," Darien commented, his relief stark.

As Masai led them further into the Myrkviðr Forest for hours, Darien's agitation had only grown. Larissa understood. Each mile they drove north was a mile they'd have to backtrack to get to Safír before the Viðnám's invasion.

The sun descended as Masai guided them on the right path at the fork in the road. Larissa racked her brain, trying to remember the geography lessons her parents had instilled in her childhood. "I think we're heading toward the Élivágar River."

"Makes sense, I guess. Weren't those rivers supposed to exist at the beginning of the world?"

"Look at you"—Larissa feigned shock—"pretending you paid attention during history."

Darien smiled. "Nope. That one was all Aagen; he loved the old stories."

Larissa's chest tightened. "So did Dal."

Silence invaded the cab. Larissa's eyes stung at the thought of Dal and Vern and their bodies burning on the farm that had been Larissa's hiding place for a year before the *draugr* found her. "Do you think they knew?"

"About you being the Princess?"

Larissa twisted the pearl ring on her finger. "Yeah."

"Aagen told me that when the woman brought me to his doorstep, he knew I was important. He didn't know who I was. Maybe it was the same for Dal and Vern."

Larissa frowned. "And Aagen said that the woman looked like my mom?"

"Hair like starlight and eyes as green as our apples is what he said. Sounds like Queen Stjarna."

"She was dead, Darien." Larissa cleared her throat. "By the time someone brought you to Aagen, she was dead."

"I know." He reached out, grabbing her hand and holding it in the seat between them. Larissa allowed herself the comfort. She was so tired of pulling away. His thumb rubbed over her knuckles, and Larissa squeezed his fingers in return. "Maybe the Norn can give us some answers."

"They have a lot to answer for," Larissa muttered.

Whatever Darien might have said in response was lost as the sight of the Élivágar River ahead. He pulled Helga over at the bank where Masai had already disembarked. Anara swooped down, landing in the back of the truck.

Larissa jumped down from Helga's seat. "Why are we stopping?"

Masai leaned over his motorcycle, lifting a strange pair of staffs and securing them to his back. "The way to the Norn lies along the Élivágar River. It runs into the Godafoss Falls. It's said that the falls were created when Óðinn's horse placed his hoof on the canyon.

The waters pour into Undarbrunnk Lake, which fills the Well of Urðr. We find Undarbrunnk Lake, we find the Norn. We'll have to hike down past the falls to the lakeside; your truck won't fit along the shoreline."

"We're leaving Helga behind?" Halla asked, standing beside Larissa with Kai at her side.

"Looks like it, kiddo." Darien clasped his sword. "Better grab whatever you need from the truck now."

"How far is it?" Larissa asked, having already tucked her gun into the holster at her side.

"Not that far, but we don't have much light left, so we ought to get going. Legend has it this canyon is home to the Huldufolk." Without waiting for a response, he strutted along the river, his feet sure and steady on the damp soil even as the setting sun cast its rays across the foamy waters.

Larissa looked to Anara, who shrugged in confirmation. What other choice was there than to follow the path the Norn had laid out, even as hazy as it was? They trailed Masai down the shoreline.

"Huldufolk?" Halla asked.

"Pappa called them the Álfar." Larissa explained.

Her eyes shone. "Elves?"

"Don't get your hopes up," Anara warned. "They died in *Ragnarok*."

"Weren't the giants supposed to have died in *Ragnarok*?" Kai asked.

Anara tilted her head. "Fair enough."

Though Larissa gave Masai space, Halla had no such inhibitions. She raced up to walk beside him, her short legs doubling the pacing of Masai. Kai trailed at a slower pace behind them, Halla's constant shadow. Her voice floated behind her over the gentle lapping of the waves.

"... but *why* did Smaragd surrender?"

Larissa winced; beside her, Anara laughed out loud. Count on Halla to ask candid questions. Larissa increased her pace, wondering if she ought to pull Halla back, but Masai looked down at her unconcernedly. "Smaragdians are peacekeepers, healers, and holders of knowledge."

Anara mimicked gagging at Masai's words, while Darien tried to cover his snort with a cough.

"Besides," Masai continued, pointedly ignoring Anara's antics. "We had no army to push back Shiko's advances even if we wanted to."

"But didn't Safír send people to help you?" Halla argued.

At that, the gaiety in Darien's face fled. All but one of Aeron's entire company had been slaughtered in Smaragd, but now Larissa wondered if that survivor had been a spy of Shiko all along, planting false information about Aeron's death.

Masai sighed. "Sometimes there isn't enough help."

Anara side-eyed Larissa. "Not when people are unwilling to help themselves."

If Masai heard, he ignored her.

"How do you heal people, like you did with the sentries?" Halla continued.

"It's our *galdr*; it comes as naturally to me as breathing does for you."

Halla sighed. "Lucky. Just one more person who has powers when I don't. At least I've got Kai, and we can be boringly normal together."

"Kai, huh?" Masai appraised the dark-haired boy walking behind him. "That's an unusual name for the south."

"Pretty sure you know I don't come from the south," Kai muttered.

Larissa's lips twitched. Despite her misgivings, she had to give it to him; nothing rattled the quiet boy.

Masai inclined his head. "True, but it's never polite to assume."

As if emboldened by Halla's questions, Larissa found herself asking, "What are the staffs on your back?"

Stopping, Masai reached for his back and pulled out the short staffs. One was heavier, while the other was sheathed on one end. "These are the weapons of my bloodline. Every kingdom had them." He held out the thicker of the staffs. "This one is called Gríð, and this"—he held out the other, unsheathing the end to reveal the sharp blade underneath—"is called Vǫrð."

"What does it mean?" Darien asked.

"*Peace* and *Protection*." Masai twirled the staffs then capped the one and returned them both to his back. "Before Smaragdians were considered pacifists, we were protectors. We protected the forest and each other. My mother always believed that the best way we could protect our people was in our servitude to Shiko, and although my people have survived, they're not living. Not really." His eyes pierced Larissa. "I'm counting on you to change that. It's the only reason I'm willing to take you to the Norn at all."

Larissa held his gaze. "Lead on, then."

Masai turned, but his foot hesitated mid-step as the snarling screech shattered the serene lapping of the water. Birds fled from the nearby trees. Blood drained from Masai's face.

"Kings and Queens," Larissa hissed, drawing her gun and racing up to where Halla stood frozen, panic written across her face. Larissa scanned the trees as the others gathered in a tight circle around her. They knew the sound all too well. Somewhere in the forest, a *draugr* was hunting. "Masai, how much farther?"

He gripped the staffs in his hands, readjusting his grip and licking his lips. "I'm not sure. I've never been this far."

Anara growled. "What?"

"The Norn showed me where to go, but they didn't give me specific mileage!"

"You tell us this *now*?" Larissa demanded.

Kai shook his head. "We're doomed."

Larissa clung to Halla's hand, wishing she'd thought to give her sister some kind of weapon. As another screech rang out, Larissa whipped her head to the forest behind her, certain that she could see the treetops in the distance quivering as if some monster was thrashing through them, hunting their prey.

Darien drew his sword. "What are the odds this is a *draugr* out in the wild that isn't actually looking for us?"

Anara's hands shifted into claws as her yellow eyes peered through the trees. "We're not that lucky. The screams are still farther than they seem. We run. Masai, you lead. If the *draugr* finds us, we fight. Go!"

33

Blood on the Rocks

Darien

DARIEN WAS SICK OF running. Fending for his life, fighting monsters that seemingly came from Hel itself, even adjusting to his new life as Crown Prince—nothing compared to his indignation over the amount of running he'd done in the past several weeks. Blunt jolts of pain shot up through the soles of his feet and entered his cramping thighs as they fled into the night. From the sounds of the ever-increasing screeches, there was no doubt that the *draugr* was hunting them, just as there was no doubt that it was getting closer.

The only question that remained was whether or not the *draugr* was alone.

Masai never let up, leading them through the twists and turns on the Élivágar River shoreline, huffing that they were nearly there. He'd had to slow his long strides as Halla and Kai struggled to keep up. When they could no longer run, Larissa grabbed Halla's hand and pulled to keep her walking as Darien did the same for Kai. Anara had shifted twice into a raven to see if she could glimpse the *draugr*, but between the darkness of night and the cover of the trees, she'd been unable to spot the creature.

When she returned from her second trip, they paused to draw in great gulps of air, waiting for Anara's report.

"Why isn't it flying?" Darien asked.

"It's tracking our scent on the ground."

"Then let's lose it." Larissa moved toward the water.

Anara grabbed Larissa's shoulder, pulling her back. "Not worth the trouble. The *draugr* will pick it up on the other side. Besides, that water will freeze your legs so badly, you won't be able to run when you need to."

"Listen," Masai hissed.

Over the pounding of his heart and the harsh breath in his ears, Darien caught another sound. It was the roar of water plummeting hundreds of feet. The sound of Godafoss Falls renewed their energy. They raced toward it, leaving the riverbank and re-entering the woods where they struggled over roots and rocks. Though muffled by the trees, the sound of the roaring falls only increased.

The ground sloped at a dangerous decline, forcing them to slow. The sound of the falls thundered at Darien's side. They were descending parallel to the falls. At a particularly treacherous part of the path where they were forced to cling onto roots to navigate a rocky drop, Halla's foot slipped, causing her to nearly land on Darien at the bottom. He caught her with a grunt, ignoring the way she turned her face in embarrassment and righting her before anyone else could see. Then they were running again.

Breaking through the trees, Darien's breath caught at the sight before him. Shaped in an enormous *U*, the waterfall stretched far in each direction before pouring buckets of water over the volcanic rock cliff into the Undarbrunnk Lake below. The lake waters lapped up toward the shoreline where Darien and the others stood.

There was little time to admire its beauty as the screeching of the *draugr*, sounding closer than ever before although muted by the falls, came from the forest behind them.

"Come on!" Masai shouted, leading them further along the shoreline of the Undarbrunnk Lake and away from the falls.

"Alright, Masai," Larissa barked, struggling to be heard over the constant crash of water. "What now?"

"There has to be an entrance somewhere around here. Myths say this lake leads into Urðr's Well."

"Then you better find it quick," Anara hissed. "Or I'm feeding you to the *draugr* while the rest of us get away."

"You could help," Masai snapped.

Darien looked, but all he saw was the falls plummeting into the lake behind them. Its water lapped up onto the volcanic shoreline where crabs scuttled from holes and underneath rocks. The forest surrounded them, but nowhere was there an obvious entrance to anything.

Movement in the trees caught Darien's attention. Darien drew his sword, the sound of the scratching steel silencing those around him. "We've got company."

They all turned toward the figure walking out of the woods toward them. Halla and Kai stood with their backs to the lake as the others peered into the trees. Emerging from the dimming woods, the man materialized.

Darien's heart squeezed in agony. His hair was longer than before, with braids woven tightly on the sides of his head. He'd shaved his beard. Though his hazel-green eyes stared at Darien in lifeless detachment, the man was clearly his brother.

A slow smile crawled up Calder's face as though he were a performer before an attentive audience. Larissa drew her gun, shielding Halla and Kai, as Anara leaned forward, her body on the edge of transformation. Even Masai gripped his staffs, his jaw set in determination.

"Well, aren't you all a long way from home." Calder leaned against a tree on the edge of the forest.

Calder's refusal to draw his weapon sparked enough of Darien's anger to overshadow the pain of seeing the man who was and yet was not his brother, but Calder wasn't looking at Darien. He examined Masai.

"Your mother lost her husband, and now you've chosen to rob her of her son as well."

Masai's grip tightened on his staffs, but he only glared at Calder in response.

"And Lovisa." He tutted in her direction. "What were you thinking? Leaving the safety of Perle and dragging your dear sister back into harm's way? Don't you care about her anymore? Or

perhaps you intend to kill anyone who gets in your way like you did Hammon."

Shock flickered across her face.

"Leave her alone," Darien forced the words out through gritted teeth.

"Ah, the *new* Crown Prince." Calder bowed mockingly before turning back to Larissa. "Did you like the gift I sent, Princess? Seemed fitting for your coronation, don't you think?"

"You're outnumbered," Larissa pointed out. "You can't win."

Calder's eyes roved over Halla and Kai. "A Diamantian? Keeping your own slaves now? You're more like the Empress every day."

Stark fear reflected on Kai's face; it was stronger than any emotion Darien had ever seen from the boy. Instinctively, he moved to block Calder's line of sight.

"It's four versus one, and that's *if* I'm being generous." Calder pushed himself off the tree, drawing his weapon as he stalked toward them. "But, why on Evrópa would you assume I'd come here alone?"

The shrieking of the *draugrs* sounded again, but this time on opposing sides of the falls. At the sound, Anara snarled, her head whipping to both sides. Although Darien couldn't see anything in the growing darkness, he knew there was more than just the one *draugr*. With Calder at the topmost point and the lake behind them, the *draugrs* had perfectly triangulated their prey. Darien's feet shifted on the volcanic rock, readying himself for the attack.

"The Empress wants to meet you, Larissa," Calder continued. Honey coated his words, slipping into Darien's ears with ease. "Something about that godsforsaken prophecy. If you agree to come with us, I'll let your friends live. Isn't that what you want? To protect those you love at any cost? Or will you let them die for you?"

Larissa raised her gun, stopping Calder in his tracks. "You can't persuade me this time, Calder. I don't want to kill you, but I will if I have to."

Calder shrugged. "As you wish, Princess."

Like twin eruptions, the *draugrs* struck from either side of the forest, their claws outstretched and their mouths open in screams that pierced Darien's eardrums. On the right, Anara lunged into her wolf form, tackling that creature to the ground and rolling with it close to the water. On the left, Masai blocked the other *draugr*'s swipe with his staffs. Halla and Kai stooped down, only to throw rocks at the creature attacking Anara.

Darien had only a second to take in the scene before Calder charged. Larissa's hands shook on the gun as the shot went off. The bullet missed, striking a tree and splintering the wood. Darien lunged in between them, meeting Calder's sword with his own.

The force of the impact reverberated in Darien's shoulders. "Larissa, help Anara!"

"I'm not leaving you." A rush of crackling energy passed under Darien's outstretched arms, the force of it bypassing him but sending Calder's body crashing back into the trees. The darkness of the night made it impossible to see where he had landed, but the rustle of the leaves made it clear Calder had retreated further into the forest.

Behind them, Halla screamed. Darien turned in time to see one of the *draugrs* swiping at Masai's unguarded legs, ripping through skin and muscle. He fell to one knee, his face twisted in pain. Darien and Larissa ran just as the creature wrapped its whiplike tail around Kai's leg, pulling the boy to the ground and dragging him across the volcanic shoreline.

Darien dashed forward, his sword cutting through the *draugr*'s tail, and yanked Kai back just as the *draugr*'s claws swiped where his body had been. The monster roared, turning its eyes on Darien and Kai. The pupilless whiteness widened in surprise. "You—"

But its words stuck in its throat as Larissa stretched out her hands, squeezing the air between her fingers. The *draugr* clutched at its throat, its purple tongue lolling about as it struggled for breath. Darien moved closer, dodging the wings that frantically whipped about. He needed a clear shot for decapitation.

A sharp yelp drew their attention to where Anara lay sprawled out on the shoreline. The *draugr* stood above her, one of its clawed feet pressing down onto the wolf's body as it roared in triumph.

"No!" Larissa spun around, directing her *galdr* toward the second *draugr* and flinging it into the Undarbrunnk Lake. The monster shrieked in torment as the water coated its skin, reminding Darien of what Anara had taught them. *Draugrs* hated water. Whether it was because the water was pure and it was not, or because it caused them pain, the *draugr* flapped its wings trying to escape the water, but its movements were sluggish and awkward.

"Get in the water!" he shouted.

Larissa ran, hoisting Anara up as she shifted back into her human form, rushing the both into the water. Halla and Kai followed, their feet splashing against the tides, but Darien's path was blocked by the first *draugr* having been released from Larissa's *galdr*. Masai hobbled to his side, leaning on his good leg and gripping his staffs. The two nodded at each other.

Darien swung at the creature's ankle, where the gray patch of skin revealed an armorless joint. Masai smacked at the *draugr*'s wing joint with one staff while shielding himself from its claw with the other. Darien's sword sliced through muscle and bone, the force jarring his hands. The *draugr* screeched but did not fall, instead pumping its wings to take it to the sky. Hot purple blood poured from the footless leg, splattering Darien and Masai who cried out in pain as it touched their skin.

Larissa shouted, water sloshing around her legs as she ran toward him. Kai held Halla back though she strained after her sister. The *draugr* dropped from the sky, his remaining clawed foot snatching at Masai's neck. Its talon scratched the surface skin, opening a bloody smile, but then the *draugr* screamed in frustration, pulling away as it batted at the raven that pecked at its eyes.

Falling to his knees, Masai flung his hands to his neck. A deep glow emanated from his fingers. When he pulled away, his fingers were bloody; the wound was no longer deadly, but superficial.

Darien stared in awe at the thin scar on his neck. "Well that's useful."

"Just a bit." He coughed, rubbing his neck as if realizing how close he'd come to a mortal wound without Anara's intervention. He took the hand that Darien offered him, rising to his feet. At the sound of Anara's shrill call, Masai let out a bellow unlike Darien had ever heard. He raced toward the *draugr*, raising his staffs to bring them down upon its head.

The crunch of the boot on the volcanic shore behind him alerted Darien not a moment too soon. He spun, hardly blocking the sword that arched in his direction and clanged against his own. Calder pushed his sword down the length of Darien's blade, drawing them close enough together that Darien could feel his brother's breath on his face.

No, not his brother. Calder.

But standing this close, how could Darien *not* see Aeron?

"You don't have to do this." Darien pushed the words out with effort, his arms straining against his brother.

"I don't have to." Calder shoved with enough strength to send Darien to the ground. "I want to."

Calder raised his blade again, then stopped, his arm frozen in the air as Larissa held him fast with her *galdr*. Masai and Anara still battled the maimed *draugr* that bled with every step. The second *draugr* now scrambled along the rocky shore, swiping at Halla and Kai as they tried to swim beyond its reach. Sweat beaded down Larissa's face as she struggled to hold Calder, who seethed in her direction, his arm shaking against her *galdr*.

We're losing, Darien realized. Masai and Anara could only hold off the *draugr* for so long. Though Anara would attack from one side with her claws, then Masai would stab from the other, their limbs moved with heavy exhaustion. Halla and Kai couldn't remain in the lake forever. Even now, Larissa's arms shook and lowered under the force of Calder's strength.

Darien rose to his feet, gripping his sword tight. There was no other way. Calder would have to die. Perhaps the *draugrs* would flee at his death. Though Calder saw Darien coming, there was no fear in his eyes, only righteous indignation, as if he could see the doubt that soiled Darien's resolve.

Darien lifted his sword.

Through the darkness, a light so brilliant washed over them that they all cried out in harmony. *Draugr* and mortal fell to their knees, shielding their heads with their arms from the radiance that rivaled the sun. An immense pressure held Darien down; he could hardly raise his head. Forcing his eyes open and peering through his arms, Darien watched three figures rise from the waters of the lake.

The one in the middle stood tall with fiery hair that flowed behind her. To her right, another was hunched over and concealed in a hooded cloak. To her left, a small figure danced across the water, her feet never touching the surface. The three moved in unison. At their advance, the *draugrs* screamed in terror and hurled themselves into the night air, plunging toward the darkness of the trees.

The figures moved toward Darien, and his eyes watered at their appearance. Closer now, he could see their red hair floating around them as their green cloaks caught in the breeze. The smallest of them looked no older than Halla.

"Verðandi," Larissa whispered beside him.

Verðandi twirled over their bodies to land beside Calder, who had been unable to raise his head. At the touch of her hand on his back, Calder's body went limp, and his sword fell from his hand. She turned toward Darien, her hand outstretched.

"Wait, no—"

There was the slightest connection; then, nothing.

34

Tree of Ash

Larissa

Soft blades of grass bent underneath Larissa's prone form. The last thing she remembered was fighting Calder on the volcanic shoreline of the Undarbrunnk Lake when the Norn had arrived. Larissa shivered, recalling the youngest goddess' cold touch. She pushed herself up, her head rising only inches above the tall grasses that swayed around her, but her gaze fluttered upward. Before her, bigger than it had appeared in her dream, stood the tree of ash and life, *Yggdrasil*.

Larissa's mouth fell open as she craned her neck back, attempting to find the top of the tree, but the branches went on for miles, stretching out of sight. In the thick branches themselves lived an array of creatures. Larissa shook her head, convinced she was dreaming at the sight of four stags resting on the lowest branches. An eagle cried out from much higher, and a squirrel scurried down the massive trunk only to disappear into the roots, chattering the whole way.

The roots wrapped around the well at the base of the tree, but the Norn were nowhere to be seen. Larissa rose, reaching for her gun only to realize its absence. Standing tall, she saw what had been hidden in the tall grasses. Darien, Anara, Halla, Kai, and Masai lay in peaceful slumber. They stirred, slowly coming to their senses as she had only moments before. Their eyes widened in shock as they took in the sight of *Yggdrasil*, but Halla leapt to her feet first, her face alive with joy.

"I knew it was real, Lara!" Though Halla hadn't said it, she wore a look that very clearly said *I told you so.*

Larissa could have laughed, if not for the additional figure on the fringe of the clearing that caught her eye.

Calder lay in the grass, his body still at rest though his chest rose and fell in a gentle rhythm. Asleep, he looked nothing like the man that had hunted them, but all too close to the boy who'd skipped rocks with Larissa and helped her sneak food out of the kitchens. Something in her gaze must have caught Darien's attention, as he too turned to see Calder. Pain flashed across Darien's face, followed by longing so physical, Larissa nearly cried.

The others noticed as well, with varying reactions from alarm to anger. Even Kai seemed shaken by Calder's presence. Larissa grabbed Darien's hand in her own, but before they could decide what to do, a voice trilled over the clearing.

"He won't wake. Not until I allow him to." Verðandi rose from the well, swinging herself up on the stone ledges, perching on the edges like a bird ready to take flight.

At her presence, Masai fell to his knees in reverence as Halla, Kai, and Darien bowed low. Even Anara cast her eyes toward the ground at the sight of the goddess, but Larissa remained unmoved. In her mind, she saw Verðandi and her mother in their palace as Shiko's sentries pounded down the door. She remembered Verðandi pulling every ounce of *galdr* from her mother's body until there was nothing left, until the light dimmed from her mother's eyes. Anger made Larissa reckless.

"Well, we're here," Larissa said. "You better have answers for us."

Though the others gasped, Anara only smirked, raising her head as she moved to stand beside Larissa.

Verðandi jumped from the well, landing lightly before them, though her toes hardly touched the ground. "Haven't you missed me at all?"

Galdr pulsed from her tiny body in such immense waves that Larissa stepped back. "What are you talking about?"

A disembodied voice rose from the well. "I told you they would not remember." An old crone, her hood still pulled around her face, rose from the well and situated herself on the outside edge, pulling out a ball of yarn from her cloak. Larissa remembered enough of her history lessons to guess that this was Urðr, the goddess who recorded the past. Urðr snorted in an ungodly manner. "Mortals never do."

Darien made a noncommittal noise of disagreement. "Considering you tampered with our memories, it might not be entirely fair to blame that on us."

"The boy might be right." The third voice, which echoed throughout the clearing, came from the base of the tree. The final Norn stepped out from its shadows, her hair a living flame that danced around her face. Larissa could only assume she was Skuld, the goddess who foretold the future.

"Boy?" Darien muttered. "I'll be of age in a few months."

"What are months to those who have lived for millennia?" Skuld asked, rotating pebbles between her fingers. Runes flashed from the faces of the rocks.

Halla bounded forward. "So you're really the goddesses of fate?"

Verðandi rose to the tips of her toes, nearly face-to-face with Halla. "Pretty amazing, isn't it?"

Larissa cleared her throat, resisting the urge to pull Halla away from Verðandi's reach. "You called for me. You said if I came, you would give me answers."

"We did." Skuld beckoned them forward, bringing them to the edge of the well. "There are many answers we can give you and many we cannot. Some answers you must earn, but first you must ask."

Larissa paused, the questions swirling in her mind, but which did she ask first? Before she could make up her mind, Anara filled the silence.

"What exactly is the prophecy surrounding Larissa?" she asked.

Urðr wound the yarn around her fingers. "The prophecy surrounding Lovisa must be earned."

"So how do we earn it, wise ones?" Masai asked, though his question was filled with more reverence than Anara's.

"In time," Skuld said. "Ask another."

Larissa shifted on her feet as the others looked to her, waiting for her to ask, but one question forced itself to her tongue. "Is my mother alive?"

The shock on Darien's face was echoed in Anara's. Halla's eyes fell, and even Verðandi looked solemn.

"No," the child-goddess answered. "Your mother died paying the price for your and Darien's safety."

"But Aagen said that my mother brought Darien to him. Hair like starlight and eyes like apples," Larissa persisted, determined to not notice that sympathy on Darien's face. "Who else could it be—"

Larissa's question died in her throat as Verðandi's small body sprouted toward the sky. Her red hair dimmed until it shone silver. Her face morphed and shifted, her glowing eyes replaced by the kindest green eyes Larissa had ever seen. At the sight of her mother, Larissa's legs shook and tears gathered in her eyes.

"This appearance was far less frightening to Aagen." Verðandi's voice was like a punch to the gut, identical to what Larissa remembered from her childhood. "For Dal and Vern, this form was reassuring."

At the mention of her parents, Halla stepped toward Verðandi. "What do you mean?"

Verðandi turned to gaze down at Halla; then, her body shrank until they were eye-to-eye. "Didn't you ever wonder why we chose Dal and Vern, and Aagen as well, to be your guardians?"

"Among other things," Anara said dryly, but Larissa felt the other girl's concern for her emanating like heat. She drew in a shaking breath, determined to pull herself together.

Verðandi turned to Urðr, who sat on the edge of the well. The crone huffed in irritation but dragged her fingers along its surface. As if compelled, Larissa and the others circled the well in unison to stare into the images that swirled across the waters.

Skuld stepped forward, narrating the scenes that played out before them. "In the years before Shiko's uprising, we sent dreams to Queen Stjarna, reminding her of what was to come. She walked with us often here in this clearing, questioning us about her mother's prophecy. We told her there was nothing she could do to stop it. When we would not give her answers, she journeyed to the Jötnar." Skuld's lips pulled back, and without meaning to, Larissa cowered back from the surge of *galdr* that stabbed out from the goddess. "Meddlesome giants. They taught her to demand the test of Óðinn to learn the knowledge she sought."

"The test of Óðinn?" Kai asked.

"He sacrificed himself to *Yggdrasil* to learn the language of the runes," Halla whispered back.

Kai frowned. "If he sacrificed himself, shouldn't he have died?"

"Not according to myth—" Halla stopped abruptly at Larissa's look.

Larissa turned her attention back to the Norn. "What knowledge did my mother seek?"

"How to save you, of course," Verðandi answered.

"Stjarna knew she could not stop the prophecy," Skuld continued. "But she wanted to rewrite it. We warned her about the cost of such an attempt, but she would not listen. She'd passed Óðinn's test, and so she gained the knowledge of the eighteenth power of the gods, the power of time."

"Time?" Darien asked, saving Larissa from asking herself.

The images on the well moved quickly now, and nausea clogged Larissa's throat. The girl in the water was clearly her, but as Lovisa, crawling through the palace tunnels after witnessing her father's death. Then Lovisa was in the room with her mother and Darien. Shiko's armies were breaking down the door, then it all stopped.

Stjarna stood hand-in-hand with Verðandi, light flowing out of her fingers and into the goddess'.

"The spell would hide your bodies in time. You would never grow old, never wake, until the time she'd allotted had passed," Verðandi explained. "It was only ever meant to be used as a last resort."

Larissa clenched her fists to keep her hands from shaking. "I don't understand."

Skuld wiped away the images from the water. "Queen Stjarna intended to send you, Darien, Aeron, and Anara to hide with the Jötnar. But Shiko attacked Perle sooner than Stjarna expected. In the end, Stjarna lost control; she reached too far trying to hide both you and Darien. She expended all of her *galdr*, hiding you for fifty years when she was only meant to hide you for days."

Larissa bit her tongue, her scream of disbelief and shock held captive behind pressed lips. Beside her, Darien paled. His hands turned to fists at his sides. Was he thinking the same thing? They'd lost so much time. And in that time, Shiko had only grown in power. If it had been days, could Larissa have stopped all the pain of the last fifty years?

She swallowed, the pressure of her emotional turmoil forcing tears to her eyes. It wasn't like her mother to make such a careless mistake in her *galdr*. All her life, she'd taught Larissa the importance of balance and restraint. Perhaps fear for her daughter had overridden her caution.

The waters rippled under Verðandi's touch and showed the youngest goddess disguising herself as Stjarna. She appeared to Aagen and then to Dal and Vern, bringing along Darien and Larissa respectively.

"Why Aagen?" Darien asked, just as Halla asked, "Why my parents?"

"There are certain ties in the tapestry of life," Urðr murmured in her gravely voice as she picked at a knot in her yarn. "Call them bonds if you will—individual life strings that become knotted together. These bonds, especially when imbued with *galdr*, are at times strong enough to override natural law. It was Stjarna's bond to Lovisa that allowed her to save her daughter and Lovisa's bond to Darien that allowed Stjarna to save him through Lovisa. They are tied together."

Heat rose to Larissa's cheeks. Darien sent her a glance from the side of his eyes.

"As strong as their tie was, we had to separate them or their presence would awaken each other's *galdrs* and memories before Anara could find them," Skuld continued. "Aagen's bond to the Safírian royalty was forgotten as his family's *galdr* diminished generations before Aagen's birth, but it never vanished. His awareness of the gift of persuasion would save Darien's life should the wrong person come poking."

Darien glanced behind them at the sleeping figure in the grass. "You mean Calder."

"Aeron," Skuld corrected. "He is still your brother."

Shocked by her words, Darien did not reply. Sensing Halla's impatience, Larissa asked again, "Why Dal and Vern?"

"Vern never spoke of it, and her mother spoke of it even less often, but she was not Safírian by birth. Her great-grandmother once lived as an aristocrat within the Perle kingdom during the reign of Queen Stjarna. Before that, her ancestors traced their heritage to Bragi."

"The god of storytelling? You're joking," Anara asked at the same time that Halla lifted herself on her tiptoes.

"What?" Halla cried. "But then, where is my *galdr*?"

"Your ancestors' *galdr* was weak to begin with and fading long before your mother was a thought in your grandmother's mind. They held onto their titles when they should have passed on to another, but Stjarna believed less in the strength of *galdr* and more in the strength of people."

Halla deflated. "So there's no chance of me having *galdr*?"

Skuld analyzed Halla, her shrewd eyes seemingly penetrating Halla's soul. "Your fate lies elsewhere."

"So that was the only reason? Vern's Perlian bloodline?" Larissa pushed, desperate for the answers. "How would that protect me?"

Verðandi laughed. "It wouldn't, but there was hardly any left of the Perlian Ancestral Bloodline anyhow. No, when necessary, we shielded you, such as when Aeron visited your farm as Calder. We shrouded your true appearance so that he wouldn't recognize you. When you were in trouble, I pressed on Darien's heart to seek you. It wasn't for protection that we chose Dal and Vern; it was because of Halla." At Halla's shocked face, Verðandi smiled. "Don't you remember? You prayed for a sister all your life. Someone you could look up to."

"You made this decision on the prayer of a child?" Darien asked.

"We made this decision based on the ties within the tapestry of life." Verðandi fiddled with the thread that spilled over Urðr's lap. "Some bindings can cross the border of life and death. Halla's thread was knotted to Larissa's long before they met."

Halla shook her head. "I don't understand."

"Nor should you," Urðr scolded, snatching the strand from Verðandi's small fingers. "Some thoughts are meant for gods, not mortals."

The water swirled again, and the images sank down like black ink spilled over paper. Larissa peered into the water, gripping the edge of the well. "You have all this power. Why didn't you stop Shiko? Why do you need us at all?"

"They can't intervene."

Larissa turned to the quiet voice, shocked to find it belonged to Kai. He'd been so quiet that Larissa had nearly forgotten his existence at all. He rubbed his hands against his pants as though they were sweaty. "Isn't that what all the stories say?"

"The boy is correct," Skuld replied. She shook her clasped hands seemingly absent-mindedly, and rocks rattled between her fingers.

"We are the Norn. We record the past. We gift the present. We determine the future, but fate is already set."

"That doesn't make any sense," Anara argued. "If you're the goddesses of fate, don't you control fate?"

Urðr huffed. "We are instruments of fate; it is not the same."

Verðandi remained silent.

Masai's deep voice resounded even though his words were soft. "Why call me? Why not show them how to get here without me?"

"Every mortal here has a purpose." Skuld rattled the stones again. "The prophecy we gave to Rúna, Lovisa's grandmother, was incomplete, though she never knew it. To reveal the whole truth, all must earn a piece of what was once known and what was never revealed. There are six pieces of prophecy, but they can only be revealed to one mortal at a time and only if you pass the test. Will you accept our test?"

Glancing at the faces set with determination around her, Larissa knew what her only answer could be. "Yes. What do we do?"

"Face yourselves." Urðr stirred the waters again as Verðandi leapt upon its ledge. She hummed softly to herself as Skuld extended her hands. "Find the truth, decide your fate, and learn the secrets of past and future."

Skuld lifted her hands, and water shot forth from the well, drenching them in its icy waters and flooding the entire clearing. Like a current, it consumed them. Larissa flailed in the water. Beside her, Darien reached for her, but his hand was torn away. Then the wave was carrying them back into the well and swallowing them within its stone mouth.

35

Missing Piece of Perfection

Halla

Halla lay on the warm ground, the smell of raspberries and summer sun wafting through the air. She dug her fingers into the soft soil, watching the clouds that floated across the sky. She could nearly make out their shapes. That one was Iðunn, holding an apple. That other cloud was Loki, bound under a poisonous serpent for his treacherous actions. There was *Yggdrasil*, its branches winding into the other clouds around it. Yet for all the clouds, it was a sunny, beautiful day. Nearly dreamlike in its perfection.

"Halla, what are you doing?"

Halla tilted her head backward. Onkel Tucker stood behind her, his hands in his overalls and a smile peeking out from behind his gray beard. A thin blue thread wrapped around his wrist. The thread fell to the ground and raced across the dirt to wrap around Halla's arm, but it never tightened or loosened with movement.

"Onkel!" Halla squealed, scrambling to her feet.

"Daydreaming again?" There was no accusation in his tone, only a hint of humor.

"And practicing," Halla argued back, holding out her hands, ignoring the multitude of rainbow colored threads that wrapped around her wrists. "Onkel, watch this!"

Halla bit the inside of her cheek, forcing herself to focus. All around her, the tall bushes of the raspberries shook under the force of Halla's *galdr*. Under such force, the raspberries fell from their leaves, but they didn't land on the ground. Rather, they swirled around Halla's head until they piled themselves neatly in the buckets at Halla's feet.

Halla released her *galdr* with a sigh of triumph. "See?"

Onkel patted her shoulder with a laugh, his thread shaking from the movement. "Well, that's certainly one way to finish your chores. It's a good thing too. Your parents are looking for you."

"Oh!" Halla nearly smacked herself in her forehead. "I forgot!"

Onkel Tucker smiled gently. "That's why I came searching."

Halla smiled back, but there was something about Onkel Tucker's face that made Halla's expression stiffen. An underlying current of grief and fear grew in Halla's stomach, warning her of some unknown danger. Then the sun warmed her skin and chased away the cold that gnawed in her intestines. She shook her head. There was no reason for such emotions. "Lead the way, Onkel!"

He led her through the endless rows of raspberries that seemed much longer than she had remembered. As they rounded the corner, the farmhouse came into view. Its squeaky front door swayed mildly in greeting. Two threads of blue ran from Halla's wrist, across the yard, and wrapped around Pappa and Mamma's hands as they waited on the front porch.

"I'll take these to the barn and come back." Onkel Tucker shifted the buckets in his hands and winked in Halla's direction. "Wouldn't want to miss your big day!"

Big day? Halla wondered, watching Tucker walk away, the thread between them lengthening with each stride. Again that tinge of sadness threatened Halla's good mood, but she pushed it aside.

"Mamma, Pappa!" Halla ran up the steps, bounding toward her parents.

Joy spread across their faces. Pappa reached down just as Halla leapt, catching her midair and twirling her around in a wide circle as Halla laughed. "Well hello, little one!" Pappa set her down, then braced his back with his hands. "Although, maybe you're not so little anymore?"

Mamma swatted at him playfully. "Well what do you expect from such a young lady? She's hardly a child anymore. Happy birthday, Halla."

Drawn into her mother's arms, Halla returned her embrace. Her mother smelled like flour and spices. No doubt she'd been working on Halla's birthday cake all morning. Mamma brushed back Halla's hair, tilting her daughter's face up. Though there was nothing but joy in her Mamma's face, Halla froze. Apprehension and dread brought tears to the back of her eyes. What was wrong with her?

"Are you okay, *bebe*?" Mamma asked, her hands smoothing Halla's hair.

Halla leaned in, squeezing her mother so tight that Mamma huffed in surprise. "I love you."

"Well, I love you too, *bebe*." Mamma laughed. "Someone's waiting for you."

Lara, Halla thought, already looking around for the sight of her sister's white braid. Perhaps she was out in the fields somewhere. But Mamma and Pappa were heading toward the front door, holding it open for Halla. Maybe Larissa was in there, already sampling Halla's birthday cake.

Halla raced in, but just as her feet passed the threshold, she stopped. The inside of their home had vanished. Instead of finding the old, broken-in couch, the chipped kitchen table, and the wooly carpet, Halla found herself in the most dazzling building she'd ever seen. She stood on a stage. The marbled floor beneath her was polished and cool to the touch.

"There you are."

Halla spun, finding not Larissa, but Kai. A deep-red, nearly black thread ran between them. But Halla had never before seen Kai like this. He was dressed in such fine clothes that Halla would have imagined in a ballroom. His dark-black hair was for once combed out of his beautiful angular eyes, which looked at her with laughter in them. "Why are you staring at me?"

"You look good."

"Surprised?"

"No, I mean," Halla babbled. "You always look good, but you look nice. Like you actually look like you tried—" Kai's raised eyebrow changed the direction of Halla's next words. "Where are we?"

"At the coronation, of course. Don't you remember?"

Oh, right, Larissa's coronation.

The great hall filled with people. Though Halla could not see their faces, she wouldn't have wanted to anyway. She was mesmerized instead by the clothes they wore and the jewelry that dripped down their throats and arms. It occurred to her then how out of place she looked in her farm clothes. Embarrassment flooded her cheeks as she started down from the stage, but Kai's hand caught her.

"Where are you going?" he asked.

"I'm not exactly dressed for this." Halla gestured down. "I don't want to embarrass Larissa."

"What are you talking about?"

The confusion in Kai's voice was enough to stop Halla's frantic escape from the stage. She looked down to see that her clothes had changed. A golden gown draped over her shoulders and the train of it ran the length of the stage and even down the marble stairs. In the front row of the crowd, Pappa, Mamma, and Onkel stared at her with pride and admiration. Halla lifted a hand to touch the long ringlets of blonde hair that fell over her shoulders. Tears returned as she ran her fingers through the soft texture. She'd always loved her long hair. The threads around her wrist trembled as she lowered her hands. The crowd quieted. All eyes were turned toward the stage, and yet, something was wrong. The crowd was looking at her.

She leaned against the boy next to her, whispering, "Kai, where's Lara?"

He raised his eyebrows. "Who?"

"Stop playing, Kai," Halla snapped, feeling rather exposed on stage. "Princess Lovisa, you know, the one who is supposed to be up here getting coronated or whatever you want to call it."

Kai's eyebrows knitted together. Then he chuckled as if trying to play off her words as a joke. "Halla, you're the Princess. This is your coronation."

Someone walked up the steps, his face hidden in mist and a crown in his hands as he approached Halla. She backed away. "No, wait, where's Lara?"

Kai laid a hand against Halla's forehead. "Are you sick, Halla? It's okay to be nervous."

"Kai! Where is Lara?"

Kai stared in confusion. "Halla, who is Lara?"

"Is something wrong, little one?" Pappa's large hand tugged on Halla's shoulder.

Halla clutched at his black suit. "Pappa, where's Lara?"

Pappa exchanged a side glance with Mamma. Mamma crouched low, readjusting one of Halla's curls. "Who, *bebe*?"

Halla stepped back from their comforting grasp. "My sister. Your daughter!"

The threads between them tightened and frayed.

Again her parents exchanged a glance. Pappa looked nervously at the crowd behind him. "Halla, you don't have a sister."

Halla backed away from them, raising her hands that glowed with *galdr*. But no, she shouldn't have *galdr* at all. Larissa had *galdr*, Larissa was supposed to be Queen. The back of the hall darkened, and shadows covered the crowd until there was only the stage left with Kai standing behind Halla, and Mamma and Pappa still discussing Halla without noticing their daughter's discomfort. Pain and sorrow struck Halla's body, so sharp and overwhelming she fell to her knees. Tears streamed down her face. The threads between them snapped.

"You're not here," she whispered in horror, but her parents couldn't hear her. Even then, their forms began to quiver and fade. "Please don't leave me again."

But she couldn't save them this time any more than she had before. Helpless, she watched as they vanished entirely. A soft hand on her shoulder was the only reminder that Halla wasn't alone. She wiped her eyes to see Kai watching her.

"You know this isn't real, don't you?"

Halla nodded, forcing herself back to her feet. "I do, but I don't understand."

"It must be the Norn's test."

"Test?" But Halla remembered. The Norn would give them a part of the prophecy in exchange for passing the test, but how did she pass? Had she already failed? "Are they testing us together?"

Kai shook his head, and a small smile flickered on his face as he brushed back his hair. Something metallic glinted from his fingers as their thread held firm. "You know the answer to that."

Halla nodded. "You're not really here either, are you?"

"You have to figure this one out on your own." Kai stepped back, kicking forward an item that lay on the ground. The golden crown rattled as it came to a stop at Halla's feet.

She shied away from it. "I don't want it."

Kai's smile grew even as his form dissolved. "And I think that will make all the difference."

"You have an interesting mind, Halla," said the gravelly voice behind her.

Turning, Halla found herself back in the clearing. She stood before *Yggdrasil*, her feet balanced on its thick roots. Urðr sat on the edge of the well before her, her hands still enmeshed in the strings on her lap.

"You have all the ambition and desire, but refused the crown." Urðr paused her hands, her sharp, wrinkled eyes capturing Halla's. "Why?"

A tremor ran through her as she looked into the eyes of fate itself. The goddess was old, fragile-looking even, and yet Halla felt fear in her presence. "It wasn't mine."

Urðr harrumphed. "Indeed. I supposed you've earned your reward." The old crone cleared her throat. When she spoke again, her voice was joined by the rest of the Norn. *"Keeper of stories, peering through facades. Past, present, future, speaker of the gods. The Norn only record, the Norn only see. Recorders, Gifters, and Augurs they shall be."*

Halla repeated it to herself under her breath three times before she was certain she would remember it. Confident, she asked, "What does it mean?"

Urðr reached into her cloak and withdrew scissors that fit neatly in one of her hands. She lifted the string in her lap and cut through the threads without hesitation. "It can mean many things."

Halla bit the inside of her cheek, knowing the old Norn would not answer her questions. A sudden itch at the back of her neck caused her fingers to search for the scar and rub it absentmindedly.

Urðr watched her movements with vague curiosity. "Do you know what your rune means?"

Halla started, dropping her hand quickly. Her thoughts turned back to the night she usually tried so desperately to forget. Fenris' hateful words in her ears, the heat of the fire, the horrified whispers of the other slaves and the scorching heat on her neck that sent her plummeting into darkness. But the Norn had asked; Halla had to answer. "I was told it was the Thurisaz rune given by the giants. That it was meant to be a reminder of suffering."

Urðr blew air between her wrinkled lips. "Perhaps that is one interpretation, the sharp thorn that lingers, but the runes are not so easily caged to one meaning. The giants saw the rune as a representation of their chaotic nature, but it was also the symbol of Thor, who used its power as means of protection for others."

Halla's mouth gaped open. "I didn't know that."

"The language of the runes has been lost over time; even we who wield them struggle to understand."

"Didn't you create them?"

Halla shrank back from Urðr's fierce gaze. "And here I thought you were intelligent. The Norn did not create this world nor anything in it."

Though she trembled, Halla had to ask, "Then who did?"

Urðr turned away, her fingers weaving the strings on her lap. "A greater Weaver than I. You should not linger here, or you might be unable to leave."

Halla looked around. "Where do I go?"

Urðr waved a hand. "Stop resisting."

Only then did Halla notice how the roots under her feet snaked up her legs and torso until they crept down her arms. Alarm coursed through her, but she did as Urðr commanded and closed her eyes, focusing only on keeping her heart still even as the roots consumed her, dragging her into the earth.

36

Monster Reflected

Larissa

"Queen Lovisa of Perle, do you swear to protect the people of this nation?"

Larissa knelt before the figure who held the crown over her head. There was nothing familiar or noteworthy about his face. In fact, the moment her gaze shifted to the crown, she had entirely forgotten what he looked like. Her eyes were on the gold crown studded with pearls, emeralds, sapphires, rubies, and diamonds. It was a monstrous thing, its sharp edges pointing toward the sky.

Yet there was only confidence in her answer. "I do."

"Do you swear to put the needs of this nation before your own?"

Larissa resisted the urge to look beside her where she knew Halla, Anara, and Darien stood just to the side of the massive gold train of her gown. "I do."

"Do you swear to maintain and uphold order and prosperity within all of Evrópa?"

Galdr tingled underneath her fingernails. Hadn't she already done so? Hadn't she already proven her worth by the title she wore and the lands she now possessed? After reclaiming the five commonwealths, Larissa had faced Empress Shiko. The battle had been bloody and fierce, but in the end, Larissa had stood victorious while Shiko's body lay crumpled beneath her. She'd returned the commonwealths to kingdoms as they had been in the years before Shiko's reign.

But peace was not easily restored. Pockets of rebellious aristocrats along with disgruntled sentries and *thræll* had brought war back to Larissa's peaceful land. The other monarchs—Anara, Masai, even Darien to a certain degree—claimed they didn't need Larissa's help. They could take care of the problems within their own kingdoms, but as the fighting increased, Larissa could no longer stand aside and allow history to repeat itself.

Verðandi came to her, confiding in Larissa all of the pain and suffering that was happening in the other kingdoms that the other monarchs had been hiding. With Verðandi's power accenting her own, Larissa did what needed to be done.

It had been easy, simply really. She blazed through the kingdoms like wildfire, wielding her *galdr* and the approval of the gods wherever she went. One by one, the kingdoms succumbed to her rule. After all, the people loved her. With the heart of the people, she was swiftly hailed as the benevolent Empress the nation needed. The monarchs could keep their rule, of course, but only under Larissa's guidance and sovereignty. Darien and Anara hadn't accepted it at first, but eventually they'd seen the necessity of Larissa's actions. Though they looked at one another in fear occasionally, Larissa knew it would pass. They would understand, and all would be as it had been.

The giants had naturally retreated to their mountains. Larissa didn't pursue them. After all, she was no monster. As long as they kept within their borders, they would be left alone, but Larissa wasn't stupid either. She'd posted her own sentries to every entrance and exit the Viðnám had taught her of the mountains. The giants could live and die in their valley; they had no place in the world Larissa was creating.

"My Queen? Do you swear to maintain and uphold order and prosperity within all of Evrópa?"

"I do." Larissa's voice rang out in the coronation hall. As the vague figure settled the crown on her head, the crowd behind her rejoiced in tears and triumph. Larissa turned, feeling the pull of her magnificent gown as it twirled with her. She tilted her chin up against the heavy weight of the crown that carried with it the responsibility of the five kingdoms, as was her right. She'd keep them all safe under her reign.

Only three figures in the crowd did not cheer. Larissa's smile became fixed on her face as she tried to ignore the restraints around Darien's, Anara's, and even Halla's wrists, chaining them together.

"Necessary only for a little while," Verðandi whispered in Larissa's ear, invisible to the crowd. "They'll come around. They know you want what is best for them, for everyone."

Larissa nodded only slightly, broadening her smile as if she could force her joy onto those closest to her. It would take time, but they would understand. Then the restraints would come off, and they would go back to who they used to be.

Larissa lowered herself onto the enormous throne that stood behind her. As she sat, the throne rose several feet into the air, and she towered over the crowd around her. But the crowd had taken on a new atmosphere. Calder strode down the aisle—no, not Calder. It was Aeron. Larissa had saved him, restoring him back to who he had been. He, more than anyone else, had understood that all of Larissa's actions had been necessary for the good of the nation.

Under her orders, he dragged two prisoners down the aisle. Though hoods covered their faces, the crowd hissed and booed as they were brought forward. Another man with an unidentifiable face dragged a third and fourth prisoner down the aisle as well until they were all lined up, kneeling before Larissa with the hoods still covering their faces.

"Grand Empress," said Aeron, "we've found the leaders of those who would rebel against the safety you offer to your new Empire."

"Well," Larissa demanded. "Uncover them."

In unison, the hoods were whisked off. Though gasps echoed across the crowd, Larissa refused to react to the sight of such familiar faces. Torsten. Jari. Haki. Halvor. In her peripheral vision, Darien stumbled toward his father, but another shadowy figure held him back. Anger raged in Larissa. How could Torsten do this? He must have known what his actions would force Larissa to do. How had he not thought about what his death would do to Darien? And die he must. They all had to pay the ultimate price for their sin.

Why hadn't they just obeyed? Then there would have finally been peace, but no. Larissa would be forced to spill even more blood, and the thought made her bite her tongue in rage.

Her fingers curled against the stone armrests. She could only spit out two words. "Why, Torsten?"

His blue eyes were like steel. Cold and uncompromising. "Because we'd already suffered under one mad Empress."

Larissa rose to her feet, descending the stairs to the floor below until she stood before Torsten. She reached a hand out, forcing his face up to meet her own. In her other hand, she gripped her gun, not knowing where it had come from. There was no need for a trial; she was judge and executioner. Even now, the crowd called out for his death. Their chants filled Larissa with confidence in her decision. Darien's pleas for mercy rang hollow in her ears. She lifted the gun, pointing it at Torsten's head.

A ray of sun shone through the stained glass windows surrounding the halls. The glint drew her attention, and Larissa caught her reflection in the red-and-blue shards. Her dress was black, not gold. Her crown was made only of diamonds that dripped in her ebony hair, which was pulled into a sharp bun at the nape of her neck. She was shorter than she'd been and she held a sword, not a gun. She gazed in astonishment at the woman in her reflection.

"You're dead," Larissa whispered to the Shiko-like reflection. "I killed you."

The reflection shook her head, turning to reveal the scar on the right side of her face. "Did you? Or did you only become me? Look at what you've done."

Larissa followed her reflection's gaze to find her sword coated in blood and Torsten's body crumpled at her feet. But how? She hadn't moved.

Darien's cry of injustice assaulted her ears as he reached his father's side, kneeling beside his body. How had he gotten out of his restraints? He glared at Larissa with an undying hatred. "What have you done?"

"Darien, I—" But Larissa's careful resolve was shattering. Beside Torsten, Haki, Jari, and Halvor also lay dying. She hadn't even gone near them. "I don't understand."

She turned to find Halla, but Anara blocked her way, hiding Halla under her arms as if protecting her. "Don't come near her!"

Larissa faltered. "I would never hurt her."

"Wouldn't you?" Anara growled, her yellowing eyes the sign of her transformation. Behind Larissa, the sound of steel alerted her to Darien's attack. She stretched out her hands, *galdr* already crackling between her fingers. They still didn't understand. How could they not understand? Everything she'd done had been for them. Why would they make her do this? Halla's eyes rounded in terror as Larissa's *galdr* surged forth—

No.

A single word, not even spoken aloud, resounded in Larissa's mind. At the word, her world stilled. The sharp tip of Darien's sword pierced the skin of Larissa's back. Anara's fangs hovered only inches from her neck, but Larissa's *galdr* was ready to surge through them both, ensuring their mutual destruction.

No!

This time, the word rang out like a mental shout. The images around her drained like dirt on a rainy window pane until Larissa stood back in the Norn's clearing. Only this time, she was alone. She looked down to find her coronation gown replaced with her jeans and jacket. She raced toward the well, nearly throwing herself inside in her rush to check her reflection. White hair with golden eyes—she was herself again. Tremors ran down her arms as she sank into the grass with her back against the well. The runes etched into the stones burned against her back, but she could not move.

"You stopped the vision," came a high-pitched voice.

Larissa stared up into Verðandi's upside-down face. The girl stood on the edge of the well just over Larissa, bending down to meet her gaze.

Larissa jumped up, putting distance between herself and the goddess. "What in Njörðr's beard was that about? Why would you show me that?"

Verðandi tilted her head. "These visions are a part of yourself. Your greatest fears and your greatest desires."

"I didn't desire that!" Larissa cried out. "I'll never desire that!"

"What?" Verðandi asked. "To keep your loved ones safe? To restore peace?"

"Not if it means becoming like Shiko! I'll die first!"

"And Darien? Halla? Anara? Will you let them die first too?"

Larissa gagged on her words. There had to be another way. A third option. "I won't become like Shiko."

"You've already killed one of her Regents," Verðandi pointed out.

"It was an accident!"

"Was it? Do you regret it? Would you take it back if it meant losing Darien?"

"No," Larissa choked out. "I would do it again."

Verðandi leapt from the well, landing beside Larissa. She reached out, grabbing Larissa's wrist. With some type of writing instrument, Verðandi sketched a rune onto Larissa's skin. The instrument burned uncomfortably, but the goddess's grip was surprisingly firm and unyielding even as Larissa jerked at her touch.

Finished with the rune that looked like an elongated *Z*, Verðandi stepped back and admired her work. "For your protection, when you need it most."

"What does that mean?" Larissa stared at the rune as its fiery glow faded into a silver scar. "When will I need it most?"

Verðandi smiled. "I can only answer one question after each test, and you've already asked about the prophecy. Or do you change your mind?"

Curiosity caused her hesitation, but practically won out. "No, tell me the prophecy."

Verðandi clapped in delight. "Wonderful! Aren't you having fun?"

Not particularly. The Larissa-Shiko reflection haunted the back of her mind, turning Larissa's saliva sour in her mouth. Was that her fate if she continued down her current path?

"I'll share with you first what we told your mother, then I'll tell you what she did not know." Verðandi's eyes glowed as she ran her hands along the runes of the well. When she spoke, Larissa swore she could hear the voices of Urðr and Skuld accompanying Verðandi. "*From within, comes destruction of peace. Chaos will reign and harmony will cease. Only the third of the Perlian line at the cost of a life can change Fate's design.*"

Larissa's skin tingled as the words washed over her. Clearly she was the third of the Perlian line who would change Fate's design, but the cost of a life? Whose? Her own? Or would Larissa be forced to take someone else's life?

Verðandi breathed deep. "Now for the part your mother did not know."

Again, the voices of the other Norn joined in. "*Where one is killed, another takes its place. Sharing the cost which all kingdoms must face.*"

Larissa repeated the words to herself, but still they held no obvious meaning. "What does it mean?"

"That's another question." Then Verðandi reached out, and Larissa found solace in the darkness.

37

Let It Burn

Anara

ANARA SPAT ASH FROM her mouth, convinced it had been water only moments ago. Her sense of hearing returned next, bringing with it the crackle of flames and the screams of hundreds. Forcing her eyes open, she lifted her body off the soot-covered ground. Her vision, though clouded in smoke, caught the details of the pillared porches and the spires rising over the city. Her city.

But she knew, as she always did when the Norn stepped into her dreams, that this was not real. Knowing this had to be part of the Norn's test did not ease the dread that pumped from Anara's heart into her veins.

"Not many can recognize our visions so quickly," came the voice of the Norn.

Skuld strode through the cloud of smoke, her eyes glowing like the fires that raged throughout the city of Brannsiden. Anara could've sworn she heard the eruption of the nearby volcanoes. She had to give it to the Norn; their illusions were thorough.

"What's my test?" she asked, coughing against the smoke her lungs refused to believe wasn't real.

"So quick to leave your home?" Skuld asked. "Don't you want to know what happened that night?"

Anara blanched, her mind burrowing through the past. The *draugr* had come in the middle of the night without warning, burning the city and slaughtering her people. Her mother's and father's screams rent the air, feeding the flames at Anara's feet. She hadn't thought of this night in years.

"Stop it!" she shouted at the Norn.

Skuld looked on mercilessly. "How can you decide whether or not to redeem your people if you don't know the depth of their depravity?"

With a flick of her hand, the smoke around them cleared. They stood in a courtyard. Several Rubinians knelt around an enormous bonfire, their heads bowed in the same direction. Anara stared in horror, recognizing so many. These were the aristocrats, those with lesser *galdr*; she'd known them her whole life. In the midst of the kneeling Rubinians, a woman dressed in a long black gown held a knife made of diamonds in one hand. Shiko peered down at those who prostrated themselves before her, speaking in an ancient language—one that Anara had always hated to study as a child. Shiko raised the dagger and sliced through the skin of her opposing arm. Blood oozed into a goblet that a man held beneath her.

Grinning through the pain, Shiko threw back her head, laughing at the sky. Her tall diamond crown never wavered from her head, even as she tilted her ear as if to listen to someone beside her, though no one was there. Shiko raised the goblet, her voice thundering over the flames.

"For too long, you have not received the consideration you deserved. Your *galdr* has been diminished by a weak ruler who hides like a coward behind his walls. Join me, and I offer you strength like none you've ever had before. Join me, and taste what real *galdr* tastes like. Join me, and you will have not only your own *galdr* but the power of *my* bloodline as well. The gods have sworn it!"

Nearly tripping over one another, the Rubinians raced toward her, accepting the blood that she drew on their foreheads in a scribbled and sharp rune that Anara did not recognize. Unable to help herself, Anara pleaded with the man nearest to her. "Don't do this. It isn't what you think!"

She reached for him, but her hands fell through the man who took no more notice of her than if she were truly a ghost. In the back of the crowd, Anara spotted a heartbreakingly familiar face.

Zoya. Her cousin's deep black hair was cut short around her face, displaying the scars that ran around her neck as a result of a recent tournament. Zoya was only thirteen, and yet she'd taken down an opponent twice her age, looking toward Anara for approval. How had Anara never seen the jealousy in her eyes?

"Please, Zoya," Anara cried, forgetting it was a vision, as her cousin stepped forward to receive her rune. "Please, don't do this! Don't make me kill you!"

Anara's words fell like dust carried away in the wind. Just as the last of the initiates received their runes, the first who had received them collapsed to the floor. Anara stepped back, gagging on the revulsion that clogged her throat. Then all of those who'd accepted the rune convulsed on the ground, arching their backs as their bodies stretched beyond their limit, as bones broke and teeth rattled to the ground. Their bodies were darkening, elongating; whiplike tails lashed out from their backs, horns sprouted from their heads, and the color fled from their eyes. Anara covered her mouth in horror watching as Zoya rose. Every inch of her cousin was gone, replaced by the monster that stood, obedient to Shiko's every command.

"Go, my servants. Bring me those with *galdr* so they might join us, and kill those who restrained you from your full potential for so many years!"

Anara ground her teeth as the *draugrs'* screeches rent the air.

"Now we follow them," Skuld commanded, her body shifting into that of a large gray owl.

Of her own accord or compelled by the vision, Anara obeyed. Her wings took her to the sky, and she found herself grateful that ravens couldn't cry. Flames leapt from the rooftops, made worse by the draft of the *draugrs'* wings They swooped over their own city, killing with abandon and spreading destruction wherever they went. Even with the ocean nearby, there would be no stopping the inferno. Rubin would collapse into ash and dust.

As it should, Anara's thoughts were bitter as she strained against the thickness in the air. Her people had chosen darkness; they'd chosen destruction. Yet, her heart still panged uncomfortably at the sight of her beloved home crumbling to the ground.

Driven by Skuld's presence, Anara flew toward the spires of her palace, darting in through the broken windows and landing on wolf's paws. She could smell the dead flesh of her enemies. That's what her people had become. *Draugrs*. Though their bodies lived on, their souls were dead. Anara had seen the truth in Zoya's eyes. There would be no choice but to hunt them tonight. To hunt Zoya.

In the foyer of the palace, Anara skidded to a halt, her claws scratching against the mosaic tiled floor. Her father and mother were surrounded on all sides by *draugrs* that leapt and slashed with abandon. Anara crouched low, preparing to launch into the fight.

Her father's shout stopped her. "Anara, no!"

"Run, Anara!" her mother called out, turning to her daughter and revealing the mortal wound that bled from her chest. Already, she was stumbling, her blood running through the mosaic grout lines.

Anara wouldn't leave them, couldn't desert them, but her world took on a twisted and hazy filter as her mother's body vanished into the ground. Another *draugr* stood over her father's broken body, howling in triumph and bloodlust. Anara whimpered, her tail tucked between her legs. She stepped back, then flailed when her back paw found nothing but air. The palace behind her had crumbled, leaving nothing but a black pit that had swallowed the rest of Rubin. All that remained of her people were the *draugrs* that licked their lips around their laughter as they advanced toward her. There was no escape from their sharp talons and barbed tails—none besides the bottomless pit behind her.

Did she dare jump? Would it be more painless? But where was her pride? Where was her fight? Anara crouched forward. She was the Princess of Rubin, the strongest kingdom of the nation. She could not let dishonor be her final act.

Will you kill them all? a voice asked from the back of Anara's mind.

If I must, Anara thought.

What of the innocents?

Perhaps there were innocents still left, out there in the city hiding from the desolation of their kingdom, but Anara's vision was overwhelmed by the monsters that cried out for her blood, having already soaked in the blood of her parents. The smallest of the *draugrs* pushed forward, its body shifting back into that of Zoya.

"You would kill me?" she asked, her eyes round and innocent.

You chose this! You're already dead, Anara cried in her mind, knowing that Zoya could not understand. They'd once been able to communicate when both in their wolf forms. They never would again.

At Anara's silence, Zoya growled, "You'll fight for every other kingdom! Why won't you fight for us?"

Anara's ears twitched back, laying flat against her head as she kneaded her claws into the tile that cracked under the pressure. Didn't they understand? She *had* fought for them. She'd already lost. There was only one choice left.

"What will you choose, Princess?" Like an image rippling across an unsettled lake, Skuld's form manifested before Anara, shaking the runes in her hands. "Have you given up on your people, or will you fight to redeem their souls?"

Anara remembered. She was not in Rubin watching the *draugrs* attack or arriving too late to save her parents. She was not about to murder Zoya again. Rubin had fallen decades ago, as had her family. She'd escaped. She'd founded the Viðnám, given so many others the chance she hadn't been able to give her people. She'd found Larissa and Darien. They'd answered the call of the Norn to learn more of the prophecy to defeat Shiko.

Stupid, she chided herself. How had she been drawn into the false vision?

She let go of the *galdr* that encased her body, allowing the fur to vanish and her limbs to return to normal. She stood before Skuld and tilted her chin up to look into the eyes of the goddess that towered over her. The woman's eyes glowed even as her face remained as impassive as ever. Anara clenched her hands to stop their shaking. Even knowing that the *draugrs* weren't real didn't stop her adrenaline from spiking at their every screech and scream.

"Can my people actually be saved?" she asked.

"That depends on you."

Was this her test? Her loyalty to her people? But where had their loyalty been to her? To her parents? Anara battled the anger and betrayal that lived just beneath her skin. "If it's possible, I will save them."

Skuld rattled the stones again, but this time she let them fall from her grasp and roll across the cracked tiles until they stopped at Anara's feet. The Kenaz rune symbolizing ancient knowledge and fire stared up at her.

Anara shook her head. "What does it mean?"

"Let it burn." Skuld reached out with her abnormally long fingers to touch Anara's neck.

At the slightest brush, Anara's throat constricted. She jerked back, clasping cold hands against the warm skin of her neck that grew hotter until Anara dropped her hands altogether. Blisters formed on her palms. Anara gagged, desperate to dislodge whatever was building in her throat, but there was nothing she could do. Her eyes welled with tears as she fell to her hands and knees, unable to breathe.

Skuld vanished. As if released from a trance, the *draugrs* charged. Of its own accord, Anara's mouth opened. Fire spewed out, coating the *draugrs*, even the smallest, whose eyes met Anara's in fear. Instantly incinerated, they collapsed to piles of ash at Anara's feet.

But the flames were not done. They poured from Anara's mouth without invitation or control. They licked the remaining palace walls and danced along the tile floors, spilling out into whatever remained of Rubin. The heat was unbearable. The air was too thick to breathe.

Just as the flames consumed Anara, blinding her with their light, she heard all three of the Norn's voices meld into one. *"Queen of monsters, dead without worth, brings baptism of fire and rebirth."*

38

A Crown and a Curse

Darien

"MY SON, THE RIGHTFUL Prince of Safír, not only defeated the Empress, but saved my life as well." Torsten clapped a hand on Darien's back as his voice boomed over the crowd. "It is with immense pleasure that I pass on my crown. We could live a hundred years and never find another as worthy."

Thunderous applause met Torsten's words. Darien's chest swelled with pride as he looked into Torsten's beaming face. Never before had his father regarded Darien like that.

The battle of Diamant had been ruthless, but it ended in victory. The vast hall encompassed the entirety of the Viðnám. Even the Jötnar were present. Darien recognized Skaði and Eluf immediately, their large frames distinct from a distance. But it was those who sat in the front row that held his attention. Anara cheered along with everyone else. Halla jumped up and down, her voice loudest of them all. Even Masai and Kai were there, smiling as if they were genuinely happy for Darien.

But at the very edge of the row, though Larissa smiled at him, tears fell from her eyes. Panic strangled Darien's heart, squeezing out the satisfaction from moments before. Larissa's presence alone was enough to remind him. No matter what he'd won in their victories, the moment he accepted the crown, he would lose her.

Another hand fell on Darien's opposing shoulder. "For decades, I was lost to Shiko's control. Only my brother could have brought me back to who I was."

Calder stood at Darien's other side, but there was no menace or anger in his expression. *No, not Calder*, came the strong feminine voice in Darien's mind. *Aeron*.

Aeron squeezed Darien's shoulder, his face on the crowds. "I willingly and gladly pass the crown onto him. To our new King, my brother!"

Darien's mouth fell open of its own accord.

Aeron nudged him hard enough that Darien staggered. "Come on, brother, keep your composure."

"But, it's your crown—" Darien started.

Aeron cut him off. "Not any more. You've earned it, Darien. You'll be the king I never could be."

Darien glanced over his shoulder at Larissa. "But—"

"Oh." Aeron's joy lessened. "Sometimes you have to do what is best for our people, Darien, not for yourself."

Flanked by his father and brother, Darien was led further up the stage to where the Safírian crown waited. He faced the crowd as his father murmured the words of protection and duty over him. Darien's eyes sought Larissa, even now, needing her reassurance. He knew she understood. Hadn't she been the one to convince him of his responsibilities?

But when he finally found her seat, it was empty. Her back was turned toward him as she made her way through the crowd. She was leaving.

Darien's legs tensed, ready to chase after her. But his people demanded a ruler. He could be kinder than his father had been, more loyal than Aeron. He could bring them into a new era of peace. Didn't he owe that to them?

Larissa's white hair faded into the shadows, and Darien could take it no longer.

Just as Torsten lowered the crown to place it on his head, Darien sprang forward, leaping off the stage and rushing through the crowd that melted around him. At the back of the hall, Larissa pushed on the grand oak doors. Under her fingers, the runes etched in the wood glowed and swirled to life. Darien reached her, grabbing her hand in his.

"Lara, don't go—"

But as Larissa turned to face him, it wasn't Larissa at all. Skuld, the goddess of fate, towered over him, her eyes glowing in judgment and her hair swirling around them both. "Your decisions define you, Darien Torstenson."

Following her gaze, Darien turned back to the stage. Only now, Aeron sat on the throne, but it wasn't Aeron. Not anymore. Calder sprawled across the chair in the lazy fashion, twirling the Safírian crown on his wrist. Torsten bowed before his eldest son, his body bruised and broken. The entire crowd sobbed as they prostrated themselves. *Draugr* sauntered through the crowd, slashing at any who did not show the proper respect.

"All thanks to you, brother!" Calder called out. He lifted the crown, setting it firmly on his head. With measured steps, he descended from the stage and crossed the massive crowd in less time than it should have taken. He stopped before Darien, a smirk permanently fixated across his mouth. "You would sacrifice our whole kingdom for her, wouldn't you? And people think I'm the villain."

Darien reached toward his hip, but his sword was gone. Even Darien's royal finery had been replaced by his farm clothes. He backed away, but Skuld blocked the exit. Her massive hand spread across his chest. His skin burned, and he jerked away. His shirt fell forward in tatters, the burnt ends filling his nostrils with the smell.

"Look well, Darien." Skuld moved in front of him, offering a small mirror for him to hold. Angling it just right, Darien stared at the shape on his chest.

Though it was not one he'd ever seen before, was not even sure it had a name, he understood its ragged edges without needing to be told.

The rune of death.

The mirror fell from Darien's hands, shattering against the floor. The hall, the crowd, his father, even Calder disappeared. Darkness crowded around him, and only Skuld remained.

"When?" Darien gasped.

Skuld shook her head. "That is not the answer you have earned, but I will tell you this." Her voice deepened, yet lightened at the same time as the voices of the other Norn joined in with hers. *"Second-born King, usurper of the throne. Hel's fingers welcome his bloodline home."*

"My bloodline?" Darien gasped. "Because of a stupid test?"

"We only read the runes, Darien Torstenson. Perhaps we read them wrong," Skuld's voice grew farther away as shadows crowded over Darien's vision. Cold fingers pulled him into the darkness. "Though we have never been wrong before."

39

The Way Back

Darien

DARIEN AWOKE TO SOFT grasses lolling around him. The branches of the great ash tree shaded his eyes from the ever-present sun. Still cold and numb from his vision, he resented the shade that blocked the warmth.

Second-born King, usurper of the throne. Hel's fingers welcome his bloodline home.

Paralyzed by Skuld's words, Darien couldn't bring himself to sit up even as he heard the others around him stir from their dreams. With effort, his fingers slid over his chest, but he could not feel the rune that Skuld had etched into his skin. Had it only been a part of the dream?

Perhaps we read them wrong. Though we have never been wrong before.

The words ran like a chill that lingered on his skin, carving out a hollow home to reside within. The Norn had predicted his death, but they hadn't said when. Even Skuld had acknowledged her reading of the runes could be wrong. He wouldn't die. If he had to fight the Fates themselves, he wouldn't die.

He forced himself to rise, noting Larissa's pale face as he did. Fear struck hard. Had the Norn marked her too? "Are you okay?"

She flinched at the sound of his voice. "I'm fine."

"What did you see?"

Her lips tightened and quivered. They rose together. Darien offered his hand to Halla, who was abnormally quiet, and exchanged glances with Anara, who touched her throat as though searching for something. Behind her, Masai and Kai silently rose to their feet. What had they seen?

How long had they been in their visions? The unmoving sun revealed nothing about the passage of time. Torsten would not wait for their return to march on Safír, and Darien needed to be there to free his people, mark of death or no. He would make the right decisions in that aspect, at least. He would put his people first.

The Norn waited for them on the roots of *Yggdrasil*. A small squirrel rested on Verðandi's shoulders, chattering away gaily in her ear. Catching Darien's gaze, the squirrel leapt back onto the expansive trunk of the tree, but instead of going up, it scrambled down and disappeared into the maze-like structure of the roots. Something rumbled deep below the earth, and two jets of smoke rose from between the roots.

As if sensing Darien's impatience, Skuld said, "It is your decision whether to share with another what you each have seen and the prophecies we've given you."

"King Torsten has already left the safety of Perle—" started Urðr.

"—he is arriving in Safír now—" continued Verðandi.

"—but Safír will not fall as easily as Perle. Unless you all return by the third day, the Viðnám will be forced to retreat," Skuld finished.

Larissa stepped forward. "I still have questions."

"You are allowed to stay," Skuld offered. "But your questions will require further tests."

Larissa's face paled. Darien stepped toward her, laying a hand on her shoulder. She looked at him, the indecision clear in her eyes. "I have to go back, Lara. I have to reclaim Safír."

"Darien—" She hesitated. "What if we can't come back?"

"You can stay, Lara," Darien said the words slowly, even as he knew there was no other response he could give. "But I can't."

He held his breath as Larissa looked back at the Norn and then to him again. He meant what he said. He couldn't force her to leave with him, but he couldn't stay. He'd seen what making the wrong choice had done in his vision; he could not let it happen again.

Though Larissa's shoulders sagged in defeat, she offered him a reassuring smile. "You fought for my people; I'll fight for yours."

"We'll come back," he promised quickly, before the doubt could creep in. Would they make it back? Would *he*? Darien shook away the thoughts; he wouldn't allow himself to think like that.

Verðandi twirled forward, grabbing Halla's hands in her own. Larissa flinched at the closeness of the child goddess, and even Kai moved toward Halla, but Verðandi only touched her forehead to Halla's. "Don't forget us, okay?"

Halla smiled. "Of course I won't!"

Verðandi's smile slid from her face. "You'd be surprised how quickly mortals forget."

"We should go," Masai's deep voice rumbled from the back of the group. It was the first time Darien had heard him talk since they'd woken up.

"Don't you think we would if we knew the way?" Anara asked, but the irritation in her tone was half-hearted.

"The way is through there." Skuld pointed at the base of *Yggdrasil*. At her command, its root shifted, forming a knotted outline of a doorway at the base of the tree. Its frame was shaped entirely by roots covered in runes. Despite their glow, the tunnel beyond the frame was pitch black.

They moved toward it only for Skuld's voice to stop them. "Aren't you missing someone?"

Darien followed her gaze and started at Calder, still slumbering in the grass. There was something about the presence of the Norn that stole his attention, making him forget the presence of his brother. Or maybe that was his own subconsciousness that couldn't bear the sight of this stranger masquerading with his brother's face.

"He isn't one of us," Darien said shortly.

"Perhaps," Skuld conceded. "But neither is he one of us. He cannot stay here. He must go back to the mortal world. What you do with him there is up to you."

A heavy pause settled over their group. Larissa's uneasy expression mirrored Darien's own.

Anara crossed her arms. "We could kill him here as easily as out there."

Masai glared at her. "You would kill a defenseless man?"

Anara moved toward him, a growl rumbling in her throat. "There's nothing defenseless about him. If the roles were reversed, we'd be dead already."

Though Anara's comment had shaken Darien, he had to admit there was truth in her words. Calder would have slaughtered them all and walked away whistling.

"But they're not reversed," Masai argued. "We are not *him*."

Kai stood behind Masai, his face pale and pinched as Anara and Masai argued. Darien stepped forward, placing himself between Anara and Calder. "No one is killing anyone. *He* might do that, but *we* don't."

Anara shook her head. "We're going to regret this."

"Maybe," Darien admitted.

Larissa joined Darien, forming a barrier in front of Anara. "If we killed him now, we'd be like Shiko." Her voice shook. "We aren't her."

"Fine." Anara threw her hands, but Darien could see that Larissa's words had worked. "But I'm not carrying him!"

"That won't be necessary," Skuld responded. With another flick of her wrist, the roots of *Yggdrasil* snaked between their feet and wrapped about Calder's body, cradling him as they pulled him through the door. His body disappeared into the darkness.

"Yeah, 'cause that's not creepy at all," muttered Kai.

Darien laughed. "Semi-sentient roots don't make you all warm and fuzzy on the inside?"

"You know? Surprisingly not," Masai answered.

Anara grunted. "Bunch of babies." She stalked off toward the tunnel and vanished beneath the roots without a glance back.

"Nothing scares her, does it?" Masai murmured. Catching Larissa's glance, he looked away. "Don't tell her I said that." Then he followed her through.

Halla turned in a wide circle, her eyes drinking in the sight of *Yggdrasil* as if trying to imprint it into her memory. Kai nudged her shoulder. "Ready?"

"Hardly," she answered grudgingly, but followed him anyway.

Only Darien and Larissa remained. For a moment, Darien feared that Larissa had changed her mind. Would she stay after all to find answers to the questions he knew still plagued her heart? She sighed, reaching for his hand, though seemingly unaware as she did so. Darien intertwined his fingers with hers. There had to be a way to fulfill his duty to Safír and to Larissa. He would find a way to do both.

Larissa fixed her gaze on the Norn. "Can I change it?"

Darien didn't understand.

Urðr focused on her weaving while Skuld rattled her stones, but Verðandi glided toward them, drawing the etching pen from behind her back and setting it to Larissa's skin. A gasp escaped her mouth as a faint rune painted her forearm before it vanished, sinking back into her skin. "When you need me most, summon me. I will come."

"Verðandi," came the thunderous reproach of the other two Norn.

Then Skuld stepped forward. "Your time is ending, and the door is closing. If you wish to leave, you must go now."

With a jolt, Darien realized the roots had been constricting; the door was half its previous size. He yanked on Larissa's hand, pulling her toward the ever-shrinking tunnel. Together they dove, sliding into the yawning mouth of the tunnel just as the roots snapped closed behind them.

Part Three

Los

Halved by life and death
Hel sits upon her throne
Unbiased to any soul
All are welcomed into her home.

-Urðr, *Book of the Past*

40

Interpretations and Confessions

Larissa

THE ROUGH VOLCANIC SHORE scratched against Larissa's cheek, and the distant roar of Gadofass Falls filled her ears. Picking herself up, she blinked to dispel the shadows that clung to her vision and saw the others doing the same. Only Calder remained unconscious on the shoreline, where Larissa secretly wished she could leave him until the water drew him into its depths. She froze, terrified by the direction of her thoughts. They felt too similar to her vision.

Darien leaned to the side, stretching his arms until something popped. "Is anyone else getting really sick of the Norn knocking us out every time they want us to move somewhere?"

"Probably just how they maintain their mystique," Anara added, cracking her neck to the side.

"I can't believe it," Halla chattered, her eyes filled with wonder. She looked at Kai, as if attempting to infect his sour mood with her own joy. "We really met the Norn!"

"If I hadn't been there, I wouldn't have believed it," Masai muttered, rubbing his head.

"Weren't you the one who supposedly knew the way?" Anara asked.

"Still"—he shrugged—"I only thought there was a fifty-fifty shot at actually finding them."

Anara snorted. "Remind me never to follow you again."

He leaned back on the palms of his hand. "I got us here, didn't I?"

"Yeah, and you needed me to save your neck." Anara indicated the thin scar that stretched across Masai's throat from the *draugr* attack.

Had that been only hours ago or days ago? It was light again, but Larissa couldn't guess how long they'd been with the Norn.

Masai's fingers caressed his neck. "I guess I do owe you my gratitude."

Anara raised a hand to her chest in mock surprise. "A Smaragdian thanking a Rubinian for being violent? And here I thought the Norn would be the most unexpected part of my day."

"I said I owed you my gratitude," Masai raised an eyebrow. "I didn't actually say thank you."

"If you two are done bickering," Larissa said, though without any real malice. Her eyes were on Darien, who crouched silently beside Calder.

Noticing him too, the others gathered around. Anara scowled, pursing her lips. Masai knelt, his fingers pulling back Calder's eyelids and pressing at the hollow of his neck. "He seems physically fine. Clearly his sleep was caused by the Norn."

"When will he wake up?" Darien asked, his shoulders taunt.

"I couldn't say." Masai rocked back on his heels, eyeing Darien. "Is he really your brother?"

Darien huffed. "He was. We need to get back on the road. The Norn said if we didn't arrive in Safír within three days, the Viðnám would lose. You'll have to help me carry him."

"What?" Anara challenged. "Not going to ask me?"

Darien chuckled. "If we change our mind about killing him, I'll ask you."

Larissa moved toward him, resting her hand on Darien's shoulder. "Do you think it's smart to bring him with us?"

Darien's back tensed under her fingers. "We can't kill him, and we can't leave him here to regroup with his *draugrs*. What other choice is there?"

Larissa sighed, letting her hand drop. Darien and Masai hoisted Calder between them. It was strange. In Calder's sleep, the remnants of Aeron were more prominent than ever before. True, he was older than when Larissa had last seen him as Lovisa, but Aeron's face was there all the same. By the strangled look on Darien's face, Larissa knew he saw it too. His pain was like poison in her veins.

The trek back up to the shoreline was far worse than the journey down to the lake. Multiple times, Darien and Masai fumbled Calder's body on the slippery slope, though they managed to catch him each time. Larissa followed in the rear, watching Halla as her small feet found stability in every root and rock Kai's hands guided her to. Larissa had to admit, the boy was growing on her enough that concern shot through her at the tortured look on his face. She didn't have to ask to know it had something to do with his vision.

She felt the same unease when she remembered the rattle of chains she'd placed on Darien, Anara, and Halla. The way Calder had smiled at her in genuine adoration. Torsten's blood staining the tiled floors. Her own reflection, looking so much like Shiko, glowing in satisfaction at the world she'd created.

Your greatest fears and your greatest desires.

Larissa's fingers tingled, encased with a soft glow as her *galdr* swirled uncomfortably within her. Kai glanced back, noticing the glow, but said nothing.

The crash of the falls faded into the rush of the Élivágar River. Not far off in the distance sat Helga. The sight of the truck grounded Larissa. Finally, something familiar.

Darien and Masai hefted Calder's body into the truck bed. Finding rope, Darien tied Calder's hands and feet together. "Lara, you'll drive. Halla and Kai can fit up front with you. I'll stay back here and monitor Calder. Anara—"

She nodded. "I'll be in the sky."

Nudged by Halla, Kai followed her to the passenger door, pulling himself up onto the bench.

"Give me a minute; I'll lead the way," Masai offered, already rummaging through the bags on the side of his motorcycle. His hand came out with a small emerald vial.

"Is that nectar?" Larissa asked.

Masai raised an eyebrow, paused in his turn as he took in their shocked expressions. "Yes."

"Where did you get that?" Darien asked.

"We ferment it in Smaragd."

Though Masai's voice was nonchalant, Anara's eyes narrowed in his direction. "And the Empress keeps all batches under strict supervision. How'd you get it?"

"Regent's son, remember?" he said, dabbing some of the nectar on his neck. The scar faded further until it was nearly gone. "Besides, it's easy to nick some when I'm the one making it."

"Well, run along home now that you're all healed up."

Masai's expression flattened as he offered the bottle to Anara. "I know the *draugr* got you too. I'd heal you myself, but I'd have to touch you—"

Anara growled.

He smirked. "I figured. So use the nectar. Don't suffer needlessly."

"I've had worse." But she snatched the bottle anyhow, dabbing it on the old and new wounds on her stomach and arms, relaxing as the nectar soaked through her skin.

Masai stuffed the bottle back in his bag. "I'm coming with you."

"Great." Sarcasm coated Anara's words. "Then you can be around when Calder slits all our throats in the night—"

Darien slammed the tailgate from inside the bed. "Can we not get into this right now? The Norn gave Masai a piece of the prophecy. He's coming, end of story."

At his harsh voice, everyone stopped. Larissa could count on one hand the times Darien had lost his temper. The tight strain on his shoulders revealed just how close he was to exploding. What had he seen in his vision?

"He's right." Larissa moved to the driver's door. "We need to get going."

"What about the prophecy?" Anara called after her.

"We'll figure it out later," she answered, shutting her door with finality.

She squished against Halla, taking comfort in her sister's presence while trying to give Kai space on Halla's other side. Guided by the raven in the sky and Masai on his bike, Larissa pulled away from the river, wishing she could leave behind Verðandi's words as easily.

When you need me most, summon me. I will come.

Larissa shivered, praying there would never be a need so dire where she would need to call on Verðandi. Her mother had done so, and look where that had gotten her. No, Larissa would handle whatever came her way without the child-goddess' help.

ᚾᛁᛝᛚᛋᚾᛁᛝᛚᛋᚾᛁᛝᛚᛋᚾᛁᛝᛚᛋᚾᛁᛝᛚᛋ

NIGHT CAME SWIFTLY, FORCING them off the roads and into a clearing just large enough to hide Helga's bulky frame. Still within the borders of the Smaragd commonwealth, Larissa couldn't shake the ominous feeling that accompanied the Myrkviðr Forest. They made camp close enough to Helga that Calder's prone and tied-up form could be seen, but far enough away that he couldn't hear them should he wake up. They couldn't risk letting him hear what needed to be discussed.

They settled themselves in a circle around the fire Masai had created—he was doing well out in nature, despite Anara's reservations. Anara's elongated ears flicked occasionally in Calder's direction, careful to listen for any movement. A dull silence fell over the group. They exchanged furtive glances, waiting for someone to be the first one to break. Larissa stared at Darien, trying to catch his eye, but he stared resolutely at the flames.

Anara blew through her lips in irritation. "Someone has to go first. *Queen of monsters, dead without worth. Brings baptism of fire and of rebirth.* That's what the Norn told me."

Thoughts raced across Masai's unguarded expression. "Monsters dead without worth? Meaning the *draugr*? Were they in your vision?"

"Yes."

Perhaps he sensed not to push Anara further, because he looked away from her then. "*A forest polluted with deception and deceit will either be cleansed or face its defeat.*"

"Well, well, well, I thought Smaragd was supposed to be better than everyone else with your peace and healing," Anara spoke dryly. "Turns out you've got your skeletons just like the rest of us, huh?"

"Is that necessary?" Darien asked, exhaustion coating his words.

Anara pondered for a moment. "Yup. Tell us, Masai, what deception and deceit is happening in this godsforsaken forest?"

Masai ground his teeth. "The prophecy doesn't even mention Myrkviðr Forest."

"But it doesn't really need to, does it? What was in your vision?"

There was a visible tightening of the veins in Masai's neck. "I don't see you explaining what you saw in your vision. All you need from me is my piece of the prophecy, and I've given that."

"Masai's right," Larissa added before Anara could reply. "No one has to share their visions if they don't want to."

"I don't mind." Halla rested against Larissa's shoulder. "I saw Pappa and Mamma and Onkel Tucker again. There were all these threads that connected us together. They were happy; it was like a dream." Her voice wavered. "But they didn't know you, Lara. It was like you'd never existed."

Larissa squeezed her sister's hand as the happiness in her voice trailed in sorrow. "It's okay. I'm glad you got to see them again. What was your part of the prophecy?"

"*Keeper of stories, peering through facades. Past, present, and future, the speaker of the gods. The Norn only record, the Norn only see. Recorders, Gifters, and Augurs are all they shall be.*" Halla made a face. "I'm not really sure what it means."

Larissa sighed. "It means the Norn aren't going to help us. Not entirely surprising, considering what they told me. *From within, comes destruction of peace. Chaos will reign and harmony will cease. Only the third of the Perlian line, at the cost of a life, can change Fate's design. Where one is killed, another takes its place. Sharing the cost, which all kingdoms must face.*"

Five pairs of eyes locked on Larissa's face. Heat crept up her cheeks at their sudden scrutiny. "Verðandi said my mother only knew the first half about the third of the Perlian line. Guess it makes sense why she was so worried it could mean me."

"*Could* be you?" Darien choked out. "There's no one else it could be. What does it mean, the cost of a life? Whose life?"

Larissa shrugged, as if the thought hadn't plagued her. "I don't know."

"Sharing the cost, which all kingdoms must face," Masai murmured almost to himself.

"Something you want to share with the rest of us?" Anara asked.

"The Norn sent us *all* dreams. The Norn pushed us together, forced us all to travel to them so that we could each receive a part of the prophecy. What if that means that Princess Lovisa isn't the only key to overthrowing Shiko's reign? What is the cost that all kingdoms must face?"

"*Larissa*," Anara corrected. "But not bad, soft-hands. Kai, what did the Norn tell you?"

With his head bowed forward, his black hair covered his eyes, Kai's hands fidgeted together in his lap. "I can't say."

"Can't say?" Anara's eyes narrowed. "Or won't?"

"Can't." Kai looked up, his eyes rebuffing Anara's accusing stare. "I didn't pass my test. The Norn wouldn't tell me the prophecy."

Shock reverberated through the group. Halla was the first to recover. "It wasn't your fault, Kai. There must have been something wrong with your test."

"They really didn't say anything? No hint at all?" Darien pushed.

Kai turned toward Darien, his expression torn. "I'm sorry. The goddess wouldn't even look at me. I didn't understand what I was supposed to do."

"Well, this just got harder," Masai muttered.

Darien laughed, without amusement or joy. "It gets worse." He took a long breath but couldn't hide his shaking hands. "*Second-born King, usurper of the throne. Hel's cold fingers welcome his bloodline home.*"

A gasp fluttered through Larissa's lips.

"And you think it means you?" Anara asked, her mind racing behind the look in her eyes.

"Even if it doesn't, she seemed to reference my entire bloodline." Darien lifted his shoulders. "But 'second-born usurper' sure sounds like me."

Larissa scanned Darien's body in fear of finding some mortal wound she had not seen before. But Darien was healthy, his breathing came easily, and his skin was flushed from the heat of the fire. His hair grew in thick waves, and even his beard was coming in more than before, though it clung to his cheeks in a shallow shadow.

"Prophecies never mean just one thing," Larissa argued.

"Did the Norn say when?" Anara asked, her voice clinical.

Darien shook his head. "No."

"Well there you have it. The Norn love open-ended prophecies." Anara relaxed. "I mean, technically, we're all dying every day." She wiggled her fingers at Halla, casting shadows across the group. "Hel's fingers wait for us all."

Halla choked out a giggle, but her eyes remained on Darien. Even Kai looked at him with apprehension.

"Anara's right." Darien rose to his feet, cracking his knuckles. "Hel's going to have to wait a bit longer before she gets the pleasure of my company."

"Where are you going?" Masai asked.

"Someone should check on Calder."

"I'll come too." Larissa jumped in her rush to not be left behind.

Helga wasn't far. Though the campfire was hidden by the thick trees, Larissa could still hear the muted conversation coming from the camp. Darien waited for her on the other side of Helga where privacy could be found. He looked up at what little of the night sky glimmered through the trees. There was something about the way the moonlight caressed his hair that summoned the longing she'd tried so desperately to ignore.

"Calder's still out," he said.

Larissa nodded, forgetting he couldn't see her. She cleared her throat. "We should have two people with him all the time. He can't persuade more than one person at the same time."

"He might be able to. I don't know. There's a lot I don't know about him anymore."

"Darien"—Larissa inched closer, her fingers brushing against his hand—"talk to me."

At her touch, he turned, but his gaze couldn't quite meet hers. "About what?"

"About your prophecy. You don't think it's some time far off in the future, do you?"

"I think there's too much to live for to die soon, but there was something else in my vision." He sighed. "Skuld marked me with the rune of death."

"Dar, look at me." Whether it was the tone of her voice or the use of his nickname, Darien's eyes finally found Larissa's. The intensity stirring behind the sea blue eyes was enough for Larissa to momentarily lose track of her thoughts. Focusing, she pushed. "Maybe you shouldn't go to Safír."

"What?" Darien stepped back, letting Larissa's hand fall. "I have to go."

"No, you don't." Larissa fought to keep her voice even. "Not if it will mean your death."

"Would you have not gone to Perle?"

She couldn't answer, and he knew it.

"Lara, my people need me. *You* made me see that. I can't be selfish, or else—" Darien's voice cut off, his eyes flashing toward Helga's truck bed.

"Or else, what? What else did you see in your vision?"

Darien's hands clenched at his sides. " My coronation day. My father was proud. He's never looked at me like that, like I was Aeron. But Aeron was there too, and he wasn't Calder, he was himself again, but he didn't want the crown. He said I would make a better King. You were there too, but I knew that if I accepted the throne, it would mean losing you."

Larissa's heart stuttered.

"You walked away," Darien's voice cracked. "I went after you, just for a minute. Just to stop you, but by the time I turned back, Calder had taken the throne. My people were slaves under the *draugrs*, and you were still gone."

"That's not going to happen. I won't make you choose, Darien." Larissa forced her voice to keep from shaking. That was what she'd been telling him all along. Their people had to come first, and yet that knowledge didn't stop her heart from strangling itself in her chest.

"Stop, that's not what I mean." A dark curl fell in Darien's face as he leaned toward her. Anger colored his voice as his hands grasped her shoulders. "I don't regret choosing you. I know I should, but I don't."

Her tongue stumbled to catch up with her heart. "What about your people?"

"I can choose them, too. I can be what they need me to be, but that won't change the way I feel about you, the way that I've always felt about you. Kings and Queens, Larissa, how can I make you understand?" He let her go, his hands running through his hair. "Nothing can change that. I know you said no distractions, and I get that the Norn are trying to show me the consequences, but there has to be a way for us to be together."

Larissa's battered heart thumped, urging her tongue to finally unravel the truth it'd held for too long. What if Darien was right? She was so sick and tired of having to pretend that she didn't love him.

He moved closer, his eyes boring into her own. "I don't believe in a world where we aren't meant to be."

Even as she wished for the world he imagined, the darkest part of her mind showed her the image from her vision with Torsten's blood on her hands and whispered, *But would he want you if he knew the truth of what you might become?*

"Maybe that world is a better place," Larissa whispered.

Darien moved closer. "There is no better place than where you are."

"You don't know what I'm capable of." Larissa's words came out as a whimper. "The Norn showed me a vision of what happens after we defeat Shiko. I made myself an Empress. I took your crown, and Anara's, and Masai's. I stopped the violence by killing anyone who stood in my way. I even imprisoned you and Anara and Halla. I became *her*, Darien. I became Shiko because I thought I knew what was best."

Darien cupped her face, the warmth of his palms spreading into her icy cheeks. "That won't happen."

"I started a war that will kill thousands. There is blood on *my* hands." Tears sprang to her eyes. "I would do it again to save you. Verðandi said my vision showed my greatest fears and greatest desires. What if this is really what I desire?"

He pulled her face closer. "Lara, listen to me. You are *not* Shiko. You envisioned a world where you kept everyone you love safe, but the Norn twisted that to test you. All the stories say that prophecies have more than one meaning. So do visions. I am not going to die, and you are not going to turn into Shiko."

Tears gathered in the corners of her eyes. "How do you know?"

"Because I know *you*." He wiped the tear that escaped, erasing its existence as he kissed her forehead. He breathed into her hair. "Besides, only the good die young, not the good-looking."

Larissa laughed, melting at his touch and curling herself against his chest. "That's the problem. You *are* good."

"Not when I'd let the world burn for you," Darien murmured.

She squeezed his jacket. "You shouldn't say that."

"We'll figure it out, Lov," he whispered into her hair. "Together."

Larissa had tried to keep her distance, and what good had it done? She was no less in love with him than she'd been fifty years ago. She pulled back, though only enough to tilt her head up to his, and ran her hand along the stubble on his cheeks. She could feel his quickening pulse as her fingers trailed to his neck.

He was right. They would find a way to save their people and have each other. She would fight for the world that Darien believed in. She raised her head to his.

"Selfish as always," came the voice from Helga's bed.

Larissa froze. Darien's body stiffened beneath her hands.

Calder was awake.

41

We're All Monsters

Darien

DARIEN SHOVED LARISSA BEHIND him as he peered over the tailgate to catch sight of Calder. He'd managed to pull his body into a sitting position, but the bindings on his wrists and ankles held. Darien regretted not tying Calder's hands behind his back as he saw the blindfold lying on the truck bed beside Calder. In that instant, as Calder's eyes caught Darien's, a foreign consciousness drove like a dagger into his mind.

Remembering his training, Darien threw up his mental shields, but not before he recognized his brother's mind. Cloaked in bitterness and agony, Aeron's consciousness remained. Darien had spent hours in his brother's mind as a child, just as Aeron had done in Darien's. There'd been no secrets in the complexities of each other's thoughts as they'd practiced training their *galdr* on one another. But this was not training. Aeron's familiarity was swept away by the dark presence that Darien could only recognize as Calder, who sent attack after attack to find a weakness in Darien's shield.

Darien held his body rigidly. The mental battle was too fierce for him to even consider moving. He reached out his own consciousness to find a gap in Calder's defenses, but there was no wall. Darien's thoughts met a pit of despair so powerful that his mind reeled back in an effort to protect itself.

"Enough!" shouted Larissa.

Calder's attack stopped instantly, though an immediate pounding replaced its presence in Darien's mind. When he opened his eyes, Larissa stood over Calder in the truck bed, her gun shoved against his temple with enough force that his head tilted away from it at an awkward angle.

"Hello, Princess." Calder's eyes raked up the gun and toward Larissa's face. "Can't blame a guy for trying, can you?"

"Do that again, and it'll be the last thing you try," she hissed.

Calder's look of approval grated on Darien's nerves. "You know, I actually believe you."

Rushing footsteps registered behind Darien only a moment before Anara and Masai burst through the trees with Kai and Halla close on their heels. Anara hissed at Calder, though she did not advance further. Masai's face was a mask of cool detachment. Halla stayed hidden somewhat in the shadows, but Kai moved closer. Fear was written on every inch of the boy's face even though Calder was subdued by Larissa's gun.

"I heard him too late," Anara explained to Larissa. "I was trying to give you two privacy. What happened?"

"It's okay," Darien said quickly, his words aimed at Kai, who stared at Calder. "It's taken care of. Lara, get that blindfold back on and tie his hands behind his back so he can't take it off." Though Calder didn't need eye contact for his *galdr*, the lack of it would certainly weaken his hold if he should try again.

Calder scoffed as Larissa knotted the fabric around his face. "So what's the plan? Torture and murder?"

"No one is killing anyone," said Masai, his easygoing voice at odds with the tension in his shoulders.

"Speak for yourself," Anara grumbled.

Calder's head turned toward them. "Still can't understand what you're doing here, Masai. Never thought you would be the one to tempt the Empress' wrath against Smaragd after so many years of mercy."

Masai's hands spasmed at his sides. "Shiko doesn't know what mercy is; neither do you."

"Do you?" Calder taunted. "Is it mercy that your traitorous actions will bring to your mother's door? She barely survived your father's treachery—"

"Enough," Anara barked. Perhaps she'd seen the way Masai's dark skin had tinged grey at Calder's words.

"Anara, darling," Calder chuckled. "I can hear you chomping at your leash to get to me."

To Darien's surprise, Anara turned from Calder, looking at Larissa instead. "We'll take turns watching him. We still need sleep, but we can't leave him alone. Two at a time should work just fine. I'll take the first shift—"

"No," said Darien. "We've seen what happens when you exhaust yourself. Sleep. Larissa and I will take the first shift. You and Masai can take the second."

"What about us?" Halla's voice, though soft, was strong.

"Not a chance." Larissa hopped down from the truck, placing her hands on Halla's shoulders. "Let us handle Calder. You get sleep."

"We're not kids," Halla protested, her chin jutting forward.

Darien could see Larissa struggling with the same exasperation that she'd shown when Darien had first met Halla hiding behind those crates of produce. She shook her head. "I know, but still. Please, Halla, just listen for once."

Kai nudged his shoulder into Halla's. "She's right. You shouldn't go near him."

Even beneath the blindfold, Calder glared in Kai's direction, but Kai only moved to stand more in front of Halla.

Noting Darien's silent cue, Anara moved toward Halla, shuffling her back into the trees. "Come on, they'll be fine." As she herded the others back through the trees, Anara threw her last sentence over her shoulder. "We'll trade in four hours."

"I'll miss you too, Anara," Calder called.

"Calder, make no mistake," Anara hissed. "If you piss me off, I *will* murder you in your sleep."

Then she disappeared back toward the camp, leaving Darien alone with Larissa and Calder. As if realizing the same thing, Larissa looked to Darien, discomfort written across her face as she gestured uneasily toward Calder.

"Oh don't go quiet on my account." Calder adjusted himself against Helga's metal frame. "It's been years, after all. Haven't you missed me?"

Nodding toward the trunk, Darien hefted himself up onto the tailgate and reached for a blanket left behind in the truck. He offered a hand to Larissa, who took it, sitting opposite him. Her touch sent his blood racing as it had been only moments before Calder's interruption. He breathed deeply, willing his mind to stay alert. Though the blindfold and Larissa's threat would most likely be enough to stop Calder's use of his *galdr*, it wouldn't stop him entirely if Calder was insistent.

Larissa stretched out her legs, entangling them with Darien's to form a barrier at the end of the truck, though Calder looked quite comfortable leaning against the cab. Darien spread the blanket over them both and settled against the metal frame, crossing his arms as the bitter cold of the night crept through his protective leather jacket. Though perhaps the cold was best to keep his mind focused on the task at hand.

"Not feeling talkative?" Calder mused. "Not quite the Darien I remember."

"You're not quite the brother I remember either."

"That's because the brother you knew died decades ago."

Darien shifted. "Then I suppose we don't have much to talk about, do we?"

"What about you, Princess? Want to tell me a story to pass the time before my *draugrs* find us and rip your little sister to shreds?"

Galdr sparked from Larissa's hands, singeing the blanket clasped between her curled fingers. Darien spread his fingers over Larissa's tensed calf. He shook his head. There was nothing Calder could do but talk, yet it seemed even without his *galdr*, his words were still poison.

Calder leaned his head back as if he could see the stars through his blindfold. "So much for old times' sake. What's the plan, then, if you aren't going to kill me? You don't seem to care much for my company."

"You'll stand trial for your crimes." Darien worked to keep his voice as disinterested as possible.

The chuckle that came out of Calder was so much like Aeron that Darien's stomach clenched, but the malice in the man's words swiftly demolished the comparison. "Torsten will never allow that. He's already given you my crown and all but buried my body. Putting the true Crown Prince of Safír on trial is the last thing he'll want. He won't dare to tarnish his perfect persona. You might not kill me, Darien, but Torsten will."

"No." Darien's voice was sharper than he intended. "You'll get a fair trial."

For Aeron's sake.

Calder's head snapped in his direction. "I already told you, Aeron's dead."

Kings and Queens. Darien hadn't realized he'd said that last part out loud.

"In that, at least, Torsten has it correct," Calder continued. "Aeron died decades ago in Shiko's prisons when you all abandoned him."

"We never abandoned Aeron—" Larissa started.

"No?" Calder sneered. "I must have missed the rescue parties you sent for Aeron. Of course, *you* couldn't come looking for Aeron yourself since you were too busy playing hide-and-seek with the Norn. At least that answers why I haven't been able to find you and why I didn't recognize you on that farm." Calder calmed, yet in his calm, Darien sensed greater danger. "Does Halla hate you? Now that she knows you're the reason why her parents are as dead as your own?"

Larissa clenched her jaw, staring fixedly on her lap.

"Maybe I *should* tell you a story," Calder continued. "I know how much you used to love them. Will you enjoy hearing how Aeron watched his men be executed in front of him as they begged him to save them? Or how Shiko dragged Aeron through the frozen streets of Diamant while *draugrs* lashed his body with their tails? Or how Aeron spent years in the icy cells splattered with his own blood and waste until he realized no one was coming?"

The horror on Larissa's face was reflected in Darien's own. At Calder's words, Larissa's *galdr* faded from her hands, and Darien's chest stilled until hardly any breath could enter or escape.

"Then why?" Darien asked. "Why would you serve her after everything that she's done to you?"

"Survival." Underneath his blindfold, Calder's lips drew back into a mocking smile. "The Empress is a monster, but at least she doesn't pretend otherwise. Shiko was the only one willing to speak truth into Aeron's life. The truth that his own brother was relieved, happy even at his supposed death. You would get everything that should have been his, isn't that right, Darien? The girl, the crown, even your father's approval and admiration. Even Aeron's father, whom he'd done everything he could to please, would easily replace him. After all, what was one son compared to the other as long as Safír thrived?"

"How could you believe any of that?" Darien interrupted, his voice rising even as Larissa shot him looks of warning.

"It wasn't a matter of belief. She pulled the truth from Aeron's own mind. Shiko helped him remember the way you and Lovisa used to scorn Aeron when you thought he couldn't see. Aeron remembered Anara's disdain and even Torsten's lack of love. It was all there in his own memories. Shiko revealed what Aeron didn't want to believe. It took time—" Calder stuttered over some memory. "Aeron was stubborn and naive. He held on to hope far longer than he should have and suffered needlessly for it. Once he accepted the truth, what was left but for him to die so that I might be born? Honestly, you killed Aeron as much as Shiko did."

A theory in Darien's mind swirled until it solidified into one horrifying revelation. He looked at Calder, really looked, searching for evidence that Aeron might still exist. Darien's thought was a wild and mad hope, yet it held a certain logic as well. "You said that Shiko helped you remember this past where we all hated you and wanted you gone?"

"Helped *Aeron*," Calder corrected. "Stupid fool should have listened earlier."

Understanding crept across Larissa's face, followed by revulsion. "Shiko's *galdr* is illusion. She lied to you, Aeron; she showed you things that weren't real."

"Call me Aeron again," Calder hissed, "and I'll kill you myself, regardless of the Empress' orders."

Darien's hand found his sword at the same time that Larissa reached for her gun, but Calder was already settling himself as if nothing had happened.

"We loved Aeron," Larissa's words were thick with emotion. "Shiko lied. Like you said, she's a monster."

"And she's not the only one. Killed any Regents lately, Lovisa?" At Larissa's silence, Calder laughed. "Stolen any thrones recently, brother? You say the Empress lies, and yet all you've done is proven her point. We're all monsters. The difference is that I don't pretend to be a hero."

42

Scent and Secrets

Anara

CALDER'S BODY AND BREATHING relaxed; he'd finally fallen asleep. Anara turned her face away from him, relying on her sense of hearing to relieve her sense of smell. Bitterness and hostility oozed as a stifling stench through Calder's pores. Another smell beneath it teased Anara with its familiarity, but she refused to breathe deeply until she was once again in open air.

"The sun should be up soon," Masai commented, his voice so low it was hardly a rumble.

She nodded, ignoring the way he stared at her. It'd been hours of Anara looking into the trees and of Masai watching her, as if waiting to see if Anara would suddenly leap up and murder Calder despite their earlier agreements. His irritating surveillance only made her want to do it more or, at the very least, peck at him until he looked away. She yawned, showing off the wolf fangs she'd grown just for Masai's sake. "Relax, soft-hands, I'm not going to kill him."

"I didn't say you would."

"Then stop staring at me like you're afraid I'll eat him."

"He might give you indigestion."

Anara looked at him, eyebrows raised. A surprised laugh escaped her lips. "Did you just make a joke about violence? Are you even allowed to do that?"

He smiled, leaning back against the hands he folded behind his head. "I told you. I'm the Regent's son; I do as I please."

"'Regent's son,'" Anara mocked. "In another lifetime, you might have been a Prince upholding your kingdom's power, but I suppose that means nothing to you. Not if you can have blind obedience instead."

Masai's eyes tightened even as his body relaxed further as if just to irritate her. "Do you always assume you know everything about everyone around you?"

"Only when I know I'm right."

"You don't even know me."

"No, but I know your bloodline." She jerked her chin toward Calder's prone body. "That's the outcome of your so-called peaceful surrender. Aeron went to defend your mother and your people, but they weren't willing to defend themselves. He paid the price for your mother's cowardice."

Masai leaned forward. "My mother saved the lives of thousands of Smaragdians, mine included."

Anara's reply was halted by the scent of incense wafting from Masai's skin. A pendant necklace fell out from behind his collar, gleaming in the moonlight. A golden boar, the symbol of Freyr's protection and prosperity, stared back at her. A woody yet spicy scent surrounded the metal. She snatched it between her fingers, yanking it—and Masai—closer to her.

"What is this?" she hissed.

Masai's eyes, so very near to her face, burned in indignation. "Let me go."

Anara sniffed the metal, knowing her proximity would only increase Masai's unease. "I wondered how I wasn't able to smell you when you followed me in your palace, but I remember *this* scent. You've put some type of incense on the pendant. It dampens other smells."

Masai ground his teeth together, the sound jarring in Anara's ears. "Smaragd has always used nature to our advantage. We have nectars for healing, sleep, and luck."

"And for disguising your scents?" she accused.

He shrugged, still held tight by Anara's grip on the pendant. The warmth of his skin permeated the air between them. "We're not violent people, but we will protect ourselves however we can. Here I thought that's something you would approve of."

Anara growled. "Not when you're enabling the Empress along with yourselves."

Masai's eyebrows tilted together. "What are you talking about?"

"Before we left Perle, a *draugr* attacked us. It was wearing a pendant that disguised its smell. Where else would it have gotten one? Didn't you say you're the one making them?" Anara dropped the pendant, its chain hanging over the thin scar on Masai's neck. Her nails sharpened to claws that scratched along the truck bed. "I should've let the *draugr* kill you and save myself the trouble."

Instead of fleeing from her reach, Masai shook his head. Underneath the heavy incense, she caught a whiff of his natural scent. It was surprisingly earthly and floral, most likely due to the flowers he distilled into nectars. "You're wrong. This was made to protect my people from her *draugrs*. Why would I share it with her?"

Anara's nails shrank at the vehemence in Masai's voice. There was no lie in his tone, but perhaps someone else in Smaragd was supplying the Empress.

At the far end of the bed, Calder stirred but did not wake. Sunbeams wove their way through the thick trees. The soft sounds of the others rising from their sleep near the campfire drifted through the leaves.

"Let's pretend I believe you," Anara whispered. "Then someone else in Smaragd is supplying the Empress. Who else would have the access and knowledge?"

Masai's lips pressed together.

"Loki's knot," Anara swore. "Kiah is supplying the Empress, isn't she?"

Silence spoke louder than his admission. She glared into Masai's eyes, so green like the godsforsaken forest Anara couldn't wait to escape. Through the trees came the others' voices as they walked back toward Helga. Not caring if she woke Calder, Anara jumped down from the bed. Masai followed, slamming the tailgate behind him. Halla's laughter drifted from nearby.

"What a great leader your mother is; you must be so proud," Anara hissed so only Masai could hear.

He advanced toward her, erasing what little space there'd been, his cheeks dark with anger. "Whatever my mother's doing is for the good of our people. What do you know about being a great leader? Your people are dead or monsters."

Anara's body shook. It'd been so long since she'd lost control of her *galdr* in anger, and she fought it now, knowing if she didn't, Anara would finish what the *draugr* had started on the lakeshore. Masai was so close; it wouldn't take much effort.

Darien emerged first from the nearby trees, followed by Larissa, then Halla and Kai. All four stopped at the sight of Anara and Masai.

". . . Is everything okay?" Darien's eyes darted from Anara to Masai then to where Calder stirred in Helga's trunk.

"Fine," Anara said, her body still trembling with the pressing transformation.

"Fine," Masai echoed, stepping back.

Anara couldn't wait any longer. "We should go; I'll scout from above."

Larissa's words were lost to the air as Anara launched herself into the sky. If only she could as easily lose the thoughts of her mind as well. But Masai's words summoned images from her vision that plagued her sight, coating it in the flames that had devoured Rubin. The screams of her people as their bodies broke under the curse of Shiko's blood rune chased her in the wind. The heat from the fire that had poured from her mouth left Anara with the taste of ash on her tongue. She flapped harder against the wind, as if she could outfly the demons in her mind.

ᚾᛁᛞᛝᚱᛋᚾᛁᛞᛝᚱᛋᚾᛁᛞᛝᚱᛋᚾᛁᛞᛝᚱᛋᚾᛁᛞᛝᚱᛋ

IT HAD TAKEN THEM hours, but they were nearly out of Smaragd. Anara glided more often than she flapped her wings, refusing to shift back to her human form for rest. She would tell Larissa and Darien about Kiah, but there was little they could do now. They already knew Kiah had chosen to act as Regent for Shiko; it shouldn't surprise them that she would actively supply the mad woman with whatever she wanted. They would deal with Smaragd *after* they reclaimed Safír.

A growing obstacle down the road caught her eye, souring Anara's mood further. She dove nearer for closer inspection. Two sentry vehicles had parked horizontally across the road, creating a roadblock for anyone crossing the Smaragd-Perle boundary line. With a frustrated caw, she turned back the way she'd come. She hadn't realized how far ahead she'd flown until she spotted Masai on his motorbike and closed the distance between them.

She cawed loudly enough to be heard over his engine. He skidded to a stop, cutting the sound. Anara felt the familiar and somewhat painful stretch and twist as her body transformed into its natural shape.

"What's wrong?" he asked.

Anara landed on her feet beside him. "Besides your constant presence?"

Masai only smiled. "I've heard attraction can often portray itself as aggression. Is there something you want to tell me?"

Anara would've shoved him off his bike right then and there if Helga hadn't pulled to a stop beside them.

Larissa rolled down her window, her brows pinched in concern. "What's going on?"

"Sentries."

Darien hopped down from the tailgate, joining their huddle away from Calder's prying ears.

Halla leaned over Larissa's lap to stare at Anara with excited eyes. "Did you say centaurs?"

"*Sentries*, Halla." Larissa shoved Halla back on her own seat. "Centaurs don't exist."

"It's not impossible; we literally just met the goddesses of fate," Halla muttered sliding down in her seat. Kai snickered beside her.

"Sentries?" Larissa asked, ignoring Halla.

"Roadblock ahead."

Larissa tugged at her braid. "Any way to get around it?"

Masai shook his head. "The forest is still too thick up to the border for the truck to pass through. Any other roads will mean hours of backtracking without the guarantee that they'll be sentry-free either."

"Kings and Queens," Larissa muttered.

Darien drummed his fingers against Helga's hood. "It'll take too much time to find another way."

"So we go through it," Anara agreed. "There's four strong fighters with us and maybe six or eight of them. We might be outnumbered, but they'll be outmatched."

Larissa glanced back at Halla in the passenger seat, who stuck her tongue out. "Stop looking at me like that, Lara. I'll be fine. I can take care of myself."

"I'd rather it not be an outright fight if we can prevent it," Larissa said slowly, even as her fingers reassuringly gripped her gun.

Anara shoved down her impatience. "Halla and Kai will be fine. We'll bury them under the bags in the trunk; they won't even be seen."

"What about—?" Darien nodded toward the back of the bed where Calder sat still bound and blindfolded.

Anara paused. Calder did present a problem.

"I'm with the Perle Princess." Masai crossed his arms. "Those sentries are most likely my people."

Anara didn't bother hiding her irritation. "They either get out of our way or we make them; it's that simple. This is war, Masai. Or do you want to go back to serving Calder and Shiko? Like mother, like son?"

Masai folded his arms, his muscles tensing against the sleeves of his shirt. "So then let's give them a chance to get out of our way."

"So they can attack us first?" Anara argued. "This is why Smaragd lost."

A vein ticking in Masai's neck was the only proof of his waning patience. "If you would stop talking for more than a second, I'll tell you my plan."

Anara made a grand mocking gesture with her hands, inviting him to speak.

"These men will recognize me, or they will at least have heard of me. I'm sure my mother has given some reasonable excuse for my absence, so they won't doubt me. Even more so, they will have heard the ghost stories of the Empress' War Dog." He jerked his head toward the back of the truck. "If we tie up everyone else in the truck bed, I can drive to the roadblock and let them know that the War Dog is taking prisoners to Safír as a bargaining tool against Torsten and his armies. Then the War Dog will drive up after me and confirm my story. We'll be let through without anyone the wiser."

Anara laughed out loud. "You think *Calder* will help us get through the roadblock? Are you insane?"

"I wasn't talking about Calder. Most people don't recognize the War Dog on sight." Masai tilted his head toward Darien. "All we need is someone of similar build and height to wear the uniform and call the shots."

Darien's face paled. "You want me to pretend to be Calder. And what, he'll just sit back here quietly tied up with the rest? He's a wild card we don't want to play. What if his gag gets loose?"

"Couldn't you persuade him to be quiet?" Halla asked from the passenger side.

Darien shook his head. "I can't break his block. There's something wrong in his mind."

Halla quieted; even Kai looked down at his feet.

Masai reached for the saddlebags on either side of his bike, digging to the bottom of one until he pulled out a small glass bottle filled with dark violet liquid. "With this, you won't have to. It's extracted from the Svefn flower and concentrated into a nectar that will knock him out for an hour at the most, so we'll need to make this quick."

Anara narrowed her eyes. "And why didn't you offer that before?"

"It's best to use it sparingly. It loses its potency with repeated usage, just like every other nectar." Masai stared at their confused faces. "You didn't know that?"

Anara rubbed the scar on her abdomen that pulsed with discomfort, then dropped her hand, realizing Masai had watched her do so. "That would've been nice to know."

Darien eyed the nectar. "He's not going to take that willingly."

"He doesn't get a choice. Stay here," Larissa instructed with a pointed look at Halla and Kai. She threw open her door, her hands already glowing with *galdr* as she approached Helga's bed. "Let's just get this done."

They moved toward the open tailgate after her. Calder waited, his body tense as he rose to his knees. His head turned back and forth as Helga rocked under the weight of Larissa and Darien pulling themselves up into the bed.

Larissa raised her glowing hands. Instantly, Calder's body stiffened under her *galdr*, but sweat beaded on her forehead. "He's fighting me, hurry up."

Darien pulled Calder to the metal floor, tilting his head back and ripping away the gag. Anara gripped his legs in case he should break free of Larissa's hold. Masai tipped the bottle into his mouth. Calder gurgled, until Darien squeezed his nose, forcing Calder to swallow the liquid. As Larissa lowered her hands, Calder cursed them, but his words slurred and his body fell limp.

Cautiously Anara released her hold on his legs as Darien did the same. She was suddenly aware of Kai's presence behind them who stared at Calder in horror. "Is he dead?"

"No," Darien said shortly. "Just asleep. Masai, help me with his clothes."

Catching his tone, Anara analyzed Darien, noting the way he set his jaw in determination as he removed his own jacket. This would be hard enough without an audience.

Anara grabbed Larissa's arm. "Let's give them a minute. And you—" She shot Kai a glance. "Weren't you supposed to stay in the cab?"

Hardly needing to be told, Larissa followed Anara back to the front of Helga. Even Kai followed, his eyes studiously downcast. Halla jumped down from the cab to nudge Kai's shoulder but said nothing. Anara crossed her arms, waiting for the rustling of Darien exchanging clothes to settle.

Masai approached. "We'll have to bind the rest of you together in the truck bed if you want this to look real."

Larissa's soft gasp drew Anara's gaze past Masai. Darien came around the truck, tugging at the black sleeves of his armored jacket. The Empress' symbol of the three diamonds intersected by the Isa rune stitched across the right shoulder looked strange on Darien. From his boots to the collar, Darien looked every bit an Empress' *Kafteinn*, but the discomfort on his face ruined the effect.

Masai shook his head. "You need to stick your nose in the air and look down on us all if you want to fool anyone."

"It wouldn't hurt if you tried to imagine killing us all every time you looked at us too," Anara pointed out. "Murderous thoughts and all go hand-in-hand with the uniform."

Darien stuck his nose in the air and glowered at them. Anara had never felt less threatened. "Any better?"

Larissa bit her lip. "Um, a little."

Halla giggled.

"Practice it on the way," Anara offered, stifling her own laughter. "You three get in the back."

"It wasn't that bad." Masai slammed his hand against Darien's back.

"No?" Darien asked.

"No." Masai's voice was too encouraging. "But you probably should practice."

Anara met Larissa's gaze, and they both nearly lost it. Kai and Halla scrambled into the truck bed, careful to skirt Calder's unconscious form. Though he wore Darien's clothes, the bitter metallic scent still clung to Calder's skin mixed with the incense of a pendant. Anara reached down, yanking it from his neck and stuffing it in her pocket to be investigated later.

Masai arranged Halla and Kai so that they leaned up against each other back-to-back and began circling the rope around their bodies. It was a fail-knot, with the loose tie hidden in Halla's hands in case they should need to unbind themselves. Anara grabbed the coil of rope Masai threw her way to bind Larissa in a similar fashion, but Larissa wasn't there.

She stood with Darien behind the truck, grabbing one of his hands. Only Anara's sharp ears caught Larissa's whisper. "What's wrong?"

Darien swallowed, letting his fingers intertwine with hers. It was such a familiar sight; Anara allowed herself a small smile.

"Calder's body." Darien stopped. He shut his eyes tight. "It's covered in scars."

Anara could hear Larissa's heart beat faster, could nearly sense the way Larissa's *galdr* welled up inside of her in response to her emotions.

Larissa ground her teeth. "Shiko."

"Yes."

In the ensuing silence, Anara nearly interrupted, but there was something too intimate about their position. Something about the way Darien's head tilted toward Larissa's, as if he found comfort and strength in simply being near her. Anara had watched Lovisa and Darien's friendship grow to something else, but this, whatever Larissa and Darien had, was so much more than that.

It wasn't just affection; it was survival, as though only they two breathed the same air. She couldn't understand why they were fighting it. Who cared about a centuries-old story of some giftless child? A love like theirs was a far better gift than *galdr*.

"Darien, if Shiko twisted his mind with some type of illusion, do you think that Aeron could still be in there somewhere?" Larissa asked.

Darien shook his head. "I don't know, but if he is . . ."

Anara moved toward them, hating her words before she said them. "If Shiko worked on him for years, getting Aeron back may be impossible."

Darien and Larissa turned to her with grief-stricken faces. They didn't know, couldn't know, what the War Dog had done for decades in the Empress' name or how many people he'd killed. No one could come back from such atrocities.

Anara raised the rope in her hands. "I'm sorry, but we need to go. That nectar will keep Calder out for only so long."

Larissa nodded, letting go of Darien's hand and pulling herself up into the truck. Anara leaned Calder's back up against Larissa's to keep him upright. Larissa shivered at the contact.

"You okay?" Anara asked.

"Oh yeah, never better," Larissa muttered. "You should trade spots with me and see how comfortable it is."

Anara smirked. "I'll have to take your word for it."

Darien walked out of sight, and Helga's engine roared. The back of the truck shook with the effort. With nothing left to say, Anara shut the tailgate and took to the sky just as Helga pulled away, following Masai's lead down the road. Soaring high above the treetops, Anara took the straightest path toward the blockade, leaving the road behind.

The sentries were right where she'd left them. Two of them remained in their trucks while the other five leaned against the outside of the armored vehicles. Though their clothing was padded, they still stamped their feet occasionally on the ground as if to beat off the chilly breeze. Anara drifted toward them, landing on the hood of one of the trucks. She cawed at the sentry that turned to look at her and clicked her talons against the metal top.

The sentry flung his hand in her direction. "Shoo. Shoo."

Anara cocked her head, pouring every ounce of disdain into her one beaded eye. The sentry edged away from her, but she heard him mumble, "Stupid bird."

Any retaliation on his part was intercepted by the sound of Masai's motorcycle. The sound alerted the sentries before the bike itself came into sight. They pulled their weapons from holsters, and although they kept them pointed at the ground, their posture was stiff and alert. Their focus was on the road before them, even as Masai's bike roared into existence before them, approaching quickly without the appearance of slowing down. The men raised their weapons.

Masai skidded to a stop in front of them, removing his helmet in one motion as he slid off his bike. His emerald earrings reflected the sun's light. "Lower your weapons, men."

"Lord Masai?" The oldest of the sentries dropped his weapon immediately, his voice filled with confusion. "What are you doing out here? The Regent said you were on a special assignment."

"I was, Aadan." Masai reached out his hand, clasping Aadan's arm with his own. "Though you should know better than to ask questions. Move the blockade and let me pass."

Aadan's face reddened. "I'm sorry, sir, but the Regent ordered that no one should be allowed to pass. She didn't give us any exceptions."

Anara cawed a warning. If these men wouldn't move, she would move them herself. The same sentry from before shot her a wary glance. Over the years, Anara had often been mistaken as an omen of the gods. She didn't mind the comparison. Masai spared her a brief glance.

"Aadan, you've served my mother well, but there is someone else on his way. If you make him wait, I can't protect you."

The sentries looked to Aadan who's hands fiddled on the grip of his gun. "Who is it?"

"Remember the Empress' War Dog?" Masai glanced at Anara. "You met him once."

Anara's feathers puffed up as she shuffled her talons. She understood. If Aadan had met Calder before, he would know that something was wrong the moment he saw Darien's dark hair.

Aadan's dark face tightened. "What is *he* doing here?"

"His prey wandered into our commonwealth. He plans to use them as leverage against the Viðnám. I'm to escort him out. That's all I can say, and I probably shouldn't have said that much. If you remember, the *Kafteinn* is not a patient man. I have no authority over him if he decides you're in his way. Now move these trucks."

As if to emphasize his words, Helga's clanking engine drew the sentries' attention back to the road to see the lumbering truck making its way toward them. Aadan hesitated for only a second, then licked his lips. "Move the trucks."

Anara flapped her wings as the truck under her moved to the side, clearing just enough space for Helga to slip through the gap. Masai straddled his bike. Even over the roar, Anara heard him say, "The *Kafteinn* is a private man. Don't tell anyone he's been here, or he'll know it was you who told. Stay safe, Aadan."

"You too, Lord Masai." Aadan's eyes narrowed on Helga's approach. "I don't trust him. Watch your back."

Masai grimaced. "And my front."

Aadan backed away, waving Helga forward. In the driver's seat, Darien stared straight ahead, the Empress' emblem a clear marker on his shoulder and chest. He pulled Helga through the gap, though he slowed as Aadan moved toward the driver's side. The distrust on his face turned to confusion which transformed into alarm as Darien pulled beside him.

"He's not—" Aadan began.

Masai revved the engine of his bike, cutting off Aadan's words as Darien leaned through the window. Anara couldn't catch his quick words under the combined noise of Helga's engine and Masai's motorcycle. The other sentries started toward their leader, then hesitated. Apparently the War Dog's reputation was enough to keep them at bay. They eyed the prisoners in the truck bed, shifting their weapons in their hands. Anara's body quivered as her *galdr* threatened to escape, as it urged her to transform into a wolf, to pounce on her prey before they could suspect the attack.

Then Aadan nodded, and Darien leaned back into the front seat. With a dazed expression on his face, Aadan waved them forward, and Helga passed through the gap, continuing down the road. Masai gave a two-finger salute from the top of his helmet as he sped his bike through the gap and down the road.

Anara remained, silent as the shadow she'd been forced to become over the years. The other sentries crowded around Aadan. His eyes refocused; his face cleared. He pushed past the other sentries and darted to the gap between the trucks, staring down the road after Helga. Darien's persuasion had not lasted long enough. Anara let her *galdr* build, readying herself for the attack. She could not let Aadan warn the others.

"Is something wrong, sir?" one of the sentries asked as Helga turned from sight.

It was Aadan's hesitation that stayed Anara's transformation.

"No," he said slowly, then with more confidence, "back to your places."

The sentries dashed into action, obediently pulling the trucks back to where they belonged, but Aadan stared down the road, whispering to himself, "I hope you know what you're doing, Masai."

Anara waited, but when Aadan went back to his post without another word, she allowed herself to release the pent-up energy stored within her limbs. She stretched her wings, taking to the air. Her thoughts bent toward Masai and what he'd done to earn such loyalty.

43

Ash-Coated Memories

Halla

THERE WAS NO REASON for Halla's exhaustion. She'd sat in the truck all day, and yet her body sagged with relief as she stretched out in her sleeping bag. She hadn't spent so much time with Lara since before her ill-fated visit to the Safírian Wall. If it hadn't been for the constant tension that twisted her intestines, Halla would have been happy for that time with her sister.

If only Kai hadn't chosen to spend the entire day sitting in the truck bed with Darien, guarding Calder after his nectar-induced nap. He'd said it was safer if there were two people watching Calder rather than one. Halla couldn't disagree; she shivered, remembering Calder's rage upon waking, but Lara had looked at Calder with pity, not fear.

They'd made camp quickly. Masai and Anara stood guard over Calder, staunchly ignoring the other. Larissa and Darien exchanged hushed whispers but stopped when they realized Halla was listening. Larissa tossed for several minutes before sleep eventually overcame her, and she'd joined Darien in sleep. Though Halla's body was tired, her mind would not surrender to her exhaustion. By the lack of snores to her side, Halla guessed that Kai was awake as well.

"Kai?" she whispered.

The sleeping bag crinkled as Kai turned. "Yeah?"

"Is something wrong?"

The rusting of Kai's movements stopped. "Why?"

"I've hardly seen you. It feels like you're disappearing."

Kai chuckled. "I've had years of practice."

"What do you mean?"

Kai was silent for so long Halla wondered if he'd fallen asleep. Then he moved closer. He breathed his words into her face. "Remember what I told you about my mother?"

Halla shivered as the night breeze ran along her exposed neck. "How she sold you?"

"Yes."

"How could I forget that? I'm still mad at her for it."

For some reason, Kai chuckled again.

"Why are you laughing at me?"

"Shhhh, Halla, you'll wake the others. I wasn't laughing at you. It's just, my mother is a fierce woman. It's funny to imagine you angry at her."

Heat rushed to the tip of Halla's nose. "Well, I am. I would tell her myself if I saw her."

Kai's humor vanished. "That would be a very bad idea."

The tone of his voice only increased Halla's growing suspicions. "She beat you, didn't she?"

Kai's silence was confirmation.

Halla scooted closer to Kai, their feet nearly touching through the sleeping bags. She lowered her voice. "It's okay. You don't have to tell me."

"My mother"—Kai's words came out in long pauses—"was not a kind woman. I think you know that. She wasn't thrilled to have me as a son. I was a liability. If it wasn't for my older brother—well, I might not have lasted long enough to be sold into slavery at all."

"Kai," Halla breathed out. "I'm sorry. I know you said you didn't think finding your brother was a good idea, but I'm sure that he would want to see you again."

"Halla, my brother—" Kai stopped. Halla could hear him swallow. "He believes in the Empress whole-heartedly, like most of our people. He would die for her. He would kill for her."

"Oh," was all Halla could say.

"I don't care about the Empress," Kai hurried to add. "If I'm honest, I don't care about the Viðnám either. I don't care who wins this war. I never have. The only person in Evrópa that I cared about was my brother. *Hel's*, I didn't even care about the gods."

Halla heard the emphasis on the past tense of *didn't*. "Did that change when we met the Norn?"

"No, I mean, they definitely affected my outlook." A hint of Kai's sarcasm resurfaced, easing Halla's discomfort with its return. "I started to change before that."

"When?"

"With you, actually."

Halla's eyes widened; her heart pitter-pattered. She wished so badly that she could see Kai's face, but the darkness of the night allowed only a dim silhouette. "Me?"

"In the barracks, I'd seen so many kids come and go from that place, and they all broke. But even after Fenris branded you, you still believed that your sister would come. I've never experienced that type of belief in someone. When I was sold, I knew my brother wouldn't come just as much as you knew that Larissa would. Then she came, and it wasn't just her; she brought an entire army for you."

Halla was suddenly glad Kai couldn't see her face. "I mean, it was for Perle too."

"It was for *you*." Kai's voice quickened. "Maybe I could have just accepted that your sister loved you more than my brother loved me. But when we were in the forest and the sentries shot at us, Larissa shoved me out of the way."

"Well, yeah. Anyone would do that—"

"No, they wouldn't, Halla," Kai snapped, then, as if catching himself, breathed in deeply. "Trust me. Most people wouldn't. Larissa didn't even like me. I could see it in the way she looked at me. I was a Diamantian, a reminder of everything she lost, and she still chose to save me. Then later, when that *draugr* had me, Darien stepped in. I still don't care about the Viðnám, Halla, but I care about you, and the others too."

Halla clutched onto the sleeping bag, unsure why Kai's words filled her with confusion. "Is that a bad thing?"

"I don't want my brother to get hurt," Kai whispered. "If the war goes to Diamant, he'll fight. And if he fights your friends, someone will lose."

"Just tell them who he is, Kai. They can show him that Shiko is wrong."

"He'll never see it that way." Kai huffed. "The Norn said the Viðnám would fail at Safír if we didn't return. I think it's going to be a bloody fight. What could I say to convince you to stay away from the fighting when we get there?"

Halla kicked her foot straight into Kai's knee. Although buffered by the sleeping bags, he still grunted in discomfort.

"I guess that answers my question."

Though Halla fumed at the question, her heart softened at Kai's sigh. "We'll be okay, Kai," she whispered.

"What about what the Norn told Darien?"

"No." Halla shook her head, her voice rising. "I don't believe that. Like Anara said, prophecies of fate don't always mean what we think they'll mean, and gods don't understand time the way we do. They wouldn't send us to help the Viðnám win at Safír just so that Darien could die."

"Halla?" Larissa's sleep-coated voice floated from Halla's other side. Halla clamped her mouth shut. Larissa's hand rubbed her back. "You okay, *bebe*?"

"I'm fine," Halla answered, not resenting the endearment like she used to. Every time Larissa used it, she heard Mamma's and Pappa's voices and felt a tug on her heart as if the word connected her to them.

"Go to sleep," Larissa murmured, draping her arm over her sister.

In minutes, Larissa's breathing evened out, signaling she'd fallen back asleep.

"Kai?" Halla whispered.

There was no answer, not even a rustle from the sleeping bag beside her.

ᚾᛁᛇᛚᚱᛋᚾᛁᛇᛚᚱᛋᚾᛁᛇᛚᚱᛋᚾᛁᛇᛚᚱᛋᚾᛁᛇᛚᚱᛋ

HALLA'S HAND DANGLED OUT of Helga's passenger side window. Though it was barely past noon, the chilly air stung her fingers, a sure sign that fall had arrived. Winter would bring long nights where the sun hardly ever made its appearance. It was the season Halla loved most, when she would be free from her farming duties and cuddle up on the couch with Mamma's hot chocolate while Pappa told stories. Onkel Tucker would fall asleep next to the fire, only to be woken by his own snores.

Tears burned the back of her eyes. It was the suddenness of the pain that still surprised her. It came from nowhere, but when it hit, her grief could nearly cripple her. Halla chewed at the inside of her cheek and stared at the midday sun, determined that its rays would dry her tears before they had a chance to fall.

They'd crossed over the Klarälven River hours ago, and though Halla had expected to feel something, anything, about returning to her commonwealth, there'd only been a hollow ache in the back of her throat. It didn't feel like home. Not anymore.

"You okay?" Lara asked.

Halla breathed in slowly until her chest nearly burst from the pressure. "It feels weird."

"What does?"

"Coming back."

"I know." Larissa's voice caught.

"I wonder if Mamma ever wanted to visit Perle." Halla sank into her seat, thinking over what the Norn had revealed. If the Empress had never attacked, would Halla have grown up in Perle?

Would she have admired Princess Lovisa from afar? But even as she considered the alternative life she might have lived, Halla rejected it. She'd much rather be an illegal second-born with Larissa than an aristocratic daughter without her.

"Lara, what will you do when you reclaim Safír?" Halla asked.

Larissa spared her a curious glance. "That's not really up to me. It's Torsten's kingdom, and Darien's; it'll be up to them. Torsten will probably imprison those who fight against him." Larissa's voice darkened. "Soon, we'll be holding as many people captive as Shiko."

Halla pulled her knees to her chest. "Like Saessae."

"I'm sorry about Saessae. We'll go back to Perle after things are settled in Safír and check on her, okay?"

"Really?" The ache in Halla's chest lightened at the thought.

"Really." Larissa smiled. "We have to start convincing the aristocratic families that we're not the enemy. It'll be a change, but starting small is the right step."

Sensing her opening, Halla took the chance. "So you'd be willing to forgive anyone who serves Shiko if they surrender, right?"

Larissa frowned. "Of course."

"But what if they don't surrender?"

Larissa glanced at Halla from the corner of her eye. Halla squirmed under her inspection. "What are you getting at, Halla?"

Halla nearly mentioned Kai and his brother but stopped herself. It wasn't her secret to tell. "What will you do with Calder?"

Larissa looked away, biting her lip and gripping the steering wheel until her knuckles turned white. "Calder will be put on trial."

"And then?"

"It's up to Torsten."

"Lara," Halla pushed.

"He'll be executed for his crimes." *Galdr* gathered around Larissa's fingers. She shook them violently as if she could shake off the glow. "Oh, Kings and Queens!"

Halla waited for Larissa's hands to settle. "You don't want Calder to die?"

Larissa shook her head. "I don't want Aeron to die."

"But isn't he Calder?"

"I don't know. If Shiko somehow twisted his mind, I have to wonder if Aeron is still inside of him. Don't we owe it to him to try and find out?"

Halla knew that *we* did not refer to her. "What does Darien think?"

Larissa's expression darkened. "He thinks taking Calder back to Torsten is a mistake. He's afraid Calder might be right, and Torsten will kill him on sight before he can reveal who he really is or was." Larissa stopped suddenly, as if realizing her musings had taken a dark turn.

"It's okay, Lara. I like it better when you talk to me than when you try to hide everything from me."

Larissa's mouth twitched up. "You're not the same little girl you were before, are you?"

Without meaning to, Halla's fingers traced the scar on the back of her neck. "No, I guess not."

"I still hate that I missed it."

Halla's brow furrowed. "Missed what?"

Larissa tapped the wheel. "Your birthday."

She laughed. "Really, Lara, we've got a lot going on right now, don't you think?"

"That's *why* I care." Larissa's voice dropped. "I only forced myself to remember my past because of you. Without you, none of this would have happened. You deserve more."

"Just don't die." Though Halla intended it to be a joke, her words fell flat. Larissa's prophecy mentioned the cost of a life, and Darien's did too. What if Kai was right? What if they were driving to their deaths?

Halla reached for her wrist to touch the medallions on her bracelet only to remember the *thræll* had taken it. She'd never replaced it. Perhaps it was for the better. She would start a new one with the rune of the Norn instead. She thought of praying to Verðandi for protection, but after meeting the goddess, Halla couldn't bring herself to utter her name. Though she'd been enthralled in the presence of the goddesses, she'd been terrified too. There was a reason the *Æsir* had lived apart from mankind for so long.

Hours passed as Halla drifted in and out of sleep. Though she wasn't tired, it felt as though Verðandi was calling her back to *Yggdrasil*. The giant tree of ash loomed in her mind, its branches shaking invitingly. In its roots, another tunnel opened, but it wasn't the same as before. Cold air blew through it, coating Halla's skin in ice.

She woke up shivering, though she was covered in Larissa's jacket. Her sister spared her a concerned look. "You're not getting sick, are you?"

"I don't think so." Though Halla's forehead felt normal, the back of her neck felt feverish. It was as though the rune itself emanated heat.

Ahead, Masai's motorbike kept pace under Anara's flight pattern, but Larissa was looking at a turn off the main road. With a turn so sharp it thrust Halla against the door, Larissa directed Helga onto a worn and beaten dirt path. Halla's discomfort was forgotten as a trickle of familiarity ran over her skin. She knew those trees; she knew that road.

With a loud caw, Anara landed on Helga's hood, cocking her beaded eye in Larissa's direction.

"Darien will understand," Larissa said sharply. "We don't have to be in Safír until tomorrow. I have to do this."

Anara rustled her wings but flew off all the same. The headlights of Masai's motorcycle flared in Helga's side mirrors, but Halla paid him little attention. She soaked in every familiar sight. Her home, their farmhouse, was just down that road and around the bend.

"This isn't going to be easy, Halla." Larissa's voice held a warning. "You can stay with Helga, but there's something I need to take care of."

Halla sobered, her breath leaving her. "Onkel?"

After the *draugr* attack, they'd given their parents a burning burial, but they hadn't had the time to find and bury Onkel Tucker. His body had been left in the fields to rot, tempting Hel's denial of entry into the afterworld.

Larissa nodded, gripping the wheel even as she urged Helga forward. "You shouldn't come. It's been a few weeks; it won't be pleasant."

"I'm coming." To Halla's grateful surprise, Larissa didn't argue even when it was clear she wanted to. "Thank you."

"For what?"

"Not treating me like a child." Halla grabbed her sister's hand. "Best belated birthday gift you could give me."

Larissa's brief smile died entirely as they rounded the bend. The trees cleared, making way for the sight that lay before them, and Halla's hope rushed out of her lungs. The farmhouse she'd been envisioning was gone. If Halla hadn't lived there all her life, she would never be able to make sense of the devastation and piles of ashes that lay before her. Larissa pulled forward until the dirt turned to char under Helga's tires. When she cut the engine, the sisters sat staring.

The largest pile of debris sat to their left. If Halla looked closely, she could see the foundational beams of their farmhouse sticking out of the rubble that surrounded them. Further off, the barn had collapsed into a pile of crumbling wooden beams. Not even the fields had escaped the fire's rage. Their precious berry fields, cultivated for generations, were scorched. It would be years before the land could be used again.

Tears streamed down Halla's face, but she didn't utter a sound. She would be stronger than last time. She would face this grief. Iðunn had not cried when she was taken from her beloved apple trees; she could not be broken. And though Halla would allow herself the tears, she, too, would not break. Movement from the truck bed shook Helga's cab, but still the sisters remained.

Footsteps drew their attention to Larissa's open window where Darien rested his hands on the metal frame. "You're sure this is a good idea?"

"No." Larissa shook her head. "But it's still the right thing to do."

Anara appeared at his side, her eyes surveying the scene of destruction. "There might not be much left to hold a burial for."

"Where's Masai?" Halla asked, noticing his empty motorcycle next to them.

"He agreed to keep watch over Calder," Darien answered. "You ready for this, kiddo?"

Halla swallowed, unable to answer, but nodded anyway. She turned in surprise as her door opened. Kai extended his hand, helping Halla scramble to the ground. Once steady on her feet, she wiped at her tears as if she could erase the evidence.

Kai's fingers fidgeted at his sides. "This is your home, isn't it?"

"What's left of it." Her voice broke.

Kai eyed the fresh trails of tears that leaked from the corners of Halla's eyes. "Why are we here?"

Halla breathed in deep, again holding it until the pain in her chest stopped the flow of tears. "When we left, we gave my parents a burning burial, but we didn't have time for my Onkel—" Halla cleared her throat. "Onkel Tucker. We had to leave him. It wasn't right. The *Æsir* requires a proper burial."

Kai's eyes scanned his surroundings. "The *draugrs* did this?"

Anara crossed her arms, having heard Kai's questions. "On Calder's orders."

Kai's face tightened as he spared a glance toward the back of the truck.

Wiping at her face, Halla moved around Helga's hood to stand beside Larissa, catching the tail end of her sister's sentence.

"—I didn't think this through." Larissa looked around. "There's nothing here we can use to mark their graves. Everything's gone."

"We'll figure it out." Darien touched Larissa's arm, bringing her attention back to him. "Let's just see what we're working with."

Larissa's shoulders released the tension they'd held all day. In all of Halla's memories, real or planted, she'd never seen Larissa so at peace as she was with Darien. Hesitant to interrupt, she hung back, but Darien caught her eye. He nudged Larissa, who motioned Halla forward.

"Are you ready?" Larissa asked.

Halla nodded, resisting the urge to take Larissa's hand. They walked through what remained of the farmhouse, Halla's shoes kicking up the ash scattered around the edges. With no walls to stop it, nature had already begun to creep back in. Weeds grew up through the gaps in the ground. She trod softly on broken boards. Burnt, fluffy insulation poured out from the walls, oddly sparkly in its own way. Her feet sank into mounds of it.

Halla breathed in deep and slow, trying to not gag on the smell. She wasn't even sure the smell was real. The others didn't seem bothered at all. Perhaps only the memories of that night assailed her nose. She could just make out the remnants of the TV; some twisted metal pots and pans were scattered on the floor of what used to be the kitchen, but there was something wrong about the size of their home. Pappa and Mamma's room had always seemed so big, but Halla passed through, thinking it looked so small.

Anara, Darien, and Kai walked behind the sisters, giving them some measure of respect and privacy, but Halla wished they would walk with them. At the back side of the crumbling house, Larissa's steps faltered, and Halla nearly bumped into her. In the center of their garden, two large scorch marks remained on the ground, but it was the third scorch mark, accompanied by three grave markers, that confused Halla.

They moved forward in unison. Halla's mind taunted her with the heat of the flames on her skin, the smell of the *draugr*'s decaying flesh, the screams of her parents. The world around her tilted. She breathed in, determined to master this grief that swallowed her whole, drowning her in the images she wished she could escape.

She couldn't fight it. She fell to her knees, the dust and ash billowing around her. She choked on it as it filled her nostrils and infected her lungs. Larissa's arms wrapped around her.

Blinking away the tears, Halla reached out to touch the gravestones. Two markers rested on top of where they'd burned her parents' bodies. They read: *To loved ones having gone from this world to the next.*

The last stone sat on the new outline, and its epitaph read: *To the unknown farmer. May Freyr, god of the harvest, reap your soul.*

Halla's fingers traced the words. "Onkel Tucker."

"I'm glad someone honored him." Larissa's words were thick with unshed tears.

"But he isn't unknown," Halla protested.

"No, he isn't." Larissa squeezed her shoulders. "And we'll continue to remember him and Mamma and Pappa too."

Vaguely, Halla was aware of Kai's presence beside her. Darien and Anara had joined them as well. Kai's fingers fidgeted even more sporadically at his sides.

"Thank you," Larissa spoke to the burial stones, laying her hands on their smooth surfaces. "All of you. You took me in when you knew the risks. You gave me a home, a family. I can't ever repay your sacrifice, but I'll try to live up to your expectations."

Larissa's voice caught abruptly in her throat. Halla leaned against her, not to be supported but rather to support Larissa as Larissa had always done for her. "You already have, Lara."

"She's right," Anara added. "You reclaimed Perle. I'm certain if Vern could see this, she would thank you for freeing her home."

Darien knelt beside Larissa. "And more importantly, you kept Halla safe."

Halla felt Larissa's eyes on the back of her neck. She shifted to shield the runic scar, but Larissa's lips pulled downward. "Not entirely." She sighed. "I guess we didn't need to come back, but I'm glad we did. If only to say goodbye."

She took Darien's offered hand, and they rose to their feet, but Darien's eyes caught on the stones, and he hesitated in his movements. He leaned forward, his fingers lightly tracing the stone itself. "I know who made this."

"What?" Anara asked. "Who?"

"This looks like Aagen's craftsmanship. He did something like this before when we lost a farm hand who fell from a tree." Darien's thoughtful expression transformed into something more similar to unexpected delight. "We can't stay here tonight, but I know where we'll be safe before we join the Viðnám in Havsiden."

"You want to go to Aagen's?" Larissa asked.

Anara nodded. "It's brilliant. It's not like we can take Calder into the city with us. It'd be better off if we were able to leave Calder under his watch until the city is taken."

Darien's delight faded. "I'm not sure that's the best idea."

"If we take him into the city, there's a higher chance he'll escape."

Larissa raised her hands to them both. "We don't need to have this conversation right now, or right *here*. But I agree. Let's go to Aagen's."

Halla's heart raced in her chest as they turned back to Helga. She wasn't ready. "I need a minute."

Larissa hesitated. "I'll stay with you."

"No, it's okay." Halla breathed in to settle the waver in her words. "I just need a minute to say goodbye. You can go."

Larissa stared in indecision.

"I'll be right there," Halla promised.

Though Halla heard the shuffle of the others as they made their way around the farmhouse, Kai stayed with her, unmoving besides his fingers that tapped in his lap. "Do you want me to leave, too?"

"No," she said quietly. "You can stay."

The memories of her parents' deaths hit her harder now without the buffer of the others' presence, but Halla didn't shy away from them. She let herself feel each hurt that she'd tried to escape. Her mind replayed the moment she'd run to her parents, thinking she'd found safety, to the moment the *draugr* had revealed itself. The smoke had nearly suffocated her under the barn trap door. She'd been so sure she was going to die. So certain that she'd already lost everyone, the thought didn't scare her.

Each smell, each sound, each sense of that night worked its way through quiet sobs and silent tears. She was grateful for Kai, for someone unconnected to that night of horror and loss. She leaned her head on his shoulder, relieved he did not pull away even as her tears soaked through his shirt.

"I miss you all so much," she cried. "The Norn showed me a dream of you. You were happy. You were so proud of me; it felt so real." Halla's fingers dug into the soil, as if it would somehow ground her back in reality, as if it might pull her away from the clouded memories of the past. "Mamma, you made a promise to the Norn that you would care for Larissa. That's what I'm going to do now. She doesn't know it. She wouldn't like it, because, well"—she laughed through her tears—" you know how she is. But I'm going to fulfill your promise, so don't worry, Mamma. And Pappa, I won't forget your stories. They helped me when I really needed them most. And Tucker, I hope you found Iðunn's apple orchard. I know you'd like it there. I love you."

Halla's whispered words died at the end, and she shuddered as the memories of that night faded toward the back of her mind. Kai shivered beside her, gripping his hands in his lap.

"Kai?" Halla lifted her head from his shoulder.

He shook his head, his dark eyes glued to the outlines scorched into the ground that surrounded them. "I'm sorry, Halla, for everything you lost. I know I said before that I didn't care about choosing sides, but this is wrong. The Empress will pay for this. I'll make sure of it."

44

Home Again

Darien

IN THE PITCH BLACK of the night, Darien heard Masai's bike rumbling and Anara's frequent caws signaling it was all clear. He'd expected more sentries on the road, but their absence did not relieve him. If there were no sentries on the roads, they must have gone to the city.

But even in the pale moonlight, Darien could not have missed the familiarity of the road. No doubt, Aagen would hear them coming. Darien would have to make himself known before Aagen assumed they were sentries knocking down his door. Though Darien's anxiety begged him to ask Larissa to keep driving straight to Safír, there was an undeniable portion of his heart that would not yield its desire to see Aagen again. He'd promised Aagen he would return, and he was going to keep that promise.

Darien's visit with the Norn had only increased his love for his adoptive father. It was one thing to love someone else's child; it was another when they knew the risk involved. There was only one true damper on Darien spirits.

Even bound, Calder still somehow managed to sprawl in Helga's bed, looking more prince than prisoner. "Not going straight to Safír, then? Going to hide like usual?"

Darien ignored him. Most of their time had been spent this way, with Calder throwing his jibes while Darien sat silently. Darien had almost gotten used to them, wouldn't have been bothered by them at all if it weren't for the moments Calder's voice would soften and a hint of Aeron would slip through.

"Leave him alone," Kai hissed.

Darien glanced at the boy in surprise. Though Kai had insisted on riding in the truck bed with Darien, he'd been silent the whole time. At first, Darien wondered if he was trying to give Halla more time with Larissa, or if he was worried Calder would overpower Darien if there was no one else in the truck bed, but Darien wasn't so sure. Something had changed in the boy after visiting Dal's Berry Farm, or what was left of it. He'd pulled himself up into the truck, and for the first time, Kai looked at Calder with more than just fear. There was anger mixed in as well.

Calder turned toward Kai's voice, his mouth stretching beneath the blindfold. "He speaks! Here I thought you might be mute."

"You're only going to make it worse for yourself," Kai threatened.

Darien winced. Didn't Kai realize he was just feeding Calder's nature? The only way to win in an argument against Calder was to not argue at all.

Calder's voice softened. "Shouldn't a Diamantian like you be on my side?"

Though Darien didn't sense any *galdr*, he wasn't about to risk it. "Enough, Calder, or I'll ask Masai to knock you out again."

Darien nearly thought about signaling to Masai then, but with each use of the nectar, it lost its potency. They couldn't risk using it if they were to need it again.

"Maybe I'll keep talking, then," Calder taunted. "Unless you're about to become interesting company? You could tell me about Lovisa's visit back to Dal's farm? Did she cry? Did she realize it was me who sent the *draugr* back to her farm and killed them all?"

Kai rose to his feet as if he would hit Calder, but a bump in the road landed him flat on his butt. Darien reached for him, silently cautioning him against further action. Kai huffed, flinging himself against Helga's tailgate and crossing his arms firmly against his chest. Darien rubbed the sapphire ring on his hand, willing himself to stay calm even as his own fists yearned to plant themselves into Calder's face.

Helga vibrated violently as the road beneath them changed from asphalt to dirt. This was it. A single word bounced around in Darien's head.

Home.

The scents of soil and apples greeted Darien like an old friend. They were nearly there. Holding on tight to Helga's side, Darien stood, waiting for the moment the farmhouse would come into view. Its windows shone with light. Aagen had heard them coming. Masai pulled his bike alongside Helga, and Darien motioned at him to fall behind as he remembered the gun that Aagen had hidden under the floorboards of the kitchen sink.

As Helga slowed in the front drive, Calder leaned forward. "Well, go on then, run along to the only daddy that actually loves you."

Darien tensed, seriously contemplating kicking Calder as a parting gift, but jumped from the open tailgate instead. Masai parked his bike behind the truck.

Masai removed his helmet, nodding toward Calder. "I'll stay with him."

Darien lay his hand on Masai's shoulder. "Thank you."

"Finally trust me now?"

"Between the *draugrs*, goddesses of fate, and Calder, you're the least of my worries."

Masai's laugh was deep. "I suppose that's true."

There was something about the tall, dark man that Darien appreciated. If they survived the next several days, Darien was determined to make Masai his friend.

Anara swooped down, landing beside the two men. She arched her eyebrow with her hands on her hips. "If you two are done, someone is waiting for you, Darien, and I don't love the look of his gun."

"Kings and Queens," Darien muttered, spinning toward the front porch where Aagen waited half-concealed in the shadows, but the light from inside his windows glinted against the metal in his hands. "Aagen! It's me!"

Darien took a step, then froze, shocked at the sight of the gun pointed in his direction. Aagen glared at him with enough seething hatred that Darien almost wondered if the Norn had erased his memory of him entirely from Aagen's mind. In the cab, Larissa reached for her gun.

"No!" Darien called to her, raising a hand in her direction and lifting his other as a show of surrender to Aagen. In his peripheral, Larissa shoved Halla down behind the dash. Anara and Masai still stood at the back of the truck; Darien would have heard them move otherwise. He could only hope that Anara would let him handle this. "Aagen, it's Darien. Do you remember?"

Aagen harrumphed. "Do you think I'm stupid, *draugr*? Leave before I make you."

Understanding almost made Darien laugh if not for the hollow of the gun still pointed his way. "When I left, I told you that I would come back and have my own story to share with you. You told me you'd like that." Aagen's face softened at the familiar words, and Darien stepped forward. "Well, I'm back, and I've got quite the story."

"Darien?" Aagen's words were a whisper. His arm fell to his side as he hurriedly thrust the gun back into his waistband. He stomped down the steps, his injured leg thumping awkwardly as he went. Before Darien could move, Aagen was there, wrapping him with his enormous arms and burying Darien's face in his long, braided beard. "My boy!"

"It's good to see you too." Darien laughed, pushing off of Aagen's chest. *This* was what family was supposed to feel like, but Darien shoved away the traitorous thought before he could linger on it.

Aagen cupped the back of Darien's head. "Look at you. Your beard is coming in. You were just a boy when you left."

Darien looked away, grateful for the shadow of hair that hid his flush. "It's only been a few weeks."

"Yet everything has changed." Aagen's voice sombered. His gaze landed on Larissa and Halla in Helga's cab. "The girls from your dreams?"

"Yes." Darien ran his hand through his hair. He stepped to the side, revealing Anara and Masai's presence behind him. Even Kai was sticking his head over the tall rails of Helga's sides. "And it's more complicated than you'd expect."

Aagen harrumphed. "With you? Complicated sounds about right. Come in and explain it to me."

Only Masai stayed behind to handle Calder as the rest followed Aagen. Darien motioned at the gun at Aagen's waist. "What were you going to do with that against a *draugr*?"

"Go out fighting. Give the others a chance."

Darien stopped at the steps. "The others?"

"Refugees." Aagen pulled on his beard. "I sent them to the next safe house."

"Safe house?"

"Safírians are taking advantage of the Viðnám's presence to flee the city while they can. This group wasn't supposed to move on for another day." He sighed. "I should try and bring them back. They're probably terrified they're being chased by a monster."

"Better to let them stay scared then to bring them back here." Darien gestured back toward Helga where Masai held tightly to Calder's bound hands. Though blindfolded, it seemed as though Calder looked straight at Darien. "We didn't come without our own monsters. He isn't a *draugr*, but he's—"

"—a *Kafteinn*," Aagen breathed out. "What in the name of Óðinn's left eye is he doing with you?"

"He's my brother. *Was* my brother."

Aagen's hand paused on his beard. "Seems we better get straight to your story."

Anara slid beside Darien with such ease it was as if she had suddenly appeared. "We'll need a place to put Calder."

Aagen gestured to the side of the house. "There's the cellar, if you think that will do."

"That'll work." She glanced back at Masai, her voice laced with meaning. "With a little help, I think."

At Anara's approach, Calder pulled against Masai's grip, but the Smaragdian held him resolutely. Darien caught the bottle Anara rifled through Masai's bag to throw his way. Larissa stood behind them, her hands glowing in case she was needed. Kai and Halla watched from the shadows. Though Calder no longer fought, his body was rigid with fury.

"You think you're on the right side, don't you?" Calder spat out. "You'll learn just like Aeron did that there isn't a right side, there's only the winning side. And when you lose, you'll lose it all. You might have stolen Aeron's crown, *Prince* Darien," he sneered, "but you'll lose it along with every person you care about, and it will be *your* fault."

Grinding his teeth, Darien forced Calder's mouth open and tipped the liquid in until Masai told him to stop. It didn't take long for the fight to flee Calder's body as he slumped to the ground.

Sighing, Anara grabbed Calder's feet. "Even unconscious, he's a pain."

Masai slid his hands under Calder's armpits. "I can carry him myself if he's too heavy for you."

Anara snorted. "I could pick him up in my sleep. I'm helping you."

As they bickered their way over to the cellar, Darien ran a hand over his stubble and joined the others where they waited with Aagen on the porch.

His adoptive father crossed his arms. "Did I hear the *Kafteinn* call you *prince*?"

"Let's get inside, Aagen. I'll tell you everything."

ᚾᛁᛝᛐᛋᚾᛁᛝᛐᛋᚾᛁᛝᛐᛋᚾᛁᛝᛐᛋᚾᛁᛝᛐᛋ

IT WAS A FEAT in and of itself to squeeze all seven of them inside Aagen's small living room. The warmth from the fireplace was stifling. Aagen paced as he listened to Darien's story, and from his occasional stomps, Darien knew he was restraining himself from interrupting.

When Darien admitted that he was the Safírian Prince, along with the man currently tied up in Aagen's cellar, Aagen had looked both impressed and horrified, muttering, "Kings and Queens."

Darien continued, summarizing as best he could, but when he recounted what had happened on Larissa's farm, he paused. "Aagen, there are three grave markers on those graves. Did you have anything to do with them?"

Aagen's face fell. "Yes. The smoke was so bad, farmers from all around the countryside drove to find the cause. We tried to put out the flames, but then the sentries arrived, commanding that we all return to our homes. I went back the next day, worried that you had passed that direction. When I found the bodies, I looked only long enough to make sure they weren't you, though it wasn't easy to tell. I made the tombstones over the next couple days and brought them back. I couldn't just leave them in the field."

"Thank you." Larissa spoke from her place on the couch next to Darien. "You honored them when we couldn't."

Aagen leaned forward, patting Larissa's knee. "You honor them still. I don't need to hear the rest of Darien's story to know that."

"Well, you might want to keep listening. You know that lost Perle Princess that the Viðnám is rallying behind?" Darien tilted his head toward Larissa.

Aagen's busy brows raised nearly into his hairline; then, he kneeled before Larissa. "Your Majesty."

Darien laughed. "Oh sure, bow for her. All I get is a measly 'Kings and Queens.'"

Aagen glared up at his adopted son. "It's hard to think of you as royalty when your drool stains are still on my pillows."

Ignoring Darien's stuttered protests, Larissa grabbed Aagen's arms and pulled him back to his feet. "My friends call me Larissa."

Aagen shook his head and thumped his good foot against the floor, but Darien caught a glimpse of the tears gathering in his eyes. "I'd heard the rumors, of course. How could I not, with the Viðnám trampling across my lands and the sentries pounding on doors? But to think that I housed the prince of Safír in my home for a year without them knowing. To think that the Perle Princess is here now! The Norn have blessed me to have met not only one but two descendants of the ancient bloodlines."

"Well—" Darien resisted the urge to laugh. "Technically, you've met four. Aagen, this is Princess Anara of Rubin and Prince Masai of Smaragd."

Anara nodded nonchalantly from her place near the door. Leaning against the opposing wall, Masai lifted his hand in a small wave.

Aagen's mouth fell open. His eyes darted to where Halla laid her head on Kai's shoulder sitting in front of the fireplace. Her heavy eyes fluttered to attention under Aagen's intense stare. "And them? Don't tell me they're some lost royalty from Diamant?"

"Nope." Halla yawned. "We're dreadfully, boringly just us. Though apparently, my great-grandmother used to be an aristocrat in Perle."

Kai coughed. "Just dreadfully boring for me, I'm afraid."

"I can't believe this," Aagen muttered, falling into his chair. "But what are you doing here? Why aren't you with the Viðnám?"

Darien briefly recounted their journey to learn the prophecy, but when he mentioned the Norn, Aagen interrupted again. "You met them? The *Norn*! But what did they say?"

"Nothing useful," Anara answered before Darien could.

Though frustrated at her lie, Darien was grateful at least that he wouldn't have to share his own bit of the prophecy again. It would only worry Aagen unnecessarily. Darien finished relaying what had happened, then asked, "But what is happening here? You said earlier that this was a safe house. What did you mean?"

The shrewd look in Aagen's eyes told Darien he did not believe Anara's lie, but he answered, "The Viðnám arrived in Safír several days ago, recruiting throughout the countryside. Jon went with them, as did the others, but with my blasted leg, I knew I would be better help here. The Viðnám is having a hard go of it. Havsiden was heavily fortified by the time they arrived. They broke through the Outer Wall two days ago, but the Second Wall holds."

Darien clenched his fists. It was just as the Norn had predicted.

"The Viðnám is sending out the innocents, the women and children and those too old to fight to get them out of the way. They come to me, and I send them on to the next farmhouse and they send them on to the next. Some hope to return home soon. Others fear the Viðnám will lose, and they're making their way to Perle. General Soren holds Lystheim until Princess Lovisa returns. Truthfully, if the Viðnám does not take Safír, I doubt that Perle will last under their control much longer."

"That's why we're here," Darien said. "The Norn said if we didn't arrive within three days the Viðnám would lose."

"I thought the Norn didn't tell you anything useful." Aagen's sharp gaze sent Darien's eyes to the ground.

Masai spoke up in his place. "They didn't tell us much."

"Hmmm. And the third day is tomorrow?"

"Yes," Larissa answered. "We were hoping to rest here before carrying on to the Viðnám tomorrow."

"Of course you can, and you should. You'll need your strength. What will you do with the *Kafteinn*?"

Darien felt Anara's stare like a physical presence. Though he didn't like it, he knew it was their only option. "We'd like to leave him here, bound and medicated in the cellar until the fight is over, but only if that's okay with you."

Aagen rose, placing his hand on Darien's shoulder. "If leaving him here makes you safer there, of course, my son."

Darien looked into Aagen's kind, lined eyes. Torsten's face flashed like an overlay on top of Aagen, but Torsten's eyes were not nearly so kind. Darien swallowed past the lump in his throat. To his side, Halla's head slumped forward as her eyes slid shut. Without needing to consult a clock, Darien knew it was after midnight. The third day had already begun.

Noticing Halla also, Larissa stood. "Is there somewhere we can rest, Aagen?"

"Yes, you and your sister can sleep in my bed. Darien's old room is available, of course, but that bed will only fit one. You," he said pointing at Kai, "could probably fit on the couch. There's room in the barn where the farmhands slept." Aagen's face turned purple. "Royalty deserves better, but I'm afraid it's the best I've got."

"It's not a problem." Anara turned the knob on the door. "I'll sleep in front of the cellar. Someone should stay close to Calder."

"I'll join your watch," Masai offered.

"Oh, and the night gets better," Anara muttered as she strode out the door.

He smiled, pushing off the wall. "I've often been told my presence makes everything better."

Their voices died off in the distance. Aagen rose to his feet, turning toward Larissa. "I can show you the way to your room, your Majesty."

"Larissa, please." She bowed down, gently shaking Halla's shoulder. "*Bebe*, come on."

Halla stirred, though only partly. Darien reached down, pulling her into his arms to carry her down the hall to Aagen's room. She seemed longer and heavier than she'd been when he'd carried her fleeing from Perle. The instant her head hit the pillow, Halla's breathing turned to light snores. Her face was even more childlike in slumber. Larissa brushed a strand of Halla's hair out of her face, then motioned to Darien and Kai to follow her back into the living room. Aagen sat on the chair he'd brought out while Kai laid himself out on the couch.

"Aagen, where will you sleep?" Darien asked.

"I won't, son. I'll stand watch outside and let the others rest. You all need it more than I do."

Gratitude flooded Darien's heart. "Thank you."

Aagen rose, but Larissa's urgent voice stopped him at the door. "Aagen, wait. I have another favor to ask."

He bowed low. "Anything, your Majesty."

"When we leave tomorrow, I'd like for Halla and Kai to stay here."

"What?" Kai's legs swung over the edge of the couch as he bolted straight up. "You didn't run this by Halla."

Larissa shot him an irritated glance. "Of course not. She would've spent all night fighting me on it." She softened her voice. "You know she won't be safe in battle. You *know* she'll put herself in harm's way without a second thought."

Kai frowned, but Darien could see that the boy was in agreement. "When I suggested something similar, she kicked me. Hard. You won't be able to force her to stay."

"I'll let it be her choice, but I need your help convincing her. She listens to you." Larissa sat beside him on the couch. "We both just want to keep her safe, right?"

Kai scooted further into the couch cushions, looking as though he wished he could disappear within them. His fingers fidgeted at his sides. "I'll try to convince her."

Though Darien hadn't known about the plan any more than Kai had, relief flooded through him. It was one thing to walk knowingly toward potential death. He couldn't bear to watch what it would do to Larissa if she lost Halla.

What will it do to her if she loses you?

The thought pushed itself forward until Darien could think of nothing else. His mind lost track of whatever Larissa was saying to Kai. No matter what the Norn had seen, Darien had to go to Safír. Besides, they hadn't foretold his death in Safír. It could happen anywhere, at any time. And really, wasn't that the same for any of them? There was no safety in war. But with that thought came the sudden fear of Larissa's prophecy.

Only the third of the Perlian line, at the cost of a life, can change Fate's design.

"Lara, can I talk to you?" The question burst from Darien's lips before he could catch himself. Kai and Larissa turned in surprise, clearly still in the middle of their conversation. Even Aagen looked at Darien in a knowing manner.

"Sure." Larissa reached her hand to touch Kai's shoulder; he stiffened at her touch. "Thank you. I'm grateful that Halla found a friend like you."

"Don't mention it," Kai mumbled under his breath, but Darien could see the tips of the boy's ears had turned red.

"Goodnight, son," Aagen called after Darien as he led Larissa down the hall.

It was strange entering his old bedroom. Nothing had changed. The thin bed was still pushed up against the wall alongside his dresser. The screen on the window was still ripped at the corner where bugs would fly in during the summer months. Darien had mended it so many times, he couldn't tell where the original tear started and where his poor patch jobs ended. It was even stranger to be in this place, knowing that so many of his memories in it were a lie, placed in his mind by goddesses of fate.

Larissa closed the door behind her, plunging the room into semi-darkness. "Is everything okay?"

Darien shook his head, though Larissa couldn't see it. He supposed he could turn on the light, but it was easier to admit to his fears in the dark. "Do you ever get the feeling we're just strings, and the Norn decide where they weave us?"

"No." Larissa's answer was quiet, but quick.

"They changed the course of our lives. They gave us false memories that sometimes feel more real than those we actually lived. And now they're prophesying that we're both going to die. For what purpose? That we *might* overthrow an Empress that has had decades to grow in *galdr*?"

Larissa's footsteps thudded softly toward him. Her fingers reached for his forearm, grounding him in that moment. "We are our own people. No matter what the Norn did to us. No matter what is expected of us. We can make our own decisions. We pull the strings, not the Norn."

"So you could just walk away from the prophecy?"

Larissa's fingers tightened on Darien's arm.

He drew closer to her. "Be honest, if I asked you to run away with me, grab Halla, and just flee from all of this, would you do it?"

Part of Darien yearned for Larissa to agree. Anara could come too, even Kai if he wanted to. Masai would probably have to come, which would annoy Anara to no end, but he would be safer on the run with them than if he were to return to Smaragd. But even as Darien imagined this hypothetical future, the images crumbled before his eyes. Larissa could not leave her people, not now that they'd accepted her. Darien couldn't leave his, not now that he'd taken responsibility for them.

Larissa drew in a shaky breath. "Darien, I—"

"I know it wasn't fair to ask. But when it comes to you, I don't want to play fair. I just want you safe." He leaned down, letting his forehead rest against hers. It was easy in the dark to pretend he was back on that shoreline with no more worries than a boy unsure how to tell a girl he loved her.

"I can't run away now." Her voice broke, but her hands tightened on his arms as though she couldn't bear to let him go. "And I don't think you could either."

She was right, but Darien wished she wasn't. "Just promise me one thing."

"Anything," Larissa whispered, never sounding more like Lovisa than she did in that moment.

Darien let his hand cup Larissa's cheek, his thumb running over her scar while his fingers wound into her hair. "Don't die."

"I *won't* die." When Larissa said it like that, Darien could almost believe her. "And neither will you. I won't allow it."

Darien smiled, a short chuckle falling from his lips. "You'll tell the Norn, then?"

"They can shove their prophecy all the way back to Asgard."

"Pretty sure that was destroyed in *Ragnarok*."

"My point exactly."

The silence lengthened, but Darien did nothing to stop it. He knew that when he did, the moment would be over, tomorrow would come, and his certainty would vanish along with the night. When would they have more than just these stolen moments?

Larissa's warm breath tickled his throat as she sighed against him. "We should sleep."

She was right; Darien knew she was right. She would need all the rest she could get to use her *galdr* at full strength. She would need everything she had to prepare for what waited for them, yet he still couldn't bear to let her go. He buried his face in her hair.

If nothing else, she will survive.

His lips brushed against her forehead as he forced his hands to release her and stepped back. If he hadn't let her go now, he never would. "You're right. Besides, if Halla wakes and you're not there, she'll worry."

He couldn't see her, but he knew the way her eyes would dart to the door, as if she could see Halla through the walls. Yet she didn't move. Instead, he felt her arms wrap around his neck as she pulled him closer, leaning her head on his shoulder.

"Dar?" she asked, her voice breathless.

"Yes?" he murmured into her hair.

"You have to promise me something too."

"Anything," he repeated.

Her hands trailed to grip his jacket. She pulled him close enough that her words were a whisper on his lips. "Don't die."

Then she slipped through the door, leaving Darien alone in the dark.

45

Brothers to the Bitter End

Halla

Halla crossed her arms so tightly, it threatened to cut off circulation to her hands. Anger boiled within her chest. If she had *galdr* like Larissa, power would radiate from her palms, but she was Halla—just Halla. With no *galdr*, only her frown and furrowed brows could adequately convey her frustration.

It was bad enough that Larissa had asked her to stay behind. It was even worse that Kai had agreed with Larissa. When she looked to Anara for support, Anara had deferred to Larissa. Even Darien had smiled at her, but said, "Sorry, kiddo."

So she stood on the porch at sunrise, torn between wanting to hug her sister goodbye and punch her for leaving her behind as the others readied Helga for their departure.

As if reading her thoughts, Larissa sighed from her place at the bottom of the porch steps. "Please don't be angry at me. I just want to keep you safe. The last time you went into a city, I lost you."

It was the waver in Larissa's voice that softened Halla's posture. Tears threatened her eyes as helplessness and acceptance warred within her. She had no *galdr*; she was a liability. For what felt like the hundredth time, Halla wished she'd been born special like everyone else. At her side, she noticed Kai risking a glance, likely checking if Halla was still angry at him. At least he was just as ordinary as she was.

Halla rushed to embrace Larissa. "I know." She buried her face in her sister's shoulders when usually she would reach only to her chest. She'd grown in the last several weeks, she realized. "Just be safe, and don't make me wait too long."

Larissa's arms tightened around her. "I'll come back to get you as soon as I can."

Halla squeezed harder, her thoughts turning to prayers. The image of the red-headed child goddess flashed before her mind. There had been a kinship between Halla and Verðandi, Halla was sure of it.

Please, Verðandi, keep my sister safe.

Halla could have sworn the wind picked up at her thoughts, lifting the short strands of hair around her face. When Larissa released her, Halla knew it was time. Her hands fell uselessly to her sides. Kai leaned his shoulder into hers.

With deliberate movements, Larissa turned, crossing the dirt road and throwing open Helga's tailgate. Anara and Masai already waited in the cab. Darien had convinced the Smaragdian it would be safer for them all to travel together. Masai eyed his motorcycle unhappily as he watched Darien say his goodbyes to Aagen. Halla leaned against the porch railing, listening to their conversation without bothering to pretend otherwise.

"You'll be safe, son?" Aagen asked.

Darien ran his fingers through his hair, the sapphire ring throwing the sun's beams around the drive. "You know, everyone keeps asking me that. You'd think I had a death wish or something."

"I know the Norn have told you more than you've told me. You've always related to the heroes in the stories, but heroes do stupid things sometimes." Aagen twisted his beard, leaning on his good leg. He thumped one hand on Darien's shoulder. "Don't be a hero. Come back, and tell me more of your stories."

Darien mimicked the gesture, squeezing Aagen's shoulder. "I'll do that, Aagen. I promise." Reaching into his pocket, Darien pulled out a small violet vial. "Masai says to administer one drop every hour to make it last longer. It will keep Calder quiet and complacent but awake, but make sure he stays bound and blindfolded just in case. Three drops will knock him out cold if necessary. I'll send someone back to collect him once I know what's happening in the city."

Aagen's large hand swallowed the bottle; with the other, he patted the gun at his side. "I'll keep him under control, and I'll keep the little ones busy too. Don't you worry."

Halla would've felt offended at the description if not for how much Aagen reminded her of Tucker. With a hand raised goodbye in Halla's direction, Darien walked away, joining the others in Helga. Halla leaned over the railing, staring at the weeds that grew up along the wooden beams of the farmhouse. If she closed her eyes, it smelled like home. When she looked up, Helga was gone.

"It's Halla, right?"

Aagen stood before her. The kindness in his eyes soothed the sting of being left behind. "Yes."

He grabbed two of the buckets that lay on the porch, holding them out to Halla and Kai. "Anyone feel like apple picking?"

Halla nearly said no, almost reassured Aagen that she did not need to be "kept busy," but the sudden normalcy of the fields called to her like an old friend.

"What about Calder?" she asked.

Aagen ignored Kai's anxious glance toward the cellar doors that had been secured with an iron rod through the handles. "Those doors can only be unlocked from the outside, and they gave him a dose before they left. We won't need to check on him for another hour."

The call of the open blue sky beckoned Halla, louder than her uncertainty. "Sounds good to me."

Kai and Halla followed Aagen out into the orchards. The buzz of the bees mixed with the sweet scent of the soil relaxed Halla's tensed muscles. They didn't have to go far until Aagen brought them to the youngest of the apple trees. They stood only a few feet taller than Halla, and the apples were small enough to fit within

the palm of her hand. She reached and twisted. The apple's smooth surface rubbed against her skin.

She turned to Kai, plopping the apple in his hand. "Consider this my repayment for the apple in the barracks."

A smile teased Kai's lips but didn't reach his eyes. "I always wanted to see where these came from."

"You've never seen an orchard before?" Halla asked, then clamped her mouth shut. Of course he hadn't.

"Diamant is primarily ice and snow, Halla." There was mild amusement in his voice.

"Diamant, huh?" Aagen asked as his nimble fingers plucked at the apples on the highest branches. At Halla and Kai's tense postures, Aagen softened his voice. "Nothing wrong with being from Diamant. We are more than our heritage. After all, look at Calder, and he supposedly came from Safír."

Halla's grin stretched across her face. She glanced at Kai, surprised to see that he looked rather sick to his stomach. Dark circles hung under his eyes.

"Are you feeling okay, Kai?" she asked.

"You don't look good, lad. Perhaps you should go lie down." Aagen's commanding voice was hard to disobey.

"Probably should. I didn't sleep well." Kai set his bucket on the ground, though he kept Halla's apple in his hand. As he stood up, his eyes caught Halla's, revealing a raw depth she hadn't seen before. "Thanks for the apple, Halla."

She watched him walk back toward the farmhouse, then out of sight. She yanked the next apple from the tree with more force than necessary. "I don't understand him."

"He's haunted by something, that's for sure," Aagen agreed. "You can nearly see the *mara* surrounding him."

"What do you mean? *Mara* come at night."

"They reveal themselves at night, but those who are truly haunted carry their *mara* with them wherever they go."

Halla set the apple into her bucket. "I didn't know that."

"Just stick by him. The best known cure for *mara* is to wrap the victim in the bonds of those around them. And he's clearly tied to you."

Halla's nose twinged with heat. "What?"

Aagen's deft hands picked the apples, holding three or four in his palm at a time. "Haven't you ever heard that every person is only a string in our grand universe?"

"Well, yeah."

"Our relationships with others cause our strings to intertwine and bind. Once two or more strings are truly tied together, they cannot be undone. That's why the *mara* fear the bonds between souls; not even their nightmares can break such bonds."

"I'm not bonded with Kai," Halla squealed.

Aagen chuckled. "Bonds take all shapes and hold all different meanings. Darien's bonding to Larissa is nothing like his bond to Anara or even to you, but I can see them all just the same."

We made our decision based on the ties within the tapestry of life.

Verðandi's voice replayed in Halla's mind, and she gasped. "The Norn said something similar. Verðandi said that some bindings can even cross the border between life and death."

"I believe that." Aagen's eyes softened. "Even though she's been gone for years now, I still feel the thread tying me to my wife. It's as taut between us as it ever was when she was alive. One day, I'll meet her again, and our tapestry will continue."

"Do you think she still feels your bond? Wherever she is?"

"I know she does."

"Can you really feel it?"

Aagen maneuvered the apples in his palms. "It's as tangible as these apples; you only have to let yourself feel it."

Halla looked at her hands, remembering the threads that had wound themselves around her wrists in the Norn's vision, but she saw nothing. Her mind traveled, searching for the ties that bound her to her parents. She closed her eyes, determined to feel the same strings that Aagen seemed to experience so easily, but after a while, all she felt was silly. Still, it was a lovely thought.

She let her head tip back, soaking the sun that filtered through the leaves and kissed her face. The *plop, plop, plop* of apples landing in the bucket created a steady rhythm along with the rustling leaves. The ends of her hair tickled her ears in the breeze. There was a shift in the air around her, and the sudden brush of thread against her palms.

Subconsciously, she reached her hands out, her fingers dancing on invisible strings that she could almost feel. There were two strings for Mamma and Pappa, a string for Larissa, for Darien, and Anara. To her surprise, Halla even found a string for Masai. And there, just at her fingertips, was a string for Kai that twanged uncomfortably under her touch. Whether it was Aagen's words that had revealed the strings or Halla's own imagination, she knew she would never again be able to ignore them. She felt the binding like it was an intrinsic part of who she was.

Just before she opened her eyes, Halla felt the presence of a last string, but she couldn't identify whom it stretched toward. The end was hidden in a cloud of mist in her mind. She opened her eyes, frowning against the unknown, then licked her dry lips. Maybe she'd had enough sun for one day.

"I should go check on Kai."

Aagen glanced at the watch on his wrist. "Let's take these buckets inside. Darien was always a better baker than I was, but perhaps you could help me make a pie out of these. Maybe that'll pull the boy out of his mood."

Halla felt her steps lighten at the thought. "I can do that."

Aagen glanced down at her. "Just don't tell Darien I told you that. It'll just go to his head."

"Never," she giggled. "It's our secret."

Aagen led Halla inside, plopping his bucket beside hers on the rickety kitchen table. Removing his gun and setting it on the small table beside the front door, Aagen walked to the sink. The sound of running water followed Halla as she roamed down the hall-way, peeking her head into Darien's bedroom and then Aa-gen's, yet Kai was not in either of the rooms. The door on the back side of the house hung open. Had Kai gone back to the orchards to find them? Her eyebrows pinched in worry as she walked back into the kitchen.

Aagen dumped the apples into the sink, letting them bob in the water. He dried his hands and looked at his watch. "It's time for another dose—what's wrong?"

"I can't find Kai."

"I'm sure he's around here somewhere." Footsteps drew Aa-gen's attention toward the front door. "There he is now."

But the footsteps were too heavy and loud to be Kai's.

"You said we could leave!" Kai's frantic voice cut through the open windows.

Fear seized Halla just as Aagen dropped the cloth in his hands. He lunged for the knife on the counter, shoving Halla behind him as the front door flung open. Calder stood in the door frame, his bindings and blindfold gone. Aagen raised his knife to throw it, but Calder spoke before he could. "Stop."

One word was enough. Aagen's hand froze in the air, the knife still in his grasp; the rest of his body had become uncomfortably stiff. Halla peered around him. Calder leaned against the doorframe with a self-satisfied smirk on his lips. Though he appeared more tired than usual, he bore no other signs of weakness. The effects of the drug had clearly worn off. Even so, his *galdr* wouldn't have helped him escape his binds or open the barred cellar door.

Behind Calder, Kai stumbled to a stop, stark horror written across his face as he took in the scene. Halla wanted to scream at him to run, to find help, but Kai looked at Calder not as though he feared *him*, but rather feared what Calder might do.

"Leave them alone. You said we could go," Kai said again, but this time his words clicked.

Calder's smile grew at the sound of Halla's soft gasp. "Figured it out, did you?"

"You let him out?" Disbelief coursed through Halla's voice.

Kai couldn't meet her gaze.

"But why—?"

"It's not his fault, really." Calder shrugged. "He cared about me long before he met you."

Halla's mouth formed a silent *o*. Kai had told her there was only one person in the world he had cared about.

"I couldn't let him be handed off the Viðnám. They would've killed him." Even as he stared at the ground, Kai's voice begged for Halla to understand.

Halla shook her head. "*He's* your brother? But how? That doesn't make any sense!"

"He's as much my brother as Larissa is your sister." Kai looked up at Calder, this time grabbing onto his arm. "Please, let's just go."

Calder pushed off from the doorway, taking note of the gun that rested on the end table. He clicked his tongue at Aagen, who still stood frozen though his eyes showed awareness, held under control by Calder's *galdr*. "It's sloppy to leave guns laying around. Someone could get hurt."

Halla's skin prickled. She rushed in front of Aagen, though her small body couldn't shield much, and threw her hands out. "Leave him alone."

It was then she realized that Calder wasn't able to control her movements; he could only control Aagen's. Maybe some of the nectar was still in his system, weakening his abilities.

"Halla—" Kai moved toward her, but Calder's hand gripped the boy's inner elbow with enough strength that Kai winced.

"Like Kai said, we don't plan on staying long." He picked up the gun, letting it settle in his grasp. "Darien thinks he can get Aeron back; I need to convince him otherwise."

Aagen's body shifted behind Halla, moving ever so slightly as he fought against Calder's *galdr*. His mouth forced out the words: "Run, Halla."

The cost of his effort was clear on his face. There was acceptance in his eyes even as he urged her to run. But even if she could get her feet to move, where could she run that Calder could not catch her?

The shot rang out. Halla flinched, screaming as the bullet tore through Aagen's chest. Hot splatters of blood landed on her face and arms. The knife in Aagen's hands fell to the ground, quickly followed by his body. Released from Calder's persuasion, Aagen moaned. Halla fell to her knees, her small hands trying to staunch the blood that poured from the hole in Aagen's chest.

He gasped and spluttered. "Halla . . . run . . ."

Kai's shouts echoed behind her, but Halla couldn't make out his words. Any minute now, Calder was certain to turn the gun on her. He had shot Aagen to punish Darien; no doubt he'd kill her to punish Larissa. Halla wouldn't give him the satisfaction of looking at him. She wouldn't let Aagen face the end alone. She wouldn't leave him like she'd left her parents.

She gnawed at her cheek until she tasted her own blood. "I won't leave you, Aagen."

He grasped Halla's hands, though it was difficult between his shaking and the blood for her to hold on. "Tell Darien . . . I love him . . . it's not his fault."

Halla nodded, choking back her tears. Even though she knew she wouldn't have the chance to pass on his message, Halla promised, "I will."

Aagen's breathing hitched, then stopped. Halla flinched at the abrupt change, then Aagen's hands slid from her grasp. Her tears fell without restraint, falling and mixing in with Aagen's blood. She bowed her head over Aagen's body, not wanting to see her own end coming.

"What have you done?" Kai shouted, his words coming at Halla as though he'd shouted from the end of a long tunnel.

"Oh don't act so innocent, Kai," Calder drawled. "You knew what I would have to do. You knew what *you* would have to do."

"What? No!"

It was the hysterics in Kai's voice that crystalized Halla's attention. Still on her knees, she glanced back at him. Kai backed away from the gun that Calder held out to him until his back slammed against the doorframe. "Halla isn't our enemy. She's never hurt anyone! You told me no one would get hurt!"

Calder's face hardened; his grip on the gun tightened. "She matters so much to you that you would turn your back on me?"

"I'm not turning my back on you, but killing Halla won't gain you anything."

"Do you still think you have a chance at her forgiveness?" Calder's voice lowered, the silky tone that Halla associated with his *galdr* seeping into his words. "You let me out. Aagen's death is on your hands as well as mine. Look at her. She hates you already."

"That's not true," Halla's voice shook; she didn't know whether she was speaking the truth. "You didn't mean for this to happen, Kai. I know you."

Calder's smile was overtly mocking. "Do you? Didn't you ever wonder how I found you at Godafoss Falls? How I knew you were going to Smaragd? Who do you think tipped me off in the first place?"

Halla's blood-coated fingers twisted into fists. "Kai?"

Guilt and regret plagued Kai's eyes, the answer evident enough in his silence.

"See? She hates you," Calder crooned. "She doesn't understand the tough choices you've had to make all your life just to survive, but I do. Let's be done with this." He lifted the gun as an offering in one hand while he squeezed Kai's shoulder with the other. "Kill her and prove you're still loyal to me."

Kai's fingers quivered as he reached for the gun. A black ring flashed on his fingers, but Halla's eyes couldn't look away from the barrel of the weapon pointed in her direction. She shook her head, not minding the tears that fell. "Kai, please . . ."

Calder grasped Kai's shoulder, nodding in approval. At Calder's touch, Kai's face hardened. Though there were no genetic similarities, Halla thought they'd never look more alike than they did in that moment. Kai breathed out. "I'm sorry, Halla."

He squeezed the trigger.

Then there was only pain.

46

Debt Repaid

Anara

Anara prided herself on her composure, but Masai's constant fidgeting in the passenger seat was enough to dissolve any poise she'd had upon leaving Aagen's farm. She gave him her best irritated glance.

He shot one back. "Couldn't you have found a better truck when you left the Viðnám?"

"Helga's been with us longer than you have; show some respect."

Masai rolled his eyes. "There's no reason for us all to arrive in this beast."

"That was between you and Darien. I don't care if the Viðnám decided to shoot first and ask questions later when you rolled up looking like someone who serves the Empress."

Masai turned his body toward Anara, his towering frame hunched over in the small cab. "Still worried I'll betray you?"

Oddly enough, she wasn't. But if Anara had learned anything from living with the wolf packs over the years, it was that strength came in numbers, and lone wolves were often left frozen solid in the snow. Not that she necessarily cared what happened to Masai. But it would be awkward to explain it to Kiah when the Viðnám marched on Smaragd if her only child had been killed by friendly fire. Then again, it would be no less than she deserved for selling Smaragdian secrets to the Empress.

"Not worried." Anara flipped her hair, eyeing the empty road ahead. The lack of sentries or Viðnám rebels could only mean that both forces were heavily concentrated in Havsiden. "I'm more concerned that you'll be a liability in the city."

He scoffed. "I can hold my own."

Anara stared pointedly at the faint scar on Masai's neck left by the *draugr*'s talon. "Like you did on the shore of Undarbrunnk Lake?"

Masai's dark skin flushed. Anara almost regretted her words. Almost, but not quite. He had fought well against the *draugr*, especially for a soft-handed Smaragdian.

"Besides," she continued as he seethed in silence. "Aren't you a pacifist and all that nonsense? I was surprised you didn't just let the *draugr* end you right then and there and say thank you with your last breath."

Masai blew the air out between his teeth. He touched the staffs placed awkwardly across his lap. "Grið and Vǫrð, remember? Peace *and* protection. Sometimes protection requires action and even offense. I've been training to protect myself since I could hold a staff. I will be *fine*. Worry about yourself."

"Why did Kiah let you train, anyway? Doesn't seem in her nature."

"It's our ancestral weapon. She wouldn't let me touch a gun, but that didn't mean she would cut me off from our roots."

Anara's lip twitched. "You don't know how to use a gun?"

He leaned against the passenger window, a satisfied smirk on his face. "I said she wouldn't let me touch one, not that I didn't find a way to one without her knowing."

"So you'll disobey her, but you'll defend her for giving away your people's secrets to Shiko?"

Levity fled through the open cab windows. "You really want to have this fight right now?"

"I'll give you a reprieve since we're nearly there, but we will have this fight eventually."

"That's assuming we both live."

She snickered. "I'm not going anywhere. You, on the other hand, we'll see."

The salty brine of the ocean rode on the wind that filled the cab. It could only mean Havsiden was close. Though Anara much preferred the volcanic shores of her own country, she could admit that there was a certain beauty to Safír's white-sanded shorelines and massive, stark cliffs. The palace itself was set atop the highest point of the farthest cliff within the city. The rest of the city was built in layers, its round-domed buildings carved into the cliff itself.

Images of Anara's past sprinkled her vision like overlays crowding the present. Unlike Perle, which had been nearly razed to the ground, Safír had survived with minimal destruction. No doubt, to Darien and Larissa, it would feel like stepping into the past. Anara would have to ensure that their own confusion between past and present did not blind them to danger. She'd seen it happen to both of them, the way their faces would go blank as they struggled with some memory or emotion they hadn't remembered before.

A low growl rumbled in her chest. Anara wasn't an anxious person, but watching over them had added a new level of anxiety to her life. She was only one person, and there were two of them, plus Masai, if she cared to look out for him as well. It would be possible but certainly not easy. At least Halla and Kai were safe with Aagen.

Masai peeked at Anara from the sides of his eyes. "You're not going to eat me, are you?"

Anara cut off the growl. "I've eaten roadkill that probably tasted better than you."

"First, I would be delicious. And second"—his nose wrinkled in disgust—"ew."

Though "ew" had pretty much been Anara's own sentiment at the time, she wasn't going to admit that to Masai. "That's the difference between Rubinians and Smaragdians. We do what we must to survive."

"Some would say that's not much of a difference at all." Masai shifted in his seat, letting his face turn toward the window. "What's that smell?"

She glanced at him from the corners of her eyes. "You're joking, right?"

As though realizing he'd said something strange, Masai's face took on a closed and guarded expression. "Why would I joke?"

"It's the sea. I know Smaragd is all about trees, but the sea isn't that far from your city."

Masai folded his arms, his jaw set as he stared straight ahead.

Anara remembered. "But you've never left the city, so you wouldn't know what it smells like."

The shock of that thought reverberated through Anara so strongly, any future sarcasm died on her tongue. The only good thing that had come from Shiko's reign was Anara's ability to roam the nation without any royal responsibility. In the last fifty years, she'd traveled almost every inch of Evrópa in her search for Lovisa and Darien. From the icy tundras of Diamant to the beaches of Safír, Anara had seen it all. There'd been so much to discover, and Anara couldn't imagine being trapped within one city. Just the thought of it made her skin itch and beg for transformation so she could escape into the sky.

The edge of the treeline was in sight; they were nearly there. A new scent mingled in with the salt and the sea, and Anara scrunched her nose. Masai caught a whiff of it only a moment later.

"*That* is not the sea," she muttered darkly.

"What is it?" he asked.

Dirt, smoke, and blood tainted the air; it was the smell of fear and decay. Tents and vehicles formed a perimeter just outside Havsiden's Outer Wall. Though Helga was able to clear the trees without opposition, Anara slowed their advance to a crawl. Her ears tingled as they shifted, becoming lupine. Shouts came from the Viðnám camp accompanied by the click of guns and the clink of metal as the rebels turned to face this new arrival. Anara stopped

Helga hundreds of feet from the perimeter, knowing it was best for the Viðnám to come to them, to see that they were unarmed.

Anara turned to Masai. "It's the smell of war."

Two armored trucks drove in their direction, but a familiar scent eased Anara's concerns. She popped her door open, walking to the front of Helga and leaning against the truck's warm hood. When one of the trucks' passenger doors opened, Anara wasn't surprised to see Halvor's relieved face.

"You're back." He glanced at the city behind him, readjusting his half-moon spectacles. "No time for pleasantries, I'm afraid. We'll escort you in."

Halvor slammed his door, and Anara hopped back into Helga, following the trucks into the Viðnám's makeshift camp. They were only able to advance so far before the road became too cluttered by the tents, trucks, and bodies of the Viðnám. Anara wrinkled her nose at the overwhelming smell of human decay. Clearly, this was where they were housing the wounded and dead from the battle. And by the heaviness of the scent, the battle was not going well.

Cutting Helga's engine, Anara leapt from the truck. Already members of the Viðnám were noticing them, calling out Darien's and Lovisa's names. Many shot her furtive looks that she ignored. More than one young woman did a double take when they saw Masai. Recognizing the attention he commanded, Masai smiled. Anara rolled her eyes and approached where Halvor waited for them.

"Come inside." He held open the flap to a nearby tent, which was guarded at both entrances by Viðnám rebels. Darien and Larissa squeezed their way through the pressing crowd, and Anara followed them both in. Masai came in last, letting the flap close behind him. The inside of the tent was spacious, complete with a large table in the middle and light hung on the walls.

Halvor looked to Larissa. "Did you find what you were looking for?"

Larissa nodded. "We know the prophecy."

He tilted his head, as though attempting to look around Larissa's body. "Where's Halla?"

"She's safe. We left her with a farmer named Aagen—"

"—oh yes, we know Aagen. He's been a great asset in helping those fleeing Safír."

"I need you to send soldiers to his farm. They'll find the Empress' War Dog drugged and bound in his cellar. The sooner he's off Aagen's land, the better." Darien ignored Halvor's raised eyebrows, examining the maps of the city strewn out on the center table. "Where is my father?"

Halvor sighed, pointing at the middle of the city right at the space before the Second Wall. "Reclaiming Safír has been nothing like Perle. Regent Omiros knew we were coming, and he prepared. It took us a full day to breach the Outer Wall. Another day to secure the Outer Section, although there are still skirmishes and pockets of sentries we're attempting to root out. We've been trying to break through the Second Wall for the past two days. Torsten gave me the charge of evacuating citizens and the wounded. The rest of the generals are inside the city as well, except for Soren, who remains in Perle."

Halvor removed his glasses to rub at his eyes, revealing the dark bags beneath. He continued, "News came in last night that a force is coming down from Rubin. They'll arrive tomorrow. We're running low on weapons, ammunitions, and food. King Torsten wants to attempt one last breach today, but if we can't get through the Second Wall, we'll have no other options but to pull back our forces to Perle."

It was just as the Norn had predicted. If they pulled back, the lives lost would have been given in vain. Anara rolled on her heels, eager to join the fight. "That's why we're here."

Darien's look was one of gratitude. "Anara's right. Hope isn't lost yet."

"We'll need whatever weapons you can give us and directions." Larissa pulled out her gun, counting the bullets that remained in her magazine.

Masai strapped his staffs to his back. "I'd take a gun as well."

Anara snorted. "*You'll* fight with us?"

Darien glared at her. "It's alright if you need to stay here, Masai. I'm sure there are many who could benefit from your *galdr*."

Masai clapped his hand on Darien's shoulder. "There are many in *there* who could use my *galdr* as well. I'll come."

Halvor narrowed his eyes. "I'm sorry, but who are you?"

Anara laughed. "Masai, son to Regent Kiah of Smaragd."

Halvor's glasses nearly slid from his face as he jerked in surprise. "I would ask questions, but we really don't have the time."

He stepped out of the tent, barking orders to one of the guards who stood nearby. Anara heard the running of feet, and then Halvor re-entered the tent. This time, a boy around Kai's age followed them in. The confusion on his face morphed into one of awe as he looked around the tent. When his eyes landed on Darien, he fell to his knees. "Prince Darien! I knew you would come."

Darien backed away, glancing at Larissa, who smirked as her eyes seemed to say, *See? It's awkward when it happens, isn't it?*

Halvor let out an exasperated sigh, yet there was genuine fondness in his voice. "Get up, Marinos, I have a job for you."

Anara recognized the scent on the boy instantly. "You found your family?"

Halvor's eyes softened and misted over. "Only by the Norn did I find them in the midst of the fighting. I brought them out of the city for their own protection, but as it turns out, Marinos is our best messenger. He knows the safest routes in and out of the city. He'll get you to King Torsten."

Marinos' large green eyes shone. "It'd be an honor. I'd be happy to help you fight as well, Your Majesties."

"You are to come straight back after delivering them and let me know the status of the battle," Halvor spoke sternly.

Watching them interact, Anara experienced genuine joy in the midst of the horrors outside of the tent. It was only right that Halvor should be reunited with his family after all the years of his life he'd given to the rebellion.

One of the guards from earlier stuck his head in through the tent flap. "Sir, there are several men and women who would like to accompany their Highnesses back into the city."

"For Óðinn's sake," Halvor muttered. "The transport truck will only seat twelve. Pick the least wounded to accompany them and tell the rest they must wait. If Rubin's forces arrive early or if we need to evacuate, we need a capable force remaining here as well."

Through the canvas of the tents, Anara listened to the man relay Halvor's instructions and the subsequent groans of the men and women not chosen to join them. The engine of the large transport trucks rumbled closer.

"That's your ride," Halvor announced.

The transport truck idled in front of the tent, but more of the Viðnám clambered around it. Masai's body stiffened as he took in the devastation. Many of the rebels were wounded, some severely so. The woman nearest to them was missing an eye. The man on the other side of the truck was still bleeding from a wound on his head even as his friends attempted to convince him to lie back down. As Darien and Larissa hopped into the back of the transport truck along with Marinos, Anara stopped, watching Masai, who walked straight to the bleeding man. The man and his friends froze.

Masai reached out, laying his hand on the man's head even as his friends shouted questions. Then Masai pulled away; the wound had closed. Masai didn't wait for their awed thanks but walked past Anara and pulled himself up into the truck.

"You do realize word will spread that you're fighting alongside us if you do that?" Anara asked as Masai squeezed in next to her.

"I can't just ignore them."

The truck rumbled into the city. Anara took stock of the rebels that had joined them. Four men and three women. All were bandaged in some way and wore identical grim expressions as they shared their weapons and ammo with Larissa, Darien, and Masai. When one turned to offer her a gun, Anara declined. It would only slow down her transformations. As they passed under the Outer Wall, Masai turned to the red-haired woman on his right, whose entire waist was wrapped in a stained bandage.

"What happened to you?" he asked.

"Shrapnel. We weren't expecting them to bomb their own cities."

"Bomb?" Larissa asked. "They didn't have those in Perle."

"They did, actually," another rebel answered. "We just didn't discover them until after we took the city. It seems Regent Hammon didn't think he would need them, but you proved him wrong, Princess." Though the man's words were spoken with admiration, Anara noticed the way Larissa's mouth twisted in distaste.

Darien leaned forward. "How goes the fight?"

"Not good," the redhead answered. "Regent Omiros is using small regiments, forcing us to split into smaller groups as well. It's prolonging the battle and making it difficult to avoid civilian casualties. The bomb that got me took out an entire city block."

Masai gestured toward the girl's back. "May I?"

Perhaps she had seen what he'd done outside the truck, or maybe it was the compassion of his deep voice that compelled the woman to turn her back toward him. He laid his hands on top of the bandages, and although Anara could tell his touch was gentle, the woman still gasped at the pressure on her wounds. A green glow emanated from beneath his palms. Anara hadn't seen anyone's *galdr* act that way apart from Larissa. When he dropped his hands, the redhead rolled back her shoulders and sighed in relief.

"Thank you, Your Highness."

Masai's eyes turned guarded. "I never said—"

"They're not stupid," Anara pointed out, crossing her arms and leaning against the canvas that covered the truck bed. "Skogkatt's out of the bag now. Might as well accept it."

"Your Highness." Another rebel swallowed hesitantly, gesturing at his leg. "If it's not too much to ask—"

As the truck rolled on, Masai moved from rebel to rebel, healing again and again where he could. Larissa and Darien watched in equal fascination, but Anara sat stiff with worry. *Galdr* had a price, and every injury that Masai healed would only drain him further, making him just one more possible victim of the war. The sounds of battle grew around them the farther in they drove.

All around them, citizens fled or hid in bullet-ridden buildings. Larissa and Darien clenched their fists, no doubt forcing themselves to remain in the truck instead of leaping to help. Smoke drifted from destroyed blocks, and still, Masai went on healing. By the time the truck was forced to stop due to the debris in the road, the rebels all stared at one another in wonder.

Masai leaned back, his shoulders sagging forward as they all unloaded from the back of the truck.

Anara stood, looking down on where he sat. "You probably shouldn't have done that."

"They needed it. It might mean the difference between life and death if they're able to run faster or fight harder."

"And they still might die anyway. You will too, now that you've weakened yourself."

Masai's eyes were hard. "Do you only think of yourself?"

Anara hissed. "If you really think that, you don't know me at all."

Only the two of them remained in the back of the truck. Masai shook his head. "I'm trying to."

"Try surviving this. Figure out if I'm a heartless monster later." Anara hopped down from the truck and approached where the others huddled around Marinos.

The young boy, Marinos, brushed his sandy-blond hair out of his eyes. "The Second Wall is a mile away. King Torsten will be on the eastern side of the Wall, Prince Darien. Follow me."

The rebels formed two lines surrounding Anara, Darien, Larissa, and Masai as Marinos weaved over the broken pavement and through the collapsed buildings. Broken statues of Njörðr, Safír's patron god, were scattered amongst the ruins. Marinos never wavered from his path, even when there was no path to see. The Second Wall loomed ever closer as the young boy kept up a stream of chatter and questions directed at Darien. Anara let the small smile creep onto her face at the obvious hero-worship.

"I can help you," Marinos argued. "I know my uncle said to return but—"

"No, you should go back," Darien cut him off, though with utmost kindness. "It's not safe here. You're just a kid."

Marinos pouted. "You're not exactly an adult either. That's something I admire about you. You don't let anyone look down on you because of your age; you just do what needs to be done."

Darien shot Larissa an exasperated look, but she only shrugged in bemused silence. No doubt it made for a nice change for Darien to take the spotlight. Marinos skidded to a stop as their company halted around them. A man stood in a crater that had split the street in front of them into two. He wore priestly robes and had a hood pulled up around his face. Tattooed runes decorated what little skin Anara could see. A silver pendant of three intersecting triangles hung on his chest.

Marinos relaxed. "It's just Brother Gorthr."

Larissa stiffened beside Anara, her hands glowing in agitation. Darien tugged at her jacket to keep her from advancing.

"You're from Perle. What are you doing here?" Anara asked.

The man pushed back his hood, revealing his bare head covered with more of the same runes. "The Hoorg do not belong to any one city; we belong to the gods."

The Hoorg. Even Anara's thoughts were filled with derision. She'd come across this particular religious sect often in her travels; not once had it been a pleasant experience.

"What do you want?" Larissa's sharp voice demanded. Clearly, she had not forgotten his role in trafficking Halla as a slave into the inner sector.

Brother Gorthr approached them, sniffing deeply. "Your party carries the smell of death."

Darien's hands tightened into fists; Larissa glanced at him nervously. Anara growled, "This whole place smells like death. Tell us why you're here."

Masai shifted beside her, twirling his staffs in his hands.

Brother Gorthr lifted his hands in surrender. "I'm here to escort you the rest of the way. You can go now, Marinos."

The boy glanced at Darien, his lower lip jutting out in defiance. "No, Halvor told me to take them to King Torsten and bring back a report."

"Take this back to Halvor." Gorthr offered a piece of paper to Marinos, who took it after a moment of hesitation. The priest turned his attention to Darien. "The King was able to locate explosives in the abandoned sentry barracks along the wall. The explosion is set to go off any minute now. If they are able to breach the wall, they'll flood into the Court of the Aristocracy. If you are here to help, you'd best get going."

Marinos shoved the paper in the inside pocket of his jacket. "Prince Darien, please let me stay and fight. This is my city—"

"It's my city, too, Marinos." Darien clasped the boy's hand. "Trust me to free it for both of us. Go back to Halvor; he's waiting for news. He needs to know what the King is planning."

Disappointment radiated from the boy, but he nodded, unable to deny Darien's orders. With one last hopeless glance back, Marinos turned and ran back the direction they'd come.

Anara slid beside Darien. "He's got heart."

"He'd get himself killed," Darien replied. Then turning to Gorthr, he said louder, "Take me to my father."

Climbing through the rumble only increased Anara's dislike for the confinement of the ground. Every inch of Anara's body begged for transformation, for the freedom of the air, but she waited. Her eyes shifted from rooftop to rooftop, looking for black-armored sentries, but the block was abandoned. Then the murmur of rebels met her ears. The Second Wall was immediately before them, just beyond the end of this final block.

"We're close," Anara warned the others.

But as they passed by the broken white-marbled building on the corner of the street, Anara sensed the slight shift in the air, the silent anticipation. Her animal instincts sent her tackling those closest to her to the ground just as the bombs went off.

The world shook with enough force that Anara wondered if the gods themselves had come back to wreak havoc on the city of Havsiden. Her ears rang, but not as painfully if she had not already shifted the interior canals to block out some of the shock. Rubble from the wall flew over them, debris scattering over their group.

Anara was up first, pulling others to their feet. Nearby, Brother Gorthr stirred under the rubble. A new cut adorned Larissa's forehead and bled red into her white hair. Seeing it at the same time, Darien scrambled to his knees, his fingers prodding near the wound.

"It's shallow," he yelled, probably louder than he thought he was. "Press something against it."

He was right, but it bled profusely under the cloth a rebel handed to Larissa.

Masai stumbled to his feet, his skin coated in dust from the explosion, and reached for Larissa. "Here, let me."

He laid his hand on her head; then, the cut was gone, leaving only a shallow scar.

Muffled cries and gunshots rang out. Down the road, the Viðnám and the Safírian sentries clashed with one another as they streamed through the Wall from either side. The rest of their group struggled to their feet, and Masai bounced between them, offering assistance wherever he could. Kneeling beside the last rebel, he paused, his hands outstretched. The red-headed woman lay at his feet, her eyes staring at the sky.

One of the other rebels stifled a sob, but still Masai did not move. Anara grabbed his shoulder. "You did what you could. We have to go."

When he didn't stand, Anara grabbed him under his arms and hoisted him to his feet. The haunted look on his face was enough to stop her next reprimand. Had he never seen death this close before?

Darien leaned down, closing the red-headed rebel's eyes. Anara looked away; she'd spent too many years staring at death. There was nothing more they could do for her. Already the scene around them was dissolving from organized lines of opposition to a melee of bodies and weapons. Guns yielded to swords and fists as each side no longer had clear enough sight to maim the other, though shots still rang out like a persistent rhythm underlying the disarray of war.

This was it.

Darien rose, touching Larissa's cheek with a bloody palm. She nodded, her hands glowing. Together, they ran toward the battle.

A fierce grin split Anara's face as the blood pumped wildly through her veins. Fear would have been the normal response, but something about the sounds of war electrified her soul like nothing else could. She knew the moment their group was spotted from the rebels' cries of celebration and the sentries' shouts of anger. Then, for Anara, there was only the fight.

Her skin trembled as the shift overcame her. She flung herself into the sky, surveying the mass of hundreds of churning bodies. In the middle of the chaos, Torsten was surrounded on all sides; the sentries had clearly been given their priority target, but Torsten killed as many with his handgun as he did his sword. Still, the endless waves of sentries pressed in, cutting him off from the rebels that tried to break their ranks.

Anara cawed loudly.

Wide-eyed, Torsten turned as Anara dove, then ducked. She transformed, exchanging her wings for paws with massive claws that she dug into the backs of two sentries. The sentries fell forward in alarm as she howled into the sky, their break in composure allowing the Viðnám to surge forward and cut their way into the midst where Torsten and Anara fought.

Torsten's lips were tight. "Glad you made it."

Anara's laugh was a low rumble in the back of her throat; then, she lunged into the men around her. They fell like paper under her sharp claws, but not without inflicting their own wounds. She felt the sting of steel and the hot graze of a bullet ripping fur from her shoulder. As the Viðnám beat back the sentries, Anara allowed herself a moment of respite. Falling back behind their lines, she returned to her human self and rested her back against the Second Wall.

Blood seeped from various wounds on her body. None were life-threatening, but the bullet's path burned like *Sutr*'s fire.

In the distance, high on the farthest cliff, the palace of Safír glimmered in the sunlight. Her white domes and large glass windows were out of place with the gore splashed on her streets. No doubt Regent Omiros was within, waiting with his final defense.

Anara scanned the fight, finding the familiar dark curls and white braid as Darien and Larissa fought side-by-side. They'd joined King Torsten. Darien's sword moved in wide arcs, more defensive than offensive. Even now, he injured when Anara knew he could have killed. When the fighting grew too precarious for gun play, Larissa raised glowing hands to shove the surrounding sentries off balance where they fell under rebel weapons. The Viðnám gained more ground into the Court of the Aristocracy, pushing against the broken lines of the Empress' forces. In the crowd, Anara caught sight of Marinos, who'd clearly snuck back to the battle in the confusion of the explosion. The boy grappled with a sentry, knocking him down with the butt of a rifle to the sentry's face, then followed Darien deeper into the commotion.

But where was Masai? His dark skin should've been a dead giveaway. Anara's lips thinned. Anxiety welled within her as she pushed herself off the wall. Where had he gone?

"Anara, move!" Masai's voice shouted in her ears; his arms wrapped around her waist, pushing her toward the ground and covering her body with his own.

The explosion erupted behind Anara in the same moment—not nearly as large as the blast that had broken the gate, but still significant enough that those closest to the Wall found themselves on the ground. The ones deemed unlucky by the Norn did not rise again.

Masai hissed painfully in Anara's ears. He rolled off of her, and she found her way to her knees. Her body was no worse than it had been before besides a new scuff on her chin from where she'd hit the ground and the lip she'd bitten through during the impact.

Masai puffed out labored breaths. He clasped his ribs, his hands glowing faintly. "I think I cracked a rib."

Anara stilled. "Did it puncture anything?"

"Let's hope not." He groaned in pain. "I would hate to rob you of my company prematurely."

As Masai's breathing evened out, Anara found she could breathe too. His shoulders sagged more heavily than his eyelids as evidence of the cost of his efforts. He wouldn't be able to keep pushing himself without repercussions. The explosion had caused a hole in the wall where she'd previously stood. If Masai hadn't pushed her out of the way, she would be dead. The realization hit just as Masai's eyes met her own.

"I should probably thank you," she said, mirroring the sentiments he'd spoken to her only days before.

One side of his mouth tugged up as his eyebrows raised. "But you're not going to, are you?"

"Maybe if we both survive this." She rose, offering a hand that he took.

He supported his healing ribs with his other hand. "I plan to make good on that promise, little wolf."

Her eyes narrowed. "I told you not to call me that—"

The windows of the palace shattered, followed by the inhuman screech of *draugrs*. Anara and Masai cried out along with hundreds of other voices as Viðnám and sentry alike covered their ears with their hands. The *draugr* screams reverberated off each other, sending shooting pains into Anara's skull. With hands still covering their ears, the sentries cheered. Invigorated, they advanced again on the Viðnám.

Anara's hands curled into claws as Masai lifted his staffs beside her, uncapping the staff he'd named *Protection* to reveal the blade underneath. The battle had only begun.

47

Divided Soul

Halla

So much pain.

Halla hardly noticed the jarring impact as her body slammed to the ground or the feel of blood rushing down her stomach. The gunshot wound in her chest made it hard to breathe. She couldn't move, couldn't think of anything besides the pain and her sister's name.

Vaguely, she recognized the sound of the door closing and of footsteps trailing away from her. Then an engine roared to life before it faded into the distance. Halla's harsh breathing evened out as the pain vanished from her chest. Was this death, then? If she could feel her parents' threads, would she be able to follow them to wherever they'd gone?

She could still feel Aagen's wooden floor beneath her body and the stickiness of the blood from Aagen's wound. Yet from her own wound, she felt nothing. Maybe this was her body's way of defending itself in her last moments, by granting her peaceful numbness. Halla waited for the darkness to take her, but if anything, her senses sharpened to everything around her.

Footsteps thundered up the porch steps. The door flung open, but Halla didn't open her eyes. Perhaps they'd come back to make sure she was truly dead.

"Halla." Kai's urgent voice rang like an alarm in her ears. His hands were on her arms. "Halla, you're okay. Open your eyes; you're not dead."

At his touch, Halla's eyelids sprang open. She jerked herself out of his grasp, scrambling away until her back hit the kitchen's cabinets. Halla's hands scrambled to her chest, searching for the wound she had felt so vividly. Though her arms and shirt were still speckled with Aagen's blood, they were clean of her own. Her skin was unblemished. Where had the hole gone?

"What? How—"

"Halla, it wasn't real." Kai leaned forward as if to steady Halla's hands that tore at her clothes.

"Don't touch me!" she screeched.

Utter pain flashed in Kai's face. "I deserve that."

But Halla wasn't paying attention to his words or even the regret that settled deep in his eyes. She stared at the ring shining ostentatiously from his middle left finger. The band was black, yet it shimmered. A thick golden line ran through the middle and within the golden line were dozens of small dark gems.

"Kings and Queens . . ." Halla whispered, her hands shaking at her sides. "Are those—"

Kai followed her gaze but did not move to hide the ring. "They're black diamonds."

"But, why? How? I've never seen it before today—" Halla stopped, clasping her hand over her mouth to smother a gasp. Kai said nothing, letting Halla's mind fill in the blanks. She lowered her shaking hand. "The Diamantians' *galdr* is illusion."

"It is."

Horror and understanding battled for prominence in Halla's mind. "Someone with that power could hide a ring."

"Or make it look like I'd shot someone. Someone with *galdr* powerful enough could even make the person that I shot believe it was real." Sadness weighed down Kai's voice. "I'm so sorry, Halla, I needed you to believe that I'd shot you. Otherwise he would have done it himself."

"Like he killed Aagen," Halla snapped, taking small pleasure in the way Kai flinched from her words, his eyes unable to look at

Aagen's body. He'd lied to her. Over and over again. She'd thought he was normal, ordinary, just like her, but he wasn't. He'd used *galdr* against her every day to hide the truth.

"He told me he wouldn't hurt you. He said we could go home." Kai mumbled the words as if reassuring himself. He lifted his eyes to Halla. "I just didn't want them to kill him. What if it was Larissa, Halla? Wouldn't you have done whatever you could to save her?"

Halla rose to her knees. "Larissa never would have needed me to save her because Larissa wouldn't be a monster!"

Fire burned in Kai's eyes as he rose in response. "You don't know what my mother did to him! He didn't deserve it, any of it, but he was kind to me, even when no one else was—"

"Your mother?" Halla whispered.

Kai's head dropped into his hands; his fingers wove into his ink-black hair, pulling at the strands.

"Is your mother the Empress?"

"She's hardly a mother," he muttered into his hands.

The kitchen spun around Halla. Aagen still lay only inches away from her, and the boy in front of her, whom she'd trusted with her very life, was the son of the Empress.

"But she *sold* you! Why would you help her by telling Calder where we were? She made you a slave!"

Kai shook his head in his hands. "I was never a slave. Talk of the Viðnám was becoming more common, but she couldn't get the information she needed. She figured if anyone knew how to find the Viðnám, it would be the ones who were the most desperate."

Bile rose in Halla's throat. Kai had never been abused in the barracks. Fenris may not have known who he was, but he knew enough to never lay a hand on him. There was a reason no one ever bought Kai: because Kai was exactly where he was meant to be.

Halla hadn't felt this sick since she'd lost her parents. She buried her face in her knees and bit down on her knuckles, determined to not be sick or cry or scream or any of the things that she wanted so desperately to do. But what should she do? Anara would've killed

Kai the instant he betrayed them. Darien would've tried to reason with him. Larissa would've—well, she probably would've killed him too.

Larissa!

"Kai," she croaked. "Where did Calder go?"

His eyes shifted away from her again. "He took Masai's motorcycle. He's heading for Safír."

"What?" Halla leapt to her feet, clinging to the kitchen counter as the world tilted on its side. Kai stood, reaching out to steady her, but Halla's daggered expression stopped his hands.

"I swear on the Norn, Halla. I didn't go to free him. I just wanted to talk to him, but he told me they'd kill him and it would be my fault if he died when I had the power to save him. He promised we could go home and regroup there. He said Safír was already lost. I wouldn't have let him go if I'd known he would kill Aagen or try and hurt you!"

"How could you not know?" she shouted. "After everything we've told you he's done. After the way he hunted us down? How can you stand there and act like you're surprised?"

Kai's fingers twitched at his side, his ring glaringly obvious now that he wasn't shielding it from Halla's view. "He's the only one who ever protected me. He is the only one who has ever loved me. I know what he is, but he gave me his word." Kai's voice rose. "He's never lied to me before. How could I know he would now?"

"They trusted you," Halla spat. "They protected you!"

"I know," Kai's voice cracked. "I'm sorry. I regretted telling Calder where you were going even before he found us, but I couldn't undo what I'd already done."

Halla chewed her lip. She had so many questions, but there was only one thing that mattered now. "Take me to Safír."

"Hel's bells, Halla, you can't be serious."

"He's going after my sister and Darien and Anara and Masai! We have to warn them. There has to be a way to get there. Or maybe you really don't care if your psycho *brother* kills them after all!"

"That's not true!" Kai shouted.

"Then help me find a way to get there!"

"What about Aagen?"

Halla clenched her fists, resisting the violent urge to slap Kai across the face as she forced herself to look at Aagen. "We'll come back," she promised Kai and Aagen and herself, "but he would want us to find Darien if there's even a chance of warning him."

Kai snatched the keys that hung near the door. "It won't be nearly as fast as Masai's bike, but we could take Aagen's truck."

Instead of joining Kai, Halla kneeled down, placing her hand on Aagen's head. Tears slid down her face. She tried to remember the words Larissa had spoken over their parents, but all she could muster was, "If you see your wife, I hope you're happy with her again."

Halla sniffed, consumed by anger and hurt, and wondered if Calder had been right. Did Halla hate Kai after all? She stalked past him and toward the barn, which Aagen's truck sat inside. She pulled herself up into the passenger side as Kai took the driver's seat.

"Do you even know how to drive?" she asked.

"Well enough." He slid the keys into the ignition, and Aagen's truck rumbled to life. It even smelled like him.

"So what, Calder just let you stay behind?"

Kai's fingers fidgeted against the wheel. "No. Though the illusion I gave him of me riding on the back of the motorcycle has probably worn off by now."

Halla shivered at the thought of Calder's anger upon realizing Kai had lied to him, but she pushed away the thought as the truck rolled down the dirt drive. She glared at Kai, crossing her arms against her chest as if the pressure alone could stop her heart from splintering. Her mind pulled at the memories, questioning the integrity of each one as it passed. Had any of it been real? Kai's kindness in the barracks? His protection of her on the road? Had it all been an illusion? Was this now just another illusion? Why hadn't the Norn known? Halla chewed her cheek. Who was to say the Norn hadn't known? Why hadn't they said anything, unless . . .

"What did the Norn actually say to you?"

Kai's foot slammed on the brake. "Sorry, sorry."

He eased his foot back onto the gas, taking the truck onto the main road, but Halla only waited for the answer to her question.

He sighed, not looking at her. "*Double-edged heart; divided soul. Betrayed or betrayer? Decide your role.* That was my part of the prophecy."

Halla shook her head, lifting her eyes to the roof of the truck, failing to stop the tears as they fell from her eyes and the breaking of her heart. She reached for the threads Aagen had shown her. Four strings pulled her to Havsiden, but a fifth still connected her to the boy beside her. It was an infinitesimal sensation, but Halla was certain; the thread between her and Kai had frayed. One strong gust and it would snap.

"Well, I guess we know which role you chose."

48

When the City Bleeds

Darien

THE AIR WAS THICK with the angry shrieks of *draugrs*, Anara's howls, the shouts of the Viðnám, the curses of sentries, and the screams of dying men. Darien hardened his heart, desperate to block out the sounds that he knew would forever haunt his mind. He threw his fist into the sentry nearest him and slammed the butt of his gun against the back of the man's head. The sentry fell to the ground, unmoving but, Darien prayed, still alive. He didn't check to see if the man rose again.

These were his people, even if they didn't want to be. He couldn't kill them.

But the blood he slipped in only solidified that others were not so hesitant in their death strokes. Larissa's hand snaked out, grabbing his arm and stopping Darien mid-fall. Her golden eyes held his, a refuge in the turmoil around them.

"I've got you, Dar."

He grasped her arm, spinning to stand back-to-back with her to wait for the next surge, but none came. Darien's breath came in pants. He used the respite to survey the battle around him. Though the sentries fell quickly, more continued to pour down the streets. To make matters worse, the *draugrs* were pushing back on the Viðnám, undoing all of the forward movement they had made. Darien hadn't yet seen Omiros, the Regent of Safír, but that didn't mean he wasn't somewhere in the tumult.

A familiar shout caught Darien's attention. Farther ahead, Haki and Jari battled one of the *draugrs*. Anara flung herself toward the creature as Masai attacked it from behind, swinging his staffs with remarkable precision.

"We have to help them!" Larissa called out.

Darien's response was lost in a dark shadow that blocked out the light of the sun. Looking up, he caught the flash of obsidian scales and bat-like wings. He shoved Larissa to the side, rolling beside her. He reached for his sword even as he rose to face the *draugr* that landed in front of them. Larissa's hands shot forward, glowing as her *galdr* caught hold of the creature. It screeched in rage. Darien raised his sword, but movement caught his eye.

Behind Larissa, a sentry raised his gun, its barrel pointed at her back. Darien turned toward her, knowing he would never make it in time.

A golden-white hawk fell from the sky, diving into the sentry's face. The sentry flailed under the new attack, and his finger clenched the trigger. Darien's body slammed into Larissa's, knocking her to the ground as the bullet whizzed over them. The *draugr* growled in triumph at its sudden freedom. Its wings pumped hard as it shot into the air, sending a current of wind rushing over Darien. The sentry's body slumped to the ground, and General Ishaan stood in his place.

He grabbed hold of Darien's and Larissa's arms in unison. Cuts decorated his tanned skin, and there was blood on his teeth. "Get up, Majesties."

"Where'd you come from?" Darien asked.

"Putting down another skirmish in the city. We didn't get King Torsten's message in time, or we would have been here earlier." Darien noticed then a new wave of Viðnám rebels had entered into the courtyard, turning the tide yet again. Ishaan's eyes roamed the crowd. "Where is my Queen?"

"There." Darien pointed to where Anara and Masai fought side-by-side against the first *draugr*.

Ishaan's eyes narrowed at the sight. "Smaragdian."

"It's coming back!" Larissa shouted, adjusting her stance and raising her hands.

Darien and Ishaan tensed as the second *draugr* swooped down once again with its talons extended. Larissa clenched her hands and yanked hard. The *draugr* cried out, its wings stilling in the air, causing the monster to plummet to the hard stone that lined the bloody courtyard. Darien placed himself at Larissa's back, his gun in one hand and his sword in the other. He wouldn't allow another sentry to attack her while she was busy incapacitating the *draugr*. Ishaan leapt onto the creature. Darien didn't need to watch to know when the creature finally died; the sudden absence of screams was enough.

Larissa slumped against Darien's back at the sudden release. She was using too much of her *galdr*; she wouldn't be able to keep this up. Darien turned to her, still supporting her. What he wouldn't give to be able to share what *galdr* he had with her.

Ishaan nodded in their direction. "I must protect my Queen."

Then, with a flutter, the Rubinian was gone. In the midst of their fight, the larger battle had progressed toward the palace, taking Anara with it.

Larissa straightened, brushing back her hair with shaking fingers. "We should find Anara and Masai."

"And my father." Though they'd been reunited briefly, the shifting current of battle continued to separate them. No doubt King Torsten would be near the front, leading his people forward. It was where Darien should be. "Do you need to rest?"

"Not while others are dying."

Darien couldn't think of an argument against that. They dove back into the chaos, always keeping each other within reach as they wove their way through the beaten and bloody bodies. Haki and Jari had also disappeared from Darien's sight. He could only hope that they were alive.

He did his best to not look at the bodies he stepped over. It wasn't fair that sentries and rebels alike bled on the streets while monsters and those with the power of the gods battled around them. A dark-skinned man fought off another sentry; his enormous mustache identified him immediately. General Sture's knife dug hilt-deep into the man before him. His mouth twisted in distaste. Immediately, he knelt next to the unconscious man, spreading his hands across the wound. The blood stopped, but the man did not stir.

At Darien's appearance, Sture rose. The Smaragdian General looked sick to his stomach. "I can't bring myself to kill them if I don't have to."

Darien had never liked the general in their council meetings, but he felt he'd never understood the man more than in that moment.

Shots, louder and closer than before, rang out, sending Darien and Larissa to their knees as they took cover. All around them, sentries and rebels cowered from the peppered pop of the bullets. Darien scanned the rooftops, spotting the shiny barrel of the machine gun as it flashed in the midday sun. Bullets rained down on sentries and rebels alike as though the man had been given order to kill without restraint. Perhaps Omiros had decided dead rebels were worth more than living sentries. Sparks crackled around Larissa's raised hands as she turned her attention to the sentry, who at the same moment turned his weapon on her.

Bullets ricocheted off the shield of energy that Larissa held like a ceiling over their heads to protect them from the gunfire. Darien took aim only to hear the click of the empty chamber. He dropped down, searching for another gun nearby but finding only the Smaragdian general. General Sture's eyes were unseeing above his bloodied mustache as he lay next to the sentry he'd only just healed.

"Dar," Larissa grunted against the bullets that pounded against her shield. "I can't hold him forever."

A caw of a raven, followed by the screech of a hawk, registered from up ahead. The two birds flew in unison toward the rooftop; then came a scream as the shooter was flung from the rooftop and landed with a thump on the ground. Larissa's shoulders slumped as she let her hands fall to her sides, and Darien snatched up a pistol lying next to a sentry's bullet-ridden body. The Viðnám cheered, but their shouts were overwhelmed by the victorious cries of the sentries. After a few cries, Darien understood the words they were shouting.

"REGENT OMIROS!"

Darien and Larissa shoved their way through the rebels, desperate to reach the front lines. Though the fighting continued behind them, the men they passed were practically frozen, seemingly transfixed by the presence of the Regent sauntering toward them. He had graying black hair and a scar across his olive nose that looked like it'd been broken before, yet his posture emitted power.

Sentries and rebels alike pulled back to form a large clearing in the battlefield's center. King Torsten waited, sword and firearm hanging from his hands, as Regent Omiros approached. With Larissa at his side, Darien pushed to the front of that crowd to stand behind his father, whose royal armor had been coated in gore and blood. Nearby in the crowd, Anara and Ishaan growled at Regent Omiros. Masai gripped his staffs, eyeing the men who stood behind the Regent.

"Regent Omiros." Torsten's voice was hard, yet underneath it, Darien could feel the pull of his father's *galdr*. It was a difficult thing to try and persuade someone without the mental connection first established, but Torsten had decades of experience behind him. "Your *draugrs* are dead. Your sentries' blood has coated this city. It is enough. Surrender your forces."

Regent Omiros' face tightened, pulling the scarred skin over his nose taunt, as he tried to resist Torsten's *galdr*. His arms raised in surrender, his gun held loosely in his hand. The sentries around him murmured in confusion and fear. Regent Omiros glared at his traitorous hands as if he could not believe their actions. His legs shook slightly as he knelt before Torsten, even as his eyes retained their fury. Omiros shifted before Torsten, a necklace falling forward, revealing an uncorked vial at the end of it with crushed red flowers contained behind the glass.

Masai gasped. "He's faking! The petals clear his mind—"

Omiros moved quickly, leveling the gun at Torsten's chest as Torsten raised his sword. Darien lunged forward at the same moment, his sword swinging through the air. The bullet shot out, passing through his father just as Darien's sword sliced cleanly through Omiros' wrist.

Only Darien heard the thump of his father's body against the crowd as Omiros' scream of rage triggered the opposing forces to crash into one another. The Viðnám charged forward, surrounding their fallen king. Darien dropped to his father's side, determined to protect him from being trampled by the fighting that raged around them.

Darien had feared for his own life, not his father's. He never would have expected his father to be the first to fall, yet there on the cobblestone street, Torsten lay in an ever-growing puddle of blood. Darien leaned over him, applying pressure to stop the bleeding. Torsten groaned under Darien's weight but did not open his eyes.

Bodies pressed in around them. Darien dared to look up. The sentries were closer now, but Omiros was gone. Then came Anara's howl as she shoved her way through the crowd with Larissa on her heels. Larissa's hands glowed with a light so bright as to be blinding. The sentries faltered at her appearance, their bullets useless against her shield. Anara, followed by Ishaan, pressed against the sentries, cutting them down with claw and fang. Seeing their comrades fall and their commander gone, the rest of the sentries fled toward the palace, leaving the Viðnám to seek their own wounded and fallen allies.

"Is he alive?" Larissa asked, falling to his side.

The Norn's prophecy rang in Darien's ears.

Hel's fingers welcome his bloodline home.

Would his father be the first of their bloodline to perish under the Norn's prediction? Masai knelt beside them, pushing Darien's hands out of the way without a word. His large hands covered Torsten's chest, glowing green against the dark-red blood.

"He'll live," Masai said shortly, his attention clearly on the matter at hand. "Maybe."

"Maybe?" Darien asked, the word cutting his throat as it forced its way out.

"I'll do what I can."

"Your Highness," another voice called from behind.

Darien looked up at General Aiko's pale face. With the absence of its usual sneer, Aiko's face was more vulnerable than Darien had ever seen it. "I will stay with His Majesty, but we can't lose our forward movement. The Viðnám can advance now and take Safír. If we wait for King Torsten to recover, everything we've done will be for nothing. *You* must lead them."

Darien's fingers reached for his father's hand, ignoring the blood that made their grasp slick. He would survive. He had to, just as certainly as Darien had to leave him. He squeezed tight. "I'll make you proud, Faðir."

Torsten's fingers caught onto Darien's, holding him in place. Darien stared in shock as his father's eyes roved open once before closing. Torsten opened his mouth, his words so quiet that Darien nearly missed them. "I know you will."

Swallowing, Darien let his father's hand fall from his grasp. Beaten and bloodied, the rebels stared at him in uncertainty. No doubt they wondered if Torsten's wound would be the end of their invasion, but Larissa lifted her chin, reminding Darien to do the same.

She leaned close enough so only he would hear her words. "We are royalty. If we are not afraid, they won't be either. You can do this, Dar."

Darien faced the crowd, lifting his own sword to point toward the palace. "Your brothers and sisters have bled too much to stop now. Today, we reclaim Safír!"

The Viðnám's response was manic and immediate. They lifted weapons and fists and shouted into the air. They rushed forward, weaving past the fallen sentries and flooding around Darien as they raced toward the palace.

A familiar face caught Darien's attention as Marinos ran toward them. What in Hel's name was he doing there? He was supposed to be outside the Wall. Darien grabbed his arm, yanking him to a stop. "You shouldn't be here!"

"I want to help!" the boy argued. The splattering of gore on Marinos's shirt showed he'd never gone back to Halvor. Blood trickled from beneath his hairline.

Darien groaned in frustration. There was no time for this. "Fine, but stay close."

The boy's eyes lit in adoration and praise.

Behind Marinos, one of the assumed-dead sentries stirred from the ground. Darien only just caught the flash of metal and the pop of the bullet. Marinos grunted, a soft, disbelieving cry, then collapsed into Darien's arms.

"Marinos!" Darien shouted, but the boy's wide green eyes had already lost their light.

Anara pounced on the sentry, swiping the gun from his hand, but he was dead. The man's last effort had cost the life of a child. A sort of numbed focus quieted the world around him as Darien stared at the crumpled body in his arms. Darien didn't even know him, but that didn't stop Marinos' blood from staining Darien's hands or dripping on his boots. What would he tell Halvor?

Darien laid the boy gently to the ground, thinking it strange that he should bother. Marinos couldn't feel it anyhow. The Viðnám continued to pour toward the palace around them as Darien stared into those unblinking eyes.

A tug on Darien's arm brought him to his feet. Larissa grabbed his face, forcing him to look at her. Her eyes were wet, but her voice was firm. "Darien, look at me. There's nothing you can do. We have to finish this."

She didn't wait for his response but yanked him forward. Darien let himself be pulled along with the tide of Viðnám, but Marinos' face remained with him. As the palace loomed ahead of them, he could not help but wonder if Marinos had taken the bullet Fate had intended for him.

49

Ransom

Larissa

BUILT ON TOP OF the cliff, the palace of Safír's white domes glinted in the sun as if unaware of the blood covering her city streets. Larissa's *galdr* easily broke apart the palace doors, flinging them across the courtyard. The mob of the Viðnám crashed against the sentries who waited within, but Larissa, Darien, and Anara pressed through. If they could find Regent Omiros, if they could remove him, then the fighting would stop.

Larissa didn't dare look at the anguish on Darien's face as they fought their way through the crowd. Larissa understood that war pumped through Anara's veins; she did what she could to protect others, and that gave her strength. But for Darien, the devastation threatened to devour him whole. Larissa knew well the guilt that came with killing someone. It would damage Darien's soul irreparably to do so, which was why she was determined to kill Omiros herself.

Anara sniffed the air, ignoring the fighting around her, and pointed toward the grand staircase. "Fourth floor."

Straggling sentries impeded their way, but they fell or fled before Larissa and the others. Panting from exhaustion, they found themselves on the top floor, looking down a long hallway. Anara breathed in deep. "Last room on the right, but he's not alone. At least three other guards. Don't bother trying to persuade him, Darien. That charm on his neck will make that nearly impossible."

"Is that why my father's *galdr* didn't work?" Darien asked, adjusting the grip on his pistol.

"As far as I can tell. Masai will have to explain later." Anara's body trembled, but Larissa recognized it as her withholding a coming transformation. "Ready?"

Larissa nodded. Just one more fight, and then she would go see Halla, and Darien could see Aagen again. His adoptive father would heal the wound left by this battle as Torsten never could. Larissa followed Anara as Darien brought up the rear. Anara kicked in the door with enough force that it cracked off its hinges, then dove to the side. Bullets flew through the doorway, missing her by mere inches. Larissa and Darien huddled in the hallway, their backs against the wall as rounds buried themselves within the opposing wall. Anara held up three fingers and slowly lowered each one.

Larissa's hand grew hot as *galdr* gathered in her palms. Her body ached in exhaustion, but she ignored it. There would be time to rest after Omiros was dealt with.

As Anara's last finger went down, Larissa launched herself into the opening of the door, raising her hands to stop the bullets in their tracks. Anara flew over her as a raven, then landed as a wolf on two of the shooters, incapacitating them quickly. Darien entered last, his gun raised at Omiros and the third guard.

But it wasn't a guard at all. The stump at the end of Omiros's arm was tied off and bandaged, no doubt by the same physician Omiros now held in front of his body as a human shield with a knife pressed firmly against his neck. Anara shifted back, joining Darien and Larissa, who each had their weapons trained on Omiros. Sweat ran down Larissa's neck. She was burning up, using too much of her *galdr*.

"Let him go." Darien's voice was like silk draping across Larissa's skin. She felt his *galdr* even though it was not directed at her.

Omiros sneered. "If your father can't order me around, what makes you think that you can, little Prince?"

"I already took your hand," Darien snapped. "I'll take your life, too, if you make me."

"If you want to shoot me, you'll have to shoot him." Omiros pulled the physician closer with his good arm, his knife nicking the man's neck.

"Please, my lord," the physician stuttered. "I have served you faithfully. Spare me."

"And you'll continue to serve me however I deem fit." Omiros dragged the man with him, backing toward the balcony that overlooked the city. He sneered at Darien. "Would you really kill him to get to me? Haven't enough of your people died today?"

Darien's throat contracted as he tensed his jaw. Larissa reached for whatever *galdr* she had left. If she could just freeze Omiros, even for a moment, Darien could remove the physician, and Anara could kill Omiros.

"Come any closer and I'll throw him over the side," he threatened.

Larissa's hands tingled. How could she signal to the others what she planned to do? What if Omiros slit the physician's throat the moment Larissa made her move?

"There's no way out for you, Omiros," Darien threatened. "Surrender or face death."

"I'll never bow to an usurper," Omiros hissed. "Just know that his blood is also on your hands."

Then he pushed the physician over the stone balcony.

Larissa's *galdr* rushed to her fingertips as she tugged at the energy surrounding the physician's body, making it thick as syrup to slow the man's descent. The flash of the knife in Omiros' hands caught her attention as he drew his arm back. She transferred her *galdr* to him, freezing his arm in the air. Already, she could feel him breaking through her grasp. Darien fired his gun. Once. Then twice.

Determination and revulsion intermixed on Darien's face as Omiros staggered back, hitting the balcony ledge with enough force that his body tumbled over the side. There was no scream but a resounding thump. Larissa rushed to look over the ledge, scanning the ground below. The bent angles of Omiros' body were proof enough. The Regent was as dead as the physician who lay beside him.

Larissa looked away.

Darien sagged back against the wall, his gun still held tightly in his hands. Larissa caught Anara's eyes. She nodded in understanding. "I'll tell the generals the Regent is dead."

Feathers burst from her skin, and she was gone. Larissa swallowed the adrenaline that coursed through her body, forcing herself to take slow, measured steps toward Darien. She reached out, her fingers trailing down his wrist and relieving his gun from his grasp. "It's okay, Dar. You did the right thing."

"The physician?" he asked.

She shook her head.

He turned, slamming his fist against the stone wall. Larissa lay her palm on his back, feeling the strain of his muscles. "You did everything you could."

"I killed him." He turned back to face her. "You had him under your control there at the end. I didn't need to shoot him."

"My control was slipping, Dar. I wouldn't have lasted long." She raised her hand, letting her fingers wind into the curly hair at the nape of his neck. She tilted her head beneath his, forcing him to meet her gaze, and repeated, "He deserved it."

"Like the sentries? Those are *my* people bleeding out there. How many have to die before this war is over? How many will *I* have to kill?"

What could she say when she'd had the same doubts? She bit her lip. "We did what we had to do. That's all we can do in war."

A shadow crossed over Darien's face. "But what will that do to *us*?"

A loud horn resounded with enough force to shake Larissa and Darien from their isolation. They looked out over the balcony to see King Torsten, supported by Masai, walking toward the palace. Halvor and the rest of the Viðnám walked behind them. What little resistance remained outside the palace laid down their weapons, raising their hands and falling to their knees in surrender.

"Your people are free." Larissa squeezed his hand. "Just like mine."

But Darien was staring at the approaching crowd. "Someone has to tell Halvor about Marinos."

Larissa glanced behind, finding Halvor in the crowd several feet below. His head hung heavy even as those around him celebrated their victory. He already knew. She tugged at Darien's arm. "Come on. They'll be waiting for us."

The trek out of the palace was made in eerie silence. Though the stairs were slick with blood, the fighting itself had stopped. As they descended the final steps, King Torsten and the Viðnám waited within the palace's expansive foyer. At the sight of their Prince, the Safírians cheered. Darien raised his chin higher, the picture of princely propriety. Sighing, Larissa pulled her hand from Darien's grasp before Torsten could see.

Surprised settled in her chest as Darien's fingers held onto her more tightly than before. He wound his fingers between hers; his message was clear. He would greet his people with her at his side. The smile grew on her face even as tears stung the back of her eyes.

The crowd around them quieted as King Torsten shuffled toward Darien and Larissa with Masai's help. Once he was close enough to lay a hand on his son's shoulder, Masai withdrew to the side. Though Torsten's eyes briefly skimmed over Darien's and Larissa's hands, his face still held a genuine grin.

"My son!" Torsten's voice boomed. "Prince Darien has rightfully reclaimed our home, our kingdom, our people!"

Darien's lips parted in shock as Torsten clapped his shoulder again, moving to the side to push Darien toward the crowd. Larissa let his fingers slide out of her grasp as the Viðnám surged forward, crowding around their prince. The Safírians wept and shouted for joy; every citizen tried to reach Darien, to shake his hand, to look him in the eye. At one point, he turned back to look at Larissa with joy etched on his face. She could only smile back, as if he could read the words in her heart. He had earned his people's love, something that not even Aeron had ever truly done, not to this degree. He'd earned his title as Crown Prince.

Beside her, Torsten spoke with Anara. "The fighting is dying out everywhere, but it will end faster if the news of Regent Omiros' death spreads. Could you—"

Anara cut him off. "I'm on it. I'm not one for sappy moments anyhow."

"I'll come with you," Masai offered. "I can be more useful out there than here."

General Ishaan slid between them, "I'll accompany you as well, your Majesty. There are still pockets of fighting, and you can't rely on a soft-hand to defend you."

Masai barked out a laugh. "If you think she needs anyone's protection, you don't know your Queen well enough."

Anara gave Masai an appraising look before turning to Larissa. "You're staying?"

Larissa nodded, waving her off. Masai and Ishaan followed, shooting each other disgruntled looks as they went. Larissa had had enough fighting. Besides, Darien's happiness was the only thing keeping her from collapsing on the stairs from her fatigue. Though her hands still burned, the rest of her felt cold. As Torsten went to stand by his son's side, laying his arm across Darien's shoulder, Larissa allowed herself to lean against the marble column behind her and close her eyes.

"Princess Lovisa?"

Larissa jerked off the column, her hand flying to her gun as her eyes snapped open. Her hand froze on her holster as she took in the small boy standing in front of her. He couldn't be more than eight or nine. Though he stared at her gun in fear, he held out a piece of paper in his shaking hand. "I was told to give this to you."

Larissa reached out, gently taking the note from the boy. "I'm sorry; I didn't mean to frighten you. Who gave this to you?"

The boy's eyes rounded. "I don't know. He didn't tell me his name."

Larissa frowned, opening the note. Fear and despair ripped through her chest in equal measure. Her heart faltered, then beat in double time. She read the scrawled words once, then twice. The cheers of the Viðnám became muted like the waves crashing on the nearby shores.

Larissa shoved her way through the crowd still clambering for Darien's attention and down the front steps of the palace. The note fluttered from Larissa's hands, but it didn't matter. She'd already memorized the whole message.

I have Halla. Come alone to the gardens if you want her back alive.

-Calder

50

Mercy

Darien

THE FEEL OF HIS father's arms across his shoulders brought Darien more pride than all of the Viðnám surrounding him. Torsten's words—*my son*—played over again and again in Darien's mind. He'd heard his father use that tone many times with Aeron, but Darien couldn't remember the last time Torsten had spoken about him in that way.

He shook hands with the Safírian citizens crowding around him, unable to ignore how their hands were covered in dirt and blood. Farther back in the crowd, Halvor smiled at Darien, but there were tears in the man's eyes as a woman sobbed against his shoulder. Their freedom had come at a price.

Darien glanced behind, hoping to take strength from Larissa's presence. Even in his moment of triumph, it meant nothing if she wasn't by his side. He'd hoped she'd understood that by the way his hand had clung to hers. There hadn't been enough time to say it, but Darien was determined he would say it as soon as he could.

But the column where Larissa had stood was bare. He froze, still clasping the hand of the man in front of him. Just because she was gone didn't mean anything was wrong. But as he continued to scan the crowd to no avail, Darien's heart constricted in his chest. Near the palace entrance, he caught a glimpse of brilliant white hair flashing through the frame.

"Excuse me," Darien said to those around him, not directing his words at any one person but at them all. He ducked under his father's arm, pushing toward the palace doors.

"Darien!" Torsten called out.

"Excuse me," Darien said again, shoving through the mass of bodies that swarmed around him. The unease in his chest rose as he was slowed by the never-ending tide of Safírian citizens flowing in through the open doorway. "Move!"

He hadn't meant it, but an ounce of *galdr* slipped through his tone. Those around him stepped back, though looking confused as if they didn't understand why. There was no time to regret his actions. Darien dashed out into the palace courtyard.

A slip of paper tumbled in the wind, getting stuck under Darien's boot. He lifted his foot and, catching sight of the scribbled words, scooped up the note. His breath fled, and his fingers crumpled the paper.

He raced toward the gardens of his childhood, the sounds of crashing waves growing louder in his ears. The gardens had been built by the cliff just behind the palace, cultivated by his mother's gentle hands. On the far side of the gardens was an expansive clearing right at the precipice from which Darien had watched the yearly Jóltide fireworks with his family.

In his mind, Darien saw Calder waiting in that clearing with Halla standing precariously close to the edge. One hard shove would send Halla's body plummeting to the sharp rocks and the violent seas below. With Halla in hand, he would be able to demand anything of Larissa.

Darien's hands went toward his sides, taking comfort in his sword, but his fingers fumbled at the empty opening of his holster as he remembered Larissa taking his gun from him. Darien swore, picking up his pace even as he panted against the exertion passing through the blooming foliage that hid the end of the garden from sight.

Darien would have to find a way to save Halla, then he and Larissa would be able to take out Calder—he'd become too dangerous to live. Darien's mouth went dry and his hands shook as he remembered the blood splattering from the bullet that Darien put in Omiros' chest. Killing the Regent, a man who'd objectively deserved it, had shaken Darien's resolve. What would it cost Darien to kill his own brother?

"Where's Halla?" Larissa's frantic voice reached Darien before he had cleared the trees.

"Nice to see you again too, Princess," Calder drawled.

"Where is my sister? Tell me or I'll blast you off this cliff."

Darien slowed behind the edge of trees, hiding his body from Calder's line of sight and peering through the foliage. Larissa and Calder were close, only feet away.

Calder shook his head, his lips twisted into a smile. "You wouldn't. You're too *good* for that, remember? You wouldn't want to become a monster like me."

"Try me," Larissa spat.

"Kill me, and you'll never know where I've hidden Halla. If you want her back, you'll come with me, and you won't make a scene."

Drawing his sword, Darien stepped into the clearing, placing himself between Larissa and Calder. "I like Larissa's plan better. Tell us where Halla is."

Calder's smile slipped from his face as he drew his sword. "Why do you always have to interfere?"

Darien tightened his grip on his sword as Larissa's hand inched toward her gun. "What else are younger brothers for?"

"I am *not* your brother!" Calder roared, running forward with his sword arcing toward Darien, who blocked it just as Larissa raised her gun. Calder's head snapped toward her. "Stop!"

Larissa froze, her eyes wide as her body buckled in command under Calder's *galdr*. Darien understood in an instant. She'd spent too much of her *galdr* in the battle, depleting what she would need to resist Calder's manipulation. Darien's arms shook as his own fatigue reminded him of the exertion he'd already expelled.

Calder sneered. "Did you really think that you would be stronger than me?"

He lunged with his sword aimed at Darien's ribs. Darien spun away, but the tip caught his shirt, ripping the material. In his periphery, Larissa's body quivered with the effort of shaking off Calder's *galdr*, and though her body moved, it was in incremental inches.

Calder struck again, but Darien parried, retreating from Calder's advance. He danced backward, always just out of reach, moving Calder farther from Larissa. If Darien could increase the distance and distraction, Larissa could break out of Calder's grasp.

As if understanding Darien's plan, Calder shouted in frustration, cutting down in a diagonal arc toward Darien. With a twist, Darien separated himself again, only to advance on Calder, forcing him to parry Darien's thrust. Calder bared his teeth under the weight of Darien's attack, but beneath his ferocity, Darien saw Aeron's patient face as he walked Darien through stance after stance. In Calder's hard eyes, Darien saw Aeron's filled with laughter. The double vision left a gaping hole in Darien's chest that he could not allow himself to give in to.

With a shove, Calder pushed himself away, his sword held aloft. "I see you've remembered some tricks."

"I learned them from you," Darien said.

Calder spat on the ground. "You've learned nothing from me."

Darien adjusted his grip, waiting for the attack. Calder shifted on his feet. Darien's body moved in response. Then the shot rang out.

Calder hissed, falling to a knee as his sword fell to the ground beside him. Behind him, Larissa held her gun steady, freed of his persuasion. He clutched at the bloody wound in his shoulder, but even from a distance, Darien knew it was a flesh wound. He stalked toward the man, kicking the sword out of his reach. He lifted his own to Calder's throat, the tip of it nicking the skin.

"Where is Halla? Tell us where she is, and we'll show you mercy."

Calder shook his head. "You always were better at showing mercy than I. You probably would've let the old man and the little girl live."

Darien's skin went cold as the sea breeze rushed over him. Behind Calder, Larissa's face turned white. The sword shook in Darien's hand. "What did you *do*?"

"That fake father of yours, what was his name? Aagen, right? At least, that's what Halla called him as she watched him die." The feral grin stretched across Calder's face even as he grimaced from the pain in his shoulder. He looked over his shoulder at Larissa. "Halla can keep him company in Helheim. I know how much you would hate for her to have to go alone."

Before his words could register, before rage and grief could splinter Darien's heart, Calder reached for his side. A loud crack shattered Darien's ears. Pain as quick and sudden as lightning shot through his heart. He fell to his knees; his chest was painfully hot, though the rest of his body was cold. Calder kneeled before him, raising the familiar gun that had once been Aagen's.

Calder stared in triumph at the blood that Darien felt pouring down his chest. "Say hello to Aagen and Halla, won't you?"

51

A Bargain

Larissa

Too late, Larissa saw the gun.

Darien's mouth opened, his face lined with pain. Fear and confusion clouded his eyes as his sword fell from his grip, as his legs gave out from under him.

A red haze consumed Larissa's vision, the same color as Darien's blood. Righteous rage boiled inside of her, desperate for escape.

Calder's finger inched toward the trigger to fire another shot.

Larissa drew on whatever *galdr* remained, dragging it up through her body, letting it scorch through her. She screamed in agony and flung out her hands, channeling every bit of power and directing it toward Calder.

No hesitation. No guilt. Only anger.

The wave of Larissa's *galdr* smashed into Calder, snatching his body and hurling it toward the edge of the cliff. He dug his hands and feet into the ground. Larissa urged her *galdr* to grow, to flow through her like a tidal wave, slamming it against Calder's desperate form again and again. Shock and disbelief battled in his eyes. Her vision still red, Larissa gritted her teeth as her *galdr* crashed over him.

Calder's scream echoed against the precipice as his body plummeted through the air, ending abruptly and replaced by the vicious crashing of waves and the pounding of Larissa's blood in her ears.

Her vision cleared at the sight of Darien swaying on his knees, his hands pressed against his chest. Larissa's feet pounded across the ground; she collapsed next to him in time to catch his body as he fell into her arms.

"Dar, stay with me." She leaned over him, her hands desperately trying to staunch the bleeding that oozed between her fingers. "You're going to be okay."

One of Darien's bloodied hands cupped Larissa's cheek. His breath came in short, shallow gasps. "I'm so sorry . . . about Halla."

Sobs racked Larissa's body, but she couldn't allow herself to think, to feel, or it would destroy her. Halla couldn't be dead, she refused to believe it. She would've known. She pressed harder on Darien's chest, certain she had to be hurting him, but he hardly seemed to feel it. "You're going to be okay. Stay with me. You promised me, Darien! You promised you wouldn't die!"

His lips turned up in a smile that didn't hide the agony in his eyes. He rubbed his thumb over the scar on her face. "Lara, you need to know . . . our responsibilities to our people . . . they mean nothing if you're not with me. If I had to choose . . . between you and my kingdom . . . I choose you . . . I'd always choose you."

"Then choose me." Larissa choked on her words. "Stay with me. Don't leave me."

"I don't want to." His voice was hardly audible now. "A thousand . . ."

The sound of approaching footsteps came from the gardens, but Larissa couldn't turn around. It didn't matter if it was the Viðnám or the sentries or the Empress herself. Darien's face, his bloody chest, filled her vision. There was no one else but him. She leaned in to hear his murmurs over the sound of the waves.

Darien's lips brushed against her ear, his words like a prayer whispered to gods who refused to listen. "A thousand lifetimes with you would never have been enough, but I would have been grateful for at least this one."

Tears flooded down her face, drops of them falling on his cheeks. "Darien—"

His eyes closed, and his hand slid from her face.

"Darien? Darien!" Hysterics tore at her throat, stripping it raw. "Stay with me! You promised!"

Larissa buried her face in Darien's neck, his curls tickling her face, but all she could smell was blood. The footsteps of the approaching crowd grew louder.

"Help us! Help *him*!" she screamed. "Please—"

"Larissa! Darien!" Anara's voice cut through the crowd of voices that cried aloud at the sight before them.

Anara's body crumpled beside Larissa. "Masai, do something!"

Hope warmed Larissa's heart, easing the hollow pain in her chest. She raised her head, making room for Masai, who knelt at Darien's side, his dark hands reaching out to Darien's chest. Though his palms glowed, the light sputtered out and faded. Sweat beaded down Masai's face. "I have nothing left. He's too far gone."

It was the guilt in Masai's voice that acted as the final blow, severing Larissa's heart from her mind. Cold paralyzed Larissa's body.

"No!" Anara screamed, shoving Masai onto the ground. "Fix him!"

"I can't!" he shouted back, rising to his feet. He caught Anara's fists in his large hands to stop her from attacking. "I'm sorry. He's gone."

Anara snatched her hands back and wrapped her arms around Larissa as if in comfort. But there could be no comfort. Larissa's fingers caressed the hair at the nape of Darien's neck, unable to recognize her own sobs. How could a world exist without him in it?

"I'm sorry, Lara." Anara's voice shook. "He was my best friend, too."

"That's my son!" King Torsten's tortured voice called out from somewhere behind Larissa, but she clung even tighter to Darien's body.

She wouldn't let him go; she couldn't.

"No, the Norn can't have him." Larissa raised her face to the sky, ignoring the crowd around them. "Verðandi! You can't have him! Show yourself!"

Though Larissa's tears continued to stream down her face, the world around Larissa slowed, then stopped. The noise ceased; even the waves silenced. Everything around her was tinged in gray, as though the very color of the world had been sucked out of her surroundings. Anara's comforting hand stopped near her shoulder. Torsten knelt, his hands frozen in the process of tearing at his beard in sorrow. Halvor and General Aiko stared at Darien, at the blood that stopped dripping from his chest.

As silent as a wisp of smoke, the small child-goddess with flowing, fiery hair and glowing eyes settled next to Larissa. Her bottom lip jutted out in a pout. "Such a shame; I'd hoped we were wrong."

"He's not dead," Larissa forced the words out through gritted teeth, but even to her own ears, she sounded like a wounded animal. "Save him."

One of Verðandi's small hands brushed back a black curl from Darien's face. "I've stopped him in time just like everyone else. You're right that his heart has a final beat left, but his soul has already gone."

"What does that mean?"

Verðandi laid her hands on Darien's chest, knitting together the gaping wound with only her touch. "I can heal the body, but I can't retrieve the soul."

Larissa's hands brushed over the closed wound in wonder. It was as if the bullet had never gone through. "I can retrieve it. Just tell me how; there has to be a way."

Verðandi looked at her with pity in her young eyes. "There is a price."

The image of her mother pouring out her *galdr* into Verðandi, sacrificing her life, played out in Larissa's mind. If Calder had been telling the truth, then Halla was gone. The thought alone turned

Larissa's world black. If Halla was beyond saving, and Darien couldn't be saved, what point was there in living?

Anara was resilient. She would survive. As for the prophecy, Larissa couldn't care less. For weeks, all she had cared about was the prophecy and her people and Darien's people, but what did those things mean without the ones *she* loved? If Darien would choose her over his kingdom, she would choose Darien over the prophecy. Every time. Let the Norn choose a different hero to save the world.

"I'll pay it." Larissa held out her hands as she remembered her mother doing so long ago, ignoring the realization of how angry Darien would be when he learned what she'd done. As if he wouldn't do the exact same thing. "If you need my *galdr*, take it. Just save him."

But Verðandi only grabbed her hands, placing them back on Darien's body. "It's a different price, and you won't pay it to me."

Frowning, Larissa rubbed away the tears that stained her cheeks. "Then who?"

The child-goddess smiled down at Darien, running a finger along his stubbled jawline. "She might not want to give him back. Hel likes pretty things too."

Larissa drew in a shaky breath. "Hel? As in, the goddess of death?"

"The collector of souls herself." Verðandi's high pitched voice chimed in the air.

"I thought she died in *Ragnarok* with the rest of the gods."

Verðandi raised an eyebrow. "Many of us survived, including Hel. I'll care for Darien's body, take it back with me, and keep it frozen in time just as before, but you must retrieve his soul if you wish to bring him back."

"And she'll just let me waltz into Helheim and leave again?" Larissa asked incredulously.

"There are bonds that tie us together. You are bound to Darien, and even Hel can't deny those bonds. Of anyone, your tie to Darien is strongest. It will lead you to him, and it will allow you entry into Helheim along with my gift."

"Gift?"

"Don't you remember?" Verðandi leaned forward, her fingers tapping on the underside of Larissa's wrist. At her touch, the elongated *Z* rune from Larissa's vision reappeared. It glowed for a moment then faded away, sinking into Larissa's unblemished skin.

"For your protection, when you need it most," Verðandi repeated.

Larissa stared at the child-goddess, not at all convinced by her innocent expression. "You knew this would happen. You knew that Darien would die, that I would make this deal, that I would go to Helheim."

"Of course we knew." Verðandi smiled. "So you will go?"

"Don't you already know the answer?"

"Then it's decided." Verðandi leapt to her feet. She bit her lip, looking apologetic. "I misspoke before. I don't need as much of your *galdr*, but I do require some of it to transport Darien back to *Yggdrasil*."

"Why?" she asked, even as she raised her hands. It wasn't that Larissa wasn't willing to pay, only that she was curious. "You have all this power; what do you need mine for?"

"Our *galdr* cannot work outside of the boundaries placed upon us by the gods. We cannot interfere with predicted fate unless we are fueled by others." Verðandi laid her hands on top of Larissa's. "This might hurt a little."

The air around their hands shimmered as *galdr* poured out of Larissa and into Verðandi. There was pain, but to Larissa's broken heart, it was bearable. If pain was the cost of Darien's safety, she would pay it. *Galdr* slogged through her body as if it took Verðandi longer than usual to find it. When Verðandi withdrew her hands, Larissa slumped over Darien's body, certain that there was nothing left within her. In a way, it felt right to be emptied of *galdr*. She *was* empty, a shell of who she'd once been.

A golden aura emanated from Verðandi as her red hair curled and flicked around her face. Verðandi bent forward, laying her hands on Darien's chest that shimmered at her touch. The shimmer extended down his body, encasing him in *galdr*—Larissa's *galdr*. Larissa watched through half-closed eyes as his body faded from sight, leaving her lying in grass and soil coated in his blood.

"We will speak again soon," Verðandi promised.

Larissa could hardly manage the word. "How?"

"In your dreams, as always, Lovisa. I will show you the way." Verðandi's voice faded to a whisper. "You have until the next full moon, when Hel's tide will collect all souls. If you do not get to Darien before then, you will not be able to reach him at all."

Larissa knew the goddess had gone as the discordant cacophony rushed over her, and color bled back into her surroundings. Without Darien's body to hold on to, Larissa was left with only her grief. She wrapped her arms around her waist, holding together what little of her remained. Anara's hand finished its arc and landed on her shoulder, but Larissa turned her face into the soil, howling in rage and sorrow, unwilling to force her body to rise and face a world without Halla, without Darien. She heard Anara's and Masai's exclamations as they took in Darien's missing body, but their words were worthless in Larissa's ears.

Then another voice pierced her turmoil. It was a voice Larissa feared she'd never hear again. Straining against the emptiness that weighed her body down into the earth, Larissa lifted her head.

Running toward her was a small girl with freckles that contrasted sharply against her pale cheeks and green eyes. Eyes just like her mother's.

"Halla," Larissa croaked, wondering if perhaps she was seeing a vision.

"Lara!" Halla threw herself beside Larissa and pulled her sister's head into her lap. Halla's hands and arms were streaked with blood. At the sight, Larissa forced herself to sit, grasping Halla's face and soaking in the flush across Halla's cheeks that proved her vitality. Proved that she lived.

Larissa didn't ask how, didn't need to know, not then. There would be time for questions later. Halla was alive, and Larissa would travel to Helheim and bring Darien back. That was enough. A sliver of hope warmed the cold, empty center of her chest where her heart had used to beat. Maybe one day, it would beat just as strongly again.

52

Fight and Flight

Anara

"WHAT DO YOU MEAN I *can't* go?"

Anara winced at the incredulity in Larissa's voice, noting the sharp undertone of fury that grew ever closer to the surface, knowing that neither emotion would do anything to sway Torsten's mind. Anara shifted to better accommodate the dull pain that covered every inch of her body, but the most potent wound was inside. They'd lost Darien. *Again*. After searching for so long, Anara had found him, found them both, but now Darien was gone. She never should have left them.

Larissa's curled hands rested on the council table before her as she glared at the blood-covered king. Though healed, Torsten still favored his right side and winced as he adjusted his position. Anara's bitter thoughts found satisfaction in Torsten's discomfort.

Masai, Halla, and Kai also sat at the table. Masai's healing of Torsten had granted him instant access to the intimacy of their council, but Halla and Kai had been included to tell them what had transpired on the farm. Masai looked away in shame when he heard of how Calder had broken through the haze created by Masai's concoction, but Anara still didn't understand how he'd been able to get out of the cellar. When she'd asked Halla, the girl had turned a green shade of discomfort, but only answered, "I don't know."

When she relayed how Aagen had fought Calder to give her and Kai time to escape, Halla had stared at the table as tears ran down her face. She'd glanced at Kai only once before looking away. The boy hadn't uttered a single word, refusing to meet anyone's gaze. Anara would have pressed, if not for Larissa's revelation of her conversation with the Norn.

Anara hadn't seen Verðandi, but she'd witnessed Darien's bloody body one moment, and the next it was gone. It wasn't impossible to think that the goddess of fate had been involved. When Larissa told Torsten of her plan to go to Hel and retrieve Darien's soul, Torsten's answer, though slow in forthcoming, was a resounding "no."

Torsten leaned forward, his movements slow and measured. "I mean what I said, Lovisa. The goddesses of fate do not give anything without a price. Hel does not give back what is hers. If you go to Helheim, you will not return. You are the only one foretold to overthrow Shiko. Maybe after—"

Anara scoffed, soft enough that only Masai, sitting next to her, caught it.

Larissa shook her head. "I only have until the next full moon, that's what Verðandi said. I can't wait for the war to end."

"And we can't afford to lose you before we've won, or all of this has been for nothing."

"I killed Calder." Larissa's voice went deadly soft. "If I don't bring Darien back, you have no one left."

Anara resisted a shiver at Larissa's words, though Kai flinched violently in his seat. There was no regret in Larissa's tone over what she'd done to Calder. It wasn't that Anara would've done anything differently, but after watching Larissa wrestle with the darkness of war, Larissa's newfound callousness was nothing less than shocking. Even Kai, typically so unruffled, looked a bit sick.

Torsten rubbed at his temples. "You think I don't know that? He was the last of my bloodline, the last of my heritage."

"That's all you care about, isn't it? Your stupid bloodline." Larissa stood, her chair falling to the ground behind her. Halla sank lower into her chair, jerking away when Kai reached out to touch her shoulder. Anara tucked away the interaction in her mind as Larissa leaned over the table. "Darien was more than your legacy; he was your *son*, Torsten."

Torsten rose, his palms flat on the table. "And *you* took him away from me! You raced off to find Calder, and Darien ran off to find you without any support. It's *your* fault my sons are dead."

"My fault?" Larissa spat. "Who gave up on Aeron the moment you heard he was Calder? Who berated Darien every chance he could when Darien didn't live up to your ridiculous expectations? No wonder the gods gave him a new father!"

"*Out*!" Torsten thundered, his shaking hand pointed at the door. "Get out!"

"Gladly." Larissa spun on her heel, nearly sprinting across the length of the hall.

Halla and Kai followed while Anara and Masai were the last to exit. Just as Anara closed the door, she heard Torsten's dry sob. Even so, Anara's heart remained unmoved. There was responsibility, and there was loyalty. Torsten had chosen the first. He would have to live with his choice.

Larissa led them down the halls of the Safírian palace to the wing where they'd been given their quarters. She flung open her door, hardly noticing as the others entered cautiously behind her. Anara's foot firmly closed the door behind them just as Larissa reached for her gun.

"What are you doing?" Halla squeaked, her eyes glued to the gun.

"Torsten can't stop me. I'm leaving. You're staying here."

"But—"

"No, Halla. Verðandi said that I could go, just me. My bond to Darien is the only thing that will get me into Helheim. And Verðandi's rune will hopefully get me out."

"But how?" Masai asked.

"I don't know." She threw a bag on her bed and shoved the nearest clothes into it. "I'll figure it out."

"What about the funeral?" Anara asked.

Fire blazed in Larissa's eyes. "There's no funeral because Darien isn't dead!"

Galdr burst from Larissa's hands in a wave of heat that sent them all stepping back out of range.

Anara moved toward her as if the heat radiating from Larissa's skin didn't burn. She understood the fire in Larissa's soul, born of loss and anger. The same flame had burned in Anara since the devastation of her people, when she'd been forced to kill her own family for survival. Anara laid her hand on Larissa's shoulder, waiting until the other girl met her gaze. Tears gleamed in her eyes.

The heat around Larissa faded, and Anara sucked in a breath of cool, salty air wafting in from the open balcony window. "If you want to fight your way out, you know I'll be by your side. But I have another plan . . ."

The body wrapped in white linen atop the funeral pyre was not Darien's, though few were privy to that knowledge. Only those who'd been in the garden knew that Darien's body had vanished, and Torsten meant to keep it that way. Another cadaver had been provided from the many unclaimed corpses in the city. Even knowing it wasn't Darien didn't ease the stabbing ache in Anara's chest as Torsten lit the pyre on fire with Queen Einsa at his side.

The flames reflected against the smooth surface of the shells and polished stones that formed the shape of a boat around the mound. It was a picturesque scene as the crowd of mourners stood in the garden with the sun lowering itself beneath the waves on the horizon. Even the pyre had an odd kind of beauty, having been constructed on the edge of the cliff right over where Darien had died, covering the bloodstained ground. The burning would allow his soul freedom to travel beyond.

Or, at least, that was what Torsten claimed as he gave his son's eulogy, speaking of Darien's bravery, his goodness, his complete dedication to his people even to the bitter end. How he'd killed the Empress' War Dog to ensure his nation's survival.

How he'd given his all.

Anara averted her gaze, unable to stand the sight. Beside her, Larissa stared out at the open ocean as the sun disappeared, plunging them in the darkness of the night. The flames of the pyre burned brighter, throwing light and shadows against the mourners. It revealed the dryness of Larissa's cheeks, the hardening of her eyes. Anara nearly wished that Larissa would wail as inconsolably as she had when holding Darien's body. The dead emptiness in Larissa's eyes frightened Anara more than any cries of desperation.

Remaining at the pyre's side, Torsten raised a hand to motion the mourners forward. They would pass, one by one, to give their final remarks that would follow Darien into whatever awaited him. As a warrior slain in battle, surely he'd be welcome into Valhöll if such a place still remained after *Ragnarok*. Anara wasn't sure. Besides, she knew where his soul was, where Larissa already planned to go, and its mistress would be anything but welcoming.

As the Princess of Perle, Larissa was first in line. Anara followed her heavy tread, ready to support her, but Larissa's spine remained stiff. She stopped at the head of the pyre, staring into the flames. Torsten stared at her but said nothing. He'd not spoken to her since their argument that morning. Einsa offered a look of sorrow and regret; it was the most emotion Anara had seen from Torsten's second-queen, but Larissa ignored them both. Her lips moved, but only air passed through. Whatever words were written on her heart, Larissa kept them to herself. She moved on, allowing Anara to step up behind her.

Anara inclined her head toward the pyre and whispered low enough that she could not be heard over the crackling of the flames. "Hold on, Darien. Lara is coming."

She stepped away, making room for Masai and the remaining line of generals, citizens, and rebels that had come to pay their respects. Wrinkling her nose in distaste, she moved toward Larissa's side. The air was thick with the smells of salt and death. After Masai's brief pause at the pyre, he walked away, continuing back through the gardens with a quick glance at Anara, who nodded minutely in response.

Beside Larissa, Halla wrapped her arms around her chest as though to keep her heart from falling out. Tears streamed down her face with abandon. Kai stood behind her, in the shadows, watching. To Anara's surprise, the boy's face glistened with tears, but his eyes were locked on the edge of the cliff beyond the pyre. Anara's gaze followed his, thinking of the rocks below. Ishaan had searched the rocks, finding Calder's blood, but his body had already been washed away by the sea. Anara considered it justice. It was right for Calder's body to be adrift, never knowing peace.

All around them, the cries of the mourners grated against Anara's keen ears. She considered changing the shape of her eardrums to block them out in the same way she wanted to filter the smells staining her nose, but it was right to experience the discomfort. Anara had no doubt that Larissa would bring Darien back. The gods had not created a love like theirs to be destroyed before it could bloom. No, Larissa would go to Helheim, and she would return.

Even so, Anara's heart wept the tears she would not allow her eyes to reveal. She wept for Darien and the pain he'd endured. She wept for Aeron as the boy she'd once loved, though she'd never had the bravery to say it. She wept for Larissa and the death of who she'd been. Even now, Larissa's face remained unmoved as the cries mixed in with the crackle of the rising flames. It wasn't strength that kept Larissa upright or her eyes dry. It was brokenness and the emptiness of loss.

The line of mourners went on as minutes dragged into hours. Though Larissa offered Halla comfort, holding her sister against her side, her composure never cracked. Anara remained beside her, accepting the condolences offered to Larissa. By the time the last mourner had passed, the flames of the pyre smoldered in the darkened mass of wood and bone. The sight of it made even Anara's stomach heave in discomfort. Her eyes stung with smoke, and her chest burned with every breath, but that too felt right.

Many, like Generals Ishaan and Aiko, remained in the shadows of the trees, but Torsten stood alone on the edge of the cliff, looking out at the dark waters. There would be more funerals. General Sture had died in the battle along with many others. Darien's funeral pyre would not be the only one burning in the city; no doubt the smell would become so intense that Anara would have to shut her windows and plug the cracks to avoid drowning in the pungent odors and burning flesh. Though Halla's tears had dried, she sniffed occasionally at Larissa's side.

Anara sensed Masai's return before she heard him. Again that sharp scent of incense rose in his presence, but so did the more floral tones of his skin.

Masai's whisper reached Anara's ears. "It's ready."

The stiffening of Larissa's body made it clear she'd heard as well. Ever so slightly, Larissa raised her hand and lightly tapped Halla's upper arm. Halla's eyes widened with awareness. Her sobs increased, and Halla's hand clutched her chest with enough theatrics that Anara worried someone would notice their ruse. Then, Halla's body slid to the ground.

Though Larissa gasped with enough conviction that even Torsten turned to look, Anara knew Halla was only acting the part assigned to her. Larissa looped her arm under Halla's as Masai did so from the other side. They never looked back as they carried Halla away from the pyre and into the gardens.

Though annoyance crossed Torsten's face, it yielded grief as he turned back to look at the oceans, as Anara had known he would. With his back turned from her, Anara slid into the shadows, unsurprised to see Kai follow the others at a distance. She frowned at the boy. He'd always been an enigma, but he walked after them like a man sentenced to death. She stalked behind him, stowing away her observations for when she could examine them later.

At the front of the gardens, Masai passed off a large-hooded, floor-length jacket that Larissa wrapped securely around her body, hiding the elegant mourning gown. As she tucked her hair back into the hood, Larissa could have passed herself off as any other mourner in the city. She bent down to embrace Halla.

"I'll be fine. I'll come back."

"You promise?" The strength in Halla's voice wavered.

Larissa brushed back the strands of blonde hair that had fallen in her sister's face. "I promise."

Anara looked at her feet, careful to not let her wariness reveal itself on her face. If the old stories were true, Hel would not give Darien back without a price, and Anara knew Larissa would pay anything. She could only hope Larissa's bond to Halla would be enough to temper Larissa's recklessness and bring her back.

As if she could read Anara's mind, Larissa looked at her. "You're not worried about me, are you?"

Anara smiled through the doubt, placing one hand on her hip. "Not at all. Just don't make us wait too long. We have more kingdoms to reclaim."

Larissa's brows tightened. "I only have until the next full moon. Then we'll know, one way or the other."

Silence permeated their group even as the sound of mourners and the smell of ash lingered in the air, only to be broken by a faint rumbling and cranking noise that Anara would recognize anywhere. Larissa's eyebrows rose. "You didn't?"

Anara's smile was genuine. "I couldn't let you go on your own."

She led them out of the gardens and crossed to the far side of the courtyard. A familiar blue pickup sat parked in the shadows of the courtyard walls, its key already turned in the ignition where Masai had left it.

"I grabbed the supplies you mentioned," Masai said to Anara. "I still say she could've taken a better truck."

Larissa walked forward, letting her hand run over Helga's rusted side. "There's no better truck than Helga."

Anara knew it was more than that. If Larissa went in Helga, at least she wouldn't have to go completely alone. Larissa pulled herself into the cab, ripping her mourning gown as it caught on the door's edge. Anara shut the door after her, hopping onto the side bars to rest her hands on the window. "Get out of the city and head northwest. If Verðandi is meant to guide you to Helheim, it makes sense to start in her direction back toward Smaragd."

Larissa pulled on the gloves that had been left on the seat, concealing her pearl ring. "You'll take care of Halla?"

"Of course."

"You'll be able to handle Torsten?"

"I've had practice."

Larissa nodded but rolled her lips together. "Anara, if I don't make it back—"

"No," Anara cut her off. "You will make it back, Larissa, not for your people or for some prophecy. You'll make it back for Halla. You'll make it back for me, because I can't lose another friend. You'll make it back for Darien, because if it came down to it, you know that's what he'd want you to do. You know that's how he would want you to honor his death."

"I can't live in a world without him."

Anara handed over the gun she'd hidden under her jacket. "Then bring him back. But you better be with him too, or I'll be making the next trip to see Hel."

Larissa laid the gun on the seat beside her, her lips twitching. "I love you too, Anara."

Anara's throat tightened, and her eyes burned. She stepped off the side bars, landing on the courtyard steps. With garbled protestations, Helga's engine growled as Larissa guided her away from the gardens, away from the palace, and down toward the Wall that protected Safír's innermost circle. As if unable to help herself, Halla's footsteps followed after Helga's truck, only stopping once Helga had gone from sight. The night wind picked up, rustling Halla's hair and pulling it away from her neck, revealing the scarred rune that seemed to glow under the moonlight. Anara laid her hand on Halla's shoulder, keeping watch as ash fell from the sky.

Epilogue
Verðandi

THE SMALL CHILD-GODDESS WAS not bothered by the chill in the air or the mist that obscured the shapes of the steps before her. On light feet, Verðandi ascended the steps, gliding across the cracked surface of the palace foyer and deep into the court of the Queen of Death. The doors of the throne room were wrapped in roots frozen in ice that cracked at her touch. With whispered secrets, the doors swung inward.

Mist consumed the throne room, hiding the cold stone floor and swirling around Verðandi's robes. It curled up her spine as if its grasping tendrils could tame the wild flame of her hair. Certain and carefree, Verðandi waved away the fog as if it were a misbehaving pet, and it sank at her touch.

Before her loomed a massive throne composed of black ice and aged by time. Its sharp edges nearly reached the high ceilings. It was massive in its scope, far larger than any human could possibly ever need. Though it was appropriate as the immense woman who sat upon it was anything but human.

"Hello, Hel," Verðandi called out as she reached the steps before the throne.

The goddess stared down at her out of one burning violet eye. Her delicate eyebrow rose in scornful curiosity, and her vivid red lips pressed against each other. Or at least, half of them did. For half of Hel's face was beautiful, with full lips shrouded in luscious black hair that hung down to her waist, complimenting rosy, glowing skin, but the other half was dead. The ragged line started at the top of her forehead and cut down her face and neck, disappearing into

the fabric covering Hel's chest. A gaping hole was all that remained of Hel's other eye, and missing lips revealed the teeth still rooted in her jawbone. On the dead side of her body, Hel's hair was white and thin. She was the physical manifestation of all life had to offer and all death had to steal.

She tapped her skeletal hand against the armchair of the throne. "What do you want, Verðandi?"

Verðandi pouted at Hel's bored tone, reaching down to pat the mist that gathered at her feet. It parted from her hands and fled at her touch. "Not even your pets like me."

The woman's red lips turned up, amused. She beckoned with her manicured hand. The mist raced to her, nestling in her palm. Verðandi could make out the shapes of eyes and teeth within the mist. "They mean no offense. They're not used to the living, or anything warm, really."

Hel shook her hand, scattering the mist that howled as it dispersed. She rose from her throne, her body towering over Verðandi and revealing the Jötnar blood that ran through her veins. The other gods had banished her to Helheim, calling her *half-breed*. Just as they had once called Verðandi.

Hel still wore the same black gown she'd donned during *Ragnarok*. Leather armor covered the soft fabric. The furs around her shoulders had come from her brother Fenris after his death on the battlefield. To the mortals who passed through her gate, she was a beauty and a nightmare.

Verðandi only smiled as she tilted her head up to gaze into Hel's face. "Did you get my gifts?"

Hel descended the steps slowly. "Did you mean to send them quite so broken?"

"Don't most things arrive broken in this realm?"

"Hmm," Hel replied, reaching the bottom of the steps. Her ragged-edged sword swung at her waist, its tip nearly touching the ground.

"They're pretty, though, don't you think?" Verðandi giggled, gazing up at the giantess.

Half of Hel's face lifted with an amused grin. "I suppose they are. And I'll have eternity to fix them."

Verðandi's smile only grew. "Maybe not eternity."

Hel's amusement vanished at Verðandi's look. "What have you done?"

"We cannot disregard the threads that bind those together."

Hel snorted. Around her, Helheim trembled, and the screams of souls from beyond her throne echoed as the earth shook. "You are playing a dangerous game, Verðandi."

"I don't know what you mean," Verðandi answered, her voice laced with sweet naivety.

"Do you remember the golden blood of the gods as it flooded this earth? The mortals might have brought about the demons, but it was the gods and Jötnar who destroyed this world in fire and ash. They played the game, and they lost."

Verðandi tilted her chin up. "That's because they didn't know the rules."

Prophecy

Keeper of stories, peering through facades.
   Past, present, future, speaker of the gods.
   The Norn only record, the Norn only see.
   Recorders, Gifters, and Augurs they shall be.
   From within, comes destruction of peace.
   Chaos will reign and harmony will cease.
   Only the third of the Perlian line
   At the cost of a life, can change Fate's design.
   A forest polluted with deception and deceit
   Will either be cleansed or face its defeat.
   Queen of monsters, dead without worth
   Brings baptism of fire and rebirth.
   Second-born King, usurper of the throne.
   Hel's cold fingers welcome his bloodline home.
   Double-edged heart; divided soul.
   Betrayed or betrayer? Decide your role.
   Where one is killed, another takes its place.
   Sharing the cost, which all kingdoms must face.

Pronunciation Guide

Aadan (Ahh-dahn)
Aagen (Eye-gin)
Aeron (Air-on)
Anara (Ah-nar-ah)
Benia (Ben-ee-a)
Brother Brunnen (Bruoo-nin)
Brother Gorthr (Gor-ther)
Calder (Kahl-der)
Dal /Pappa (Dale)
Darien (Dare-ee-in)
Einsa (Ine-sah)
Eluf (Ee-loof)
Fenris (Fin-rihs)
General Aiko (Eye-KOH)
General Ishaan (Ee-shawn)
General Soren (Sore-in)
General Sture (Stur)
Haki (Hah-key)
Halla (Hahl-la)
Halvor (Hall-vore)
Helga (Hell-gah)
Hovmester (Hove-mess-ter)
Jari (Yar-ee)
Jon (Yawn)
Juni (Joo-nee)

Kai (KI)
Kelby (Kel-bee)
Kiah (KI-ah)
Larissa (Lar-is-sah)
Lovisa (LOH-vee-sah)
Marinos (Mare-ih-nohs)
Masai (Mah-sI)
Meya (May-ah)
Mikkel (Mee-kell)
Norn
    Skuld (Scoo-ldt)
    Verðandi (Verr-thawn-dee)
    Urðr (Orrth-thr)
Regent Hammon (Hey-mon)
Regent Omiros (Oh-mer-ohs)
Rúna (Rroo-nah)
Saessae (Say-say)
Shiko (Shee-KOH)
Sister Wren (Ren)
Skaði (Skah-thee)
Stjarna (Shtar-nah)
Torsten (Tour-ston)
Tucker (Onkel Tucker)
Vern/ Mamma (Vurn)
Zoya (Zoy-ah)

Commonwealths

Diamant (Dee-ah-mont)
Perle (Pur-la)
Safír (Sah-feer)
Smaragd (Smear-ogd)
Rubin (Roo-bEEn)

Capitol City: Ishjem (Eess-yem)
Capitol City: Lystheim (Lies-tee-im)
Capitol City: Havsiden (Hahv-sy-din)
Capitol City: Treheim (Tray-Highm)
Capitol City: Brannsiden (Brahn-sy-din)

Mythological Glossary

Æsir: group of gods who live in Asgard, the heavenly realm

Árvakr and Alsviðr: horses that pull the sun across the sky

Aurvandil the Valiant: saddest of the stars

Baldr: god of light, wisdom, and courage

Bragi: god of storytelling

Eir: goddess of protection and mercy

Fenrir: monstrous wolf-son of Loki

Freyja: goddess associated with love, fertility, and war

Freyr: god of harvest and protector of farmers

Frigg: goddess of children

Hati & Skoll: wolves who eat the sun and moon

Hel: goddess of death, Queen of Death

Iðunn: goddess of spring and keeper of immortality

Jörmungandr: giant sea monster/ son of Loki

Kári: god of the north wind

Kvasir: a wise god and poet

Loki: trickster god

Mani: god who pulls the moon

Mimir: god of wisdom

Njörðr: Safír's patron god of the sea

Óðinn: high chief of the gods, great wanderer

Ragnarok: the defeat of the Æsir

Skrymir: smartest of all giants

Sól: god who pulls the sun

Sutr: greatest of the fire giants

the Norn: the three goddesses of fate; Recorders, Gifters, and Augurs

Thjazi: giant who stole Iðunn

Thor: god of thunder, strength, and protection of the human realm

Tyr: god of warriors and heroes

Vanir: group of gods of fertility, wisdom, and the ability to see the future

Víðarr: son of Óðinn, god of vengeance

Vör: Perle's patron goddess of wisdom

Yggdrasil: an immense and central sacred tree at the center of the world

Runes

DAGAZ

Dawn, Awakening, Certainty, Illumination, Completion, Hope

HAGALAZ

Hail, Nature, Wrath, Being Tested, Overcoming Obstacles

ISA

Ice, Clarity, Stasis, Challenges, Introspection, Watching & Waiting

THURISAZ

Thorns, Reaction, Defense, Conflict, Catharsis, Regeneration

JERA

Turn of the Year, Cycles, Completion, Changes, Harvest, Reaping

EIHWAZ

Balance, Enlightenment, Death, The World Tree

SOWILO

Sun, Health, Honor, Resources, Victory, Wholeness, Cleansing

LAGUZ

Water, Intuition, Emotions, Flow, Renewal, Dreams, Hopes & Fears

KENAZ

Fire, Torch, Illumination, Clarity, Truth, Revelation

Letter to the Reader

Thank you for reading *Tree of Ash*, and your continued support of *The Runic Saga*! Your kind words, reviews, and DMs motivate me and encourage me like nothing else.

Catch up with Larissa, Halla, Darien, Anara, Kai, and Masai in Book Three.

Until then, you can get updates and exclusive behind-the-scenes on your favorite characters and my writing process by joining my newsletter or following me on social media (@KaylaAnnAuthor). Those who sign up for my newsletter will receive sneak peeks at upcoming character art and ARC reading opportunities!

If you loved *Tree of Ash*, you can make a huge impact by leaving a review!

Supportive readers like you make all the difference when you leave a review, even if the review just says, "Good stuff." Reviews left on Amazon, Goodreads, and social media help to share this book with others and increase its visibility.

Keep reading for a sneak peek at Book Three!

Acknowledgements

First and foremost, I give all glory to God. It is through Him that I have the ability and the passion to write.

To my critique partners, Morgan, Michelle, and Jakob, you are truly the foundation of my writing. I'm so grateful for your willing and even eager desire to read my stories at their ugliest forms. Thank you for the invaluable feedback that you provide.

To Amanda and Angela, you are not only my author support group, but you are my close friends. You are always there for my writing and publishing questions, but you're more than that. You are my cheerleaders, my advisors, my teammates. I'm so grateful for you both.

To my husband, you are my encourager, my steady hand who reminds me to take a breath and eat some chocolate.

To my beta readers, thank you for being brutally honest with me in the kindest way possible. Thank you for the DMs and emojis of shock and love and excitement. To my Street Team, thank you for encouraging me along the way by sharing my work and spreading the news. To my supportive reviewers who shared your loved of *Well of Dreams* and motivated me to continue writing, thank you.

To my readers, thank you for allowing me to share this world with you.

To all of the authors who share their stories, thank you for inspiring me to do the same.

Kickstarter Acknowledgements

Thank you to every single person who backed my Kickstarter campaign. It is **because** of my generous backers that I was able to continue the series of my dreams including professional maps and illustrations. Thank you so much.

Ashley C Martin	E. A. Hendryx	Kelsey M.	Rachelle Degoumois
Abby A.	E. Kim	Kelsie L Brown	Rebecca Hill
Abigail B.	Elizabeth Crawford	Kim Roger	Rebecca J. Thompson
Addison Horner	Elle Cage	Kimberlee Graham	Rheanna North
Adelle Williams	Ellen Pilcher	Kimberley - noribooreads	Rosa Thill
Aimee Moore	Elodie Nicoli	Kristina	RosieDragon
Alexander L. Parker	Elyse C.	Krystina Roupe	Ross and Linda Rither
Alexandra Corrsin	Emily Condos	Kylie Burrage	Ruby Sutton
Alexus Nelson	Emily Gamm	Kyliegh Romine	S Simmons
Alice Ferion	Emma Friis	Licia Moss	Sabrina Lozier
Alicia Guess	Emma Hill	Linda Moss	Sam Christopher
Alyssa Diederich	Emma Jacks	Lisa Moody	Samantha Keil
Alyssa Pressley	Emma Shirley	Liz DuRoss	Samantha Mendell
Amanda Balter	Erica Rue	Louise Davis	Samantha Newberry
Amanda Simas	Erika Gfeller	Lukas Baker	Sangeetha
Amber Toro	Erval Mikkaelson	Lydia Woodward	Sara Francis
Amy Rietveld	Eve Weaver	Madison Parker/Laflin	Sarah F. Frederick
Angela Morse	Faith Randolph	Maria Gilbert	Sarah Kruhm
Angela Powers	Fleur DeVillainy	Mariah L. Rosewood	Sarah O
Anna Barroso	Franchesca Caram	Marina Hatfield	Sarah S.
Anna L	Gabriella Tejada	Mark R. Patrick	Scott Casey
AnnMarie	Georgianna J Myers	Marlene Renteria	Seamus Sands
April L. Miller	Gerald P. McDaniel	Meg Fitzpatrick	Serena Devlin
Ashley Hagood	Giulia Santucci	Megan Astell	Shanon M. Brown
Ashley Sills	Grace Migay	Megan Caudill	Shelby Groves
Astrid MacLaren	Hannah Pennington	Megan Crist	Shiloh I Reeves
Benjamin Weaver	Harla Kadrie	Megyn "Sapphi" MacDougall	SJ Reed
Bethany Atazadeh	Heather Cera	Melissa Graham	Sky Warren
Billye Herndon	Heiko Koenig	Michael H.	SLM
Bonnie Tadlock	Hope Windsor	Michelle Forman	Stacy Ward
Brian Grimes	Isabel K	Mike McCue	Stephanie Crachiolo
Brieane Shanahan	J Bruckner	Morgan G.	Stephanie Meredith
Brittany Mack	Jakob & Michelle Baker	Morgan Rither	Stephanie Price
Brittany Wang	Janine B	Morgan Steele	Sue Frecker
Brooke Gendreau	Jeanna H.	Moriah	Tara Hundley
C.J. Milacci	Jeff & Angela Mooney	Natalie Colburn	Tarian
Cara Welch	Jen Woodrum	Natasha Rueschhoff	Tedra Trimm
Carissa Anne	Jennifer H	Nathan Keys	Terri Hernandez
Carmella Grace	Jes Drew	Nicita	Terri Seanard
Carol MacLennan-Gonzales	Jesseca W	Nicole Johnson	Terry Juell French
Carolyn Selli	Jessica Beatty	Nicole Sanders	Theresa Williams
Cassi Krotzer	Joanne Long	Nicole Triptow	Tiara Blake
Christy Austin	John Lollini	Nivita Starling	Tiffany Goldman
Connie Jo Lawson	Judy Bawroski	Olivia Renner	Tyleah Merino
Corinne Brucks	Jules Dyrud	Pamela Hart	Tzvia V
Cortney Babcock	Julia N. White	Patricia Armstrong	V. M. Lyton
D. E. Carlson	Julie	Pauline Le	Valerie Galderisi
Danielle Harrington	Julie Janis	Priscil	Vanessa Perry
Dawn Montoya	Kaitlyn Deann	Qavee	Vicki Hsu
Dayna Perez	Kasandra Forester	R Jensen	Victoria
Deanna Magee	Katherine Malloy	R. Dugan	Victoria Clemm
DM Gearhart	Katherine Shipman	Rachel Rohde	Xyvah
Doug and Lori Parker	Kayla Sharp	Rachel Vance	Yara Dijkstra

Keep reading for a
sneak peek at
Book Three

Book Three

Larissa

PITCH BLACKNESS PRESSED IN against Helga's rusted blue frame from every side as Larissa drove down the long, narrow road. It was straight enough that Larissa drove without headlights, careful not to alert anyone to her presence. After driving for nearly two days, she'd reach the border between Perle and Smaragd within the next few hours. Then she'd have to find some place to stash Helga before she continued on foot.

Larissa rubbed at her eyes, desperate to stay awake. She only had until the next full moon, maybe three weeks, before Hel claimed Darien's soul permanently. Verðandi hadn't said how far it was to Helheim, only to drive northwest back toward *Yggdrasil* and Verðandi would guide her from there. Larissa thought of Darien's broken body lying at the base of the enormous ash tree, the goddess's small hands at work mending it as his soul remained trapped in the depths of Helheim.

Larissa gripped the steering wheel more tightly, but her hands slid against the wetness that hadn't been there before. She raised a shaking hand, knowing that the blood on her palm was Darien's. Her own screams echoed in her ears, her sobs as she cradled Darien's lifeless body. His final breath, a proclamation of his love, lingered like a scar across the hardened heart that thudded against the memory. Larissa could smell it, the powder of Calder's gun, the metallic scent of Darien's blood, the salt of the ocean.

If only she'd seen the gun. If only Larissa had called on Verðandi earlier. What if she had summoned the child goddess before

Darien's soul had been stolen by Hel? Could she have saved him then?

Her breath came in short gasps as she tried to wipe away the blood that refused to leave her fingers. She let go of the steering wheel, desperately scrubbing at the dried blood. Hadn't she washed this off before she left? Calder's own scream of fear as Larissa's *galdr* flung him over the cliff, sending him plummeting to his death, rose with the screech of Helga's tires.

Too late, Larissa noticed the turn in the road. Too late did she grab for the wheel only for it to be yanked from her grasp at the impact of Helga's tire against the divot in the road. The truck spun as Larissa screamed into the night. The seat belt jerked against Larissa's chest, knocking the air from her lungs. A certain weightlessness took over her body as Helga's tipped, her tires scrambling for purchase. Then Helga flipped, and Larissa flung her hands up to protect her face as the sound of shattering glass accompanied the sharp pains over her exposed skin. There was a jarring crunch, then nothing.

ᚾᛁᛪᚠᛋᚾᛁᛪᚠᛋᚾᛁᛪᚠᛋᚾᛁᛪᚠᛋᚾᛁᛪᚠᛋ

"THERE ARE EASIER WAYS to speak with me, Larissa," came the girlish voice of the goddess Larissa knew all too well.

Larissa groaned; every inch of her body ached and stung. She forced open her eyes only to find that her world was dark and upside down. She stared at Verðandi's feet. Larissa reached for the seat belt release, only to have to reach up instead of down. It was then she realized Helga lay completely upside down. The seat belt released, and Larissa crumbled to the roof of the cab. Her hands groped for her travel bag that had been on the passenger seat and dragged it out with her through the empty front window frame.

"No, don't bother helping me, I'm just fine," Larissa spat out as she crawled past Helga and lay panting on the asphalt, making an assessment of her bruised and throbbing body. Shallow cuts decorated her neck and hands, though thankfully, her long mourning jacket had protected most of her body from the glass. Darien's blood no longer coated her palms, no doubt only a hallucination brought on by exhaustion. Nothing felt broken, but every movement hurt.

She dared to look at Helga, already knowing what she would find. Smoke billowed from the hood, and the cab was nearly completely crushed. Larissa winced looking at it, wondering how she'd gotten out. There would be no return trip for Helga, and Larissa couldn't help but wonder if this was only foreshadowing her own outcome if she continued on toward Helheim. But even if it was, she could not abandon Darien, not when there was a chance she could bring him back.

(End of Sneak Peek)

Sign up for my newsletter or follow @KaylaAnnAuthor for updates on *The Runic Saga*.

About the Author

Kayla Ann is a traditional and self-published author. Her traditionally published book, *Agency in the Hunger Games*, explores the importance of personal agency in a world determined to strip away individuality. Her debut self-published YA novel, *Well of Dreams*, explores similar themes of fate versus free will. Kayla Ann writes in her limited free time when she is not teaching the next generation of readers, playing board games with her husband, or serving as personal chef, hairdresser, playmate, and story-teller to her young son.

www.ingramcontent.com/pod-product-compliance
Lightning Source LLC
Chambersburg PA
CBHW020051310726
48970CB00007B/2519